TO SPARK A MATCH

Books by Jen Turano

LADIES OF DISTINCTION

Gentleman of Her Dreams: A LADIES OF DISTINCTION Novella from With All My Heart Romance Collection

A Change of Fortune

A Most Peculiar Circumstance

A Talent for Trouble

A Match of Wits

A CLASS OF THEIR OWN

After a Fashion

In Good Company

Playing the Part

APART FROM THE CROWD

At Your Request: An APART FROM THE CROWD Novella from All For Love Romance Collection

Behind the Scenes

Out of the Ordinary

Caught by Surprise

AMERICAN HEIRESSES

Flights of Fancy

Diamond in the Rough

Storing Up Trouble

Grand Encounters: A HARVEY HOUSE BRIDES COLLECTION Novella from Serving Up Love

THE BLEECKER STREET INQUIRY AGENCY

To Steal a Heart

To Write a Wrong

To Disguise the Truth

THE MATCHMAKERS

A Match in the Making

To Spark a Match

THE MATCHMAKERS | BOOK 2

To SPARK A MATCH

JEN TURANO

BETHANYHOUSE

a division of Baker Publishing Group
Minneapolis, Minnesota

Published by Bethany House Publishers
Minneapolis, Minnesota
www.bethanyhouse.com

Bethany House Publishers is a division of
Baker Publishing Group, Grand Rapids, Michigan

Printed in the United States of America

Library of Congress Cataloging-in-Publication Data
Names: Turano, Jen author.
Title: To spark a match / Jen Turano.
Description: Minneapolis, Minnesota : Bethany House, a division of Baker
    Publishing Group, 2023. | Series: The matchmakers; 2
Identifiers: LCCN 2023026688 | ISBN 9780764240218 (paperback) | ISBN
    9780764242168 (casebound) | ISBN 9781493443680 (ebook)
Subjects: LCGFT: Romance fiction. | Novels.
Classification: LCC PS3620.U7455 T59 2023 | DDC 813/.6--dc23/eng/20230607
LC record available at https://lccn.loc.gov/2023026688

Scripture quotations are from the King James Version of the Bible.

Author is represented by Natasha Kern Literary Agency.

Baker Publishing Group publications use paper produced from sustainable forestry
practices and post-consumer waste whenever possible.

23 24 25 26 27 28 29   7 6 5 4 3 2 1

For Rachel Kortmeyer.
Thanks for the years of girl talk, listening to far too many
mediocre bands to count, and being an all-around
fabulous friend! I look forward
to the adventures ahead of us.
Love you!
Jen

One

HUDSON RIVER VALLEY
LATE OCTOBER 1888

If strolling through the drawing room with the hem of her gown trapped in the folds of her bustle, giving the two hundred upper-drawer society members attending Mrs. Ogden Nelson's intimate dinner party an unfettered view of her drawers, was a precursor of things to come during the approaching New York Season, then Miss Adelaide Duveen was now of the belief she should abandon her quest—or rather, her mother's quest—of acquiring one of those oh-so-coveted society matches and simply embrace her spinster state for the rest of her days.

Doing so would undoubtedly save her the bother of additional mortifying moments, which were inevitable if she kept pursuing what seemed to be a futile attempt to find a gentleman who was willing to overlook what society saw as numerous flaws and court her.

"Honestly, darling," Phyllis Duveen, Adelaide's mother, said, bustling up to join her as Adelaide backed out of a charming parlor that, unfortunately, contained a gathering of young ladies in it. "Any thoughts on how this latest catastrophe occurred? I

7

mean, it's not every day—or any day, for that matter—that a lady strolls about in such a questionable state of dishabille."

"What thoughts could I possibly have about my recent fiasco?" Adelaide returned as she continued down the hallway, pausing in front of a portrait of a terrifying older gentleman with muttonchop whiskers who was undeniably a long-deceased relative of Mrs. Nelson, given the distinct resemblance the gentleman bore to their hostess. "It's not as if I intended on giving everyone a glimpse of my undergarments."

"Your fiascos are never intentional," Phyllis murmured before she took hold of Adelaide's hand. "Nevertheless, I must say this is one of your most unusual mishaps to date. I truly have no idea how such a circumstance could have transpired."

"I imagine my latest calamity was a result of my attempting to readjust this monstrosity of a bustle. I was unaware that my hem got stuck in the dastardly contraption, which then resulted with me making a complete ninny of myself after I returned from the retiring room."

Phyllis frowned. "Why were you readjusting your bustle? I gave your lady's maid specific instructions to secure it with additional ties so you wouldn't have to fuss with it this evening."

"It wasn't Marta's fault. It was the bustle's fault for shifting, or perhaps Mr. Hayworth is to blame since he's the one who insisted his gown needed such a massive bustle to begin with. Why he designed such a gown for me is somewhat puzzling, though, because bustles are decreasing in size this year." Adelaide gave her skirt a twitch. "The thought did cross my mind that you haven't abandoned that nonsense about making me look more voluptuous through designs that add inches to what even I know is a boyish figure. I then discarded that notion because we supposedly came to an understanding about unusual design ploys after I attended that ball in Newport dressed like a peculiar version of a cake, what with all the frills and lace Mr. Hayworth added to that particular abomination."

"I may have forgotten to mention the change in strategy to Mr. Hayworth, probably because he was so enthusiastic about having you try out a new type of bustle—one he invented himself," Phyllis admitted. "From what I understand, he's included coiled springs between the wires, which he's hoping will allow you to sit with greater ease."

"My bustle is spring-concocted?"

"Apparently, but after your latest incident, I'm going to suggest you don't attempt to sit down often because, now that I consider the matter, coiled springs may be a certain recipe for disaster."

Adelaide glanced over her shoulder to the bustle in question. "I certainly would have abandoned this gown for a less problematic one if I'd known about the coils."

"Which would have been a shame because the blush hue of your gown does wonders for bringing out the color in your eyes."

"My eyes are brown. It's difficult to bring out any other color except brown, no matter what hue my gown might be."

"An excellent point. Perhaps I should have said the blush is in direct contrast to your dark hair, which lends you an air of, ah, mystery."

Adelaide choked back a laugh. "Simply because my hair is black does not mean I'm mysterious."

"Sophia Campanini has black hair, and she's considered very enigmatic indeed."

"Sophia Campanini is a premier opera singer, something I'm most assuredly not. Everyone considers opera singers mysterious. However, it's difficult to say whether Sophia's hair is actually black. She's known to frequently wear wigs. Case in point, a few weeks ago I spotted her strolling along the Ladies' Mile wearing a platinum wig that was drawing everyone's attention."

Phyllis's eyes began to gleam. "Ooh . . . platinum."

"Do not even consider hying yourself off to the nearest wig-maker and procuring platinum locks for me."

"But that might be exactly what's needed to give you that cloak of mystery that seems to be eluding you."

"Mystery eludes me because I'm simply not mysterious."

"That could very well change if we attach a noteworthy wig to your head."

Adelaide arched a brow. "Do you honestly believe, what with how I cannot manage to keep a bustle in place, that I'd somehow be capable of keeping a wig securely fashioned to my head?"

"Another excellent point, which is why it's fortunate Sophia Campanini is scheduled to perform after the midnight supper. I'll simply have Mrs. Nelson introduce me to the famed opera singer, who I believe has already arrived, given all the oohs and aahs I heard before your unfortunate mishap."

"I highly doubt Sophia Campanini will be keen to speak with the mother of the lady responsible for detracting attention away from what she undoubtedly was expecting to be a grand entrance. Even if people were oohing and aahing over her appearance, I'm sure that was cut short after everyone spotted me in all my unmentionable glory."

Phyllis gave a bit of a shudder. "Perhaps it would be best if I simply seek out the advice of my hair stylist. I imagine she's well versed in the language of wigs."

"Or you could put this less-than-amusing idea of yours aside and forget about wigs altogether."

"That's some wishful thinking on your part, because I'm now of the opinion that having you sport an unusual hair color is exactly what's needed to set you apart from the crowd."

"I believe my propensity for mishaps, my love of books, my lack of proficiency with most feminine arts, my enormous collection of cats, and my questionable fashion sense already sets me worlds apart from the crowd—and not in a favorable manner."

"*I'm* the one responsible for your fashion choices."

Adelaide gave her mother's arm a pat. "And you've been very diligent with attempting to discover what fashions suit me, even if we've yet to land on a style that shows me to any sort of advantage. Nevertheless, with that said, I'm putting my foot down about the wig. The last thing you'll want to see is me losing a wig in my soup during the first course of a formal dinner."

"I bet a little touch of glue would prevent that from happening."

"We are not *gluing* anything to my head. Besides, no one will suddenly conclude that I'm an intriguing lady merely because my hair is an unusual color. If you've neglected to remember, I'm twenty-three years old and have been out in society for five Seasons, both winter and summer. It would be next to impossible to convince anyone I'm anything other than peculiar. Wandering around with a wig on my head will only succeed in increasing the notion society already holds about me."

Phyllis seemed to deflate on the spot. "Oh, very well, no wig. But we'll need to think of something to distract everyone from this latest incident. I don't imagine anyone is going to easily forget the sight of your drawers, what with how they seemed to be sporting some manner of embroidered animals with pointy ears on them."

"They're cats," Adelaide said. "Although they don't resemble cats—more along the lines of bats, but that's because Mrs. Bainswright, the woman who made the undergarments for me, has yet to master the art of embroidery, probably because I've been the one teaching her. I'm not what anyone would call proficient with needlepoint."

"I'm not acquainted with a Mrs. Bainswright."

"Maude and her husband, Alfonso, own Bainswright Books on Bleecker Street."

"I've never heard of that bookstore," Phyllis said before she frowned. "But since Mrs. Bainswright took the time to embroider such an unusual gift for you, it seems as if you spend particular time in this mysterious shop, something I was unaware of."

"There's no need for you to start looking all suspicious," Adelaide said. "I've not been hiding anything from anyone, except that Bainswright Books is my favorite bookstore. I've only done that, though, because it's a shop society rarely frequents. If word got out that, in addition to being a treasure trove of rare tomes, Mr. Bainswright also stocks some of the latest romance and dime novels, Bainswright Books would soon see an influx of the social set and would no longer be the refuge I enjoy away from the Four Hundred."

"Aren't you depriving Mr. Bainswright of potential well-heeled customers by keeping the delights of this shop to yourself?"

"The Bainswrights aren't particularly enthusiastic to serve members of the upper crust, especially the ladies, no matter if they're well-heeled or not. Society ladies expect to be catered to, and Mr. Bainswright is not exactly what I'd call a catering-to sort. The only reason he keeps an impressive selection of dime novels for sale, as well as copies of papers such as 'The Fireside Companion,' is because Mrs. Bainswright devours such riveting reads like candy. Mr. Bainswright, on the other hand, would be content to avoid readers who enjoy what he calls 'fluff pieces,' because he prefers to devote his time to his rare book section, which is where his profitability lies."

"How does he make a profit from rare books if he doesn't cater to the society set?"

"Gentlemen who are interested in acquiring rare books rarely go through the bother of tracking them down on their own. They hire agents for that. Those are the men Mr. Bainswright deals with."

"But where does Mr. Bainswright acquire rare books from?"

"He has a variety of sources—men who purchase items from estates as well as people who need funds and dust off old tomes and novels they won't miss. The latter does concern me, since some of those sellers are a rather shifty lot."

"You spend time in a bookstore that caters to shifty sorts?"

"It's an unavoidable hazard, given that most bookshops dealing in rare books attract dubious characters."

"With the abysmal state of your luck, darling, I'm going to encourage you to avoid this bookstore, lest you find yourself tangling with those questionable characters."

Adelaide waved that aside. "Mr. Bainswright keeps a shotgun at the ready, one Mrs. Bainswright has assured me he knows how to use." She smoothed a wrinkle from her sleeve. "But speaking of Mrs. Bainswright, she's bound to be disappointed about my latest catastrophe. She was convinced her gift was going to bring me some much-needed luck in the romance department, because she read a plot line that revolved around unusual unmentionables in one of her favorite dime novels. I'm afraid she was off the mark about the luck business, because I'm sure no gentleman will go out of his way to seek me out tonight."

"Gentlemen would have a difficult time doing that when it's obvious you're currently in search of a quiet room to hide out in for the remainder of the ball." Phyllis stepped closer to Adelaide. "You must realize there's no need for you to bury yourself away simply because you've once again suffered an embarrassing episode. Frankly, I'm convinced we can use this latest debacle to secure you every dance being offered tonight."

"The last thing I want is to secure sympathy dances from gentlemen I know you're going to browbeat into taking to the floor with me."

"I have no idea why you believe I stoop to browbeating," Phyllis said, with a far too innocent bat of her lashes.

It was impossible for Adelaide to resist a snort. "You've made a habit of badgering gentlemen ever since I made my debut, which means browbeating is inevitable where you're concerned.

13

If you haven't noticed, gentlemen have begun fleeing from you the moment you begin breezing your way across a ballroom. They know your particular attention presages another episode where you'll wield guilt like a weapon to have them fill up my woefully lacking-in-names dance card."

"I've never seen a gentleman flee from me."

"Of course you have, which is exactly why you've recently begun prevailing upon your friends to pester gentlemen on your behalf, something I'm now going to insist comes to an immediate cessation."

Phyllis smiled rather weakly. "An immediate cessation may not be possible because Mrs. Oliver Wetmore already told me she's secured Mr. Barton Delafield's agreement to partner with you for the second dance of the evening. He's apparently partnering Miss Thelma Cutting for the first waltz, although he mentioned to Mrs. Wetmore that if he'd not requested Miss Cutting's hand for that dance, he would have been more than amiable to taking to the floor with you for the waltz, something I took as very encouraging indeed."

"If Mr. Delafield truly wanted to dance with me, he'd have asked to add his name to my dance card when I ran across him in the receiving line. However, since he didn't broach the topic of dancing then, I'm certain he won't suffer any lasting ill effects when he realizes I've disappeared during a dance he only grudgingly agreed to in the first place."

"Mr. Delafield wouldn't need to suffer at all if you'd set aside your mortification and rejoin the festivities."

"I'm looking at my most recent calamity not as an incident where I need to hide myself away because of embarrassment but as a convenient excuse to indulge in something I genuinely enjoy—reading. I'm in the middle of a book about mummies, which I'm sure I'll find more satisfying than dreading the approach of gentlemen who've been pressed into requesting the honor of dancing with me, which they never feel is an honor."

"I'm certain many of the gentlemen who've needed a touch of convincing to waltz you about a room find themselves completely charmed with your company after a dance is completed."

"My *charm* is exactly why those gentlemen never ask for a second dance in any given evening."

Phyllis released a sigh. "I'm sure they'd be only too happy to do so if you allowed them to know you'd enjoy a second dance."

"I discontinued doing that during my first Season out after I mentioned to Mr. Harold Seward that I enjoyed dancing the Star Quadrille, which was scheduled after dinner that evening." Adelaide gave a sad shake of her head. "The moment I was done speaking, Mr. Seward began hemming and hawing about how he was committed to other ladies for the remainder of the ball. He couldn't get away from me fast enough, and to this day, he's never invited me to dance with him again."

Phyllis's lips thinned. "It was not well done of Harold to treat you so shoddily, especially during your first Season out."

"Harold Seward did me a favor because he showed me, as nothing else could, that I was never going to be considered a diamond of the first water, nor considered any type of catch, except for the most desperate of fortune-hunters, whom I've sufficiently dissuaded over the years by using that charm you just mentioned. But enough about my lack of success within society. It doesn't bother me, which means it shouldn't bother you either."

"I only want to see you happy."

"I *am* happy, just not the particular type of happy you want me to be. However, because I know you're going to fret about me removing myself from the festivities, know that I won't read for the entirety of Mrs. Nelson's dinner party. Rest assured, you'll see me make an appearance for the midnight supper. I'm bound to be ravenous by then, and I certainly won't want to linger in that regrettable state."

Phyllis began fiddling with the buttons on one of her silk

evening gloves. "I suppose that's somewhat reassuring, but you must at least allow me to convince Mrs. Nelson to rearrange your seating at dinner. She has you sitting between Mr. Vernon Clarkson and Mr. Leopold Pendleton. Those two gentlemen are not suitable dinner partners because they're positively ancient."

"*Au contraire*. I enjoy Mr. Clarkson's and Mr. Pendleton's company. They're amusing and adore regaling me with stories about the adventures they experienced in their youth."

"It would be more helpful if you'd be amused by the exploits of a younger gentleman, one who is currently experiencing those escapades instead of having done them fifty years ago."

"If only there were any young, adventurous gentlemen who longed to sit beside me at dinner parties."

"We'll never discover the answer to that if you refuse to allow me to meddle with seating assignments."

"No meddling, and with that out of the way, I'm off to read my book. You may at least take comfort in knowing that reading should not allow me to experience any additional shocking incidents this evening."

"That's small comfort, especially when the topic of your unmentionables is going to be fodder for wagging tongues for the foreseeable future." Phyllis brushed a piece of lint from Adelaide's gown. "Half the guests in attendance tonight will be repairing to the city soon, whispering behind gloved hands about your latest incident."

"You could take some comfort in the fact that Cousin Charles saved me earlier from plunging into the backyard fountain," Adelaide said. "Society would have been even more aflutter if I'd suffered two catastrophes in one evening."

"You never mentioned almost falling into a fountain."

Adelaide scratched her nose. "I didn't see the point because Charles saved me from a drenching, although . . . if he hadn't saved me, that might have been a less embarrassing incident to suffer through since I would have been left sopping wet, which would have given me the perfect excuse to return home early."

"That still would have left tongues wagging, but why were you and Charles in the back courtyard to begin with? His mother, your dear aunt Petunia, is determined to see him wed in the next year. He'll hardly be successful with that if he takes to lurking out of sight during society events."

"Charles is making himself scarce because Miss Jennie Gibson is in attendance tonight. Aunt Petunia is apparently of the belief Jennie would be the perfect match for him."

"And I'm in full agreement with that because Jennie Gibson is completely darling and is well on her way to being declared an Incomparable in the coming Season."

"And that right there is why Charles is hesitant to even approach the lady. Incomparables have made it a habit to give him a wide berth, which is why he'll continue skulking by the fountain unless Aunt Petunia manages to track him down."

"You know she'll ask me if I've seen him."

"But since you haven't seen him—merely heard me mentioning where he is—you can have a clear conscience telling your sister that you haven't taken note of him all evening." Adelaide began moving down the hallway, sticking her head into a room that, unfortunately, had three gentlemen gathered by a far window, their heads bent together and looking quite as if they were discussing matters of business.

"Perhaps you should suggest to Charles that he consider hiring a matchmaker, as so many gentlemen did over the Newport Season," Phyllis said after Adelaide backed her way out of the room and began wandering down the hallway again.

Adelaide slowed to a stop, this time underneath a portrait of a well-dressed lady with a pampered poodle sitting on a chaise beside her. "There's no point in doing that because Gwendolyn, the only matchmaker Charles finds remotely approachable, has decided to set aside any future matchmaking endeavors and embrace her life as the new Mrs. Walter Townsend."

"Which is regrettable, given the tremendous success Gwendolyn enjoyed during the summer." Phyllis fiddled with the clasp of the diamond bracelet encircling her wrist. "I'm still holding out hope that she'll realize she's destined to make one last match before she hangs up her matchmaking gloves for good."

Adelaide laughed. "I'll give you this—you are resolute in your determination to see me settled. Nevertheless, if you're hoping that last match would revolve around me, know that Gwendolyn offered numerous times to help me out in the gentleman department. I told her I couldn't possibly accept her assistance."

"Why in heaven's name would you have refused what you should have seen as a godsent opportunity?"

"I highly doubt God spends His time worrying about sending me a matchmaker simply because I'm not a beacon for marriage-minded gentlemen. Besides, even though Gwendolyn proved to be beyond competent with securing matches, I'm not your typical society lady. I come with far too much baggage. It could've strained the friendship Gwendolyn and I developed if she'd taken me on and discovered I'm a hopeless case."

"You're not a hopeless case."

"You're my mother, so you're required to say that, but I'm a realist. In fact, after the troubling event that occurred earlier, I'm beginning to consider abandoning the marriage mart altogether and simply accepting my fate as a confirmed spinster. My time in the city will be far less stressful as well as less mortifying for everyone involved."

Phyllis blinked. "There's no need to be hasty. Why, showing everyone your unmentionables wasn't even that noteworthy. I imagine everyone has already forgotten about it."

"You just said tongues would be wagging for the foreseeable future."

18

"Not if we nip this situation in the bud." Phyllis lifted her chin. "I say we return to the ballroom and proceed as if nothing happened."

"And *I* say, given that I almost fell into a fountain and then experienced a bustle mishap, we should err on the side of caution and keep me well removed from everyone for an hour or so."

"Oddly enough, that makes a certain amount of sense." Phyllis settled a stern eye on Adelaide. "I will, however, expect you at dinner."

"I told you, I'll be ravenous by then, and you know I'm not one to ever pass up a ten-course meal."

"I'm not sure it's a good thing you're more excited about a meal over enjoying the company of the guests here this evening," Phyllis grumbled before she gave Adelaide a quick peck on the cheek, then turned and glided away.

Anxious to get down to some serious reading, Adelaide strode into motion, slowing when she caught sight of a door that was cracked open at the very end of the hallway. Making a beeline for it, she gave it a tentative push, wincing when it creaked. Her wince turned into a grin a second later, though, when she stepped into the room and discovered it was a well-appointed library, and better yet, devoid of people.

"Much better," she said as she spotted a comfy-looking fainting couch and hurried over to it. After perching on the very edge of it—done so because her bustle wouldn't allow her to do anything *but* perch—she opened the large reticule that certainly didn't favor her gown and riffled through the contents, pulling out her copy of *My Winter on the Nile: Among the Mummies and Moslems* by a Mr. Charles Dudley Warner. She flipped to the page she'd marked with a ribbon, then stilled when, from out of the corner of her eye, she noticed the heavy damask drapes moving ever so slightly.

Rising to her feet, she moved to shut a window that a servant had evidently forgotten to close, not wanting Mrs. Nelson's drapes to become ruined by the storm everyone was saying would hit by midnight. She came to a rapid stop, though, when a pair of shoes captured her attention, ones that most assuredly belonged to the man she just realized was lurking behind the drapes—a man who was even now beginning to step out from the folds of expensive damask, his features cloaked in the shadows the wall sconces were unable to banish.

It took all of two seconds to fling her book in the direction of a gentleman who was obviously up to some manner of shenanigans before she opened her mouth to release a resounding scream.

Unfortunately, before she could get so much as a croak past her lips, the man grabbed hold of her arm and slipped his other hand over her mouth, stifling a scream that no one would now be able to hear.

Two

❧

"Don't scream. I won't harm you."

Recognition was immediate and had Adelaide forgetting all about screaming, although she had no control over the fact that the hair on the nape of her neck stood to attention—something that frequently occurred whenever she heard the voice that had just whispered into her ear.

It was a voice a lady was hard-pressed to forget because it was smooth like velvet and suited this specific gentleman, who was thought to be a bit of a rogue—or at least he looked the part, what with his raven hair, formidable physique, and a face that recalled images of fallen angels or gentlemen who spent their time pursuing danger.

Gentlemen who looked as if they courted precarious activities always seemed in possession of voices that practically caressed a person's ears, that pesky business responsible for ladies' hearts going pitter-patter with alarming frequency—not that Adelaide permitted her heart to do any skittering about when Mr. Gideon Abbott was in her vicinity. Such a thing would be sheer folly because rumor had it that Gideon was not interested in settling down into wedded bliss. That rumor was reinforced by the fact that he never showed particular attention to any lady, not that the ladies didn't try to attract his consideration.

"Gideon?" she finally whispered when she realized he was waiting for a response from her, even though the response she attempted to give him was almost indecipherable since his hand was still covering her mouth.

Seemingly convinced that she wouldn't scream, he removed his hand and released her arm, which allowed her to turn and face him, her gaze traveling over the gentleman who'd just scared her half to death.

It came as no surprise to find him doing justice to the formal evening attire he was wearing. The pristine cut of his jacket highlighted his broad shoulders and trim waist, suggesting he was in possession of a tailor who knew exactly how to dress a gentleman to perfection.

"Why am I not surprised to discover it's you?" were the first words out of Gideon's mouth, pulling Adelaide from her perusal. "Honestly, Adelaide, I would think you'd have better things to occupy yourself with other than retreating to a library during a dinner party. Care to explain what you're doing here?"

A shiver of delight shot through Adelaide, due no doubt to Gideon's use of her given name, which wasn't a novel experience, since he'd begun addressing her informally after he'd rescued her from a most unpleasant fate a few months before, one that could have resulted in a rather grisly death if he'd not been close at hand to save her. She forced herself to meet his gaze, her sense of delight fading when she detected a hint of vexation in his eyes.

Truth be told, she wasn't unaccustomed to exasperating people on a somewhat frequent basis, but in this instance, she'd done nothing exasperation-worthy. She lifted her chin. "I believe a more pressing question would be what were you doing lurking behind those curtains?"

It was rather irritating when, instead of answering her, he gave her arm a pat.

"I'm afraid the unintentional fright I gave you has allowed you to misinterpret the situation, but now is hardly the moment to discuss the matter." Gideon began nudging her toward the door. "I've just noticed you're looking concerningly peaked, which is entirely my fault."

"Of course it's your fault. You scared the stuffing out of me."

"Which was apparently responsible for you heaving a book at me."

"You're fortunate a book was the only weapon I had at hand."

Gideon stopped moving. "Do you normally have *other* weapons readily available?"

"Well, no, because I don't make it a habit to arm myself when I'm attending dinner parties, since I'm not usually confronted by men who are skulking about."

"I wasn't skulking."

"I beg to differ. But if you're so opposed to me believing you're the type of gentleman to prowl about in a most suspicious fashion, all you need to do to deprive me of that notion is explain what you were doing in the library before I wandered in here."

Gideon completely ignored her request as he pulled her into motion again. "Not that I want to offend you, but you've now taken to looking pale as a ghost. Permit me to get you settled in a spot far removed from the guests, who are bound to notice your pallid state, which will undoubtedly have them asking questions I know you won't want to entertain. If you'll recall, I saw how frustrated you got that time you caught on fire and were then left with a barrage of inquiries after we got the flames put out. Since you've now suffered another fright, one that has clearly left you out of sorts, know that after I get you settled, I'll fetch you a cool drink, which should put some color back in your cheeks."

Considering her cheeks felt as if they were blooming with color, due to the notion Gideon was obviously not keen to explain the skulking, it was evident the man was making a less-than-subtle attempt to remove her from the library. Frankly, he seemed to be going to herculean lengths to distract her from whatever it was he was up to by being far too solicitous of what he kept suggesting were her tender sensibilities.

She came to an abrupt stop, forcing him to do the same. "I'm fairly certain this library, being at the end of a very long hallway, is as far removed from the guests as we're going to find."

He didn't miss a beat. "True, but now that I think about it, it's actually too far away from the festivities, because it's not close to where refreshments are being served. Given the ashen hue of your face, it's clear you're in desperate need of a beverage before you find yourself succumbing to a fit of the vapors."

She dug in her heels when he attempted to prod her into motion again. "I'm the lady who suffers mayhem on a frequent basis. As you just mentioned, I once caught myself on fire. I didn't suffer a fit of the vapors when I suddenly went up in flames, which means I'm not a lady who is going to succumb to vapors merely because you startled me when you materialized from behind those curtains. But speaking of Mrs. Nelson's drapes, you've yet to explain what you were doing behind them. Most people aren't prone to disappearing into the folds of window dressings during a dinner party."

He arched a brow. "Most people also aren't prone to retreating to libraries when a night's festivities are soon to begin, and in this case, that would be dancing. Mrs. Nelson brought in a complete orchestra, which isn't something most ladies care to avoid."

"I'm not most ladies. Besides, it's not a crime to avoid dancing. Loitering behind curtains, on the other hand, suggests something a little more sinister."

Annoyingly enough, Gideon neglected to cough up an explanation. Instead, he took to regarding her for a few seconds before he cocked his head. "May I assume your decision to remove yourself from the guests is because you've experienced some manner of turmoil already?"

"It wouldn't be a normal evening for me if some manner of chaos didn't occur," she returned. "But it wasn't really a noteworthy bout of turmoil. I mean, granted, tongues will be wagging about my latest incident for weeks, but in all honesty, what I experienced was a, um, wardrobe sputter, if you will."

"How unfortunate," he said before he grinned, the sight of it causing her pulse to accelerate the tiniest bit, something she strove to ignore because it certainly would never do to allow this gentleman's far-too-appealing grin to leave her behaving like a giddy schoolgirl, not when it had been eons since she'd been in a classroom. Besides that, she had the sneaking suspicion Gideon used his grins much like weapons, pulling them out whenever he needed a distraction. Unfortunately for him, she was determined to remain undistracted.

"May I dare hope you'll appease my curiosity and tell me exactly how this sputter occurred?" Gideon asked as he placed his hand on the small of her back and gave her a gentle nudge toward the door again.

She refused to budge, having no intention of allowing him to whisk her out of a room he evidently didn't want her lingering in, not until she discovered exactly what he was up to.

Summoning up the limited acting abilities she possessed, Adelaide began fluttering a hand in front of her face. "I'm afraid I'll need to do that telling at some later date because you may be on to something regarding my emotional state. I'm suddenly feeling all sorts of lightheaded, which means we'll need to stay here until I get my nerves under control."

Gideon's grin disappeared in a flash. "You just told me, and vehemently no less, you're not a lady prone to vapors."

"Perhaps my life of mishaps has finally caught up with me."

She gave another flutter of her hand. "Why, I'm even beginning to feel rather weak in the knees. Given that unfortunate development, I'm sure you'll agree I should immediately sit down before I crumple to the floor."

Instead of ushering her to the nearest chair, Gideon took a step away from her and gave her a thorough perusal. "You don't look as if you're about to faint. In fact, your face is no longer pale, and your eyes have begun sparkling with what appears to be amusement."

"I'm sure they're doing no such thing. If they're sparkling at all, it's probably a sign I'm about to swoon. I've been told ladies' eyes every so often start sparkling right before those eyes roll back in their heads."

"Why do I get the distinct impression you just conjured that bit of ridiculousness out of thin air?"

Swallowing a laugh, she feigned a wobble, which caused Gideon to immediately steady her with another hand to the small of her back, although instead of leading her to the fainting couch, he headed for the door again.

"There's a billiard room just down the hallway that has a comfortable-looking settee in it," he said. "Your weak knees will certainly appreciate being able to rest there."

Adelaide sidestepped away from him, releasing a breathy sigh that she hoped he'd take for additional distress. "I don't believe my knees are strong enough to make it out of this room. Since I've already drawn far too much notice with my wardrobe sputter and have no desire to attract additional attention if I swoon and you're then forced to carry me about, if it's all the same to you, I'll rest here, in the library, on that fainting couch I was lounging on a few moments ago, one that's simply too comfortable for words."

"You seem rather articulate for a lady in danger of swooning."

"I've been known to chatter away at the most unusual of times."

"Why do I get the feeling you're being contrary on purpose?"

"Because you possess a skeptical nature?"

"That's not the reason."

She pressed her now-curving lips into a straight line. "I'm sure it *is* the reason because I'll have you know that while I do have the ability to turn contrary upon occasion, it's not a trait my mother approves of, which is why I strive to suppress it if at all possible."

"You don't seem to be having much luck doing that right now."

"I'm sure that's on account of my weak knees, which are turning weaker by the second."

Gideon ran a hand through his hair, blew out a resigned-sounding breath, then took hold of her arm. Instead of drawing her over to the fainting couch, though, he began steering her toward a small slipper chair that was situated on the opposite side of the room. "I believe this chair will be far more comfortable for you. It's located directly beside a shaded lamp, which should help soothe those nerves of yours."

She wrinkled her nose. "You must not have noticed the size of the bustle I'm wearing because I don't think it'll fit in that chair. I was forced to perch on the very edge of the fainting couch earlier, and that's far larger than the chair you've now chosen for me."

"Perching doesn't sound comfortable, even though you claimed the fainting couch was lovely to lounge upon. Besides that, perching won't do for weak knees because you'll be required to put pressure on them to retain your balance. That's why you're now going to let me hie you off to the billiard room, where no perching will be required."

Unwilling to allow what was obviously a very determined gentleman to get his way, Adelaide didn't hesitate to plop into the chair he'd suggested, earning a furrowing of the brow from Gideon in the process. Before she could do more than smile over the fact she was still in the library, her bustle gave an odd sort of groan, which turned into an even odder pinging noise, and then, a mere second later, she found herself hurtling through the air.

Before she knew it, she was sprawled on the floor—on her stomach, no less—her plummet to the ground leaving her winded. Or perhaps her breathlessness was a direct result of something sharp, undoubtedly a piece of a coiled spring that had obviously sprung, jabbing her underneath her rib cage.

"Are you alright?" Gideon asked.

She turned her head and found him kneeling beside her, his green eyes unusually wide.

"I would love to say I'm fine," she muttered, "but I'm beginning to wonder if suffering numerous mortifying incidents in any given evening can be detrimental to one's well-being."

"A valid concern for certain, but any thoughts regarding how you ended up on the floor?"

"I believe Mr. Hayworth is to blame."

"Who?"

"My mother's dress designer. He's been experimenting with bustles of late, and I'm an unwitting subject of his latest experiment. I believe the coiled springs he installed on my bustle were not meant to withstand a plopping and thus staged a rebellion."

The corners of Gideon's lips quirked. "You've just suffered a bustle uprising?"

"Indeed, one that's left me suffering from a sharp piece of metal that seems to be stabbing me."

His amusement disappeared in a flash. "Allow me to get you unstabbed."

"You can't help me resolve my current situation considering the culprit is my bustle. The rules of etiquette would consider any bustle assistance to be untoward on both our parts."

"Given that you're currently sprawled on the floor with the skirt of your gown askew, giving me a glimpse of what I can only say are rather unusual unmentionables—not that I've given them more than a cursory look, and only because, well, it was an unavoidable sight—I believe we can agree there'll be nothing untoward with me helping you set yourself to rights."

Adelaide couldn't quite suppress a groan. "I've exposed my unmentionables again?"

"I'm afraid so, but I'm now getting a clearer picture of what was involved with that wardrobe sputter you mentioned."

Before Adelaide could think of a response to that, Gideon swept her upright and went to work rearranging a bustle that had shifted once again.

The thought sprang to mind that there was something to be said about a competent gentleman, one who at times seemed to be quite like the heroes in her favorite dime novels.

"There. Better?" Gideon asked, tugging her skirt into place a minute later and pulling her out of thoughts that were rather ridiculous, given her current situation and because the gentleman in question was hardly a man she should allow herself to dwell on in a fanciful fashion in the first place.

"Much," she managed to utter. "Thank you."

"You're welcome, and with you now reassembled and unstabbed, allow me to escort you to the billiard room, where plopping won't be required, which should alleviate the danger of you suffering an attack from your bustle again."

"You do realize that your determination to see me well removed from the library is only succeeding in piquing my curiosity, don't you?" Adelaide asked.

"There's nothing to be curious about. I'm merely determined to get you settled in a room where no marauding bustles can go on the offensive because of furniture that's ill equipped to deal with the unusual fashion accessories that are seemingly all the rage."

"Or you want me out of this room because you're soon to have some manner of clandestine meeting with someone."

Gideon's lips twitched. "I'm going to assume, since you hurled a book at me earlier, and one you apparently brought with you to a dinner engagement, that you're an avid reader. I'm also going to assume, what with how you possess an impressive imagination, that you enjoy reading novels complete with clandestine meetings every other chapter."

"That's a lot of assumptions on your part, although I will admit spy novels are my genre of choice these days. I've recently become acquainted with Mr. Frank Reid, a most marvelous detective who showed up on the pages of a story titled *The Old Sleuth* as a series compilation that was first printed in *The Fireside Companion* back in 1872."

"You'll have to tell me all about this Frank character after I see you settled in the billiard room."

"I won't be getting settled anywhere until you answer a few questions—those being whether or not you're soon to have a clandestine meeting with someone, and why an esteemed member of the Four Hundred would have a questionable meeting with someone to begin with."

"I'm not preparing for any type of meeting, nor am I a spy, which is probably the next thing you'll accuse me of since you just admitted you enjoy spy novels."

Adelaide drew in a sharp breath. "That would explain a lot about you."

"The fact that I'm not a spy?"

"The fact that you *are* one."

Gideon was smiling one of the most charming smiles she'd ever seen him use before, one that, in Adelaide's humble opinion, seemed practiced. "Why would you think me being a spy explains much about me?"

She refused to allow his smile to divert her from the conversation at hand. "Because you're always around whenever I find myself in dire predicaments, as if you have a sixth sense about such matters. The spies I've read about always possess those types of senses."

"I was standing five feet away from you when you went up in flames. The only sense I had at that particular moment was that you were on fire and someone needed to put you out."

"You saved me from tumbling over a cliff in Newport this past summer."

"Because you and I had only just finished playing a rousing game of Annie Over and I happened to be near you when you stumbled."

"But there were other gentlemen standing closer to me, yet none of them possessed the reflexes needed to stop me from plunging to an unpleasant death. Spies are notorious for being quick on their feet."

"So are gentlemen who start their days by taking a run through Central Park."

She wrinkled her nose. "Given your responsibilities to your family business, I would think that you wouldn't have time to do anything but get yourself fed and off to work most mornings."

"Ah, but you see, I'm not involved with the day-to-day operations of the family business. My brother, James, took over responsibility for that after my father died." He gave a bit of a shrug. "I've been relegated to seeing after our social responsibilities as well as our philanthropic ones, which doesn't require me to attend to any matters at the break of dawn."

She had the uncanny feeling there was far more to that story than he was divulging. "I would think your mother represents the Abbott family within society."

"Mother has retreated to Paris, where she finds the climate more accommodating to her rheumatism."

Her toe began tapping against the wooden floor. "But if you're the social face of the Abbott family, why don't you attend more society events, or linger longer at the few functions where I've seen you?"

His eyes twinkled. "How delightful to learn you've been observing me."

She waved that aside. "I'm a confirmed wallflower, Gideon. I have a lot of unoccupied time on my hands at any given event, so don't read too much into that." She frowned. "But returning to your family responsibilities, don't you find philanthropy and social obligations rather dull after spending years attending the Naval Academy and then going into service with the navy?"

"You know I attended the Naval Academy?"

"You're an eligible gentleman from a well-connected society family. Talk has always been rampant about you." She caught his eye. "I must admit I'm now surprised that talk hasn't centered around matters of espionage. I once overheard a general speaking with my father, and he mentioned that the navy was the first branch of the military to embrace an official intelligence-gathering department. Now that I think about that, well . . . so much about you makes perfect sense."

"You were eavesdropping on your father?" he asked.

She gave an airy wave of a gloved hand. "Completely by accident. I was wandering around the back terrace of our Hudson estate and the French doors to my father's office just happened to be open, and . . . there you have it. Unintentional eavesdropping."

"Or intentional lurking. But to address what is obviously a vague theory about me on your part, I'm no longer with the navy, so no, I'm not some type of secret agent. With that now firmly settled, allow me to retrieve the book you hurled at me. After that, I'll get you settled somewhere no one will stumble upon you, which will allow you to return to reading whatever riveting story I'm sure you're anxious to dive back into."

"I'm finding this conversation far more intriguing than the mummy story I was reading earlier."

It came as no surprise when he completely ignored that as he strode across the room and plucked her book from the floor. As he straightened, she took a step toward him, but stilled when, from out of the corner of her eye, she noticed something on the floor—something that was sticking out from behind the fainting couch, and something that certainly explained Gideon's determination to see her well removed from the library.

She lifted her chin as Gideon rejoined her, earning a sigh from him in the process.

"You look like you have additional questions," he said.

"Indeed. The most burning of which regards the shoe I just spotted—one that's behind the fainting couch, and one I assume is attached to someone's leg."

Three

❧

"Huh. Would you look at that?" Gideon said, directing his attention to where Adelaide was nodding. "There *is* a shoe, and one that's definitely attached to a leg." He was by her side a second later, taking hold of her arm and prodding her toward the door. "Allow me to see you well removed from what could certainly develop into a perilous situation."

"Nice try, Gideon, but I'm not going anywhere," Adelaide said, slipping out of his hold and hustling over to the fainting couch, her mouth dropping open at the sight that met her eyes.

A man truly *was* lying prone on the floor, dressed in black, with a cap pulled low over his brow. His hands were tied in front of him with what appeared to be a drapery cord, but he wasn't moving a muscle, which demanded an explanation.

"It's little wonder you didn't want me lingering in the library," she said, turning to Gideon. "In all honesty, I'm feeling quite idiotic for not noticing there was an unconscious man behind the couch I was perched on earlier. Given that his hands are tied, I'm going to assume he's not dead because there'd be little point in securing a man who'd breathed his last, but what happened? Or better yet, who is he?"

Gideon's forehead furrowed. "Don't you think instead of pressing me for answers, you should be skedaddling out of here like most normal ladies would do?"

"I've never been deemed what anyone would consider normal." She returned her attention to the unconscious man, leaning forward and peering at his face. "Good heavens. That's Frank."

"You know him?" Gideon asked.

"Not personally."

"Then how do you know his name's Frank?"

"He's a frequent customer at Bainswright Books. I once overheard a conversation he was holding with a few men, and one of those men called him Frank." She straightened. "And not that I can say this with certainty, given that the men moved away from the rack of books I was, ah, lingering behind, but his last name might be Fitzsimmons."

Gideon gave his chin a scratch. "I know I'm going to regret asking this, but you weren't intentionally eavesdropping on these men, were you?"

"It's hardly my fault if I happen to be in spots where conversations can be easily overheard, nor is it my fault that I seem to be one of those ladies no one seems to notice."

"You're quite mistaken if you believe you're a lady who doesn't stand out in a crowd."

Pleasure immediately coursed through her, but before Adelaide could appreciate the feeling to its fullest, Gideon crossed his arms over his chest. "May I assume there was a reason you were snooping around that day in the bookstore when you listened in on Frank and his friends' conversation?"

"I won't deny I may have decided to lurk behind a specific bookcase that particular day, but I had a good reason for doing so. Frank never struck me as a bibliophile, and yet I'd seen him wandering around Bainswright Books quite often and rarely with any books in hand. There was also something about the way he dressed that piqued my curiosity." She glanced back to Frank. "Not that you can tell this at the moment, given the manner in which he's currently garbed, which seems to be burglar-chic, but he's normally a very dapper dresser, although on the flashy side, something one doesn't often see down on the far side of Bleecker Street."

"If that's where this Bainswright Books is, I'm going to suggest you discontinue patronizing that establishment. With your unfortunate habit of courting disasters, you should steer clear of questionable areas in the city."

Adelaide waved that aside. "Bainswright Books has the largest assortment of books in the city, and it's how I've amassed a collection of dime novels I wouldn't have been able to find anywhere else. There's absolutely no chance I'll stop shopping there. However, that has nothing to do with this most unusual situation at hand." She gestured to Frank. "I currently have numerous questions regarding poor Frank, such as why you've tied him up and why he's still not moving. I don't see any blood, unless the black he's wearing is concealing that."

"There's no blood because I used a blackjack on him."

"Ah, so you *are* responsible for Frank's condition."

Gideon raked a hand through his hair. "I have no idea why I admitted that to you. I was intending to suggest you return to the dinner party before Frank regains consciousness, which could pose a danger to you."

"He hasn't so much as stirred a single muscle, so I'm safe for now, and . . ." She smiled. "Don't feel bad about your unintentional admission. I've been known to fluster people at the best of times, and this is hardly the best of times." She took a step closer to Gideon. "Since I'm in no immediate danger, if we could return to the blackjack—I have no idea what that is, but it sounds exactly like something a man who spends his time engaged in clandestine activities would know about."

Gideon settled a frown on her. "You're very tenacious about my supposed involvement with matters of intrigue."

"Tenacity, I'm afraid I must admit, is another fault of mine."

"May I assume you strive to keep that fault hidden from your mother as well?"

"Of course, but if we could return to the blackjack?"

"I'd rather discuss the benefits of escorting you to a room that doesn't have an unconscious man in it."

She settled for sending him a quirk of a brow, which resulted with him blowing out a rather resigned-sounding breath.

"You're incorrigible," he muttered before he dug into the pocket of his jacket and pulled out an object that had a knob attached to a short shaft. "This is a blackjack, or some people refer to it as a blackjack sap. The top is weighted with balls of lead underneath the leather, and when wielded properly, it can deliver a blow that's capable of knocking a man out."

"Did you hit him in the head? Because if so, we might need to summon a physician."

"I hit his neck—or more specifically, a certain artery in his neck. He went down like a stone, but he won't suffer any lasting harm. The effects usually only last for an hour, give or take."

"Did you learn how to do that in the Naval Academy?"

"No. An old friend of mine taught me before I entered the Academy. But since there's no telling exactly how long Frank will remain unconscious, we'll need to talk about Roland later."

"He's the one who taught you how to wield a blackjack?"

"He is, although I probably shouldn't have mentioned him to you either."

"I'm not going to tell anyone about this Roland character, but may I assume he's in the intelligence business?"

Gideon took her by surprise when he suddenly smiled. "He's a partner at an accounting firm."

Adelaide frowned. "Seems somewhat odd that a man who

taught you how to use an unusual weapon would enjoy the rather dull business of rectifying monetary accounts."

"Indeed, but now isn't the moment to discuss Roland or the nuances of accounting in general. The night is getting away from me, and I need to resolve a mess I never intended on making."

She considered Frank again. "I can see where Frank would pose a problem for you, especially if you *are* involved in matters you don't want society to learn about. However, since I've obviously found you out, or at least have some rather interesting suspicions about you at this point, I don't believe it would be too much to ask for you to explain why you used a blackjack on him."

"Are your knees going to go weak again if I don't appease your curiosity?"

She curtailed a grin. "My knees are now in fine form, thank you very much. Using them as an excuse would be churlish of me at this point, something my mother disapproves of almost as much as contrariness, although . . ." She gave her nose a scratch. "It's curious, now that I think on it, that you've humored me as long as you have, considering you've knocked a man out in the midst of a dinner party, and yet you've wasted time speaking with me instead of throwing me over your shoulder and carting me off to the billiard room."

"I'm not a gentleman who resorts to caveman tactics."

"Perhaps not under normal circumstances, but I imagine you'd consider doing exactly that if you were under a dire time constraint, which I suppose you are to a certain extent. However, given that you didn't usher me directly out of this room suggests you really do have a calamity on your hands—one you have yet to figure out how to resolve."

"Maybe *you* should consider becoming involved with intelligence gathering because you're far too intuitive for your own good," Gideon muttered.

"If I thought an intelligence agency would take on a woman, I'd be first in line. Sadly, we women are gravely underestimated, which means I highly doubt I'll ever be given such a wonderful opportunity. With that said, though, perhaps I could assist you with your current situation. I've been known to figure out plot twists when I'm only two chapters into a spy novel."

"This isn't one of your novels."

"It's reading like fiction to me, and besides, what have you got to lose by allowing me to help you?"

Gideon returned his attention to Frank. "I suppose it wouldn't hurt to put our heads together, but . . ." He caught her gaze. "Discretion in this matter is a must. No one can know what transpired in this library tonight."

"Discretion is my middle name."

"Your middle name is Winifred, after your maternal grand-mother."

"You know my middle name?"

"I made a point of learning a little about you after you went up in flames, but to return to Frank, in all honesty, I had no idea who he was until you told me. Unfortunately, I've heard more than a few rumors about him, ones that suggest he's an up-and-coming crime boss, who, as you mentioned, is known to be a flashy dresser."

"I can't say I'm surprised about that," Adelaide admitted. "I did detect a menacing air about him, which is another reason why I was doing all that lurking. I'll now need to apprise Mr. Bainswright of Frank's reputation at my earliest convenience—not that Mr. Bainswright will ban him from the store, since I'm relatively convinced there are more than a few dubious characters roaming the aisles on any given day."

One of Gideon's brows shot up. "You know there are questionable customers frequenting this bookshop and yet you continue to patronize it?"

"We've already discussed why I love this store, so moving

on." Adelaide nodded to Frank. "How was it that you became embroiled in an altercation with Frank?"

"Believe me, it wasn't premeditated. I was merely doing a favor for a, well, acquaintance, if you will, who received a note earlier this evening, asking her to meet with a fervent admirer tonight in this very library. She, of course, was reluctant to do so, and asked me to investigate the man for her. When I stepped into the library, I asked Frank if he was waiting for this acquaintance of mine, and the next thing I knew, he was charging at me with a pistol gripped in his hand. I had no choice but to defend myself."

"And how fortunate for you that you're evidently capable of taking on a pistol-wielding man *and* living to tell the tale."

"Indeed, although I would have preferred to not have been forced to engage in such a troubling circumstance tonight, what with how it'll be difficult to explain the situation to anyone if I can't get Frank out of here without being seen."

"I'm sure questions would be asked regarding how a gentleman of leisure was capable of dispatching a known criminal boss without suffering a scratch, just as I'm sure there would also be questions about why you felt compelled to meet with Frank at Sophia Campanini's request."

"I never said Sophia Campanini asked me to approach a mysterious admirer."

Adelaide stifled a snort. "Please, it doesn't take a master sleuth to figure out that less-than-difficult puzzle. It would be an unusual circumstance for a lady of the Four Hundred to receive such a note from an admirer. Sophia Campanini, on the other hand, being a very in-demand opera singer, is probably accustomed to admirers sending her notes in the hope she'll grant them a few moments of her time. Given that she's rumored to enjoy her admirers lavishing gifts on her, she might not care to meet with an unknown admirer on her own but would certainly want someone to investigate him for her, especially if the admirer in question possessed deep pockets."

"That's some rather impressive deductive reasoning on your part," Gideon admitted.

"That you would acknowledge that suggests I'm quite right about this matter. One of the questions now remaining is why Sophia Campanini would specifically seek you out and ask for your assistance."

"It would be best if I don't disclose those details to you."

Adelaide's toe began beating a rapid tattoo against the Aubusson carpet. "We've come too far for you to turn nondisclosure on me now. However, since you seem reluctant to elaborate, I'm going to assume that Sophia approached you because she's somehow aware that you're a gentleman who knows how to handle delicate situations, although . . ." She tapped her finger against her chin. "I haven't puzzled out how she'd know that, unless . . ."

"Unless what?" Gideon prodded after a good minute passed in silence as Adelaide tried to figure the matter out.

She tilted her head. "I'm going to hazard a guess and say you're involved with some type of private enterprise that concerns itself with delicate matters." Her lips began to curve when Gideon winced ever so slightly.

"That's it, isn't it?" she asked. "You're no mere gentleman of leisure, but are using skills you obviously honed during your stint in the navy for some secret organization, and . . ." She stepped closer to him. "I bet you're involved with that accounting firm you mentioned, one run by your old friend Roland. But he doesn't run an accounting firm, does he? It's more along the lines of an investigation agency, using the whole accounting business as a front."

Gideon's mouth went a little slack. "How did you arrive at that conclusion?"

"You smiled when you mentioned the accounting firm."

"Perhaps I find accounting amusing."

"No one finds accounting amusing, not even accountants.

But returning to Roland the Accountant—may I dare hope he uses that as a code name, quite like criminals do?"

"What code names have you ever heard criminals use?"

"Boris the Butcher springs to mind."

"You know Boris the Butcher?"

Adelaide raised a hand to her throat. "That almost sounds as if you know a real Boris the Butcher, whereas the one I was speaking about was in one of my books."

Gideon sent her an overly innocent smile. "I was referring to a Boris I read about in a book as well."

"Considering you're undoubtedly involved with the hazy world of clandestine operations, one would think you'd be more proficient with lying."

His brows drew together. "Why do you think I'm lying?"

"Your right eye twitched. But if we may return to the situation at hand? *Are* you involved with Roland the Accountant?"

"He doesn't go by Roland the Accountant, merely Roland Kelly, but allow me to point out that I'm beginning to believe *your* name should be Adelaide the Persistent."

"If I'm ever fortunate enough to need a code name, I'll choose something far more intriguing, such as Adelaide the Avenger, or . . ."

"Adelaide the Annoying?" he finished for her when she faltered.

"I'm sure you do find me rather annoying at the moment, but I assure you, my ability to irritate you will significantly decrease if you'll simply tell me how Sophia knew she could ask you to intervene with this so-called admirer. Considering he attacked you, I have to believe it wasn't admiration he holds for Sophia but something of a far darker nature."

"That would appear to be the case, but . . ." Gideon released a breath. "I'm not comfortable revealing too many details about what I do, because there's a reason I've taken such pains to keep my true occupation a secret. I don't want to expose any innocent parties to the risks involved with my chosen profession."

"Which is admirable, but I've uncovered your secret." She nodded to Frank, who'd still not moved a muscle. "With that said, if we don't figure out how to get him out of here, society as a whole may soon know your secret as well."

"You might have the right of that, but again, I'm not comfortable disclosing much."

"A few basics will suffice, and know that I won't breathe a word to anyone." She held up her little finger. "I'll even be willing to pinky promise."

His eyes crinkled at the corners. "I don't believe anyone's offered to pinky promise with me since I was in short pants."

"No one should ever be too old to pinky promise," Adelaide said, holding out her little finger and doing her best to ignore the jolt of something interesting that raced up her arm the second his little finger curled around hers. She gave his finger a quick shake, retrieved her hand, and summoned up a smile. "With that out of the way—to the basics. What exactly are you involved in?"

"I'm sure you're going to take great delight in this because . . ." Gideon sent her a hint of a smile. "You were exactly on the mark about me being involved with Roland Kelly. We're business partners, and yes, we delve into matters of deception and duplicity, normally for titans of industry, although Sophia Campanini hired us a few months back to investigate the background of a gentleman who was enamored with her."

"How did she know your accounting firm was a front for an investigation agency?"

"Sophia has a lot of connections throughout the city, most of them wealthy gentlemen. It wouldn't have been difficult for her to learn about Roland, although the only reason she discovered I'm involved with the accounting firm is because she saw me engaged in conversation with the gentleman she wanted investigated, and she put two and two together." He rubbed his chin. "I had to have a chat with her about discretion and may have had to promise her priority service from the firm whenever she needs assistance with any delicate matters."

"Bet that rankled."

"Given that Sophia enjoys the reputation of being a demanding woman and has taken to contacting the firm over the most trivial of matters, yes, it's somewhat annoying."

"But it seems as if she truly did need someone to intervene on her behalf tonight, what with how Frank Fitzsimmons reacted to your appearance."

Gideon shot Frank a glance. "I'm sure one of the first questions I'll ask him after I get him well removed from the Nelson estate is why he went to such lengths to meet with Sophia. He must have had a matter of great importance to discuss with her since he took the time to travel from the city to the Hudson. Most criminal bosses would have sent an underling to deal with Sophia, which does lend a certain sense of menace to whatever she's gotten herself involved in."

"Indeed, which means the sooner you get him roused from his unconscious state and talking, the better."

"My only obstacle with that is I haven't the foggiest idea how to get him removed from the library without being seen. While I could say I wandered into the library and was attacked without provocation, authorities will then most certainly be called in."

"And you'll lose your opportunity to interrogate the man," Adelaide said. "Since that will leave too many questions left unanswered, what you need right now is a distraction." She caught his gaze. "It just so happens I'm more than experienced with creating chaos."

Gideon shook his head. "I can't allow you to place yourself in another embarrassing incident because I have a dilemma on my hands."

"Of course you can because I owe you."

"How do you figure that?"

She moved across the room, drew aside a curtain that revealed French doors leading to the back terrace, and smiled as a plan immediately began to form. "You've saved me from unpleasant fates numerous times. I could have been horribly disfigured if not for your quick actions as well as dead if I'd gone over a cliff, but because of your intervention, I'm still here, alive, kicking, and not deformed. That means I'm going to assist you tonight, whether you want me to or not."

"I think we need to add stubbornness to what is rapidly turning into a long list of attributes I doubt your mother would approve of."

"Mother is perfectly aware of my faults. She just doesn't care to acknowledge them. However . . ." Adelaide twitched the curtain back into place before returning her attention to Gideon. "Perhaps it would be to my benefit if you were to mention some of those faults to Mother because, if she learns that gentlemen believe I'm odd, stubborn, contrary, and perhaps a touch tenacious at times, she'll resign herself to the inevitable."

He quirked a brow. "And that would be?"

"That she'll need to content herself with having a daughter who's destined to remain a spinster."

"I doubt you're destined for spinsterhood."

"And I'll respectfully disagree, but now is hardly the moment to discuss my spinster status, not when I have some chaos to attend to."

Gideon frowned. "I'm not convinced that should be our first approach to solve my quandary."

"In this situation, it's the only approach to use if you want to get Frank Fitzsimmons well removed from here without being seen. That means you need to stop arguing with me and let me get on with things."

"What exactly are these things you're going to get on with?"

She shrugged. "I only have a glimmer of an idea right now,

one I hope manifests into something more once I put the rudimental aspects of it into motion. With that said; after I get on my way, you'll need to crack open the French doors behind the curtains, then give me five minutes. I believe that's enough time for me to draw attention."

"How will I know you're finding success with your plan?"

"By the screaming, of course."

Gideon's eyes widened. "There's going to be screaming?"

"It would hardly be a worthy distraction if there wasn't screaming." With that, Adelaide strode into motion, slipped around Gideon, scooped up her reticule from the fainting couch, and headed for the door, pretending she didn't hear the protests he voiced as she hurried into the hallway.

It took her less than a minute to find her way to the kitchen, smiling at a footman who didn't hesitate to find her a few pieces of bread when she told him she needed it to settle a queasy stomach. After thanking the man, she headed through a door leading to the back courtyard, nodded to some of the other guests, then set her sights on her cousin, Charles, who was still sitting by the fountain, exactly where she'd left him what seemed like eons ago.

"I've brought bread," she called in an overly loud voice, knowing it would attract attention from the guests lingering on the terrace.

Charles frowned as she drew to a stop beside him. "Why are you bringing me bread?"

"I thought you might enjoy feeding the swans. It could put you in a more charitable frame of mind."

Charles directed his frown toward three swans that were heading their direction. "From what I've observed about these swans as I've contemplated the dismal state of my life out here, they're not what I'd consider friendly."

"Perhaps some bread will change that." Adelaide waved one of the slices at the swans, leaning over the edge of the fountain in what she hoped would be seen as a casual move. "Why, look how graceful they are, Charles, and . . ."

Anything else she might have been thinking about saying got lost when the swans began emitting a trumpeting sound right before charging her way.

All too quickly, they were almost upon her, but when she turned to remove herself from the situation, her bustle shifted and threw her off balance, and before she knew it, she was tumbling into the water.

Regrettably, even though she'd been planning on purposely falling into the fountain at some point to provide Gideon with the distraction he needed, she'd certainly not been intending to plunge headfirst into downright freezing water, nor had she even considered the notion that her foray into the fountain would be accompanied by an attack of vicious creatures that seemed to have murderous intentions on their minds.

Four

⚜

Gideon reined Zeus, his temperamental beast of a stallion, to a stop and swung from the saddle as the events of the previous night cavorted through his mind yet again.

He'd not been in accord with Adelaide's plan to provide him with a much-needed distraction, but she'd given him a diversion of epic proportions.

It had barely taken her the five minutes she'd claimed to need before the sound of screaming reached him, an occurrence that caused guests to stream from Mrs. Nelson's house and rush to gawk at what was unfolding around a fountain in the back courtyard.

He'd missed the actual event since he'd slung Fitzsimmons over his shoulder and hauled him to his waiting carriage once he realized the guests had been sufficiently distracted. Thankfully, he'd not taken note of a single person witnessing the odd sight of a member of the Four Hundred lugging an unconscious man away from a dinner party.

By the time he'd gotten Frank ensconced in the carriage, where two of his associates who doubled as groomsmen assured him they'd keep him secured until he returned, the screaming, shrieking, and obvious mayhem had come to an end.

Wanting to ascertain Adelaide had survived whatever havoc she'd enacted, he'd slipped through the shadows and back to the courtyard, nodding to guests who were strolling toward the ballroom. The name he heard whispered time and again left him with the distinct impression Adelaide's plan might have exceeded the term *chaotic*.

It hadn't taken long before the particulars of Adelaide's latest disaster reached his ears, with Miss Cynthia Wilcox hustling to his side and taking hold of his arm, all aflutter to discuss everything that had transpired moments before. To say he'd been taken aback regarding the details of what Adelaide had experienced—and in aid to him, no less—was an understatement.

It didn't come as much of a surprise that she'd chosen the fountain to use as a diversion. She'd obviously been intending to suffer a plunge into the water, or at least a near tumble. However, it was doubtful she'd been expecting an assault by swans, that unfortunate circumstance responsible for her almost drowning after the birds attacked. Fortunately, her cousin, Mr. Charles Wetzel, had been close at hand and jumped into the fountain to save her.

Charles's rescue attempt evidently didn't go smoothly because additional swans went on the rampage as he, from what Cynthia Wilcox disclosed, tried to valiantly fight them off as he managed to get Adelaide's head above water amidst an assault by creatures everyone, up until that point, had considered tranquil birds that lent a beautiful atmosphere to Mrs. Nelson's well-maintained estate.

Tranquility had been in short supply once the birds went on the offensive. And if attacking swans wasn't a peculiar enough sight for the guests, the peculiarity, in Cynthia's opinion, had turned downright remarkable when Chef Gagneux, Mrs. Nelson's famed culinary artist, rushed toward the fountain in an attempt to save Adelaide and Charles, all while balancing two gold platters filled with one of the main courses.

By the time Chef Gagneux reached the fountain, the swans were in a frenzy, and after one of the birds took note of the chef and his flagship dish, *Canards a la Rouennaise*, the madness of the situation increased tenfold.

From all accounts, no one was exactly certain if the swans abandoned their assault on Adelaide and Charles because they were infuriated that Chef Gagneux was attempting to draw their attention with a dish made from pressed duck and had taken offense that their near relations were being served up on a platter, or if they didn't mind that at all and simply wanted to sample the dish for themselves, which, frankly, was a far more troubling thought.

Nevertheless, whatever the reason, the swans set their sights on Chef Gagneux and proceeded to engage in a full-on assault.

It was evident the chef's determination to save Adelaide and Charles only went so far because he didn't hesitate to throw Mrs. Nelson's expensive platters at the advancing swans, his culinary masterpiece going airborne the second he let the plates fly. Pieces of pressed duck began raining down on the assembled guests, as did the sauce that accompanied the duck, which was why many ladies, including Sophia Campanini, immediately took leave of the dinner party, their gowns splattered with droplets of what looked exactly like blood.

The besieged chef didn't linger to notice the damage his dish caused. The last anyone saw of him, he was bolting across the back courtyard, swans nipping at his heels, yelling over his shoulder he wouldn't be back to complete the midnight supper—in fact, he wouldn't step foot on the estate again until Mrs. Nelson got rid of every swan once and for all.

To say Mrs. Nelson was displeased with Adelaide was an understatement.

According to Cynthia, Mrs. Nelson gave Adelaide a blistering dressing-down regarding the inadvisability of feeding bread to her swans in the first place, since they maintained a specific diet fed to them by her staff. She then launched into a tirade about how careless it had been for Adelaide to give her esteemed guests a glimpse of her unmentionables, which Mrs. Nelson emphatically stated had been well beyond the pale. After that, she accused Adelaide of ruining her dinner party, especially given that the entertainment for the evening, that being the incomparable Sophia Campanini, had departed in high dudgeon. Mrs. Nelson had then finished her rant by demanding Adelaide leave her estate posthaste before additional foolishness could occur.

Such a demand evidently didn't go over well with Adelaide's mother. Phyllis apparently rose magnificently to her daughter's defense, delivering a scorching diatribe to Mrs. Nelson regarding etiquette as it pertains to one's guests. She then took to delivering her own dressing-down, chiding Mrs. Nelson over having the audacity to blame Adelaide for the sorry behavior of savage swans, which, in Phyllis's opinion, had no business being given access to a fountain where any innocent guest could have been accosted.

Cynthia's eyes had widened at that point in the conversation before she'd disclosed that Mrs. Nelson, at the suggestion her swans were savage, began swelling up like a hot air balloon. Before she had the opportunity to explode, though, Phyllis whisked a soggy Adelaide over to a waiting carriage, along with a waterlogged and severely tattered Charles Wetzel, and off they trundled from the Nelson estate.

It was clear that Adelaide's misadventure, which had been carried out in service to him, was going to keep the tongues wagging for months to come, which meant . . .

He owed her.

That was exactly why he was now at Miss Camilla Pierpont's Hudson estate, hoping his very good friend would be willing to extend him a rather large favor.

"Mr. Abbott, good morning, sir. Miss Pierpont didn't mention you were expected today."

Stepping around Zeus, Gideon discovered Freddie, one of Camilla's grooms, standing a few feet away, warily eyeing Zeus, the wariness increasing when Zeus released a snort and tossed his head.

"It's an unscheduled visit, Freddie," Gideon returned. "But the morning was beckoning, and since Zeus enjoys a brisk gallop, I decided to ride him over here."

"Dare I hope that galloping left Zeus in an amicable frame of mind?" Freddie asked.

"I've never experienced Zeus being anything other than ornery, gallop or not, but we can always hope."

"That we can," Freddie agreed with a quirk of his lips. "He does have a certain charm, though, which is why I know I speak for all the grooms employed on the Pierpont estate when I say we always relish the opportunities to tussle with Zeus whenever you come to call on Miss Pierpont." He squared his shoulders and moved to take the reins from Gideon. "I'll get Zeus settled in a stall, perhaps bribe him with a few apples, and pray for the best."

As Freddie led Zeus away, although it was hardly an encouraging sign when Zeus began nickering in a menacing fashion, Gideon headed for the house. He was greeted at the front door by Mr. Timken, the Pierponts' butler, who was already holding the door open for him.

"Mr. Abbott, what a pleasant surprise," Mr. Timken began in a rather loud voice, obviously done to be heard over the organ music that was all but shaking the walls. "Miss Pierpont will be delighted to see you, as will the rest of the staff because . . ." He took Gideon's hat and leaned close. "She's playing 'Toccata et Fugue' this morning."

"An interesting choice to start any day."

"Or morose," Mr. Timken countered. "But it's better than

what she was playing before this selection, which was Chopin's Nocturnes. That left half the staff in tears."

"An unfortunate circumstance, to be sure."

"Indeed," Mr. Timken agreed. "I sent everyone to do a touch of cleaning up to the attic since it's far enough removed from the music room to where the songs Miss Pierpont is choosing are a little muffled." He leaned closer. "I'm hopeful, given that nothing seems to keep her attention for long these days, that she'll decide to spend a few hours painting by the river, although painting is hardly going to stave off the ennui she's been suffering of late."

"Camilla's finding life on the Hudson dull?"

"It's my belief Miss Pierpont is finding life in general tedious, but I believe she may have experienced some excitement last night. She mentioned something about utter pandemonium at Mrs. Nelson's dinner party." Mr. Timken caught Gideon's eye. "Talk around the breakfast table between Miss Pierpont and her aunt Edna, or rather Mrs. Robinson, revolved around a Miss Adelaide Duveen."

Gideon suppressed a shudder. "What did they say happened?"

"I'm afraid the conversation was cut short when Camilla stated she was going to spend the morning playing the organ and Mrs. Robinson suddenly remembered a scheduled engagement. She then all but bolted out of the dining room and departed from the house ten minutes later."

"Probably a prudent decision on Edna's part."

"Quite, since it spared her a morning filled with mournful musical choices." Mr. Timken shook his head. "Unfortunately, I don't believe pursuing less-than-adventurous activities will alleviate Miss Pierpont's boredom. However, now that you're here, and since she values your counsel, you might want to consider suggesting she take on a young lady to sponsor during the upcoming Season. She's neglected to dabble in her matchmaking efforts of late, which I believe is one of the reasons for her ennui."

"It's doubtful I'll be successful convincing Camilla to return to matchmaking," Gideon said. "She's been extremely vocal regarding what she considers a spectacular failure with her efforts regarding Miss Leonie Warwick, otherwise known as Lady Westward these days. Add in the notion that Camilla was also disgruntled over the attitude of society ladies on the marriage mart this past summer in Newport, and I'm relatively certain she's abandoned all interest in matchmaking pursuits."

Mr. Timken glanced up at the chandelier in the entranceway and winced when it began rattling, undoubtedly because Camilla had reached a particularly robust section of the song. "I don't know why she'd consider a match between Miss Leonie Warwick and an earl to be a failure," he shouted.

"Camilla doesn't believe Leonie held any affection for Lord Westward and only married him because he's an aristocrat," Gideon yelled back.

"Miss Pierpont does pride herself on making love matches," Mr. Timken returned. "Still, I witnessed Lady Westward driving through the streets of New York after the wedding ceremony with her new husband and she looked downright ecstatic to me."

Thankfully, the chandelier stopped rattling when the volume suddenly decreased as Camilla reached a new stanza.

"Camilla would say Lady Westward only looked that way because she procured a coveted title, whereas Camilla wanted her to secure a match steeped in affection." Gideon smiled. "You'll be pleased to learn, though, that I'm here today because I have a proposition to present to Camilla, one that could see her boredom set aside for the foreseeable future."

Mr. Timken raised a hand to his chest. "Do not say you're going to propose marriage again to our dear Miss Pierpont, something her parents have been angling to arrange for years."

"Given what happened the one and only time I initiated the idea of marriage between us, no, that's not what I have in mind."

"I suppose broaching marriage, because I well recall what happened the last time you did that, might be a bit risky," Mr. Timken muttered before he winced when the organ began playing in earnest again. "But no sense dawdling here with me. You have a proposition to present, and here's hoping Miss Pierpont will be receptive to that, which should distract her from her music, at least for an hour or so. I'll tell her you're here."

"I can see myself to the music room, Mr. Timken," Gideon said. "You should go rescue the staff from the attic."

After Mr. Timken inclined his head and they exchanged grins, Gideon headed down the hallway, stopping to give Gladys, Camilla's poodle that everyone claimed to be a disgrace to her breed, a scratch. After earning a single wag of the pom at the end of her tail in return, Gideon continued until he reached the doorway of the music room, stopping just over the threshold as he took a moment to consider one of his oldest friends.

It wasn't a surprise to find Camilla dressed in the first state of fashion as she continued playing the organ, wearing a morning gown of delicate silk, with a matching ribbon woven into her blond hair.

Camilla, of course, would never consider leaving her room in a state of dishabille, no matter if she was planning on staying in for the day or not. She was considered by everyone to be the consummate lady, schooled since birth in all the feminine arts and rules of etiquette. Because of that, she knew exactly what was expected of a lady born into a Knickerbocker family, and she'd striven to live up to the high standards of her family name.

She'd mastered a variety of musical instruments before she was ten, organ included, perfected the art of social conversation before she was twelve, and was known to be one of the most beautiful and charming ladies to ever grace the Four Hundred.

Deemed an Incomparable when she'd made her debut at seventeen, Camilla hadn't lacked for suitors, although Gideon had not been in New York when she'd officially entered high society. He'd been traveling the world, working for the newly formed Naval Intelligence Agency, but he'd received letters from Camilla giving him updates, although the delivery of her letters had been sporadic. That was why he'd been unaware of a catastrophe in the making that developed during Camilla's first Season—one that was set into motion when Camilla made the acquaintance of George Sherrington, or rather the Earl of Shrewsbury.

She'd fallen madly in love with him at first sight, and Lord Shrewsbury proclaimed, at least according to Camilla, that he returned that sentiment. However, disaster was imminent after Camilla told her parents she'd found her true love. Hubert Pierpont, Camilla's father, had taken one look at George Sherrington and had seen him for exactly what he was—a fortune hunter. He'd then refused George's request for Camilla's hand in marriage, which had resulted with Camilla doing something she'd never done in her life.

She'd rebelled.

She informed her father she was going to marry George anyway, even after Hubert told her he would not give so much as a single penny of her dowry to a man he considered a complete and utter scoundrel.

Being madly in love, Camilla opted for love over fortune, erroneously believing Lord Shrewsbury would, of course, be of the same mind and wouldn't blink an eye over marrying her even though she would come into the marriage penniless.

Unfortunately, Lord Shrewsbury's response had been exactly what one would expect from a fortune hunter.

Once he discovered marriage to Camilla would not see his coffers sufficiently plumped up, George informed her that, regrettably and without his knowledge, his mother had arranged for him to marry another society lady, Miss Eleonora Deerhurst. Miss Deerhurst had been out four Seasons, and her father had not thought twice about offering Lord Shrewsbury a substantial fortune to marry his daughter, especially when it allowed the Deerhurst family to not only get Eleonora finally married off but also allowed them the privilege of adding an aristocratic title to their family tree.

What Gideon found most repulsive about the situation, though, was that instead of admitting to Camilla that her greatest allure for him had been her money, Lord Shrewsbury told her that she was the love of his life and would always be his one and only, but as a true gentleman, he was honor-bound to marry Miss Deerhurst since their engagement announcement had already been sent off to the papers.

From the letters Gideon received from Camilla after the fact, she was heartbroken as well as furious with her parents. She'd vowed then and there to never marry, unwilling to put her heart in jeopardy ever again, even though she was an only child, and as such, her parents' only hope for continuing the Pierpont bloodline.

Camilla hadn't batted an eye over that, content to allow the Pierpont lineage to die with her, no matter how much that thought distressed her parents.

Hubert Pierpont had been determined to change Camilla's mind and had even gone so far as to approach Gideon to try and convince him that he, being one of Camilla's closest friends, should consider marrying Camilla.

Even though Gideon had been in no position to take on a wife, what with how he was never in the country, he'd not been able to refuse Hubert's proposal because Camilla had clearly been suffering, and he couldn't abide seeing her in such a sorry state.

His offer of marriage had not gone well.

Camilla had thanked him very prettily for extending her

such an honor—right before she'd punched him, which had been completely unexpected. She told him to discontinue with the ridiculousness of thinking she'd ever want to marry a man she considered a brother, having practically grown up with him since their respective brownstones abutted each other in the city and their Hudson family estates were less than a quarter mile apart.

That had been the last time they'd ever spoken of a marriage between them.

A wrong note bellowing from the organ snapped Gideon from his memories, his lips curving when Camilla released what almost sounded like a grunt before she lifted her fingers and then, to his complete astonishment, banged her head against the organ keys, the horrible sound that was subsequently produced leaving the windows trembling.

"Having an enjoyable morning, I see," he said, advancing into the room as Camilla's head shot up, her forehead now sporting red marks across it from pounding her head against the ivories.

"Gideon. I wasn't expecting you this morning," Camilla said, rising gracefully to her feet and gliding over to meet him, giving him her hand, which he dutifully kissed.

"I hope you don't mind the unannounced visit."

"You know I always enjoy your company, and it's not as if you interrupted anything of importance." She grimaced. "Did you hear me make a muck of that last stanza?"

"Would it be ungentlemanly of me to admit I did?"

Her eyes crinkled at the corners. "Well, don't tell anyone. I have a reputation as a great musical proficient to uphold."

"My lips are sealed." He tucked her hand into the crook of his arm and led her over to a settee upholstered in seafoam green, waiting until she got settled before he joined her.

"It's quite unlike Mr. Timken to not announce your arrival, even with you being considered a member of the family" was the first thing Camilla said after Gideon sat down.

"I offered to see myself in because your butler needed to rescue the servants from the attic."

Her forehead puckered. "Why would all the servants be in the attic? They normally wait until we're ready to close the house for the winter before they venture up there."

"I believe your questionable musical choices were responsible for Mr. Timken suggesting everyone remove themselves to a less . . . raucous floor."

"I was playing Chopin and Bach. Their music could never be considered raucous."

"Perhaps I should have said melodramatic choices instead." He smiled. "You do realize you set every chandelier to shaking, don't you?"

A sigh was her first response. "I'm afraid I didn't notice that, but I'll make sure to apologize to the staff after you leave. I should have realized my selections were a little much for the morning." She leaned back against the settee. "But enough about my music. Shall I assume you're here to apologize for neglecting me last night?"

"You know I did nothing of the sort," Gideon countered. "I distinctly remember greeting you after I made it through the receiving line."

"True, but you then abandoned me when Sophia Campanini arrived and sent one of her sycophants to fetch you."

"Surely you don't believe I'd rather spend time in Sophia's company instead of yours, do you?"

She gave his hand a pat. "Of course not. Sophia Campanini is a far too demanding woman to appeal to a gentleman like you. And I wasn't suggesting I felt abandoned because you went off to speak with her. I felt neglected because you never bothered to seek me out afterward to tell me exactly what she wanted."

"Why would you be interested in what Sophia wanted?"

"Because I imagine it had something to do with the accounting firm. I've also been dying to hear how an opera singer learned you're involved with that enterprise, especially when you've taken extreme measures to keep your involvement with the firm secret."

Gideon refused a sigh. "How did you come to the conclusion Sophia is aware of my association with the accounting firm?"

"Because she's not a woman you'd normally spend time with, and I've noticed you in her company more than once. Three weeks ago, I saw you speaking with her in Central Park, and before that, you were engaged in conversation with her after one of her performances." Camilla's nose wrinkled. "Granted, I suppose I could be wrong and you're not immune to her charms. If that's the case, I'll stop nagging you about why you were speaking with her. However, if you are, heaven forbid, enamored with her, you may prepare yourself to be lectured about the hazards of becoming involved with a woman who is more interested in what expensive gifts a gentleman is willing to lavish on her over the gentleman himself."

"I'm not enamored with Sophia Campanini."

"Wonderful, although I didn't actually imagine you were, which means I'm right and she needs the type of assistance that only the accounting firm can provide. All that remains now is for you to appease my curiosity and tell me exactly what that matter concerned, at which point I'll no longer be annoyed with you over your neglect last night."

Gideon shifted on the settee. "I'm afraid you're going to have to remain annoyed then because we've been over this numerous times. Simply because I disclosed my real occupation to you because you're one of my oldest and dearest friends does not mean I'm going to discuss any of our cases with you. For one, that would be a breach of client confidentiality, and two, as I've told you at least a million times, my occupation comes with risks, ones I don't want you anywhere near."

A narrowing of a brilliant blue eye was Camilla's first response to that before she lifted her chin. "You didn't tell me about the accounting firm because I'm your oldest friend. You told me because I was completely affronted on your behalf when you didn't sign up for another tour with the navy after your father died. From what I understood at the time, your brother, instead of bringing you on as his partner in the family business, relegated you to representing the family at social events and managing Abbott philanthropic endeavors. I found that completely unacceptable and was determined to speak my mind about the matter." She smoothed a hand over her wrinkleless skirt. "You knew full well that James wouldn't have lasted five minutes with me and would have spilled your secret without a second thought. That right there is why you coughed up details about the accounting firm, even though they were stingy details and only grudgingly disclosed."

"I'm sure I wasn't grudging about the matter."

"We'll need to agree to disagree about that."

Gideon fought a sigh because, in all honesty, Camilla was probably right about the manner in which he'd told her about the accounting firm, due no doubt to the fact he'd had no intentions of telling her what he was doing until she'd misunderstood the situation with his brother and had decided to act on his behalf.

Frankly, until his father died, Gideon had been eager to sign up for another tour with the navy because he enjoyed the intelligence work he did for the government. However, mere days after the unexpected death of the patriarch of his family, certain vultures of industry had descended on every Abbott enterprise, intent on hostile takeovers.

James had sent him a telegram apprising him of the concerning situation, adding that he wasn't certain he'd be able to save the family businesses. Gideon, who'd been trying to find passage home for his father's funeral from where he'd been stationed in Egypt, had reached out to Roland Kelly, a man who'd been his bodyguard throughout his youth and taught Gideon almost everything he knew about weapons and self-defense. Roland was also the man who'd pushed Gideon into pursuing a career in service, believing Gideon wasn't meant to live a life of leisure, but a life filled with purpose instead.

After Gideon left to attend the Naval Academy, Roland continued offering members of society protection against kidnapping attempts and the like, but he'd decided to turn his attention to private inquiry work after foiling a blackmail attempt against Mr. Edmund Sinclair, who'd insisted on paying Roland a hefty bonus for stopping the threats against him.

With his contacts throughout the city, Roland had grown his business at a steady rate and hadn't hesitated to investigate all the threats being leveled against Abbott business ventures. Gideon hadn't been surprised when Roland settled matters quickly, but he *had* been surprised when Roland pitched an unexpected business proposition: Roland wanted Gideon to bring everything he'd learned as an intelligence agent and come work with him as a partner in his company, the accounting firm. That proposition was what finalized Gideon's decision to leave the navy.

After speaking with his immediate supervisor in the navy and learning that the government would be more than happy to have a man with Gideon's particular skillset working in the private sector, which would still make him available to take on government jobs where discretion was a must, Gideon had agreed to Roland's proposal and not extended his tour of duty. He'd then suggested to James that he take over representing the family at society events, something James hadn't balked at in the least because he loathed society and had been only too willing to turn over what he considered nonsense to his younger brother.

Adopting the role of a philanthropic gentleman of leisure allowed Gideon to use his fashionable upper-drawer status to infiltrate circles Roland didn't have access to, while also allowing the accounting firm to increase profitability, since industrial espionage was on the rise and men of industry needed those with Gideon's talents to safeguard their business interests.

"So, returning to Sophia Campanini, may I at least assume you've been successfully handling whatever it was she wanted you to handle for her?" Camilla asked.

Gideon pulled himself from his thoughts and smiled. "Nice try, but again, I'm not disclosing sensitive information to you. You'll simply need to content yourself with the notion that I'm not enamored with the opera singer and leave it at that."

It came as no surprise when Camilla immediately took to pouting, a look she'd perfected over the years and one that was normally successful with getting her anything she desired.

Unfortunately for Camilla, he wasn't swayed by any of her perfected feminine charms.

He crossed his arms over his chest and took to regarding her, earning a bit of a grunt from her a few seconds later.

"Fine, don't tell me," she grumbled. "Although if you've not been successful with whatever it is, you should consider filling me in because I'm convinced I could be a valuable asset to the firm since I have the eyes and ears of society at my disposal. Add in the fact that no one would ever suspect me of being involved in clandestine affairs and it's a win-win situation for everyone involved."

"You're never going to work for the accounting firm. It would be far too dangerous."

"Gathering intelligence for you at society events would hardly put me at risk. Besides, as I'm sure you're aware, I'm once again suffering from extreme ennui. It's so extreme, in fact, that I've resorted to delving into melodramatic music to stave off my boredom, something that could very well see me losing numerous members of my staff."

"Then it's a good thing I've come to call, because I've come up with a solution that should hold your boredom at bay for the foreseeable future, which will spare your staff additional impromptu concerts on your part." Gideon leaned closer to her. "I'm in need of a favor. One only you can grant."

Camilla blinked before she raised a hand to her throat. "On my word, but you want me to come out of matchmaker retirement and finally make you a match, don't you? And," she continued before he could get a single protest out of his mouth, "even though I've officially hung up my matchmaker gloves, for you, my dear Gideon, I'll be more than happy to do exactly that. In fact, we can plan out a strategy today, decide what young ladies appeal to you, and then I'll get right to work. We'll have you engaged within the first month of the New York Season and to a lady I know you'll find a spark with, one that will then ignite into flames."

Gideon swallowed. "I'm not really the type prone to any sparking, let alone spontaneously bursting into flames."

"Of course you are. You simply haven't explored those hidden depths I know you possess."

"My hidden depths have nothing to do with sparks and flames, but before you argue with that, I have to tell you that the favor I need has nothing to do with me."

Camilla frowned. "You don't want me to find you the lady of your dreams?"

"Since I have no intention of settling down in the near or distant future, given the demanding and dangerous nature of my profession, no." He reached out and took hold of her hand. "But before you get yourself all worked up, know that the favor I need to ask of you is far more important than assisting me with my love life, or lack thereof."

"Finding true love is always of the utmost importance."

"Not for me it's not."

Her shoulders sagged ever so slightly. "Oh, very well. Since you're apparently not keen to have me find you the love of your life, which, to be clear, I could most certainly accomplish, what is this favor you need from me?"

"I'd like you to take Miss Adelaide Duveen in hand."

Camilla yanked her hand from his. "Surely I misheard you, because you couldn't possibly have said you want me to take Adelaide Duveen—as in the lady who allowed everyone to get a glimpse of her unmentionables and then got attacked by rampaging swans—in hand."

"That would be the lady, and yes, I'd like you to help her."

"Why?"

Gideon had known that question would certainly come up, but he'd yet to formulate a credible response without disclosing too much to Camilla. He summoned up what he hoped was his most charming of smiles. "I don't think the reasoning behind the favor is really relevant to the conversation."

Unfortunately, Camilla didn't see the smile because she was distracted by a fly that had had the audacity to invade her music room and was currently circling her head.

"How could it not be relevant?" she finally countered as she sent the fly careening through the air with one deliberate slap. "I wasn't even aware you were overly familiar with Adelaide Duveen, and yet now you want me to make a match for a lady who is currently considered society's most veritable pariah."

Gideon scratched his nose. "Actually, Adelaide isn't keen to marry."

"You want me to convince her otherwise?"

"Not at all."

"Then what, pray tell, do you want me to do with her?"

He summoned up another smile, hoping this one would be more effective than the last. "I want you to convince society to abandon their notion that Adelaide is peculiar and to begin thinking of her as an Incomparable, or better yet, a diamond of the first water."

Five

―――――――――――

"If I'm understanding correctly," Camilla began, reining her horse, Fiona, to a walk and garnering Gideon's attention, "Miss Duveen helped you out of a bit of a pickle last night, which, unfortunately, has left her facing censure from society yet again."

Gideon nodded. "I believe that sufficiently sums it up."

It was not encouraging when Camilla sent him a rolling of her eyes.

"No, it doesn't. You've not told me what type of pickle you were in, or how it came to be that Miss Duveen became involved in the matter in the first place."

"I knew it was taking you far too long to change from a morning gown to a riding habit," Gideon muttered. "You evidently used the time you left me lingering in the music room to drum up numerous questions regarding last night's event, ones you know I'm not at liberty to answer."

"It took me a mere thirty minutes to change."

Gideon's brows drew together. "You told me, after you surprised me by saying you wanted to speak with Adelaide without delay, that you needed to fetch a hat for the ride and that you'd be back in a jiffy. A jiffy suggests you'd be a few minutes, not thirty."

"I couldn't very well ride over to the Duveen house in a morning gown. It would be unseemly." Camilla lifted her chin. "And I don't know why you'd be surprised I'd want to speak with Adelaide as soon as possible, especially when you're being less than forthcoming with pertinent details."

"You can't interrogate Adelaide about last night because, while it's true she became involved in what was the most unlikely of circumstances, I didn't provide her with more than a cursory outline of the situation either."

"I'm sure she knows more than I do" was all Camilla said to that before she kneed Fiona into a gallop, Gideon urging Zeus to do the same because he really had no choice but to catch up with her.

The last thing he needed was for Camilla to meet with Adelaide without him present because the ladies would undoubtedly put their heads together and that certainly wouldn't bode well for him.

"Don't you think it would be a more prudent use of our time, instead of having you try to worm information out of me about last night, for me to tell you a little background about Adelaide?" he asked once he caught up with her. "You admitted you don't know much about her, other than that she suffers the reputation of being thought peculiar within society. Surely you're going to need to know more than that if you decide to grant me my favor, and the first thing you need to know is that Adelaide isn't peculiar at all. She merely possesses an unusual attitude toward life."

"If you think that's going to encourage me to take her in hand, you're sadly mistaken," Camilla said. "Society doesn't embrace ladies with unusual attitudes. And given the two debacles she experienced last night, it might be downright impossible to convince the Four Hundred she's an Incomparable."

"If anyone can accomplish that, it's you," Gideon argued. "You're one of the most innovative leaders within society, and where you lead, others will follow."

"Your confidence in my abilities might be overstated," Camilla muttered before she took a deep breath. "However, I have been suffering from boredom of late, and taking on Adelaide would cure that particular condition."

"Does that mean you'd like me to tell you more about her?"

"I suppose it does, but don't think for a second that we won't revisit the topic of what transpired last night at the Nelson event."

Being only too willing to turn the conversation to something that didn't revolve around the debacle of the previous evening, and knowing he'd think of something else to distract Camilla once she broached that subject again, Gideon spent the next ten minutes answering Camilla's pointed questions about Adelaide.

"Her image will need a complete overhaul," Camilla mused as they turned onto the lane that led to the Duveen mansion. "But it'll still be tricky to restore her reputation, especially when society is considering giving her the cut direct."

"But Adelaide's from a Knickerbocker family."

"Which may save her from complete societal ostracization, but we'll worry about that later." She bit her lip. "Do you think there's a possibility Adelaide would give up a few of her cats? It's one thing to have a cat or two around to keep mice in hand, but you said she has twenty of them, which evokes images of a mad cat lady who speaks to cats as if they were human and has a great love of knitting."

"Adelaide probably does speak to her cats, but I'm not certain about the knitting. I am sure, though, that she'll be unwilling to part ways with any of what she calls her 'little darlings.'"

"That's too bad since cats haven't been considered fashionable in decades, if not centuries, but I suppose it's a good sign she might not spend her time knitting, since embroidery is the needlework of choice these days."

"I don't think Adelaide enjoys needlework either because she mentioned she's woefully lacking when it comes to any of the feminine arts."

Camilla reined Fiona to a stop. "You do realize that even though I was highly successful as a matchmaker, I'm not a miracle worker, don't you? How in the world do you expect me to find success with Adelaide when she seems to be the most eccentric woman to ever grace the Four Hundred?"

"I say we use her uniqueness to our advantage. She's one of a kind, which makes her stand out in any given crowd."

"Hmm . . ." was all Camilla said to that before she urged Fiona into motion again, a comfortable silence settling between them as they traveled around a turn in the road before steering their horses onto a gravel drive that led directly to the front door.

"Good heavens, is that Mrs. Duveen?" Camilla suddenly asked, pulling Fiona up short as she nodded to something in the distance.

Gideon squinted in the direction Camilla was peering and blinked when his gaze settled on a lady wielding hedge trimmers against a poor hedge that was now devoid of most of its branches, while a groundskeeper stood off to the side, rubbing a hand over his face as if he didn't quite know what to make of what seemed to be the massacre of perfectly innocent shrubbery.

He kneed Zeus forward and brought him to a stop five feet away from the lady with the hedge trimmers, who did, indeed, turn out to be Phyllis Duveen.

"Mrs. Duveen?" he began, swinging from the saddle and moving closer. "Is something amiss?"

Phyllis stilled for the briefest of seconds before she turned, the sight of her causing Gideon's eyes to widen because she was looking quite unlike her usual well-put-together self.

Her face was flushed with color, and she was actually perspiring, although she didn't seem to notice that, nor did she seem to notice that she'd suffered a scratch across her cheek, undoubtedly caused by all the attacking-of-the-hedge business she'd evidently been doing for quite some time, given all the branches that were littering the drive and the row of hedges that were looking downright pitiful.

After dashing a tattered sleeve over her forehead, Phyllis took a step forward, handed the hedge trimmers to a relieved-looking groundskeeper, then settled a strained smile on Gideon.

"Mr. Abbott. Isn't this a delightful surprise," Phyllis began. "I wasn't expecting callers today, especially after the unfortunate events of last night, so do forgive me for being in such an, uh, unusual state of disarray."

He nodded to the hedges. "May I assume the unfortunate events of last night are why you've taken to pruning the shrubbery?"

"It's more due to the consequences of last night," she admitted before she glanced at the hedges and winced. "I suppose it's a fortuitous circumstance that you've come to call because I'm not sure the hedges are going to be salvageable after what I've done to them."

"Consequences?" Gideon forced himself to ask.

Phyllis's lips thinned. "Society has apparently had enough of Adelaide's antics. We've been receiving notes since the crack of dawn rescinding invitations to dinners, teas, luncheons, and even philanthropic meetings."

A weight settled in the pit of his stomach. "People are uninviting you from scheduled events?"

Phyllis grabbed the hedge trimmers from a now very startled-looking groundskeeper and began attacking another hedge with them. "Too right they are, although Ward McAllister sent around a note an hour ago stating that society will be more than happy to receive *me* again during the upcoming Season,

70

given my Knickerbocker status. He then, dreadful man that he can be, cautioned me against bringing Adelaide to any event because the powers that be—probably Ward himself, along with a few other society matrons—have decided she's unsuitable to hold the title of a member of the Four Hundred. From what I've gathered, society is fully prepared to give her the cut direct if she tries to participate in any of the festivities come January."

She clipped off another branch, eliciting a groan from the groundskeeper, before she returned her attention to Gideon. "All I can say is thank goodness my other two daughters, Sarah and Ellen, are already successfully settled and are currently out of New York, having decided to holiday at one of our homes in Florida. I've already fired off a telegram to them, telling them to stay put for the winter since the Season this year is undoubtedly going to be rather chilly for anyone associated with the Duveen name."

"A circumstance that will not come to pass if I have anything to say about it," Camilla said, sliding gracefully from her saddle and gliding up to stand directly beside Phyllis.

Phyllis's brow furrowed as she thrust the hedge trimmers back into the groundskeeper's hands, who immediately turned and hurried away, probably not wanting to allow Phyllis another opportunity to prune additional hedges. "Miss Pierpont, what are you doing here?"

"It's a long story," Camilla began, "but know that Gideon and I have taken the liberty of descending on you unannounced because we'd like to help Adelaide regain her footing within society after what transpired last night."

Phyllis raised a hand to her chest. "Good heavens, Miss Pierpont. Are you suggesting you want to sponsor Adelaide during the upcoming Season? I was under the impression you'd stepped away from matchmaking."

"I *have* put my matchmaking days behind me, but securing

Adelaide a match is not what we have in mind." Camilla smiled. "A reputation restoration is."

"I don't believe I've ever heard of anyone attempting one of those before, but . . ." Phyllis frowned. "You must realize that such an endeavor would be challenging to say the least. Besides that, I'm finding it beyond curious why the two of you want to assist Adelaide with her unfortunate image in the first place. It's not as if either of you enjoy a close relationship with my daughter."

"I'm in need of a challenging endeavor," Camilla said before Gideon could think up a credible response. "As I mentioned, I've given up matchmaking, but I've realized that decision has left me at loose ends of late. Frankly, I've been dreading the idea of participating in another Season, but then this morning, as Gideon and I were discussing the unfortunate event—or rather, events—your daughter experienced at the Nelson dinner party, a fascinating idea sprang to mind, one where I'd use my position within society to aid Adelaide."

"That's an unusual scheme to spring to mind."

"Indeed, but it's one that could be beneficial, not only to Adelaide, but to me as well, since it'll give me a noble purpose for the foreseeable future. Adelaide obviously needs a transformation, and who better to help her with that than me—a lady with an indisputable position within society, and a lady with far too much time at her disposal." She reached out and took hold of Phyllis's hand. "I also find it deeply disturbing that society would even contemplate the idea of casting out one of its own members, and for something as trivial as marauding swans."

"You're forgetting the unmentionables incident."

"A circumstance that was also trivial, because what lady hasn't returned from the retiring room with an article of clothing out of place?"

"I can't think of a single lady besides Adelaide who's ever experienced such a thing," Phyllis muttered.

"Be that as it may, it wasn't as if she harmed anyone." A glint appeared in Camilla's eyes. "You mark my words, after I'm done with your daughter, no one will remember last night's misadventures."

Phyllis worried her lip for a moment. "Which is a delightful thought to be sure, but I'm not certain Adelaide will be agreeable to your proposal. Truth be told, she seemed somewhat relieved after the rescinded invitation notes began streaming in this morning that she wouldn't have to suffer through society events anymore."

"If I'm successful, she'll be enjoying her time within society, not suffering through anything," Camilla countered. "But I suppose we won't know if I can change Adelaide's mind about society in general until I speak with her. Shall we repair to the house where I can broach the matter with her?"

"She's not in the house." Phyllis nodded to a path that cut through the hedges ten feet away from them. "She wandered down that path about an hour ago. If I were to hazard a guess, I'd say you'll find her by the river under a large maple tree, reading a book about mummies."

"Then that's where we'll look first," Camilla said.

Phyllis dusted a few leaves from her sleeve. "While you're off to speak with her, I'll arrange for a light luncheon to be served. I'd be ever so pleased if the two of you would agree to enjoy a meal with me, which may spare my poor hedges additional attacks."

"You don't want to accompany us?" Camilla asked.

"It's not that I don't want to be present to see Adelaide's reaction to what she'll certainly find a most unexpected proposition," Phyllis began, "but it would be doing her an injustice if I'm privy to that exchange. Adelaide knows how upset I am about society turning on our family. If I'm there when you explain what you want to do with her, she'll agree without truly considering the matter. That wouldn't be fair to her because she'll be the one who has to put herself in front of society again, a decision she shouldn't make lightly."

After wishing them luck and saying something about tracking down her groundskeeper to apologize, Phyllis turned and hurried down the lane, disappearing through a hole in the hedge a moment later.

Taking Camilla's arm, Gideon headed for the path that led them around the house and toward the river.

"I think it might have been to our benefit that Phyllis wasn't herself today," Camilla said, taking Gideon's hand as he helped her over a fallen tree.

"How so?" Gideon asked.

Camilla edged around the trunk of another fallen tree, apparently not keen to scramble over it, and smiled. "From what I know about Phyllis, she's been very determined to see Adelaide settled into wedded bliss. If she'd been her normal inquisitive self, she would have pressed us on exactly why you want to assist Adelaide with her unfortunate reputation."

Camilla's smile turned into a grin. "And even though you're very good with skirting topics you don't care to discuss, Phyllis is a mother on a mission. She would have cajoled until she learned the details of last night, and then, once the full truth came out, she would have expected you, as an honorable gentleman and the person who was responsible for one of the fiascos Adelaide suffered last night, to repair Adelaide's reputation through marriage." Camilla caught his eye. "Given that you've been vocal about maintaining your bachelor status, I imagine that isn't a prospect you want to entertain."

It was rather surprising when Gideon found he couldn't immediately voice his agreement to that.

Yes, he had no intention of marrying in the near or distant future, what with the nature of his chosen profession, but he couldn't claim the thought of becoming involved with Adelaide wasn't a little . . . appealing.

There was something about her that piqued his interest, something that drew him toward her and brought out a protectiveness that had seen him deliberately positioning himself close to her at society events in order to be readily available on the chance she found herself in trouble.

He'd told himself again and again that it was simply his nature to be protective of women in general, but he didn't seek out other ladies to watch at any given event, which meant there was something more to his desire to ascertain Adelaide wasn't placed in harm's way, something that needed to be considered at length. But certainly not now when he was in the company of a lady who'd previously spent the majority of her time securing matches of the affectionate sort.

He knew only too well that Camilla could turn relentless when she set her mind to something, and if she suspected he might possibly hold a touch of affection for Adelaide, well . . .

"We need to return to the house," Camilla suddenly said, pulling him from his thoughts as she took hold of his arm and spun him around before she began tugging him in the direction they'd just traveled.

"Because?" he asked.

"I may have just spotted Adelaide, but considering there was a gown fluttering from the branch of a large tree—one that doesn't seem to have a lady in it—I believe she might have, unusually enough, abandoned that gown. Given that there's a chance she's now inappropriately attired, it'll be best if we get ourselves well removed from her vicinity, because if Phyllis were to learn you'd gotten a glimpse of her daughter in such a state, you'll definitely be meeting Adelaide at the end of that proverbial aisle before the Season even begins."

Six

The odds were definitely not in her favor these days.

Adelaide sat frozen in place while the voices she'd detected got closer, contemplating how it was possible she once again found herself in the most implausible of quandaries.

Normally, unexpected visitors appearing on Duveen land wouldn't be cause for concern, but considering she'd been forced to abandon her gown because it kept getting snagged on tree branches, impeding her rescue attempt of a stranded kitten, it was a disconcerting predicament to be sure.

Add in the fact that the tree she was currently sitting in had lost at least half of its leaves, leaving her less-than-completely concealed, and it was evident she shouldn't expect her luck to change anytime soon.

Holding her breath when the voices stopped and praying they'd stopped because the people had moved on, she tilted her head, relief flowing through her when she caught not a whisper of conversation, which hopefully meant . . .

"Adelaide, is that you?"

She closed her eyes as recognition struck. "Would you believe me if I said no?"

A laugh was Gideon's first response to that. "Care to share what you're doing up there?"

"Not particularly." She shifted on the branch, which caused additional leaves to fall, leaving her more exposed than before. "If you could give me a few minutes, I'd be more than happy to speak with you back at the house."

"I can't leave you stuck in a tree."

"I'm not stuck. I simply can't climb down right now because I might be missing a key article of clothing."

"Would that be the gown that seems to be stuck on one of the branches?"

"I'm afraid so."

"Is there a reason you're not wearing it?"

"If you'd ever attempted to scale a tree while wearing a gown you wouldn't need to ask that question."

"Fair enough. May I presume you're in your current predicament because you were trying to escape from another rampaging creature?"

"Two animal attacks in such a short period of time would be remarkable even for me. But since you don't seem keen to go away without some type of explanation, I heard a cat mewling and discovered it stuck fifteen feet from the ground. I couldn't very well have left the poor thing up here."

"Don't you have a footman who could have rescued it?"

"Cats are unpredictable. There was every chance a footman would have startled it and caused it to scoot farther up the tree."

"You weren't worried you were going to alarm it?"

A snort escaped her. "Please. I may alarm society members on a frequent basis, but cats understand me. With that said, this kitten and I seem to have suffered a misunderstanding because as soon as I was close enough to snag it, the little darling bolted down the tree, jumping from branch to branch and then scampering out of sight. I think it may still be hiding amidst what's left of the leaves, but I thought it best to leave it alone for a bit."

"Or you thought you'd leave it alone because you're actually stuck up there but are too stubborn to admit it."

"I never get stuck in trees. But if you must know, I decided to take a few moments to appreciate the soothing sound of the rustling leaves. After the day I had yesterday, and then the troubling notes my mother received today, I was enjoying a moment of unexpected serenity—until you showed up."

"I'm sure serenity has been rather lacking for you after the incident with the swans."

"Indeed, but now isn't an opportune moment to discuss the circumstances of last night. I am, after all, inappropriately attired. With that said, off you go. I'll need a good ten minutes, and then I'll join you at the house where we can discuss swans, cats, or better yet, Frank Fitzsimmons. I assume, since no word has reached my ears through the servant grapevine about you in the company of an unconscious member of the criminal persuasion, you were successful getting him away from the Nelson house undetected."

"You didn't mention anything about an unconscious member of the criminal persuasion being present last night."

Adelaide stilled for the briefest of moments, having completely forgotten Gideon had obviously been speaking with someone before he'd called out to her. Who that someone was remained to be seen, but her voice sounded familiar, and . . .

Mortification was swift when she finally placed the voice with a face, and it took a great deal of effort to resist the urge to scramble higher into the tree because . . . her morning only needed this.

Why Camilla Pierpont had accompanied Gideon was curious to say the least, since it wasn't as if Adelaide had ever spoken to the lady except to exchange the expected pleasantries. Nevertheless, the fact that the most proper lady in society was currently in the vicinity of the tree she was perched in, while barely clothed, was the icing on a far-too-concerning cake.

"Miss Pierpont," she finally forced herself to call. "I didn't realize you were with Gideon."

"Miss Duveen, good morning," Camilla called back. "I must beg your pardon for descending on you without notice, but I willingly admit that my unexpected appearance has turned advantageous for me. You see, Gideon, being Gideon, has been less than loquacious about what he was up to last night. I had a feeling you'd have some details about the matter, and it turns out I was right about that."

"Oh dear," Adelaide said.

"Indeed," Camilla agreed. "But before you apologize to Gideon for divulging one of his many secrets, know that I would have eventually gleaned all the particulars from him. I'll also be much obliged if you could expand a little about this Frank character, who is apparently a criminal."

"I don't actually know anything else about him, except that Gideon was forced to render him unconscious when Frank went on the attack," Adelaide called back, stilling when additional leaves that had been giving her relatively little concealment in the first place began drifting to the ground, probably because she'd shifted on the branch. She glanced down to where Camilla and Gideon were standing, relief flowing freely when she caught sight of the tops of their heads, which meant, at least for the moment, they weren't looking upward.

"Why did Frank attack him?" Camilla called next.

"I have no idea. Gideon will need to explain that because I'm sure he discovered why Frank tried to assault him when he questioned him at some point last night after getting him well removed from the Nelson dinner party."

"That's a discussion that can certainly wait, at least until you're out of the tree," Gideon said, which, if Adelaide wasn't much mistaken, was his way of trying to redirect the conversation.

Unfortunately for him, she wasn't willing to accommodate

his desire for redirection, not with all the questions she'd been dying to ask him, ones that had left her unable to sleep and had seen her rise from her bed before dawn.

"I think now is the perfect moment to continue this discussion since there's relatively little chance anyone will overhear us," she called back.

"You told me not two minutes ago that you wanted me to make myself scarce. Now you want me to launch into a discussion about Frank while you're still, if I need point out, in a state of questionable attire."

As arguments went, that was a fairly valid one. However, she wasn't willing to concede defeat just yet. Thankfully, a perfectly credible response suddenly sprang to mind.

"Satisfying my curiosity may help me recover that state of serenity that went missing the moment you showed up underneath my tree," she began. "Besides, if you ask me, it'll be to your benefit to appease Miss Pierpont's inquisitiveness, at least to a certain extent, because that won't allow her time to formulate in-depth questions you know you won't want to answer. I say there's nothing like the present to placate her curiosity."

"I don't see why I need to placate Camilla at all. I did tell her that learning too much about my activities could place her in jeopardy, something I mentioned to you as well."

"But she already seems to know a little about the, ah, clandestine activities you participate in when you're not assuming the role of upstanding member of the Four Hundred."

"I *am* an upstanding member of the Four Hundred."

"Did I not just imply, Miss Duveen, how adept Gideon is at avoiding topics he doesn't care to discuss?" Camilla asked before Adelaide could respond. "I'm sure he would like us to now divert the conversation to his position within society, but since that's not actually in question, allow me to return to this Frank person and what you, Gideon, learned after you interrogated the man."

"I'm beginning to feel decidedly outnumbered" was Gideon's only response to that.

"And I'm sure I should feel sorry about that, but, no, I don't," Camilla said. "I feel more sorry for poor Miss Duveen, who must be becoming rather chilled by now. That state is only going to increase until she can become suitably clothed again, something I'm going to assume isn't going to happen until you explain what transpired with Frank, at which point she'll then agree to get out of the tree, and then we can continue on with other matters from there."

Gideon released a bit of a grunt. "Fine. Since the two of you are apparently in unreasonable frames of mind, because Adelaide wouldn't need to be chilled at all if she'd simply climb down now, here's what I can tell you about Frank's motives . . . absolutely nothing. I never got an opportunity to question him. After I secured him in my carriage, I returned to the dinner party to check on Adelaide, and by the time I returned, I discovered that my men had been set upon by Frank's men. My men were overpowered, Frank was whisked away, and that was the end of it."

"He got away?" Adelaide asked.

"Indeed."

"That certainly puts a concerning twist on the situation," she said. "May I hope you were at least able to speak with Sophia last night and that she lent valuable insight as to why Frank might have wanted to speak with her?"

"All Sophia told me, after I caught up with her at her permanent suite of rooms at the Fifth Avenue Hotel, which I couldn't do until almost midnight since I had to take my men to the doctor for stitches, was that she'd never heard of Frank Fitzsimmons. She then insisted she had no idea why a known criminal would want to meet with her. After that, she told me it was very late and that she had an early rehearsal come morning before she had one of her many bodyguards show me to the door."

"Didn't she want you to have Frank investigated further in order to discover exactly why he wanted to meet with her?"

"She had me shown out before I could suggest that."

"A suspicious action if there ever was one," Adelaide said.

"I thought so," Gideon agreed. "But since Sophia employs an entire brigade of bodyguards, I'm not overly concerned about her safety, although the accounting firm will begin looking into Frank, whether Sophia wants us to or not."

"Because you didn't believe Sophia when she said she didn't know why a criminal would want to speak with her?"

"Exactly, although I also need to run Frank down because his men were responsible for injuring two associates of the firm."

"How will you do that?"

"We have contacts on the street, but I'll also assign a few men to do some surveillance on Sophia. Frank went to extraordinary lengths to meet with her, and even though he was thwarted last night, I doubt that will be the end of the matter."

Adelaide leaned forward. "I imagine surveillance work would be right up my alley."

"Absolutely not," Gideon didn't hesitate to shoot back.

"But no one would suspect me, a harmless wallflower, of dabbling in reconnaissance work, which would be to your advantage," Adelaide argued. "Besides, my family owns a box at the Metropolitan Opera House, which means there really wouldn't be anything suspicious about me taking in a few of Sophia's performances."

"An excellent argument," Camilla said, piping up. "And along those same lines, I must point out once again that no one would suspect me of involving myself in matters of deception either, what with my reputation of being the consummate lady who never puts a toe out of line. Plus, if you were to agree to allow Miss Duveen and me to take on a few surveillance projects together, you would no longer need to worry about the ennui I've been suffering. And if we worked together, there'd be little danger to either of us since there's safety in numbers."

"I shudder at the thought of you and Adelaide pairing up. And besides that, I've already provided you with a project to stave off your boredom," Gideon said. "Believe me, given the subject matter you've agreed to take on, tedium will no longer be a problem."

Adelaide pushed aside the two leaves that were left on the branch she was perched on, her gaze settling on Gideon, then drifting to Camilla, who was whispering something to Gideon she couldn't quite catch, but something she was quite convinced revolved around her. She cleared her throat.

"I don't happen to be that subject matter you just mentioned, am I?" she called.

"We'll discuss that after you return to the ground," Gideon said.

"Which sounds like a yes to me, so I'll be down in a jiffy."

"I'll station myself at the bottom of the tree as you make your descent in case you fall."

"I won't fall."

"Given your history, I say you have at least a seventy percent chance of doing exactly that."

"I rarely suffer tumbles from trees."

"*Rarely* suggests it has happened before."

"Children," Camilla interrupted as Adelaide opened her mouth to voice another argument, "this is hardly the time for a squabble. You, Miss Duveen, need to climb down from the tree, and you, Gideon, will keep your back turned and maintain your distance because, again, Miss Duveen is improperly dressed. I'll wait underneath the tree and attempt to catch Miss Duveen if she falls."

"No one is standing under the tree," Adelaide countered. "With that settled, I'm coming down, and I'd better not find either of you waiting for me."

Ignoring Gideon's mutters, Adelaide began her descent, scooting across the limb where her gown was stuck. After untangling it from a small branch, she stilled when an ominous creak met her ears, followed by the distinct sound of a branch breaking. Before she knew it, she was whizzing through the air, wincing as branches slapped against her face. Squeezing her eyes shut, she barely had time to pray for a soft landing before she slammed into something hard—something that, of course, turned out to be Gideon.

Seven

Opening her eyes, Adelaide blinked a time or two as Gideon's chin swam into view right as she realized he'd somehow managed to catch her without either of them dropping to the ground, even though she had to have been a dead weight when she'd plummeted into arms that seemed to be forged of steel.

"Would this be the moment where I get to say I told you so?" Gideon asked.

Pulling her thoughts away from his arms, which was rather difficult since they were wrapped around her and holding her close to a chest that seemed just as hard, Adelaide strove to ignore the heat that was settling on her cheeks. "I suppose you're justified for an I told you so, given that I did tumble out of the tree, but only because that branch broke at the most unsuspecting of times."

He caught her gaze. "Perhaps I was too conservative in my estimate that you had a seventy percent chance of tumbling. I'm thinking ninety percent might have been more accurate."

"And while I'd love to argue with that, you may be right," Adelaide muttered, squinting as she caught sight of a small bundle of black fur perched on a limb directly above them, one that suddenly launched itself through the air.

Before she could get a single word of warning out of her mouth, the furry missile landed directly on Gideon's head. A second later, she found herself relinquished to the ground, landing with an *umph* in a pile of leaves as Gideon fought to disentangle a now rampaging kitten from his hair.

Pushing herself to her feet as the kitten began hissing while it kept its claws firmly attached to Gideon's head, Adelaide stood on tiptoe, wrapped her hand around the kitten, and gave it a tug—to no avail. She tugged again.

"You do realize that hurts, don't you?" Gideon grumbled.

"If you didn't have so much hair, this wouldn't be an issue."

"I'll make certain to broach that matter with my barber the next time I pay him a visit, on the off chance I'm in danger of suffering another assault by a miniature feline that's far fiercer than it looks."

"It's just scared," she said before she returned her attention to the kitten. "No one's going to hurt you," she cooed, which earned her a blink of an eye from it before it released a pitiful-sounding mewl.

Taking that as a sign it might now be agreeable to relinquishing its hold on Gideon's hair, she reached up and gave it another tug, smiling when she managed to pluck it from his head, even though she earned another wince from Gideon in return.

"How delightful to learn there actually was a stranded animal," Camilla said, stepping up beside Adelaide and eyeing the kitten, who was already nuzzling its tiny head into the crook of Adelaide's neck.

"You thought I made it up?" Adelaide asked.

"That did cross my mind," Camilla admitted. "The morning started off unusually warm for October, although that's no longer the case, and there was a possibility you simply shucked out of your dress because of that. A kitten in need of rescue would have been a perfect excuse to explain that odd situation."

"I don't make it a habit to shuck off my garments without due cause."

"I would hope not."

"Well, quite," Adelaide said before she turned to Gideon, who was now presenting her with his back, something that recalled her to the notion she was lollygagging around in her unmentionables. Heat immediately settled on her cheeks again. "Perhaps now would be an excellent time for you, Gideon, to become better acquainted with a kitten I believe I'll call . . ." She held it away from her, looked it over, and smiled. "He looks like a Harvey."

"He seems more like a Menace than a Harvey, but it's not a surprise to learn it's a male, considering it didn't hesitate to attack me," Gideon muttered.

"I'm not naming him Menace," Adelaide countered. "That would hurt Harvey's little feelings. And just so you know, female cats go on the offensive just as often as males do, but I imagine Harvey attacked you because he thought you were a threat to me." She cuddled Harvey close. "That suggests he would make an excellent guard cat for someone who often finds themselves in precarious situations."

"That isn't your way of suggesting I take ownership of Harvey, is it?"

"He'd be perfect for you."

"On the contrary. That little monster just yanked a great deal of hair from my head, and its claws punctured my scalp. Besides, I already have a temperamental stallion and a beast of a dog that would probably view Harvey as a snack. Furthermore, the last thing I need to add to my household is a kitten with a questionable nature. I prefer not having to sleep with one eye open at night."

"I'll give you a day or two to rethink the matter," Adelaide said, earning a snort from Gideon before he strode into motion, without taking up Adelaide's suggestion he get better acquainted with Harvey no less, his rapid pace lending the impression he was determined to put some distance between them as quickly as possible.

Blowing out a breath as the realization struck that Gideon probably wasn't going to change his mind, Adelaide turned to Camilla and summoned up a smile. "Would you be a dear, Miss Pierpont, and hold Harvey while I get myself suitably attired?"

"I've never held a cat before in my life."

"Then this will be a lovely first for you," Adelaide said, stepping close to Camilla and handing Harvey over to her without a by-your-leave, ignoring that Camilla's eyes had widened to the size of small saucers. "There. Isn't he darling? And listen, he's beginning to purr."

"Sounds more like growls to me," Camilla argued. "I think he's considering going on another rampage."

"He won't do that if you snuggle him directly up against you."

Eyeing Harvey somewhat warily, Camilla drew the kitten close, her lips curving when he began purring in earnest. "I suppose he is somewhat sweet," she admitted. "But I'm not keeping him, and you shouldn't either, considering you already have twenty cats."

"But I've already named him, and it's downright impossible to turn my back on a cat I've given a name," Adelaide said, making her way to where her gown was now lying in a pile of leaves.

"I imagine you name all your strays straightaway so you have a ready excuse for taking them in."

After giving the gown a shake, Adelaide sent Camilla a wink. "You've found me out, Miss Pierpont, but it's not that I make a concerted effort to collect cats. Strays simply find me. I can hardly neglect their sorry plight." She gave her gown another shake. "I've been holding out hope that someone in society will decide cats are in fashion again, and when that happens, I'm confident I'll be able to decrease the number of cats I own."

"I don't know of anyone, except yourself, who prefers cats over dogs," Camilla said.

"That's simply because cats are misunderstood creatures. Compared to dogs—not that I have anything against those, except the ones that want to eat my darlings—cats are far easier to take care of. They don't need to be walked, and they don't need much in the way of attention, although they don't prefer being as solitary as most people believe them to be. They also don't make a lot of noise—not like those yippy dogs society members travel about town with." She stilled for the briefest of seconds before she winced. "You don't happen to own one of those yippy dogs, do you?"

Camilla laughed. "No need to fear you've just offended me. I own a poodle—Gladys is her name—but she's a disgrace to her breed. She doesn't know how to prance, refuses to let me put bows in her hair, and certainly doesn't do any yipping because she'd consider that using far too much exertion. People think she's ancient, but she's only five. She's merely lazy and prefers spending her time lounging in sunny spots or snoozing beside the fireplace."

"Perhaps she'd become livelier if you were to introduce an energetic kitten into your household."

"Nice try, but no."

"May I dare hope that your use of the word *no* occasionally means you're taking a matter under consideration?"

"No."

Adelaide decided to try another angle. "Just look at it this way. You'd be helping stray cats everywhere if you'd take Harvey in. People look to you for guidance in matters of fashion. If you were seen moseying around the city with an adorable kitten in tow, I know everyone would soon be clamoring to follow suit."

"An impressive argument, Miss Duveen, but I think not."

"That definitely doesn't sound like a final answer, so we'll revisit the idea in a few days, after you've had an opportunity to truly ponder the benefits of adding an adorable kitten to your life." Adelaide tossed the gown over her head and yanked it into place, emerging a second later to discover Camilla's brow had furrowed. "Is something the matter?"

"You're wearing a gown that's at least three sizes too large for you."

Adelaide glanced down, smoothed a hand over wrinkled fabric, and nodded. "It's definitely large, but I sometimes like my clothing roomy, because I enjoy being able to move with ease when I'm wandering around the grounds."

"You chose that on purpose?"

"Of course. It was either this gown or one that's even larger, but the larger one, unfortunately, was beginning to unravel, and unraveling paired with me is never a great combination."

"Do you have such overly large garments at your disposal because you lost a great deal of weight at some point?"

Adelaide brushed a leaf from her sleeve. "I've always been slender, but before you ask, most of my wardrobe is ill fitting." She smiled. "My mother got a bee in her bonnet this past summer that I'd draw Mr. Walter Townsend's attention if I looked more voluptuous, given that his late wife possessed a most enviable figure." She sighed. "It was a failure of epic proportions, although not a failure for my dear friend Gwendolyn Brinley, who now goes by the name of Mrs. Walter Townsend. Nevertheless, since Mr. Hayworth, Mother's dress designer, put a lot of effort into creating a large wardrobe for me, I try to make use of the pieces, especially since they're remarkably comfortable if I don't wear them over the bustles and all the stuffed undergarments I'm supposed to include to enhance my form."

"You wore stuffed undergarments during the summer?"

"It was an unfortunate state of affairs since I was sweltering throughout my time in Newport and lost weight, something that certainly didn't allow me to obtain that curvaceousness my mother wanted me to acquire." Adelaide smiled. "Thankfully, Mother has abandoned that harebrained idea, especially after what happened last night with that monstrosity of a bustle Mr. Hayworth invented for me."

"It sounds to me as if you need a new dressmaker, since I don't know any credible ones who'd create ill-fitting garments for their clients."

"In Mr. Hayworth's defense," Adelaide countered, "it's not entirely his fault my garments rarely fit me. I don't have the patience for fittings or shopping in general. That's why I give my measurements to my mother, and she takes it from there."

"You're going to have to abandon your aversion to fittings if I'm going to succeed with the proposal I'm here to present to you," Camilla surprised her by saying.

"Proposal?"

Camilla took a step closer. "I fear with finding you in a tree, your plummet to the ground, and then the kitty cat skirmish, the intention of our visit has been overshadowed." She turned Gideon's way and called, "Adelaide is properly dressed now, so you may join us to disclose why we're here."

A second later, Gideon was striding their way, settling one of his charming smiles on Camilla once he stopped in front of her. "I thought it would be best for you to explain."

It was immediately clear that Camilla was immune to his charming smiles because instead of divulging all, she shook her head. "Absolutely not. It was your idea."

A sliver of trepidation began working its way up Adelaide's spine when Gideon turned his charming smile her way.

The trepidation increased when he suddenly took hold of her hand.

"First, allow me to thank you for your assistance last night, something I've neglected to do until now," he began. "As a gesture of my appreciation for your support, I've asked a favor of Camilla, one she's agreed to grant me."

Understanding was immediate and caused Adelaide's mouth to gape open until she had the presence of mind to snap it shut. "Do not say you've coerced Miss Pierpont to come out of matchmaker retirement to take me on, because I told you last night that I'm content with my spinster status." She held up her hand when Gideon opened his mouth. "Besides that, and of equal importance, is this—I came to your assistance because I felt indebted to *you*. If you now attempt to do me another service, I'll be beholden to you once again. Frankly, I'm not certain I'm up for repaying another obligation. My attempt to do that last night, while surprisingly successful, given the diversion of attacking swans, didn't go off as I intended and has left society contemplating giving me the cut direct."

"And that right there is why you need to at least hear me out because it's my fault you're facing societal ostracization," Gideon countered.

She waved that aside. "You're not to blame for my unfortunate societal state. The Four Hundred has been less than receptive toward me since my first Season. I've simply given them the perfect validation to part ways with me without suffering even a smidgen of guilt, since I singlehandedly was to blame for pressed duck raining down on esteemed guests last night."

"Flying pressed duck was certainly not something I ever expected to witness," Camilla muttered.

"I don't believe anyone could have anticipated that particular incident," Adelaide said, turning to Camilla. "But ducks aside, if we may return to this proposal, while I appreciate the offer, I need to respectfully decline. As I said, I'm no longer interested in securing a match. And while my refusal will most assuredly disappoint my mother, I don't want to be the reason you suffer a crushing defeat, something I know you've never experienced before."

JEN TURANO

"We aren't proposing a sponsorship on the marriage mart."

Adelaide blinked. "You aren't?"

"No," Camilla returned. "Although I thought that's what Gideon had in mind when he first raised the topic of taking you in hand."

Adelaide shot a glance to Gideon, who sent her another charming smile before taking a marked interest in a cloud passing overhead. She returned her attention to Camilla. "I know I'm going to regret asking this, but what do the two of you have in mind for me?"

"I'd like to refashion you into a diamond of the first water."

A snort escaped Adelaide before she could stop it. "That's certainly unexpected, and forgive me, Miss Pierpont, but that's a feat I'm afraid will be impossible for even you. Frankly, it could very well see society ostracizing *you* because they'll conclude you've taken leave of your senses."

"Are you questioning my abilities, because I assure you, it won't take all that much for me to get society to abandon their decision to give you the cut direct. That will then allow us to move forward with convincing them you should be considered in high demand."

Adelaide gave her nose a scratch. "It's not that I doubt you exert a great deal of power within society, but I don't believe you're grasping how deeply tainted my reputation is amongst the upper crust." She stepped closer to Camilla. "And while I truly appreciate that you'd be willing to attempt to reinvent me, you won't persuade anyone I'm a diamond of the first water. That title has eluded me for a reason—I'm simply not fashionable."

"And we'll have to agree to disagree about that because once I have time to devise a plan, I'm convinced I can change society's perception of you."

"It would have to be some plan."

"True, but after I consult with your mother, because mothers always know these things, about exactly what went wrong

93

with your debut and then your subsequent failure to take within society over the following years, I'm sure something will spring to mind."

"I would prefer to keep my mother in the dark about this matter."

Camilla winced. "She might already know why I'm here."

Adelaide arched a brow Gideon's way, garnering a wince from him as well.

"Would you believe we encountered your mother on the drive leading up to the house when we first arrived and that she very quickly discerned why we were here?" he asked.

"It's more likely you apprised her of the situation because you're hoping to persuade me to accept your proposal by using my mother's disappointment if I don't do exactly that to strengthen your case."

Gideon was sporting yet another charming smile a second later. "It's almost uncanny how competent you are with figuring matters out."

"Involving my mother was hardly fair, especially when she's been beside herself this morning," Adelaide countered, finding it rather difficult to resist the urge to throttle the man.

"I don't believe I can argue with that," Gideon said far too cheerfully.

The urge to throttle him increased. She drew in a deep breath, slowly released it, and turned her attention to Camilla to avoid further impulses for bodily harm. "Since Gideon is hardly being helpful about this matter, I'm going to prevail upon you to see reason. You've been involved with society from the moment you drew breath, so you must know it'll be a futile endeavor to convince them I'm an Incomparable.

"I'm not like other society ladies. I don't dance well, I'm not possessed of a voice like an angel, nor do I have a flair for fashion. I simply don't fit the mold of what society expects of their Incomparables or diamonds."

"You definitely don't fit the standard mold," Camilla admitted.

"Now we're getting somewhere," Adelaide said. "Which means this is the point in the conversation where I thank you again for your offer, decline it, and suggest we repair to the house for some refreshments and additional talk of one of you agreeing to take Harvey in."

"We just need to create a different mold," Camilla said, completely ignoring everything Adelaide had just said.

Gideon was nodding a second later. "But you're a genius, Camilla, because that's exactly what we should do. What do you have in mind?"

Camilla walked around Adelaide, looking her up and down before she stopped in her tracks and smiled. "I've got it."

"Got what?" Adelaide forced herself to ask.

Camilla gave Adelaide one last perusal and took a step back. "We'll turn you into something far more intriguing than any old diamond or Incomparable."

"But society adores their diamonds and Incomparables," Adelaide argued.

Camilla's eyes began to sparkle. "True, but I say it's time to introduce something innovative into fashionable circles. Something bold."

"Nothing bold is going to replace diamonds or Incomparables."

"It will if we convince society those are passé, especially since society is known to be rather fickle."

"They may very well be fickle, but they're staunchly attached to fawning over the ladies who are deemed the most fashionable in any given year."

"Well, quite," Camilla agreed. "However, I don't believe they'll be able to resist what I'm going to convince them is just as desirable—perhaps more so. A true original."

Adelaide gave her nose another scratch. "I don't think society is suddenly going to abandon their love of the most beautiful ladies on the marriage mart to embrace an original like me."

"And I beg to differ because I believe we can change their perception of what should be considered in vogue, especially with Gideon's assistance."

A bit of wariness clouded Gideon's eyes. "I don't remember you mentioning anything about needing me to assist you with Adelaide."

"Your part just came to me—and all because of Miss Duveen's idea about turning cats stylish," Camilla said as she repositioned Harvey, who tried to burrow underneath the neckline of her gown, and lifted her chin. "I think she may very well be right in that it would take only one well-placed society member strolling around New York in the company of a feline companion to have the upper crust clamoring to own cats. It then stands to reason that the same strategy can be used in Adelaide's case. We simply need to have a gentleman considered in high demand pay particular attention to her—and that gentleman, of course, would be you."

Eight

DECEMBER
NEW YORK CITY

Over the month and a half since Adelaide had agreed to Camilla's proposition—done so not because Gideon thought she truly wanted to improve her standing within society, but because she believed her agreement to be taken in hand would be a relief to her mother—he'd begun to realize that she was, indeed, an original, and a fascinating original at that.

He'd also begun to suspect that Camilla might succeed with effectively reintroducing Adelaide into society, what with how she'd already seen success with the whole Adelaide-avoiding-being-ostracized business. All she'd had to do to accomplish that impossible feat was arrange a tête-à-tête with Mr. Ward McAllister.

During their little chat, Camilla had presented Ward with a proposal he'd been unable to refuse—she would host a spectacular ball during the Season and give him carte blanche to plan out every detail of that event with no expenses spared. All Ward had to do in order to be given the privilege of organizing what would certainly be the talk of the Season was get

Adelaide reinstated as a member in good standing within the Four Hundred.

It had taken Ward a mere day to persuade the upper crust they'd been far too hasty with their decision to banish Adelaide, and the rapidity of his success was all due to the insinuation that anyone who refused to accept Adelaide back into the fold would face his personal displeasure.

Evidently no one wanted to incur Ward's discontent because within days of his involvement in the matter, Phyllis began receiving callers, all of whom seemed anxious to let bygones be bygones.

And just like that, Adelaide was once again considered a bona fide member of the Four Hundred.

Camilla had then set her sights on the next part of her campaign—laying the groundwork to have Adelaide declared the celebrated success of the upcoming Season.

To err on the side of caution, Camilla didn't want Adelaide participating in any society events until their grand reveal of the new and improved Adelaide at the first official ball of the Season, that being the Patriarch Ball held during the first week of January. However, she wanted Adelaide's name on the lips of society members often, which is why she'd been bustling around the city, injecting Adelaide into conversations whenever she could, mentioning things about how delightful and refreshing Adelaide's unusual attitude toward life was, as well as referring to Adelaide as her "darling Adelaide" or her "very dearest of friends."

According to Camilla, society was not unreceptive to listening about Adelaide. In fact, they seemed intrigued by the notion that an upper-crust leader was becoming intimate friends with a lady they'd only recently thought of expelling from their midst once and for all.

Oddly enough, instead of receiving satisfaction from Camilla's early success, Gideon found himself somewhat disheartened because . . . he was becoming accustomed to spending a few hours with Adelaide most every evening at Camilla's home on Fifth Avenue. During that time, they strategized, practiced their dancing, and once even convinced Adelaide to sing for everyone, something Camilla put a rapid end to after Adelaide's singing set Gladys, Camilla's dog, to howling. That had been telling in and of itself since Gladys never bothered to exercise her voice, what with how she evidently found that to be far too bothersome.

His amusing evenings with Adelaide would be limited, though, if she found herself in high demand during the rapidly approaching Season, a depressing notion if there ever was one, which was curious since it had been his idea to encourage society to embrace her in the first place.

"I'm afraid Sophia Campanini really *is* hiding something from us, especially when the girl she recently solicited us to find, one Lottie McBriar, seems to be working for Frank Fitzsimmons."

Gideon pulled his gaze from the hansom cab they were currently tailing and turned toward Roland Kelly, the man who'd once been his bodyguard and mentor, and who was now his business partner.

"Sophia hasn't been upfront with us ever since I told her Frank tried to kill me in the Nelsons' library," Gideon said. "Frankly, I was surprised she reached out to us again, considering Sophia seems to have taken pains to avoid me whenever I've gone to the opera. With that said, I knew almost immediately when I answered her summons yesterday that she wasn't telling me the truth about why she needed me to find Lottie McBriar—who Sophia knows by the name of Jane Smith—a girl she just happened to hire as one of her dressers two days after the incident with Frank on the Hudson.

"Sophia's never shown an interest in her staff before," Gideon continued, "and yet she wanted me to believe she was concerned about Lottie's disappearance after Lottie told her she needed to tend to a dying mother and never returned to the theater to continue dressing Sophia. Sophia actually managed to squeeze out a few tears as she begged me to find Lottie, claiming she was worried the girl may have contracted whatever dire illness her mother supposedly had."

Gideon caught Roland's eye. "It's more likely that Sophia realized the significance of when she hired Lottie and might very well have concluded that Lottie left her service not because of a dying mother but because she'd completed whatever task she'd been sent by Frank to accomplish."

"One would think," Roland began, "given Sophia's slightly conniving nature, that she'd have realized that something wasn't exactly aboveboard the moment Lottie introduced herself as Jane Smith."

"I doubt Sophia even caught Lottie's name. From what I've been told, Sophia has a difficult time retaining staff and was probably desperate for a dresser when Lottie showed up." Gideon looked out the window again. "I found it rather telling that it didn't take much for us to uncover Lottie's true identity after three employees from the Metropolitan Opera House told us they knew Jane Smith was actually Lottie McBriar from Five Points. It speaks volumes that not one of those people shared that information with Sophia during the time Lottie was working for her."

"It'll be interesting to see if Sophia is more forthcoming with any theories she may have about what Frank Fitzsimmons wants with her, especially after we tell her Lottie was undoubtedly sent to secure a position with her on Frank's orders, done so after he was unsuccessful in meeting with her at the Nelson dinner party."

"Sophia will only share her thoughts about Frank if she decides he's a true threat to her," Gideon returned. "Hopefully after we shadow Lottie today, we'll have more of an idea of

JEN TURANO

what she may be up to, although I have an obligation I can't neglect this evening, which means my time's limited out on the streets today."

"May I assume this obligation revolves around Miss Adelaide Duveen and Miss Camilla Pierpont?" Roland asked.

Gideon smiled. "Of course. Camilla is determined to turn Adelaide into the premier talk of the upcoming Season, and not the sort of talk that usually surrounds Adelaide. That's why I've been spending so many evenings at Camilla's, squiring Adelaide around the ballroom as Camilla's aunt Edna accompanies us on the piano."

"I wouldn't think a Duveen would need dance lessons."

"Adelaide has a history of trampling more than her fair share of feet over the years. Camilla's decided Adelaide's occasional clumsiness is a direct result of nerves. She wants us to become comfortable dancing with each other so we won't stumble about during the opening dance at the Patriarch Ball."

"How's that going, the becoming-comfortable business?"

"Hard to say for sure since my feet have been thoroughly abused of late, but unlike Camilla, I don't think it's Adelaide's nerves. I believe it's more a case of her being distracted."

"Distracted by . . . ?"

"Badgering me. She's determined to become involved with the accounting firm and seems to have difficulty badgering and dancing at the same time."

Roland settled back against the seat. "Adelaide Duveen wants to come work for us?"

"I'm afraid so."

"Why?"

"I suppose after having pored over countless spy novels throughout the years and then enjoying what can only be considered uncanny success with the Fitzsimmons debacle, she's come to the conclusion she could be an invaluable asset to us."

"She might actually have a point. She did, after all, help get

101

you extracted from a situation that could have seen society learning your secret."

"True, but Adelaide is a magnet for trouble. The last thing I want to be responsible for is placing her in precarious situations. Unfortunately, she ignores what I consider sound reasoning on my part and insists on debating the topic with me every time we take to the floor."

"Perhaps you should consider scheduling time with Adelaide outside the evenings you spend at Camilla's to spare the state of your feet. That might allow her to concentrate on her steps."

"I don't think it would be in my best interest to encourage additional badgering time. Doesn't seem like that would be all that enjoyable for me, although Adelaide would relish it because she's convinced she'll wear me down in the end. Besides that, though, Camilla wants me to restrict the time I spend in Adelaide's company and not have us be seen out and about in public until the Patriarch Ball."

"I thought Camilla wanted you to show Adelaide particular attention."

"Oh, she does," Gideon said. "But she thinks it'll make more of an impact on society if I wait to do that until Adelaide arrives at the official opening of the Season, looking quite unlike herself, what with how Camilla is giving her a style renovation. Camilla has also decided that I'm to approach Adelaide in a besotted fashion and then adopt a smitten expression before I take hold of Adelaide's hand and beseech her to grant me the honor of two dances as well as secure her company at dinner."

A snort was Roland's first response to that. "I'd love to be there to see that because I wouldn't think you're capable of summoning up a smitten expression, let alone pulling off a credible beseeching scene."

"Camilla came to that very same conclusion after asking me to show her my smitten look," Gideon admitted. "She immediately set up a meeting for me with Mr. Morton Gimbel last week."

"The actor?"

"One and the same. Camilla's a sponsor of Gimbel's latest show, which is why he agreed to give me some pointers in the acting department."

"I would have enjoyed seeing that as well."

Gideon grinned. "There wasn't much to see. Mr. Gimbel gave me a few exercises, which I apparently failed, then told me I would never have a career treading the boards. In all honesty, I was somewhat offended because I've often assumed different identities and have done so with great success, although . . ." He tilted his head. "I've never been tested by assuming the role of lovesick suitor before. Nevertheless, when Mr. Gimbel began pointing out how deficient I was with acting in general, I'm afraid I may have become slightly irritated. That then led him to state that, while I was incapable of summoning up a smitten expression, I was rather good at evoking a threatening one."

"I doubt Camilla wants you gazing threateningly at Adelaide come the opening ball of the Season."

"Quite, which is why she's now tasked me with the unpleasant business of practicing those exercises Mr. Gimbel gave me in front of my mirror every morning. Don't tell Camilla this, but I'm not making much headway in the improved smitten-expression department."

As Roland immediately began to chortle, Gideon directed his attention out the window as the carriage began to slow and then pulled to the side of the street, coming to a stop five carriages behind the hansom cab they'd been following. "Looks like Lottie has some business to attend to on Bleecker Street."

A moment later, Duncan, an associate who doubled as his groomsman, opened the door and leaned into the carriage. "Lottie just entered Herzfeld Haberdashery, but she kept looking over her shoulder before she disappeared inside, as if she might suspect she's being followed."

Roland glanced to Gideon. "It'll be up to you to shadow her then, because you look more like a gentleman who'd shop in a haberdashery than I ever would. I'll have our driver take me down to Clinton Street and park there. I'll keep a lookout and take over for you if she continues down the street."

Sending Roland a nod, Gideon stepped from the carriage and patted his jacket to ascertain the pistol he never went anywhere without was easily accessible. After instructing Duncan to linger on the sidewalk to be available to tail Lottie once she left the store, Gideon began sauntering for Herzfeld Haberdashery in the casual manner he'd perfected over the years. He was greeted directly inside the door by a dapperly dressed gentleman who inquired what he was shopping for, then stepped aside with a smile when Gideon told him he was merely browsing.

It didn't take long to spot Lottie McBriar standing in front of a counter that housed a cash register as a man wrapped something in brown paper. Edging around a rack of ready-made jackets, Gideon lingered on a tweed one done up in a muted shade of green, glancing to Lottie out of the corner of his eye every few seconds.

It wasn't a surprise, given her involvement with the criminal set, that she wasn't a girl who stood out in a crowd, dressed in a simple gown of inexpensive muslin, her brown hair tucked underneath an inconspicuous hat, a large, battered reticule hanging from her wrist.

What was a surprise, though, was her articulate speech once she began speaking to the man after he tied up the package with twine and handed it to her.

"Thank you, Mr. Herzfeld. Mr. Fitzsimmons is always pleased when his customers are prompt with their . . . fees." Lottie tucked the small package into the large bag looped around her arm. "I'll be certain to tell him that you had everything ready for me today instead of having me wait, a consideration that not all of Mr. Fitzsimmons's customers afford me."

Mr. Herzfeld sent Lottie a small smile before he inclined his head, his smile fading after she turned on her heel and strode for the door.

As Lottie breezed out of the shop, Gideon lingered for a moment before following her, keeping an eye on Mr. Herzfeld, who had taken to muttering something about Frank Fitzsimmons being the bane of his existence. A bane, no doubt, because Frank was evidently extorting the locals—something Gideon would need to address in the foreseeable future.

After two minutes had passed, he told Mr. Herzfeld he'd be back another day to shop when he had more time, then headed through the store and out the door, Duncan brushing past him to tell him Lottie was now wandering around a perfumery. Stepping into the shop next to the perfumery, Gideon waited until he saw Lottie stroll past, gave her thirty seconds, then followed her, hanging back on the crowded sidewalk as she spent the next thirty minutes walking down Bleecker Street, stopping in various stores, probably to retrieve payments for Frank, before she went into Nina's Bakery. Delicious smells wafted into the street after she opened the door.

Gideon was tempted to follow her when his stomach rumbled, but before he could act on the temptation, Lottie was out the door again, clutching a pastry wrapped in paper, one she began nibbling on as she continued down the street. When she disappeared into a redbrick building with a green-striped awning over the front door, he increased his pace, coming to a stop when he took note of the sign over the door, one that said *Bainswright Books*—a shop he'd been meaning to investigate for the past few weeks since Adelaide had mentioned she frequently visited this particular bookstore.

Allowing another thirty seconds to pass before he reached for the doorknob, Gideon stepped into the store, smiling when the scent of old leather and dust tickled his nose. Glancing around, he found himself in a surprisingly large room, one that suggested that at some point the owners had acquired the adjacent building, knocked out a few walls, and then created a store that was filled to the brim with tables and shelves stuffed with books. A circular staircase with a wrought-iron railing located halfway down the wall on the right suggested there were additional books located on the second floor.

He began weaving his way around a table displaying an impressive collection of dime novels, faltering just a touch when he realized Lottie was standing five feet away from him, her lips thinning when her gaze met his, lending the impression his cover might have been blown. Inclining his head to her in the hopes she would think he was a polite gentleman out for some shopping, he headed for a table stacked high with a vast assortment of leather-bound books, a plan to salvage the situation presenting itself when he discovered Adelaide perusing a stack of books a table away.

The very sight of her caused a feeling of anticipation to thrum through him, something he experienced every time he arrived at Camilla's house for another evening of dancing.

It was becoming remarkably evident that Adelaide was the breath of fresh air he'd not even realized he needed, one that dispersed the stench of malfeasance that clung to him after mingling with men who relinquished their morals at the first hint of profitability. A moment in Adelaide's company left him feeling charitable toward the world again, most likely because she was a lady who'd experienced her fair share of unkindness and yet it hadn't left her bitter—far from it.

Shaking aside his thoughts when he realized he was standing stock-still, grinning as he considered Adelaide, he strode into motion, stopping directly beside her and praying she'd play along with the plan that had sprung to mind to distract Lottie McBriar from any suspicions she might have about him.

"Forgive me for being so tardy," he began, his words causing Adelaide's head to shoot up as she turned his way. "I forgot what store I was supposed to meet you at today and have spent the past thirty minutes wandering around Bleecker Street, hoping to catch sight of you."

Adelaide didn't miss a beat, although her eyes began sparkling in a most telling fashion. "I'm certain I must bear some of the blame for that, Mr., ah . . ." Her voice trailed off as if she'd just realized he might not want her to use his name. A second later, she hitched a smile into place, revealing a dimple by the side of her mouth that he'd never noticed before. "I know we discussed shopping at this bookstore because you wanted my assistance with picking out a present for your, ah, grandmother. However, I may have also mentioned I needed to purchase some new, um . . . furs today, which might have left you confused regarding where to meet me. There's a furrier five shops down."

"Furs?"

She gave a bob of her head. "Rumor has it the first big storm of the year is brewing offshore. I'm afraid my furs from last winter aren't in the best of shape."

"Perfectly understandable," he said, suppressing the oddest urge to laugh as he extended his arm to her, which she immediately moved to take. "Have you found any books of interest that may be a suitable gift for my . . . grandmother?"

"I'm afraid I haven't because I may have become distracted with adding some books to my private collection, a hazard of being an avid reader. Nevertheless, now that you're here, we can browse together." She leaned closer and dropped her voice to a whisper. "In case you were wondering, I don't actually own any furs."

"I wouldn't imagine you would, given your fondness for cats."

She beamed a smile at him, something that left him losing his train of thought for the barest of seconds until she patted his arm. "You mentioned your grandmother enjoyed . . . poetry?"

Gideon shot a quick glance to Lottie, who was now perusing a shelf of history books halfway across the first floor. "Poetry is a favorite, but she mentioned an interest in the French Revolution a few months ago."

"Then we'll visit the history section first." She nodded to the shelves where Lottie was now climbing up a ladder to reach the top shelf. "I'm sure there'll be something over there, but if we're unsuccessful, we can always prevail upon Mr. Bainswright. He knows where every book in the store is housed, but he's currently assisting my chaperones today, Mr. Vernon Clarkson and Mr. Leopold Pendleton. Given that both those gentlemen were keen to see some of Mr. Bainswright's rare books, we might have to wait awhile before Mr. Bainswright can assist us."

"Do Vernon and Leopold often chaperone you around town?"

"Truth be told, given my advanced age, I rarely travel with a chaperone. Vernon and Leopold simply ran across me as I was waiting to board the El. They were concerned that I was alone and then insisted on accompanying me, even though I told them I'm perfectly capable of traveling around the city unescorted." She grinned. "They then spent their time as we traveled on the El discussing my swan debacle, lending me their advice about how best to avoid a similar fiasco in the future."

"What advice did they give you?"

Her eyes crinkled at the corners. "They suggested I take up running."

"I bet you found that helpful."

"Hardly," Adelaide countered. "Running requires a certain level of athleticism, which is not an attribute that comes easily to me. Nevertheless, I'm quite accustomed to Vernon and Leopold lending me all sorts of entertaining advice, something they enjoy doling out whenever I'm in their company, which is often, since society hostesses tend to seat me next to them at a variety of functions."

"Aren't you somewhat young to spend dinners in the company of men who are members of the elderly set?"

"We wallflowers are often relegated to tables with widowers and the like because the fashionable set would balk over what they'd surely see as an indignity." She smiled. "But before you get affronted on my behalf, know that I enjoy Vernon and Leopold's company. They led quite exciting lives in their younger days and enjoy regaling me with stories about those times."

Gideon chanced another glance to Lottie, who was still on the ladder, leafing through a book. He frowned and returned his attention to Adelaide when something she'd said suddenly settled. "You don't actually make it a habit to travel on the El by yourself, do you?"

"Certainly. It's far faster than a carriage, what with how it can bypass all that nasty congestion on the streets."

He rubbed a hand over his face. "How are you still alive?"

Her dimple popped out again as she grinned, immediately drawing his attention and causing him to lose his train of thought.

"My uncanny ability to continue breathing has often been a subject for contemplation within the Duveen household," she began, snapping his thoughts back into working order. "But now is hardly the moment to delve into that peculiar circumstance." She lowered her voice. "If I'm not mistaken, you're currently in the process of tailing someone, although given your unusual greeting, I suspect you're worried you may have been found out. I'm now assuming you're once again in need of my assistance to help salvage your situation and know that I'll be more than happy to oblige."

Nine

༄

Gideon's thoughts faltered when Adelaide flashed him a smile, his attention fixated on a dimple he'd begun to find downright irresistible. He cleared his throat and struggled to concentrate on the conversation at hand. "I wouldn't say my situation has deteriorated enough to where it needs to be salvaged, but how did you arrive at the conclusion that I might need your assistance again?"

"What else could I have possibly concluded?" she asked. "Surely you must know that authors of spy novels always include a scene where an agent uses the appearance of an unexpected acquaintance as a distraction plot. They then have that person approach the suspect being shadowed in an offhand manner. Because of my familiarity with those plots, if you'll confirm which patron you're following, I'd be happy to subtly strike up a conversation with them to ferret out some pertinent information for you."

"There will be no subtle striking up of anything because what I'm doing here is a confidential matter."

"But I've already figured out what you're doing so there's really no reason for you to be stingy with the details."

"Except that you don't need to know any specifics, because, as I've told you numerous times, I deal in matters of intrigue, which, again, could endanger your life if you know too much."

"I would think it's more dangerous for me to be left in the dark because who knows what convoluted scenarios I may come up with." She released a touch of a sigh. "Besides, including me in your operation today will most assuredly see me returned to a more genial frame of mind."

"You seem amiable enough to me."

"That's merely a ruse. I'm actually quite miserable, given the agonizing morning I endured at Camilla's bequest."

"Nice try, but you're an avid reader, and you're in a bookstore no less," Gideon argued. "I would think any lingering anguish would have vanished the second you stepped through the door." He frowned. "If memory serves me correctly, though, you were scheduled to meet with Camilla's dressmaker for a few fittings, which is hardly an excruciating way to spend a morning."

A grunt was her first response to that. "A *few* fittings? I was forced to endure being a human pincushion for three hours. *Three hours.* Agony doesn't effectively describe the misery I suffered."

Gideon swallowed a laugh. "Harrowing morning or not, I'm still not going to appease your curiosity about who I *might* be following."

"There's no *might* about it, and I've already discerned who your target is" She sent a discreet nod Lottie's way.

He couldn't help being impressed, not that he was going to admit that to her because that would definitely lead to more badgering on her part.

"How'd you figure that out?"

"You keep sneaking glances at her."

It was an unusual circumstance to be sure, being found out by a lady who was far too perceptive for her own good.

"May I dare hope she's an intelligence agent from another

country, sent here to ferret out some deep, dark secret, but you've now uncovered her mission and are about to bring her to justice?" Adelaide asked, drawing him from his thoughts.

"You might want to consider selecting a new genre of choice because those spy novels have sent your imagination into uncharted territory."

Disappointment clouded Adelaide's eyes. "She's not a spy?"

"Hardly. She's simply the subject of a missing person's case. Her employer hired us to find her."

Adelaide shot a look to Lottie. "She doesn't look like she's missing to me."

"Indeed."

Adelaide tapped a finger against her chin. "Could it be that she abandoned her job because she might be a thief and left her position because she stole something from her employer and no longer needed to pose as the help?"

"Uh . . ." was all Gideon could think to say to that.

"I'll take that as a yes," Adelaide said. "However, in order to avoid drawing her suspicions, we should take a turn about the room and pretend we're browsing for that book for your grandmother."

With that, Adelaide took hold of his arm and began ushering him around tables heaped high with books, slowing to a stop when a gentleman dressed in a well-tailored suit stepped up to them, inclining his head toward Adelaide and smiling a smile that, in Gideon's opinion, was far warmer than it needed to be.

"Miss Duveen," the gentleman exclaimed. "I was hoping you'd be here today. I wanted to discuss that mummy book you recommended. I found it to be a fascinating read." The gentleman's gaze drifted to where Adelaide's hand was still clutching Gideon's arm, then shot up and settled on Gideon's face. "I don't believe I've had the pleasure of meeting your . . . escort."

"Gideon Abbott," Gideon supplied after Adelaide's eyes went wide, as if she still wasn't certain what name she should be using since he was in the bookstore on behalf of the accounting firm.

"A pleasure, Mr. Abbott," the gentleman returned. "I'm Mr. Jeromy Hopkins, and—"

"Ah, Miss Duveen," another gentleman, who was sporting a large mustache and wearing an eye-wincing green jacket, interrupted as he bustled up to join them. "I see Mr. Hopkins is once again monopolizing your time, but, my dear, I must beg a few moments. That book you encouraged me to purchase regarding the Australian goldfields, well, it kept me up long into the night last week. I've been dying to discuss it with you. Please tell me you've been considering that idea for a book salon a few of us broached with you a while back, because a gathering such as that would allow us to share our take on the stories you recommend. It would also alleviate the hours many of us spend lingering about this very store in the hopes you'll make an appearance."

A trace of irritation swept over Gideon because he had the sneaking suspicion these gentlemen weren't lingering to discuss books with Adelaide. It was far more likely they were loitering about because they enjoyed her company—perhaps too much—an idea that left him in a more annoyed state than ever. Before he could whisk Adelaide away from her admirers, though, she was beaming a smile at the men, one that left both gentlemen gazing back at her in a far too adoring fashion.

"I'm delighted you enjoyed my suggestion, Mr. Osborne, although I have to admit *Robbery Under Arms: A Story of Life and Adventure in the Bush and in Australian Goldfields* took me forever to get through. While I enjoyed the story, I thought it went on a little too long, although I know you appreciate hefty reads."

Disappointment flickered through Mr. Osborne's eyes. "I take it that wouldn't be a novel you'd care to include during a book discussion?"

"I'd much rather delve into an author such as Mrs. Gaskell. Her *Mary Barton* was an intriguing read, and it's not a long story, so we'd have plenty of time to examine the work at length."

Mr. Osborne brightened. "That almost sounds as if you *have* been considering the salon idea."

"I must admit I find the notion of an evening spent discussing books to be intriguing. The only problem is that my schedule is currently filled with, ah, charity appointments, which won't leave me any time for other events until after the new year. But where are my manners?" She nodded to Gideon. "Gideon, allow me to introduce you to Mr. William Osborne. Mr. Osborne, Mr. Gideon Abbott."

William's gaze sharpened on Gideon. "Are you any relation to Mr. James Abbott?"

"He's my brother."

"Ah, so you're one of *the* Abbotts," William said, whipping out a card and pressing it into Gideon's hand. "It's an honor to meet you, and if you ever have need of a book agent, I'd be happy to be of service."

Before Gideon could do more than nod, Jeromy Hopkins shouldered William out of the way where he promptly pressed a card into Gideon's hand as well. "I'm also an agent, Mr. Abbott."

"As am I," another gentleman said, brushing Jeromy aside as he thrust his card into Gideon's hand. "I'm Mr. Clement Robards. Ain't no one better in the business at finding rare tomes than me."

As Jeromy and William immediately began voicing their protests to that statement, Gideon pocketed the cards, wondering if he was soon going to have to step in before a bout of fisticuffs occurred. Thankfully, the gentlemen seemed to realize they were hardly making a good impression, and after Jeromy muttered something to Clement about telling tall tales, they returned their attention to Gideon, smiles now firmly on their faces.

"What type of books do you collect?" Jeromy asked.

"I'm sorry to disappoint all of you," Gideon began, "but I prefer procuring new pieces to add to my art and antique weaponry collection. However, my older brother has an extensive library he's always adding to. I'd be happy to pass on your information as well as any referrals you can give me pertaining to the clients you represent."

Oddly enough, the men exchanged glances before William cleared his throat. "While we can certainly provide your brother with references, what you must understand is that book collecting is a delicate matter. Confidentiality is a must these days, especially after what happened with Mr. Thomas Garrett, another book agent, a few years back. Mr. Garrett made the mistake of mentioning within earshot of his footman a specific title that one of his clients, Mr. Richard Hartford, longed to acquire. It didn't take long for word to get out that Mr. Garrett was searching for a first edition copy of *A New Voyage Around the World* by William Dampier."

"Madness quickly ensued," Clement added. "Not only was Mr. Hartford inundated with book agents wanting to replace Thomas Garrett, which Thomas took umbrage over, but every serious collector in New York decided they desperately needed that book as well. I remember scouring all my sources, but alas, I was unsuccessful."

"All of us were thwarted after the criminal set got involved," William grumbled. "Once they heard how in demand that specific book was, our sources were set upon by hoodlums. They, unsurprisingly, were the ones successful with finding the few editions that were lurking around. They then approached the most known collectors, Mr. Richard Hartford included, and got an exorbitant price for their copies. We book agents were left out in the cold."

"Is the criminal element still actively involved in book collecting?" Gideon asked.

"Of course they are," William said. "It's a lucrative business, but good heavens, here we are, waxing on and neglecting our dear Miss Duveen in the process." He turned a smile on Adelaide, who missed the smile because she was watching Lottie, who'd climbed from the ladder and was now standing a table away from them, flipping through some books. Given the way her head was tilted, it was obvious she was eavesdropping on their conversation.

"I don't feel neglected in the least," Adelaide said, turning her attention to William. "It's fascinating to hear the intimate details of book agenting, and I'm hopeful all of you will expand more about your business when we begin meeting for our newly formed book salon. As I said, our meetings would need to wait until January, but I'm looking forward to gathering with like-minded individuals, although I hope we'll be able to encourage a few ladies to join us as well." She batted far-too-innocent lashes Gideon's way. "I wouldn't want to be the only lady in attendance since ladies and gentlemen always have differing perspectives about books. It would certainly make our deliberations more engaging if we can find other ladies to attend, although . . . wherever are we going to find some willing recruits?"

Gideon suppressed a groan when Adelaide returned her attention to Lottie and then began strolling toward her, purpose in her every step.

The potential for another fiasco was significant.

Before he could take a single step to stop her, she was in front of Lottie, who was eyeing her warily when she wasn't sneaking glances to the front door, clearly contemplating whether she should make a break for it.

"Forgive my intrusion," Adelaide began, "but since you're the only other lady customer here today, may I dare hope you'd be interested in attending a new book salon we're in the process of forming?"

"A book salon?" Lottie repeated.

"Indeed, one where we'll discuss the written word at length."

"An intriguing notion, but I suppose it would depend on where this salon will be held," Lottie said.

"If Mr. Bainswright is agreeable, we'd hold it in this shop." Adelaide's brow puckered. "But forgive me yet again. I've failed to introduce myself. I'm Miss Adelaide Duveen."

"Miss Duveen, did you say?" Lottie asked.

Apprehension was swift when Adelaide didn't hesitate to nod, which was certainly problematic since Lottie was now in possession of Adelaide's real name, something that could possibly pose a problem, considering Lottie was involved with Frank Fitzsimmons.

"And you are?" Adelaide asked.

"Jane. Jane Smith."

Adelaide beamed a smile. "What a lovely name. And with the expected pleasantries out of the way, dare I hope you have an interest in joining us?"

"I'm not sure I'd like discussing books while customers are roaming about," Lottie said. "Seems like that might be rather distracting."

"Oh, we wouldn't hold our salon during business hours. We'd wait until after the shop closes for the day."

"I see," Lottie muttered before she picked up a book lying on a table and considered the spine. "When will these salons take place?"

"We haven't ironed everything out, but after we settle on a date and time, I'll arrange for Mr. Bainswright to post a notice on the window beside the front door. You'll simply need to check the window for details."

Lottie set aside the book. "I'll make sure to do that. But now, if you'll excuse me, I'm in the mood for a heavy read. So far nothing has caught my eye."

"Mr. Bainswright got in a new shipment early this morning

from one of his frequent suppliers," Adelaide said, nodding to a crate that was sitting on the floor beside an empty table. "He hasn't had time to display or shelve those books, but I know he's already catalogued them. I myself found three unusual books in the crate to add to my collection. Perhaps you'll enjoy the same good fortune and find a special treasure for yourself today as well."

"Do you think Mr. Bainswright would be agreeable to all of us looking through the crate?" William Osborne asked, stepping forward and settling another overly warm smile on Adelaide before Lottie could do more than glance at the crate in question.

"Since profitability is Mr. Bainswright's greatest motivation, I'm sure he'd be delighted if everyone rummages through it," Adelaide said, which was all it took for every book agent to rush for the crate, crowding one another as they began pulling books out and stacking them on the empty table in what seemed to be proprietary stacks.

"Perhaps there *is* a treasure lurking in there for me," Lottie murmured before she glided over to join the men, somehow slipping past William and Jeromy and all but shouldering them out of her way, earning mutters of discontent from the gentlemen surrounding her.

"You realize you may be responsible for causing a riot, don't you?" Gideon asked, earning a grin from Adelaide before she took his arm and tugged him away from the madness now surrounding the crate.

"I'm sure it won't turn that concerning," she said, coming to a stop in front of a display of *Frankenstein* novels that was well removed from any customers. "Besides, Jane Smith claimed to be looking for a heavy read, and I noticed a few of those when I rummaged through the crate earlier. I felt compelled to mention the newly arrived books because we book lovers receive a great deal of satisfaction over helping fellow readers find the perfect read."

"You also seem to have felt compelled to invite her to a book salon you know Camilla is going to have a fit about. You mentioned starting it up in January, but if you've forgotten, that's when the Season launches in earnest."

"I'll work something out with Camilla. I couldn't very well have neglected such a fortuitous opportunity, not after hearing all that about the criminal set's involvement with book collecting."

"I'm afraid you've lost me."

She gave his arm a pat. "That does seem to happen often, but hear me out. What if Jane is involved with the less legal means of acquiring books for collectors? She could be here today because she's scouting out potential acquisitions or picking up any rumors being bandied about by the book agents."

"Three book agents just told me that discretion is now a must for everyone in the business."

"Believe me, I spend a lot of time with book agents, and discretion is not always in play," Adelaide countered. "I'm sure Jane knows that, and, if she is involved with using less-than-ethical means to acquire sought-after books, she won't be able to resist the lure of book gossip that will certainly swirl around a salon. I would think you'd be able to see the advantages of having her in attendance, especially if you haven't solved whatever case she's involved with come January, because it'll put you in close proximity to her. That might allow you to uncover much-needed clues regarding the improprieties she probably enacted against her former employer."

"The way your mind works is almost beyond comprehension," Gideon muttered.

Adelaide grinned. "I'll take that as a compliment as well as a sign you're beginning to realize I truly would be an asset to the accounting firm, even if you're too stubborn to admit it."

Ten

"I don't think I was actually complimenting you," Gideon said, raking his hand through his hair and leaving it decidedly rumpled.

"Now, don't be like that," Adelaide argued. "Negativity doesn't become you. However, there's no need to discuss this matter right now, not when we could be making better use of our time by keeping a close eye on Jane. She might be meeting someone here, and we wouldn't want to miss that opportunity, would we?"

"There's no *we* in any of this."

"There you go again with the negativity."

"And there you go again with being tenacious, something I might have to mention to your mother."

Her lips twitched. "If you think threatening me with a potential lecture from my mother is going to deter me, think again. Besides, Mother has more to concern herself with right now than something as trivial as that."

"Society mothers always make time for lecturing."

"I would normally agree. However, Mother is currently engaged in a somewhat contentious situation with Camilla regarding color choices." Adelaide picked up a book, glanced at the title, then set it aside. "Mother believes I'd look quite fetching in sun colors, a notion that leaves Camilla shuddering. I fear a war of wills is teetering on the brink of erupting, and unfortunately for my mother, I don't think she has a chance of winning, not when Camilla has such a flair for fashion."

Gideon arched a brow. "Given that you're currently wearing ivory, a shade that's somewhat commonplace for ladies, I'm not certain why your mother is at odds with Camilla."

"Camilla hasn't chosen ivory for my new wardrobe. This is one of my older frocks, worn today because Camilla believes the new and improved color palette she's chosen for me will make more of an impact if we unveil it at the start of the Season. Making an immediate impression is also why I'm not venturing back into society until the Patriarch Ball, another matter that has my mother at odds with Camilla." She picked up another book, realized she'd already read it, and set it down. "But since I'm hardly a lady who enjoys waxing on about fashions or color hues in general, allow me to return to more pertinent matters, more specifically, your reluctance to recognize what an indispensable asset I could be to the accounting firm. If you'll simply set aside your nonsensical misgivings and tell me what you need to learn from Jane Smith, although I doubt that's her real name, I'll get right to work."

"I'm sure her name *isn't* Jane Smith, but speaking of names, you providing her with your name lends credence to the notion that you're not well-suited for matters involving surreptitious situations. You've now given a girl who's known to associate with members of the criminal persuasion the means to locate you."

Adelaide frowned. "Fabricating an alias in this bookstore would be a less-than-prudent decision since everyone knows who I am. Besides, you didn't withhold your real name when the book agents sought out an introduction, which left me concluding there wasn't a reason to worry that providing my name would be an issue. With that settled, what information may I ferret out of Jane for you today?"

"There will be no ferreting. That'll have her suspicions about me cemented for certain."

"On the contrary. Jane won't find it odd in the least if I return to speak with her because I can feign an interest in all those books everyone seems to be wrestling over." She nodded to where William and Jeromy were now engaged in a tug-of-war with a leather-bound book Adelaide had decided against because it dealt with the dreary subject of mathematical equations.

"No."

Adelaide resisted a sigh and tried again. "But you can hardly lurk about watching her now since she's of the belief that you're here to find a present for your grandmother."

"I don't need to lurk anymore because Duncan, one of my associates, is observing her now."

"Observing and speaking with a suspect are two entirely different kettles of fish."

"True, but again, this is a girl who's undoubtedly immersed in the city's underworld. The last thing we need is for you to become involved in a situation that gives new meaning to the term *perilous*."

"Fine." Adelaide dusted her gloved hands together. "Since you're in a nonnegotiable frame of mind, we'll shelve this discussion for later."

Gideon flashed a grin. "There's nothing to shelve, but I must admit your persistence is, curiously enough, rather charming."

Her heart, clearly being in a traitorous frame of mind, took to beating far too rapidly at the sight of his grin, something it had taken to doing often over the month and a half they'd spent together.

It was bad enough she found herself in his arms practically

every evening, although she really couldn't blame her heart for fluttering madly about while dancing because he *was* Gideon, after all—a gentleman in possession of far too many attributes that were known to make a lady wish for the unobtainable. Regrettably, she was simply a bluestocking with a penchant for finding herself in the most ridiculous of situations, who certainly wouldn't appeal to someone like Gideon and . . .

"What? No witty comeback arguing the point that you're persistent?" Gideon asked, pulling her from thoughts that were beyond nonsensical.

She lifted her chin. "I fear I have nothing witty to say because my poor mind has grown weary of debating this subject with you."

His grin widened. "I highly doubt that. It's more likely you're thinking through a change in strategy and are intending to implement that when I least expect it."

She resisted a grin of her own. "You're a very suspicious sort, aren't you? But before you argue with that, and since you apparently have no reason to skulk about the store right now, I'd like you to meet a dear friend of mine, Mrs. Bainswright. She's currently sitting beside the cash register, with no customers to serve, so this will be the perfect time to perform an introduction."

"I'd be delighted to meet your friend, but give me a moment." Gideon gave a discreet nod to a man browsing through a table close to where the book agents and Jane were still rummaging through the crate. "I need to have a word with Duncan."

"Shall I come with you?"

"And have you immediately attempt to coerce information out of the poor man? I think not."

"You're very annoying."

Sending her a wink, which she returned with a roll of her eyes, Gideon ambled off in the direction of Duncan before she called after him that she was going to ask Mrs. Bainswright if she had any suggestions for appropriate books for his grand-mother, which earned her another wink from him in return.

Refusing to dwell on how all the winking was sending heat cascading over her cheeks, Adelaide made her way across the bookstore, stopping beside Mrs. Bainswright, who was scratching Harvey and eliciting a purr from the kitten in return.

"It's a shame your other cats don't seem tolerant of Harvey," Adelaide began. "He seems to like you."

Mrs. Bainswright smiled. "He does indeed, the poor little mite, but there's no question my other cats don't enjoy him. I think it's because they're older and Harvey's still on the rambunctious side."

"None of my other cats have taken to him either," Adelaide said. "But I haven't lost hope I'll find him the perfect home, which is why I've been taking him with me wherever I go. If I don't find him a home before January, though, I'll have more places to showcase him once society events begin in earnest. Someone is bound to fall in love with his adorable personality at some point."

"He's certainly a sweet kitten," Mrs. Bainswright agreed. "And while I don't know of anyone who's longing for an energetic addition to their family, I do have a few regular clients who might be willing to give some of your older darlings a good home. Mrs. Silverman was in just yesterday and lost one of her cats to old age, and then Mr. Walker mentioned how lonely he's been of late, what with how the weather's changing and it's difficult for him to get out as much since his rheumatism kicks in during the colder months."

"How wonderful—I mean, not the part about Mrs. Silverman's cat dying or Mr. Walker's rheumatism—but that they may need feline companions. I'm afraid I'm beginning to become overrun with cats. And while you've helped me find new homes for a few of my lovelies, I keep finding new strays on an alarmingly frequent basis. I've had to resort to dispensing my large collection to the Duveen homes here in the city and on the Hudson, and I even left a few cats behind in Newport. The problem with that, though, is I worry they're not getting the individual attention they deserve."

"I'm sure your many feline friends are simply happy to have a roof over their heads and plenty of food to eat," Mrs. Bainswright countered. "You mustn't be so hard on yourself. But cats aside, I've just noticed you're not carrying any additional books to add to your treasure pile today. Nothing else strike your fancy?"

"I'm afraid not, but the three books I found earlier were treasures indeed, so I'll be leaving today as a very satisfied customer." Adelaide glanced to the embroidery hoop beside Harvey's wicker basket. "Starting a new project?"

Mrs. Bainswright picked up the hoop and smiled. "I'm making you a little something to go with the cats."

Adelaide's gaze sharpened on the fabric. "Is that a chemise?"

"You need a matching good-luck set." Mrs. Bainswright handed Adelaide the embroidery hoop. "You'll notice I've decided to branch out a little from my last project."

Adelaide squinted at the stitches. "Are these . . . birds?"

"Butterflies, dear. I thought they'd add a touch of whimsy when paired with the cat drawers, what with how cats enjoy playing with butterflies."

"Right before they eat them."

Mrs. Bainswright laughed. "Good heavens, I never considered that." She took the embroidery hoop back from Adelaide and gave it a closer look. "I don't imagine it would take much to turn these into birds, although . . . cats do seem to enjoy eating those as well."

"Perhaps flowers would be your best option," Adelaide said. "But while it's very sweet of you to embroider another garment for me, I hate thinking of all the hours you'll put into that project." Adelaide nodded to the magnifying glass lying on the table. "You've been straining your eyes again, something I certainly don't want you to do on my account."

"I've used a magnifying glass for years, my dear, and as for all the hours I've spent on this latest project, they'll be well worth it in the end because you, my darling girl, need all the luck you can get."

"If you've forgotten, I wasn't exactly fortunate the one and only time I wore the cat unmentionables."

"On the contrary," Mrs. Bainswright argued. "You managed to acquire the assistance of Miss Pierpont a mere day after you wore the cat drawers, which was very fortunate indeed, but . . ." Her sentence trailed off as her gaze settled on something behind Adelaide before she leaned closer and dropped her voice. "Don't look now, but there's a very handsome gentleman standing a few feet behind you, one I would definitely consider a dish. You should laugh as if I've just said something amusing. Handsome gentlemen always seem to appreciate ladies with a sense of humor."

Apprehension was immediate when Adelaide took note of the gleam now residing in Mrs. Bainswright's eyes, one that was normally indicative of an impending introduction to whatever male customer caught her eye whenever Adelaide was browsing through the store. Wanting to evade yet another matchmaking attempt on Mrs. Bainswright's part, Adelaide turned her head as casually as possible, meeting the amused gaze of Gideon, who unquestionably was a very handsome gentleman and who'd obviously overheard Mrs. Bainswright calling him a dish.

"You're not laughing," Mrs. Bainswright whispered before she swept past Adelaide, not stopping until she was directly in front of Gideon. "Good afternoon, my good sir. I don't believe I've ever seen you in my shop before, Mr. . . . ?"

Gideon immediately presented her with a bow before he took the hand Mrs. Bainswright was holding out to him and placed a kiss on it. "Mr. Gideon Abbott, and you are, of course, Mrs. Bainswright. Adelaide has mentioned you often, and always in glowing terms."

Mrs. Bainswright immediately began fluttering her lashes in what could only be described as a very flirty and very un-Mrs. Bainswright–like gesture. "What a charming gentleman you are, Mr. Abbott," she cooed before she paused, stopped with all the fluttering, and narrowed her eyes on Adelaide. "You've obviously been holding out on me, dear, because you never breathed a word about this gentleman to me before."

"I beg to differ," Adelaide argued. "I told you he was working alongside Camilla on our little, uh, charity project," she finished, noticing that Jeromy Hopkins was flipping through books stacked on a nearby table, within earshot of their conversation.

Mrs. Bainswright returned her attention to Gideon, gave him a thorough perusal, then leaned into Adelaide. "And here you said the embroidered cats weren't lucky, which clearly was not the case because . . . good heavens."

Before Adelaide could summon up any type of response to that, Mr. Bainswright, in the company of Vernon Clarkson and Leopold Pendleton, strolled up to join them. To her astonishment, Mr. Bainswright was beaming from ear to ear, an uncommon occurrence to be sure, considering he was in the company of members of the Four Hundred, something he tried to avoid if at all possible since he didn't enjoy catering to what he called "the quality."

"I see both of you have found a few gems," Adelaide said as Leopold staggered up beside her, carrying a stack of battered leather-bound tomes that could very well be the reason behind Mr. Bainswright's smile.

"Indeed we did, my girl," Leopold boomed. "This is a treasure trove of a shop, and I could spend days perusing the shelves as well as spend a large chunk of change procuring works I know will keep me entertained on many a cold winter's evening."

A mere second later, Jeromy Hopkins was standing beside Leopold, eyeing the stack of books Leopold was going to purchase with a telling gleam in his eyes. A second after that, he was pressing his card into Leopold's hand, before he turned and did the same with Vernon. "Jeromy Hopkins at your service, gentlemen. I'm a book agent and a dear friend to Miss Duveen. I'm sure she'll vouch for me when I say if you're in the market for a specific book, I'm the man to see."

A second later, William Osborne was thrusting his card into the hands of Leopold and Vernon, who were now looking rather taken aback, probably because it wasn't a normal circumstance for members of the Four Hundred to be practically accosted by book agents.

"I'm sure Miss Duveen will be only too happy to give you a glowing report regarding my credentials as well," William said. "Especially when talk around the city is that I'm the best agent in the business."

As Jeromy's eyes flashed with temper, Adelaide cleared her throat, knowing a change of topic was desperately needed before a brawl erupted. "I'm certain everyone here realizes both of you are well-regarded within the industry, but before I forget." She turned her attention to Mr. Bainswright. "We've been toying with the idea of creating a book salon and were wondering if it would be possible to use one of your back rooms."

Mr. Bainswright removed his spectacles, began cleaning them with his sleeve, and frowned. "Who'd be attending such a salon?"

"I imagine we'll open it to anyone who shares an affection for great works of literature," Adelaide said. "And since bibliophiles can never resist buying new books, I'm sure you'd enjoy some robust profits after we're done with our meeting."

Mr. Bainswright slid his spectacles back into place, his eyes appearing overly large behind the thick lenses. "I'm never opposed to additional sales, although we'll need to discuss times for when this salon can take place. Certain hours and days are busier than others."

"Miss Duveen thought we might hold the salon after hours," Jane said, edging up to join them. "That would work better for me since I have obligations to attend to during the day, as I imagine most of the book agents do as well. After hours would also allow us freedom to browse around the shop uninterrupted, which I know would be profitable for you, Mr. Bainswright."

Mr. Bainswright cocked his head to the side. "I don't think it would be much of an imposition for me to linger after hours every now and again, not if it'll aid my bottom line."

"Your bottom line will unquestionably benefit from a salon," Clement Robards said, brushing past William to dump a large stack of books on the counter, his hair in complete disarray. "And, for me personally, having time to peruse the racks after hours would certainly spare me the horror I just endured." He tugged down a jacket that was hiking up past the waistband of his trousers. "I was in fear for my life when other customers noticed our interest in the new shipment and took to muscling me out of their way."

"Looks like you did alright," Mr. Bainswright said, nodding to the stack Clement had come away with.

"I would have done better if Jeromy hadn't grabbed a handful of books from the crate and declared ownership without even bothering to look at the titles," Clement grumbled.

Jeromy dusted lint from the lapel of his jacket. "I don't know why you're getting annoyed with *me*, Clement, considering Miss Duveen had the advantage over all of us because she was given the right of first perusal."

Adelaide suddenly found herself pinned under the accusatory gazes of the book agents.

"It wasn't as if I could have been expected to refuse Mr.

Bainswright's offer of a preemptive peek into the crate," she said. "I mean, honestly, what true book aficionado could possibly pass up such an opportunity?"

Jeromy heaved a sigh. "A valid point, Miss Duveen, and forgive me if I've come across as accusatory in any fashion. That was not my intention. To make up for my lapse in judgment, I think you should now share with us what treasures you found. I'm sure all of us will valiantly strive to keep our disappointment over not finding those treasures for ourselves in check."

It took a great deal of effort to refuse a grin. "I'm usually the first to want to share any new book acquisitions I make, but given that most of you are unquestionably disgruntled about my being given that first peek into the crate, I believe this is where I say I'm running behind schedule and need to get on my way."

"She found something extraordinary for sure," William grumbled.

Clement nodded. "I bet she uncovered some first editions."

"Or a rare out-of-print novel," Jeromy added.

Adelaide resisted a sigh. "Not that you'll probably believe me, but there wasn't anything overly special about the books I found. I don't recall the titles, but one was an ancient-looking herbal with water-stained pages, one was an old diary that was literally falling apart at the seams, and the last one . . ." She tilted her head. "I don't recall what that one was, but it might have something to do with music. However," she continued, "since Mrs. Bainswright has already packaged my purchases for me, I won't get to refresh my memory until I'm at my leisure, which won't be until tomorrow, because I actually do have a pressing engagement soon, one I need to leave for after my escorts for the afternoon pay for their purchases."

As the book agents immediately took to looking grumpy, Mrs. Bainswright made her way behind the counter, retrieved a package wrapped in brown paper, and handed it to Adelaide.

"I'll let you know how the progress goes with the embroidery," Mrs. Bainswright whispered. "Although you may not need as much luck as I originally thought." She sent a subtle nod Gideon's way, who, thankfully, didn't see it because he was watching Jane stroll toward the front door.

"Gideon is merely a friend," Adelaide said as she checked to make certain Harvey was well-settled in his wicker basket, completely ignoring the look of skepticism Mrs. Bainswright was now sending her way.

After securing the clasp on the wicker basket, Adelaide stepped back from the counter to allow Vernon and Leopold room to complete their transactions. Once a great deal of money was exchanged for their books, which left Mr. Bainswright rubbing his hands in glee, Adelaide gave Mrs. Bainswright a kiss on the cheek before walking with Leopold and Vernon toward the door.

Gideon met them there, taking Adelaide's wrapped parcel from her before he held the door open for everyone, Leopold nodding his thanks as he all but stumbled out of the store, carrying a good twenty pounds of books in his hands.

"What say we save an additional ride on the El for another day?" Leopold suggested, catching Adelaide's eye. "I know you find it faster, but I have a feeling this pile of books is only going to get heavier the longer I hold it."

Adelaide smiled. "I would be more than agreeable to hiring a hack to return us to Fifth Avenue, but please, allow me to take a few of your packages before you hurt something."

"The day I let a lady carry anything for me is the day I cease growing older" was all Leopold said to that before he began hobbling toward a line of hired hacks, Vernon following a few steps behind.

Adelaide returned her attention to Gideon, who was squinting at something in the distance. "What is it?"

"Jane looks to be heading into that fur shop you mentioned earlier."

"Then what are you waiting for?" Adelaide asked, taking her parcel from him and giving him a nudge. "Go after her."

"I should see you settled in a hansom cab first."

"And allow her to slip out of sight? Please. I'm perfectly capable of walking a few yards on my own."

"Are you certain?"

"Very. Now go."

After telling her he'd meet up with her later at Camilla's, Gideon melted into the crowd bustling down the sidewalk.

Turning, she set her sights on her self-appointed chaperones, who were waiting for her a half block away. Hurrying to join them, her pace slowed to a crawl when she realized that Leopold and Vernon were both watching her with clear speculation in their eyes.

"Is there something you've neglected to mention to us?" were the first words out of Leopold's mouth when Adelaide finally stopped in front of the gentlemen.

She fought the urge to fidget. "I don't believe so."

Leopold's brows drew together. "I don't recall you ever mentioning, Miss Duveen, during any of the numerous dinners we've enjoyed together, that you're well acquainted with Gideon Abbott."

It was obvious a distraction was desperately needed, especially when she knew full well the two gentlemen were once again turning their thoughts to matchmaking, something they'd done in the past with less-than-successful results.

She summoned up a smile. "There's really no need for the two of you to continue addressing me as Miss Duveen. As was mentioned, we've shared numerous dinners together and have even now enjoyed a rollicking ride on the El, which means I give you full leave to use my given name."

Leopold presented her with a bow, pausing mid-bow when he began to wobble due to the weight of the books he was carrying. "How gracious of you, Adelaide, and you must address me as Leopold and Mr. Clarkson as Vernon." He managed to straighten. "But names aside, I believe we were discussing the matter of Mr. Abbot." He nodded to Vernon. "I detected a spark."

"As did I," Vernon agreed. "A spark that has the potential of turning into so much more." He inclined his head to Adelaide. "We will, of course, be delighted to assist you with nurturing that spark if you're unsure how to proceed with such matters."

Clearly, the conversation was delving into uncharted territory.

"There's no need to assist with any nurturing because Gideon and I are friendly acquaintances and certainly don't have any sparks erupting between us," she settled on saying.

It came as no surprise when they ignored all of that.

"We'll need to construct a strategic plan," Leopold said.

Vernon nodded. "Agreed, one where a spotlight is finally cast on our dear Adelaide." He began looking Adelaide up and down. "I believe a renovation may be in order. You should be dressed in darker shades, my dear, mixed with some gold and jewel tones, and . . ." He tilted his head. "A new hairstyle wouldn't be remiss. After all that, we'll need to orchestrate an entire campaign, one that will ignite that spark and see you on your way to a romantic happily ever after."

"There will be no campaign, nor will the two of you once again attempt to dip your toes into any matchmaking scenarios." She narrowed her eyes. "You know neither of you are very good at that. And before you argue the point, need I remind you of what happened when the two of you were convinced Mr. Lyle Hammerston had fallen to his knees because he was overcome with fondness for me?"

Leopold rubbed his nose. "Anyone would have assumed that."

"Lyle fell to his knees because I stepped on the hem of that ridiculous cape he'd taken to wearing about town."

"Since we didn't see that firsthand, we assumed it was admiration that had him on the floor," Vernon returned before he shook his head. "Poor Lyle was rather taken aback when Leopold and I approached him with suggestions regarding how he should go about courting you."

"I'm sure he was, but with that incident now firmly returned to your memories, I'm certain you'll agree you're mistaken about any spark, and we'll put this conversation behind us."

"Did you detect a hint of wistfulness in Adelaide's voice just now?" Vernon said, once again ignoring everything she'd said.

"Indeed," Leopold agreed. "She's in denial because of all the romantic disappointments she's suffered over the years, but . . ." He caught Adelaide's eye. "No need to worry about being disappointed this time, my dear. We're here to enlighten you every step of the way, and we'll expound upon that while in the comfortable confines of a hired hack." He glanced to the package of books he was carrying. "These really are growing heavier by the second."

"Then allow us to put all talk of sparks aside," Adelaide said, nodding to an idle hack that was waiting for new fares. She strode into motion, with Leopold and Vernon following her.

She made it all of ten feet before a boy stumbled into her, causing her to lose her footing. Before she could find her balance, another boy brushed against her, right before a third boy ran past her, snatched her wrapped parcel out of her hands, and darted through the crowd.

"Get back here . . ." was all she was able to call out before one of the other boys grabbed hold of her basket, wrenched it away from her, and sprinted off, leaving Adelaide with no choice but to give chase because the thieves were now making off with something far more valuable than her books—that being Harvey.

Eleven

"It's unlike Adelaide to be late."

Gideon turned from the window and settled his attention on Camilla, who was checking the elegant watch encircling her wrist for the umpteenth time.

He moved to join her on the settee. "It's only ten past six, and Adelaide didn't leave the bookstore until after four. I imagine she's running behind because she agreed to return home in a hired hack instead of taking the El."

"Why Adelaide insists on riding an elevated train when she has numerous carriages at her disposal is beyond me, even if the El is faster," Camilla muttered as she continued fiddling with her watch.

"I've never been on the El before," Mrs. Robinson, Camilla's aunt Edna, said, rearranging her skirts on the dainty chair she was sitting on before she reached for her second cup of tea. "Adelaide's been trying to convince me I haven't lived until I've traveled about the city on an elevated track. I must say, I find the notion oddly appealing."

"You do recall you're the lady who suffers from queasiness

when you're taking your well-sprung barouche out and about, don't you?" Camilla asked.

"Adelaide thinks the El has a different type of motion that may soothe my stomach."

"Or leave you tossing up your accounts."

"That is always a concern," Edna murmured right as the sound of voices reached the parlor.

Before Gideon could do more than rise to his feet, Adelaide, in the company of Leopold and Vernon, stumbled into the parlor, all of them looking the worse for wear.

Vernon was missing his hat, his hair standing on end. Leopold had a large tear on the side of his trousers and dried leaves clinging to his jacket, his right eye suspiciously puffy, and Adelaide was covered in a variety of stains, her hair straggling about her shoulders as she clutched her wicker basket to her chest as if she were never going to let it go.

"What happened?" Gideon demanded, striding to Adelaide's side and taking her arm, surprised when she didn't hesitate to let him assist her into the first available chair, a circumstance that spoke volumes.

"It was an ambush," Leopold proclaimed, hobbling across the room, where he made a point of inclining his head to Camilla and Edna before he lowered himself onto a fainting couch, wincing ever so slightly.

"An . . . ambush?" Gideon repeated.

"Indeed," Vernon said, presenting Camilla and Edna with a bow before he joined Leopold on the couch, wincing as well as he got himself settled. "We were accosted before we had an opportunity to rent a hack."

"I shall bring more tea," Mr. Timken, Camilla's butler, said from the doorway, his expression stoic as ever, although his glance lingered on Vernon and Leopold before he said something about fetching a bottle of brandy as well as cheese and bread, before he bowed himself out of the room.

"Brandy would be most appreciated," Leopold said, rubbing his leg, "as will cheese and bread because I, for one, worked up quite the appetite retrieving poor Harvey from someone who was determined to hang on to him."

Edna sat forward, a hand to her throat. "Someone tried to kitty-nap Harvey?"

"Indeed, although I don't believe he was their objective. My books were," Adelaide said, flipping open the basket and retrieving Harvey, who, quite like Adelaide, was looking disheveled, his fur matted with dirt and his expression forlorn.

"You need to start from the beginning," Gideon said, pulling up a chair beside Adelaide and taking a seat.

She dashed a strand of inky black hair out of her face. "It all began as we were making our way toward a line of hansom cabs. Everything was normal until a boy jostled into me, almost knocking me off my feet. Jostles happen all the time, so I wasn't alarmed, until another boy slammed into my other side, and then someone, it might have been the third one who showed up, but I'm not positive about that, snatched my parcel. As that boy was dashing away, I was suddenly confronted with another miscreant, who grabbed hold of my basket, wrenched it out of my hand, and raced down the sidewalk."

"Adelaide didn't hesitate to give chase," Leopold said, settling a smile on Adelaide. "And while I know, my dear, that Vernon and I recently suggested you take up running in case you're ever set upon by mad swans again, you are surprisingly fleet of foot. I was truly impressed when you hurtled over the small fence bordering that park and continued running without missing a stride."

"Leopold and I weren't that fortunate," Vernon added as he took out a handkerchief and began dusting dirt from his jacket. "Leopold snagged his trousers on a wrought-iron stake, ripping them in the process. And while I thought I was going to clear the fence, I ended up facedown in the dirt."

"By the time we got ourselves collected," Leopold continued, "Adelaide was in the midst of a bout of ineffective fisticuffs with the thief who'd snatched her basket, neither of them landing many punches, which suggests our dear Adelaide might benefit from some instruction in hand-to-hand combat. We were just about to intervene when Adelaide snatched the thief's hat and . . . lo and behold, what we thought was a lad turned out to be a lass." He touched his puffy eye. "That girl then dropped the basket, and in her attempt to flee, barreled into me. I snagged hold of her arm, and you could have knocked me over with a feather when she made a fist and planted it smack into my eye."

"We've obviously lost our touch," Vernon said rather forlornly. "There was a day when Leopold and I could take on numerous outlaws at one time, but today we were bested by a young girl."

"And a tree," Leopold added.

Gideon arched a brow. "A tree?"

"The lid to the basket came undone when the girl dropped it," Adelaide said. "Harvey shot out of it as if he were on fire. He then dashed through the park and clambered up the tallest tree."

"I offered to rescue him," Leopold said.

"Which failed horribly because you got stuck," Vernon said, earning a harrumph from Leopold in return.

"I wasn't stuck. The tear I suffered from the fence debacle allowed my trousers to get snagged on a limb. They were stuck, not I."

"Adelaide had to scale the tree to rescue you, but"—Vernon hurried to add—"not because I didn't want to do the extrication myself." He shook his head. "The second Adelaide realized I was reaching for a branch, well, bossy doesn't begin to describe her immediate attitude." He caught Gideon's eye. "She told me in no uncertain terms that my rheumatism was sure to become aggravated if I climbed a tree. She then ordered me to stand back before she scrambled up the tree, an impressive feat considering she was wearing a gown.”

Adelaide caught Gideon's eye. “Before you ask, I didn't abandon my gown at any point because I didn't believe it would be proper for me to shuck it off in the middle of Greenwich Village.”

It came as no surprise when silence descended over the parlor, the looks on Vernon's and Leopold's faces making it rather difficult for Gideon to resist a grin.

“Was abandoning your gown an option you were considering?” Leopold finally asked.

Adelaide's eyes began to twinkle. “I only contemplate those types of actions when I'm relatively convinced no one will happen upon me.”

“A, ah, prudent contemplation if there ever was one,” Leopold muttered. “But to continue our story, after Adelaide got my trousers free—er, not that I took them off, she simply got the fabric unstuck—she helped me reach the ground and then climbed up the tree again and rescued Harvey.”

Even though he was in the midst of a concerning circumstance, to be sure, Gideon was finding himself plagued with the distinct urge to laugh over the telling of what had to have been a most trying situation, even though it appeared Adelaide and her elderly chaperones had weathered an attack quite well— give or take a few bruises, some dirt, ripped trousers, and one traumatized kitten, who was now sound asleep on Adelaide's shoulder, emitting little snores.

“We then had to find a hired hack,” Adelaide continued. “That turned into a bit of a debacle because most of the drivers thought we were looking far too derelict to allow us access into what everyone knows are questionable interiors in the first place.”

“It took us seven attempts before we finally found a driver willing to take our money,” Vernon said. “I had to offer him triple his normal rate to drive us here.”

"All in all, it was a troubling afternoon," Leopold said. "Poor Adelaide not only had to rescue me and Harvey as well as participate in a bit of a brawl, but she also lost her new books to thieves, although . . ." He frowned. "I find it interesting that Vernon and I weren't relieved of our recent purchases."

Gideon shot a glance to Adelaide. "You were the only victim of theft?"

"Indeed, and if you ask me, that was telling." She turned to Mr. Timken, who was pushing a tea cart into the room, and waited until he passed tea all around, along with glasses of brandy to Vernon and Leopold. She took a sip of her tea, then set aside the cup and caught Gideon's eye. "Someone evidently wanted one of the books I bought today and took extreme measures to get it."

"Were the books valuable?" Gideon asked.

"Not at all. One was an illustrated copy of medicinal herbs, but it was in grim shape, which was why Mr. Bainswright sold it to me for a few dollars." She nodded to Edna. "I'd forgotten what one of the other books was until I saw you. It was a collection of sheet music I thought you would enjoy since you've taken on the responsibility of playing for our dance sessions every evening."

Edna smiled. "What a thoughtful young lady you are, my dear. I'm sure I would have enjoyed some new songs to play."

"I'll see if Mr. Bainswright has a similar book the next time I return to his store," Adelaide said. "I'm afraid I won't be able to replace the last book I purchased because it was a diary written by a young lady around the time of the Revolutionary War. The handwriting was old and faded and would have been difficult to decipher, but I thought it would make an interesting read. Mr. Bainswright sold it to me for less than a dollar, given that it was in even sorrier shape than the herbal one was."

Gideon frowned. "How does he make a profit if he charges so little for his books?"

"He always buys unsorted crates at a set rate from the supplier of the batch of books I got mine from today. Sometimes he uncovers treasures and sometimes he barely manages to break even." She smiled. "I believe he enjoys the possibility of discovering unknown gems, which is why he continues purchasing from that particular man."

"Do you remember the titles of the books that were stolen from you?" Gideon asked next.

"I'm afraid not, but I'm sure Mr. Bainswright would be happy to look up my missing titles. He keeps a log of every book he puts on the floor to sell." Her eyes suddenly took to gleaming in a rather concerning way. "Dare I hope you're inquiring about the titles because you think we should launch an investigation, one where we'll need to let the right ears on the street know we're on the lookout for my books and will pay handsomely for any information leading to their recovery?"

"*We* won't be doing anything."

She waved that straight aside. "You need to discontinue your aversion to the word *we*. Besides, it was my books that were stolen, and it was me, along with Vernon and Leopold, who had to fight valiantly to get poor Harvey back. That means there definitely needs to be a *we* in this particular instance."

Before Gideon could argue with that, Leopold sat forward. "Forgive me for interrupting, but it almost sounds as if Adelaide has become involved with that business you've taken such pains to keep quiet, Gideon."

"Would anyone like some cheese?" was all Gideon could think to ask as a distraction as he made his way over to the tea tray and began fixing up small plates, ignoring the startled look from Mr. Timken, whose job it was to serve the cheese, and who was unaccustomed to anyone blithely taking over his duties.

Edna, surprisingly enough, hurried to assist him, which earned a widening of Mr. Timken's eyes, something she neglected to notice as she went about the business of handing

141

Camilla and Adelaide small plates of cheese. She then grabbed two plates Gideon had finished preparing before she headed Vernon's way, fluttering her lashes in his direction as she thrust a plate into Leopold's hands, who barely managed to grab hold of it because Edna had already turned her back on him and was once again batting her lashes at Vernon right before she settled herself between the two gentlemen. That unexpected development left Vernon smiling and Leopold practically falling off the settee.

"This day just keeps getting more and more interesting," Adelaide muttered, which earned her a nod from Camilla, who'd not said much since Adelaide and the gentlemen had arrived, which was quite unlike her, and suggested she might very well be wondering exactly what she'd agreed to get herself into by taking Adelaide on.

"Where were we?" Vernon asked, drawing everyone's attention, although Edna had been keeping her attention centered on him, something that was probably responsible for Vernon being somewhat flushed.

"I believe we were discussing Gideon's occupation and Adelaide's involvement in that," Leopold said before he took a bite of cheese and turned an expectant eye on Gideon.

"I never knew Gideon had an occupation, other than being a gentleman who can lunch," Edna said, leaning toward Vernon and smiling a smile Gideon had often seen Camilla put to good use when she wanted to coerce information out of someone. "Truth be told, I don't see him lunching often, which could very well be explained due to this mysterious occupation of his."

Gideon cleared his throat. "I don't believe this is exactly the moment to delve into that, not when we're already running behind schedule with our dance practice this evening."

The smile slipped from Edna's face as she crossed her arms over her chest and took to looking exactly like the high-society widow she was, one who'd been known to strike terror into the hearts of the upper crust with a glance, an ability that had been the reason behind Camilla convincing her aunt to take up the role of chaperone for her.

"Your secret occupation has now come out into the open," Edna began. "It would hardly be fair to deny me at least a summary of what that occupation entails, especially when it sounds as if dear Adelaide has been swept into this secret. With me being the oldest lady in the room—although I'm not that old, being a mere sixty, er, something—it's my obligation to ascertain that whatever shenanigans you've allowed Adelaide to become involved with will not damage her reputation."

Gideon gave a tug on a tie that was beginning to feel overly tight. "Contrary to what Adelaide seems to believe, she's not involved in any business I may be engaged with, nor will she be in the future. It should also be noted that Camilla, who has been less than subtle with her attempts to convince me she should be brought on board with my, uh, firm, will not have that desire appeased either. And, as another aside, I'm not involved in shenanigans, but in a legitimate business endeavor."

"But what exactly is this business?" Edna pressed.

Seeing absolutely no way to extricate himself from what was turning into an honest-to-goodness inquisition at the hands of a determined society matron, Gideon summoned up a smile. "I'm invested in an accounting firm."

"My late husband was invested in many ventures, but he never took pains to keep his interest in those businesses quiet, something Leopold mentioned you've been doing," Edna shot back. "May I assume you're doing so because there's some question about the legality of this business or perhaps the men involved with you?"

"My firm is completely on the up-and-up."

"Who else works at this firm?" Edna tossed at him next.

"Ah . . ."

"Roland Kelly," Camilla supplied.

"Traitor," he muttered, garnering a wink from Camilla before she calmly took a sip of her tea, the wink lending the impression she was a tad put out with him for reiterating his refusal to allow her to become involved with his firm.

Edna tilted her head. "Wasn't Roland Kelly your former bodyguard?"

Gideon settled for simply nodding, knowing that was hardly going to stop the interrogation but not wanting to provide her with too much information if he could help it.

"Roland never struck me as the type of gentleman to concern himself with poring over dreary ledgers," Edna said.

Vernon released a chuckle, immediately drawing Edna's attention.

A batting of lashes soon commenced, which left Vernon rather red in the face again. "You're familiar with Roland Kelly?" Edna asked sweetly.

"He did some work for a friend of mine a few months back," Vernon admitted.

Edna gave another flutter of her lashes. "Accounting work?"

Vernon shot a glance to Gideon. "This is where I believe I'll retreat from the conversation and leave the rest of the explaining up to you."

"You might as well give her a summary, Gideon," Adelaide said. "I haven't gotten the impression Edna is a lady who's easily thwarted."

Gideon raked a hand through his hair. "You're probably right, but don't think it's escaped my notice that ever since becoming involved with you, my secret doesn't seem nearly as secret anymore."

After settling back in his chair, Gideon took a few minutes to explain the basics of what the accounting firm was to Edna before he turned to Leopold. "With all that said, and before Edna thinks up additional questions she'll undoubtedly demand I answer, I have a pressing question of my own—How did you and Vernon become privy to my affiliation with the firm?"

Leopold shifted on the settee, almost falling off because of the limited space he had since Edna had joined them. After righting himself, he smiled. "As Vernon said, a friend of ours procured the services of your firm. He was rather stingy with the particulars, only saying that he had a Mr. Roland Kelly looking into a matter of industrial espionage for him. His reluctance to discuss the matter left us curious. We asked a few discreet questions at the Union Club and learned that if a person needed assistance with delicate matters, Roland was the man to see."

"We then saw you riding with Roland in Central Park not long after that," Vernon added. "Didn't take much for us to put two and two together, especially since Leopold and I became involved in intrigue after our stint in the service was up when we were barely thirty." He smiled. "It's difficult to return to a sedentary lifestyle after one has been involved with adventures for so many years."

Edna's eyes grew wide. "I never heard a whisper about any intrigues the two of you may have been involved with. I always thought you spent your time managing your families' many business interests."

Vernon gave Edna's hand a pat. "Which is exactly what we intended for everyone to believe, but no. We did have other, far more exciting lives, although that was eons ago."

"I had no idea," Edna said, fanning her face with her hand. "I now find myself all aflutter over the idea I'm in the presence of, from what it sounds like, swashbuckling gentlemen."

Camilla sidled next to Gideon and dropped her voice. "You need to do something before Aunt Edna, who is behaving quite unlike herself, suffers a fit of the vapors."

Knowing that could be a distinct possibility because he'd witnessed Edna swooning often over the years, especially when she got overly excited, Gideon nodded before he directed his attention to Leopold and Vernon. "Have the two of you ever considered returning to a more adventurous lifestyle?"

Leopold sat forward. "Are you offering us a job?"

"It might be worth discussing."

Adelaide's eyes immediately began flashing. "You're going to offer them a job when you won't even consider bringing me on?"

He refused a sigh. "They evidently have experience in clandestine affairs, whereas, if I need remind you, you're a lady who got ambushed by book thieves just today."

"And that I was the specific target of those thieves means I'm directly involved in this latest fiasco, and as such, deserve to be included in any investigating I know you're already considering doing," Adelaide said, completely neglecting to address the pertinent facts he'd just laid out that explained exactly why she had no business involving herself in investigating anything.

"Can't you simply accept that I may know best in this instance and graciously concede defeat?" he asked.

"Not when I know I could be invaluable to this particular investigation," she argued. "You mark my words, one of those agents—or one of the customers present today at Bainswright Books—had something to do with the attack on me. I'm in the best position to nose around to discover the identity of that person since I spend a great deal of time at that bookstore and wouldn't draw anyone's suspicions."

"Or you could trust that I'm very good at what I do and leave it at that. I'll visit Mr. Bainswright tomorrow and have him look up the titles of the books that were stolen. If we're lucky, perhaps one of our informants has heard about a request for a certain title a book collector wants, and we'll then track that person down."

"But the books I purchased had only just been delivered to the store. Collectors wouldn't have known of the new titles. That means there's something else afoot."

Gideon scrubbed a hand over his face. "Difficult as this is for me to admit, that's actually a valid point."

"And suggests I'd be a true asset to this particular case."

"No."

Adelaide's eyes narrowed. "Why not?"

"I believe we've already addressed that, and ad nauseum to boot. To point out the obvious, though, the book, or books, that someone desired has now been taken out of your possession. Given that there were three members of the criminal persuasion sent after you, you were fortunate to have escaped relatively unscathed. If you start snooping around, you could place yourself in danger. One of my main objectives when I became involved with the accounting firm was to keep people safe from threats. I would be failing with that goal if I agree to let you dabble in matters you have no business dabbling in."

Her eyes flashed with temper. "You're not responsible for keeping me safe, Gideon, no matter that there are times when it seems as if you've appointed yourself my very own personal guardian."

He found he had no ready argument to that because . . . she wasn't exactly off the mark.

For some reason, after she'd gone up in flames months before, he'd found himself feeling the most unusual urge to protect her—mostly from herself and the odd happenstances that dogged her almost every step.

He'd dwelled on his protective attitude toward her numerous times, but he'd yet to come up with a theory to explain why he'd adopted the role of her protector, or why, during the past month and a half, he'd begun wondering what was going to happen if Camilla succeeded with convincing society Adelaide was a lady who deserved to be considered in high demand. That could very well mean his protectiveness toward her might need to wane, especially if society gentlemen began appreciating the Adelaide he'd come to know and admire.

"What I'd like to know, and this is circling back to a discussion Vernon and I were having with Adelaide," Leopold began, "is exactly how you, Gideon, became so closely acquainted with her. We spend many an evening dining with Adelaide at society events, and yet we've rarely noticed the two of you together. That has me wondering if there's something you've been keeping from society."

"Oh . . . here we go," Adelaide muttered before she wagged a finger in Leopold and Vernon's direction. "Before the two of you decide to clear your schedules for an upcoming wedding, allow me to put to rest once and for all the romantic notions I know are tumbling around your minds. Gideon is not my secret suitor. Instead, he's been pressed into service by Camilla because she decided to take me on as a new project."

Leopold's mouth made an O of surprise before he turned to Camilla. "You're going to attempt to procure a match for Adelaide this Season?"

"She doesn't want a match," Camilla countered. "In fact, I'm not convinced she's completely onboard with me taking her on in the first place."

"After suffering through all the torture you've been forcing me to endure, I'm in full agreement with you there, even though accepting your assistance has made my mother ecstatic, when she's not arguing with you about color choices," Adelaide admitted, earning a bit of a grin from Camilla in return.

Leopold sat forward and settled eyes that were brimming with curiosity on Camilla. "If it's not a match you're intending for Adelaide, what are you attempting to do?"

"I'm going to turn her fashionable."

"Are you really?" Vernon breathed.

"Indeed," Camilla returned. "Although I must admit that might be more difficult than I first anticipated, given that she's not exactly been receptive to all the changes I've suggested."

"It's not that I'm unreceptive," Adelaide argued. "I simply

don't enjoy being tortured for hours on end as a fiend of a dressmaker sticks pins into me."

"Miss Ellington is not a fiend. She's an exceptionally innovative designer who may have stuck you a few times, but only because you can't seem to hold still."

Leopold and Vernon exchanged rather telling looks before Leopold rubbed his hands together.

"This is wonderful news," he began. "Vernon and I have longed to turn society's perception of our dear Adelaide around for years but have been uncertain how to proceed. With you at the helm, Miss Pierpont, and with us to lend you any assistance you may need, success is all but guaranteed."

Camilla blanched. "While I appreciate the offer, as the old saying goes, too many cooks in the kitchen could very well spoil the broth."

It came as no surprise when a rousing debate erupted, Leopold and Vernon professing that their assistance was imperative for Camilla's plan to succeed since they knew everyone in society, while Camilla countered with arguments that included more idioms such as "less is more."

And while a part of him knew he should probably intervene on Camilla's behalf because she was only taking Adelaide in hand because of him, Gideon was reluctant to do so because, if nothing else, the debate seemed to have distracted Adelaide from her determination to help him.

He could only hope that she'd stay sufficiently distracted until he'd had time to seek out Mr. Bainswright, procure the titles of the books that were stolen, then get right to work uncovering whatever plot was afoot before Adelaide realized he was going forward with her case without her.

Twelve

Adelaide stepped from her carriage and set her sights on Gideon, who was strolling down the sidewalk adjacent to Bleecker Street in the direction of Bainswright Books. It didn't take a genius to realize he was on a quest to speak with Mr. Bainswright before the store opened for business, something Adelaide had known he was going to do, especially when he'd gone to extreme lengths the evening before to keep the conversation directed away from the theft she'd experienced.

He apparently had yet to understand she wasn't a lady who was distracted easily, especially when her curiosity was aroused, and it was certainly roused now, what with how she'd somehow managed to land herself into a most intriguing situation.

Truth be told, she was feeling somewhat guilty for allowing Gideon to believe she'd been sidetracked from the situation at hand, joining in with the lively debate between Camilla, Vernon, Leopold, and even Edna, who'd decided, for some unknown reason, that Camilla needed to accept the older gentlemen's assistance with relaunching a new and improved version of Adelaide into society.

Camilla had evidently seen that as a direct aunt-betrayal and had insisted Adelaide and Gideon get right to their dance time, where, concerningly enough, everyone had immediately taken to critiquing her performance.

Evidently the thought had never entered anyone's mind that shouting out suggestions to her wasn't going to have her steps improving. She'd trampled Gideon's feet too many times to count, which left him limping thirty minutes after they'd taken to the floor.

That was why, once she and Gideon were on the opposite end of the ballroom, far removed from their critiquing audience, she'd suggested they formulate a plan to extricate themselves from a situation that was becoming less productive by the second. Oddly enough, as she and Gideon began conspiring together to bring the evening to a rapid end, their dancing improved, something that suggested she was quite capable of dancing in a proficient manner if given a proper incentive as well as gaining control of nerves that always seemed to come into play whenever she was in Gideon's arms.

Their improved dancing was why Camilla hadn't put up much of a fuss when Edna begged a short reprieve from the piano, at which point Gideon, per their plan, declared a forgotten engagement he simply couldn't miss. After sending Adelaide a wink, he'd made a speedy retreat, Adelaide following a few minutes later after Leopold and Vernon had all but shooed her toward the door, explaining they needed uninterrupted time to discuss different strategies with Camilla to ensure Adelaide would truly find herself in high demand once the Season began in earnest.

Smiling at the memory of the horror she'd seen on Camilla's face, Adelaide reached into the carriage, retrieved the basket holding Harvey, told her driver she'd be back within the hour, then headed for the bookstore, slipping into the alley she'd seen Gideon disappear down.

"Awfully early for you to be out and about."

After swallowing a shriek, Adelaide settled a scowl on Gideon, who was leaning casually against the brick wall of the bookstore, amusement in his eyes. "You just frightened me half to death."

"Which was my intention because you have no business skulking down an alley. If you've forgotten, you were set upon by criminals only yesterday. Far be it from me to point out the obvious, but criminals tend to lurk about backstreets, especially in this part of the city."

"I come down this alley all the time by myself because Mr. and Mrs. Bainswright often invite me to visit before the store opens. They enjoy having a cup of tea in the backroom before their day begins and can't hear anyone knocking on the front door."

"Once again I find myself wondering how you're still alive," Gideon said, moving to join her.

"Perhaps the nine lives my cats possess have rubbed off on me."

He took hold of her gloved hand and pressed a kiss to her fingers, which immediately sent her pulse galloping madly about. "An interesting theory, but if true, you've undoubtedly squandered at least eight of those. You may want to consider proceeding with extreme caution from this point forward."

"Where's the fun in that?" she asked before she retrieved her hand and held out the basket. "Here. Hold Harvey. I need to find my key."

"You have a key to the bookstore?"

"I check in on the place whenever the Bainswrights go on holiday."

"Do not tell me you do that checking without anyone with you."

"My cousin Charles accompanies me every now and again."

"I'll take that as affirmation you do, indeed, come here unattended at times, leaving you vulnerable to the miscreants who roam this very street."

"I've never had a problem until yesterday." She opened her reticule, rooted around the contents, and extracted the key. "Shall we?" she asked, pausing after she inserted the key to look over her shoulder. "Don't be alarmed when I begin shouting to announce my arrival. The Bainswrights are incredibly hard of hearing. If they're not in the backroom, I'll need to yell to attract their attention." She gave the key a twist, opened the door, and stepped inside, Gideon following directly behind her.

A quick glance around showed no sign of the Bainswrights.

"Mr. Bainswright?" Adelaide shouted, moving through the room. "It's Adelaide."

To her alarm, Mr. Bainswright suddenly rushed into the room, his spectacles askew, brandishing a rifle. A second after he appeared, Gideon was standing in front of her, his hands raised above his head, Harvey apparently taking exception to that because he immediately began mewling from the confines of the basket Gideon was dangling in the air.

"Put down the rifle, Mr. Bainswright," Gideon shouted, his voice booming around the room, which caused Mr. Bainswright to freeze on the spot and squint in their direction.

"Mr. Abbot. How did you get in here?"

"He's with me," Adelaide said, stepping around Gideon.

"Good heavens, child," Mr. Bainswright began, lowering the rifle. "We weren't expecting you this morning, but thank goodness I didn't shoot you. I'm afraid after what the wife and I walked in to find this morning, I'm in an agitated state."

"What happened?" Adelaide demanded, crossing the room and stopping beside Mr. Bainswright, who was gripping the rifle with white-knuckled fingers. Gideon joined them, handed her the basket with a still-mewling Harvey in it, and carefully took the weapon away from what Adelaide only then noticed was a visibly shaking hand.

"We've been robbed—or perhaps not, because I've yet to find

any missing books—but poor Mrs. Bainswright is in a right state over the matter."

"How did the robbers gain access to the store?" Gideon asked as Mr. Bainswright turned and began shuffling out of the room.

"That's the peculiar thing. There's no sign of forced entry, which is why we were shocked to discover the first floor in shambles."

"Professionals then," Adelaide muttered, earning a nod from Gideon as they followed Mr. Bainswright, who stopped once he reached the main room and gestured around. "As you can see, someone seemed to be looking for something, and not from the valuable section of books I keep upstairs. Those rooms weren't touched, which puts a rather curious twist on the situation."

Adelaide set the basket on a table and took a second to un-latch the lid, finding an outraged Harvey in the process, who jumped out and began wandering around the table, presenting Adelaide with his back. Her gaze traveled over the books strewn about the floor, the tables nearest to the crate Mr. Bainswright had purchased yesterday all but empty, except for a few stray novels. Books had also been pulled from a bookcase that shelved historical books, autobiographies, and journals, the manner in which those books now littered the floor suggesting someone had been in a hurry. "How curious that only one bookcase was emptied," she said, moving closer.

"Especially when the books on that shelf aren't valuable," Mrs. Bainswright said, straightening from behind a stack of books she'd been looking over, one of Mr. Bainswright's in-ventory ledgers in hand. "I've yet to find a single book missing from our inventory, although I can't say for certain nothing was taken. Whoever broke in here tore the page from yester-day's sales out of our accounting book—but not all the sales, mind you, only the ones from transactions that occurred in the afternoon."

"Sales that were rung up starting around the time Adelaide made her purchases?" Gideon asked.

Mrs. Bainswright frowned. "How did you know that?"

Adelaide moved closer to her. "Because I was robbed not long after I left the store."

"You were robbed?" Mrs. Bainswright repeated.

"I was, but interestingly enough, the thieves didn't attempt to steal Mr. Pendleton's books, or Mr. Clarkson's, for that matter."

"You think they were only after your books?"

Adelaide bit her lip. "I did, but it doesn't make sense that after relieving me of my parcel, they'd then break into the store." She turned her attention to Mr. Bainswright. "May I see your inventory list from that crate you got yesterday? I don't recall the titles of the books I purchased, but perhaps those may explain why someone was so desperate to acquire them."

As Mr. Bainswright hurried into his office, Adelaide approached Mrs. Bainswright, who was looking rather peaked, and steered her over to her favorite chair. After helping her get settled, she told Gideon to keep an eye on her while she went off to make some tea.

The last thing she expected to see once she returned was Gideon sitting in a chair beside Mrs. Bainswright, holding her embroidery hoop and explaining how to do a proper cashmere stitch.

"See? This stitch allows you to cover more territory on the fabric than the one you've been using," Gideon said. "That'll save you a lot of time filling in the bodies of the flowers you're creating."

For a second, Adelaide allowed herself the luxury of simply watching Gideon with Mrs. Bainswright, her heart giving an odd flutter when he handed her the embroidery hoop and smiled in an encouraging manner when the elderly woman began plying the needle into the chemise.

There was something incredibly sweet about a man who courted danger taking the time to help a woman who'd suffered a horrible morning find a bit of peace. It was also incredibly surprising that he seemed to know his way around an embroidery hoop in the first place.

Gideon took that moment to look up, flashing Adelaide a grin. "Before you ask, yes, I know how to embroider. I learned when I was in the navy because we frequently had time on our hands as we were sailing around the world. It's a hobby I enjoy to this day."

"You actually like needlepoint?" she asked, advancing into the room to set the tea service on a table, ignoring the way her pulse had ticked up a notch at the sight of his grin.

"I find the repetition soothing as well as enjoy presenting my completed projects to my mother, who now has my needlepoint pillows proudly exhibited in her parlor in Paris." He smiled. "Mother has been pestering me to learn how to crochet because she'd like some throws to go with the pillows, but I readily admit the manuals I've found explaining the art of crochet aren't very helpful. I've yet to make much headway with the lap robe I've started."

Mrs. Bainswright shot a telling look to Adelaide, one that suggested she was waiting for Adelaide to offer to teach Gideon the finer points of crocheting. Resisting the inclination to roll her eyes, not only because she had no idea how to crochet, but also because Mrs. Bainswright was clearly trying to manipulate the situation, she settled for sending Mrs. Bainswright a slight shake of her head, which resulted in Mrs. Bainswright sending *her* a rolling of the eyes before she placed a hand on Gideon's arm.

"I know how to crochet, my dear man, and I'd be happy to teach you," Mrs. Bainswright began before she turned an overly bright smile Adelaide's way. "I'm sure you'd enjoy learning a few pointers from me as well. I say we coordinate our schedules so I can share everything I know about crocheting with both of you at the same time."

Before Adelaide could argue with that nonsense, although there was a part of her that wouldn't mind being on hand to watch Gideon learn how to crochet, Mr. Bainswright hurried back into the room, carrying a large ledger.

After setting it on the table, he flipped it open and ran his finger down a page. "Ah, here we go. Seems like you bought *Six Characteristic Pieces* by Frederick Brandos, a reprint of *Culpepper's Complete Herbs*, and a diary written by a Juliette Watson, although I recall being unable to make out the author's name for certain, given the dismal condition of that diary. In all honesty, I was disappointed with the books Mr. Elmendorf sold me yesterday, but since he was the only supplier to approach me this week, I was hesitant to turn away his collection."

As Adelaide set about pouring the tea, Gideon rose to his feet and frowned as he considered Mr. Bainswright for a moment. "I can't help but wonder if the circumstances surrounding the theft of Adelaide's books are somehow tied to this Mr. Elmendorf. What can you tell me about him?"

Mr. Bainswright accepted a cup of tea from Adelaide before he sat down on a straight-backed chair, his knees giving a bit of a creak. "There's not much to tell," he began. "Elmendorf has sold me books for about two, maybe three years. Frankly, he doesn't have a great eye for valuable books, which is probably why he likes to sell to me in bulk, asking a set price for an entire crate instead of requesting specific dollar amounts for each book. I've never lost money on what I buy from him, although I haven't made a lot of money either."

Mrs. Bainswright settled a fond look on her husband. "You know you only buy from him because he's always got a down-on-his-luck story to tell, and underneath your bluster, you're a big softie."

"That was supposed to be our little secret," Mr. Bainswright grumbled.

"Gideon and I won't tell anyone," Adelaide said, handing Mrs. Bainswright a cup of tea. "But I think we should make it a point to speak with Mr. Elmendorf to see if he remembers where he acquired the books I purchased yesterday. That might give us a clue as to why anyone wanted one of those books so desperately that they resorted to theft. Do you have an address for him?"

Mr. Bainswright scratched his chin. "Can't say that I do. He comes to me, not the other way around."

Adelaide caught Gideon's eye. "We're going to have to have someone watching the store at all times, not just for protection for the Bainswrights, but to have a chat with Mr. Elmendorf the next time he comes around."

"I see we're back to the *we* business, and while I agree that men will need to be dispatched to oversee activity at the store, you're not going to become further involved," Gideon said.

"That's like allowing me to become immersed in a spy novel, then taking it away from me right when the good stuff begins."

"This isn't one of your spy novels."

"Well, quite, because it's actually happening and I'm a player in the intrigue."

Gideon's eyes narrowed, but before he could voice the objections Adelaide knew he longed to make, a meow drew her attention. A glance upward left her smiling when she caught sight of Harvey stuck on the very top of a bookcase. After picking her way through scattered books lying on the floor, she reached for the rolling ladder, but before she could begin climbing, Gideon was standing directly beside her.

"Allow me," he offered. "Camilla would be put out with both of us if you suffer a fall and break a limb. That would undoubtedly be the thing that would leave her throwing up her hands in defeat."

JEN TURANO

"Camilla is far too determined to find success with me to admit defeat, even if I were to suddenly incapacitate myself." Adelaide smiled. "However, since ladders and I don't always have an understanding, I concede your point, so up you go."

Gideon blinked. "I wasn't expecting you to be so reasonable about the matter."

"I don't make it a habit to be unreasonable."

"How interesting, because you certainly seem to make that a habit with me" was all he said before he sent her a wink and headed up the ladder.

Thirteen

As Adelaide watched Gideon whisk Harvey from the top shelf, she was suddenly struck with the notion that he might have just made a legitimate observation.

She *did* seem to have the tendency to contradict him often, which was curious because she usually found it easier to agree with everyone instead of stating her true thoughts on any number of topics—or perhaps she agreed because, difficult as this was to admit, she'd always hoped that by being affable, society wouldn't behave as harshly toward her.

Curiously enough, though, when she was with Gideon, she didn't try to appease him or always agree with him, which suggested she was comfortable simply being herself around him, probably because she knew their friendship was destined to remain along the same lines of the relationship she shared with her cousin, Charles.

"He seems to have attached himself to me."

Pulling herself from her thoughts, Adelaide watched as Gideon stepped from the ladder, Harvey clinging to the front of his jacket, his little claws dug into the fabric.

Her lips began to curve. "I believe you've made yourself a new friend."

"He's meowing up the wrong human if he thinks I'm going to befriend him. I still haven't forgiven the large amount of hair he deprived me of when he attacked me."

"He's not attacking you now," Adelaide pointed out as Harvey began nuzzling Gideon's jacket with his head, right before he released a meow and turned bright green eyes on him.

Gideon resettled Harvey into the crook of his arm, gave him a scratch behind his ears, then narrowed his eyes on Adelaide. "Don't get any ideas. Simply because I'm willing to hold him for a few moments doesn't mean I'm going to take Harvey home with me."

"But he seems to adore you, and my other cats still aren't warming up to him."

"Which is unfortunate, but I doubt your cats would try to eat him, something Moe, my dog, might certainly do."

"Why do you have a dog that might have a hankering for kittens?"

"I'm not sure Moe's got a hankering, but he's a beast of a dog with a spirited disposition, and it certainly wouldn't be in Harvey's best interest to tempt Moe's willpower." He gave Harvey another scratch. "And before you ask how I acquired a beast of a dog, I found him being mistreated down by the Battery. He'd stolen a bone from a butcher, who was trying to get the bone back by chasing Moe with a cleaver. I wasn't in accord with the means being taken to retrieve a bone from an obviously starving dog, so I deprived the man of his cleaver, paid him for the bone Moe wasn't keen to drop, and brought Moe home with me."

Her heart, unsurprisingly, skipped a beat. "How were you able to deprive the man of his cleaver?"

"It wasn't difficult," Gideon said with a shrug. "If you hit a nerve exactly right on an arm, it goes numb."

"You'll have to show me how to do that sometime."

"I doubt you'll ever have a reason to learn hand-to-hand combat."

"It might have come in handy yesterday," Adelaide argued.

"Perhaps, but since I've decided you're going to need someone following you until I figure out exactly who made you a target, there's no need for you to worry you're going to need such skills."

"I don't need a guard, not when I no longer have possession of any of the books I purchased yesterday."

Mrs. Bainswright suddenly cleared her throat. "I'm afraid, my dear, that might not be the case."

"What do you mean?" Adelaide asked.

Mrs. Bainswright nodded to Harvey's basket. "I tucked one of your books in there because poor Harvey kept straining his tiny neck yesterday to see what was going on in the store. That couldn't have been comfortable for the little darling, and one of the books you purchased fit perfectly in the bottom. After putting his little blanket over it and then resettling Harvey on top of it, he was more comfortable." She bit her lip. "I'm afraid I forgot to mention that, and since you still have possession of your basket, it stands to reason you still have one of the books."

Adelaide hurried to the basket and flipped aside Harvey's blanket. "It's still here." Tearing off the wrapping, she revealed the ratty old diary written by Juliette Watson. She lifted her head and caught Gideon's eye. "This certainly explains why someone broke into the shop last night. They must have been after this diary."

Before Gideon could respond, Mr. Bainswright joined her, sliding his spectacles into place. "Don't know why someone would be after that book. It's only the musings of a young lady from a bygone era."

Adelaide turned the book over, frowning when she spotted a red X marked on the spine. Given that the mark wasn't faded, it was clear someone had recently added it to the cover. "What do you think this means?" she asked, showing the X to Gideon.

"Might be there to distinguish it from other books," Gideon said. "If I were to hazard a guess, I'd say there's probably something hidden in the pages."

"No time like the present to find out," Adelaide said, opening the tattered cover and carefully flipping through the book, stopping when she discovered a small piece of folded paper. She plucked it out, considered the paper for the briefest of moments, then handed it to Gideon.

"Have you suddenly taken ill?" Gideon asked.

She laughed. "Not in the least. I'm simply trying to prove I'm not unreasonable all the time. Besides, since you were the one to suggest there might be something hidden, it's only fair that you should be the one to discover if there's anything of worth written on that paper."

The corners of his lips lifted. "That was very gracious of you."

"Don't expect that state to last if you discover something of interest and refuse to share with me."

He tilted his head. "You do realize I'm simply trying to keep your involvement in this matter to a minimum because, given the lengths that have already been taken to retrieve this book, something dire is afoot."

"Of course," she said before she squared her shoulders. "Nevertheless, while it's noble of you to want to keep me out of harm's way, it's hardly as if I can magically become uninvolved now. Someone stole that ledger page from Mr. Bainswright, which means whoever wants the diary now knows I purchased it." She wrinkled her nose. "Since that girl wrestled my basket away from me, perhaps someone saw Mrs. Bainswright tucking a book into it."

Mrs. Bainswright shook her head. "I doubt anyone would have seen me do that because it was on the back counter. No one would have been able to discern what I was doing unless they were standing right next to me, which no one was."

"None of the book agents made a point to talk to you as you were wrapping up my purchases?" Adelaide pressed.

"Not that I recall."

"What about a girl who possibly goes by the name of Jane Smith?"

"You might also know her as Lottie McBriar," Gideon added.

Adelaide arched a brow his way. "I don't recall you mentioning Jane possibly being a Lottie."

It was less than amusing when Gideon sent her another charming smile. "Didn't I?"

"You know you didn't, that little tidbit withheld, no doubt, because you're remarkably stingy with details regarding matters you don't want me involved with."

"Can't argue with you there."

"You're very annoying."

His smile turned more charming than ever. "Can't argue with that either."

Adelaide opened her mouth to address that bit of nonsense, but before she could get a single word out, Mrs. Bainswright moved to stand beside Gideon, beaming a smile at the irritating man.

"How lovely to discover you're such an agreeable gentleman, Mr. Abbott. Why, it's not many a man who can cheerfully admit they can be annoying upon occasion." She gave his arm a pat. "You're also obviously a chivalrous sort, determined to keep our Adelaide safe." She shot a rather knowing look Adelaide's way. "Most ladies appreciate chivalry."

Gideon's smile turned into a grin. "I believe Adelaide may be the exception to that."

"That would appear to be the case," Mrs. Bainswright muttered before she lifted her chin. "However, Adelaide's unusual attitude toward chivalry aside, I don't recall speaking with a

Jane or a Lottie, but I believe I know the girl in question. She comes into the shop often, but she seems to be a finicky reader because she rarely purchases anything, even though she seems to enjoy perusing the history section."

"Was Lottie the girl with the book agents yesterday?" Mr. Bainswright asked.

"She was," Gideon said.

"I've seen her often in the store as well," Mr. Bainswright began, "although she's not much of a talker, which suits me just fine, but like the missus said, she doesn't buy much."

Gideon considered Mr. Bainswright before he frowned. "I hate to broach what is likely a delicate matter, but has Lottie ever come into the store at the directive of a man by the name of Frank Fitzsimmons? He might be collecting money from the shop owners on Bleecker Street in exchange for protection, or more likely, in exchange for not being harassed by his associates."

"I don't pay extortion money, Mr. Abbott," Mr. Bainswright declared. "However, I was approached a year or so ago by some men who were throwing around the name Fitzsimmons, as if it was a name that would see me capitulating to their demands. I was having nothing to do with that nonsense and told them to tell this Fitzsimmons character I'd burn the shop down before I handed over a penny to his band of motley louts."

"And no one pressed the matter?" Gideon asked.

"Never heard another word about it. Why do you ask?"

"I ask because learning you're not being extorted, when I believe most businesses in this area are, lends credence to a theory I'm forming about the role your shop is playing within the criminal underworld."

Mr. Bainswright's eyes widened. "What theory is that?"

"I haven't completely figured it out, but if I were to hazard a guess, I'd say that Frank Fitzsimmons didn't press the issue of the extortion money because you threatened to burn down your store. I'd also say Lottie spends time in this shop not because she's an avid reader, but because she's here to leave or retrieve messages that have something to do with Frank Fitzsimmons's burgeoning criminal organization."

"We're catering to criminals without even knowing it?" Mrs. Bainswright whispered.

"I'm afraid that might be the case," Adelaide said. "But I can assure you and Mr. Bainswright that we'll be able to sort everything out since we now have a glimmer of an idea of what might be transpiring here."

"How in the world would you be able to do that?" Mrs. Bainswright asked.

Adelaide shot a look to Gideon, who, even though he wasn't always keen to disclose anything about his business, didn't hesitate to take a few moments to explain the accounting firm to the Bainswrights, ending with "And know that I'll personally see to your case, starting with the paper we found in the diary and going from there."

"I forgot all about that paper," Mrs. Bainswright admitted.

"I'm sure that's what Gideon wanted all of us to do, since he's determined to keep me uninvolved in this matter," Adelaide said. "But I say, now that we've been reminded of it, we should get down to the business of seeing if it has anything of worth written on it."

"I was going to wait until I returned to the office before looking it over since I don't have a magnifying glass on me," Gideon said.

"Mrs. Bainswright keeps a magnifying glass at the ready because of her needlepoint," Adelaide said, resisting a grin when Gideon narrowed his eyes on her. "Would you like me to fetch it for you?"

"I may not actually need it," he muttered before he unfolded the slip of paper. Taking a second to glance it over, he then did the unexpected and handed it to her.

"You're actually going to share the contents with me without any badgering on my end?" she asked.

"I can be magnanimous upon occasion."

"It's more likely that this is one of those occasions where I'm expecting to see a treasure map, but I'm soon to discover it's someone's abandoned greengrocery list."

"It's definitely not a grocery list."

A sense of anticipation began swirling through her as she took the paper, her level of anticipation turning to downright delight as she gave the paper a cursory glance. "It's a cipher."

"You know what it is?"

Her brows drew together. "Why do I get the distinct impression you only handed it to me because you believed I wouldn't know what it was?"

"It's uncanny how you're beginning to read my mind," Gideon muttered.

"I'm sure it is, just as I'm sure you realize I'll now expect to be included in the deciphering process." Adelaide pretended she didn't notice when Gideon took to scowling. "However, since we can't do any deciphering right this very minute because we'll need a codebreaker, allow us to return to the Bainswrights' unfortunate situation." She stepped closer to Mrs. Bainswright. "I think, what with the troubling things we've uncovered about your store, such as it's undoubtedly being used as a hub to trade secrets, that you and Mr. Bainswright may want to take a well-deserved holiday as soon as possible."

Mrs. Bainswright turned to Mr. Bainswright. "I'm afraid Adelaide may have the right of it, my dear, but I don't think a holiday is what we need. I think it's time we got around to doing what we've been putting off for ages—something we can no longer delay since we can't very well allow nefarious dealings to be carried out in our beloved shop. That could very well see us accused of being accomplices to criminal activities."

"I fear you're right," Mr. Bainswright agreed. "And since

landing behind bars because of ridiculous naïvety on our part is not something either of us would enjoy, I say we agree here and now to finally retire, effective immediately."

A weight settled in Adelaide's stomach. "You're going to close the bookshop?"

Mrs. Bainswright waved that aside. "We would never consider closing the bookshop, dear. We'll be giving it to you, of course, which has been our intention from practically the moment we met you." She settled a lovely smile on Gideon. "And since you, my darling man, seem to be more than equipped to deal with the nefarious dealings that are taking place here, I expect you to promise me here and now that you'll look after our Adelaide and promise to do your very best to get these criminals routed from her new store as quickly as possible."

Fourteen

"Have you taken complete leave of your senses?" Camilla demanded, advancing toward Adelaide, who was standing on a dais in the middle of the music room, wincing every now and again as Miss Ellington, Camilla's favorite dress designer, readjusted the waistline of a dark green gown Gideon thought looked delightful on Adelaide, even though it was filled with pins.

He cleared his throat, drawing Adelaide's attention. "I told you Camilla wasn't going to be pleased to learn you're taking possession of Bainswright Books."

"And I'm sure you're feeling rather smug that you were quite right about that," Adelaide said, a decidedly grumpy expression on her face. "Don't think for a second, though, I don't realize why you insisted on coming with me to attend yet another torture session disguised as an innocent fitting, complete with sharp, pointy objects that seem to have it out for me, no matter their tiny size. You're hoping Camilla will convince me that operating a bookstore is a bad idea, something you've been unsuccessful doing."

Gideon certainly couldn't argue with that, although while

it was true he'd known Camilla would be appalled to learn of Adelaide's new venture, that wasn't the only reason he'd insisted on accompanying her.

For one, there was the distinct possibility Adelaide was in danger, given that the thieves who'd accosted her the day before would now almost certainly believe she still had possession of the diary, what with how it had clearly not been left behind in the store.

And two, he'd wanted to spend additional time in her company.

It was a curious state of affairs because he'd never found himself dwelling on a lady for any length of time, nor had he ever longed to keep company with one. His thoughts and time were usually consumed with matters of intrigue, but these days, intrigue was taking a backseat to a lady who fascinated him more than anyone he'd ever known.

He looked forward to the conversations they shared, whether they be about books, cats, or current events, and he enjoyed making her laugh, the sound of her laughter doing odd things to his stomach. The first time his stomach had taken to lurching about while in her company, he'd thought it was due to an overly spicy dish, but when it had happened again, and then again, he'd no longer been able to deny that it wasn't the food he'd consumed that was responsible for the odd state of his gastronomical issues—Adelaide was.

"You're not going to deny it?" Adelaide asked, rescuing him from thoughts that had apparently caused him to forget he was in the midst of a conversation.

"Deny what?" he had to ask, having forgotten what they'd been talking about.

"That you accompanied me here because you want Camilla to talk me out of taking over the bookstore."

"You really are becoming very proficient with figuring out my motives."

Adelaide opened her mouth, but before she could voice the argument she clearly longed to make, Miss Ellington straightened, stuck a pin back into the cushion attached to her wrist, and nodded.

"That should do it," she said briskly. "I'm sure you'll be pleased to learn, Miss Duveen, that that's the last dress we need to fit today, but don't get overly excited. Tomorrow we'll need to move on to the final alterations of the ball gowns. That endeavor will take at least three full days to get everything exactly right."

Adelaide's mouth dropped open. "Three full days of me standing here while you impale me with pins?"

"I've barely stuck you at all today, and if you wouldn't fidget, there'd be no sticking to begin with," Miss Ellington said before she gestured to the door. "If you'll follow me, I'll get you out of that gown, which will put an end to any impaling you're still experiencing."

As Adelaide stepped gingerly from the dais, then moved at a snail's pace out of the room, muttering something about torture, Camilla walked over to the coffee cart and poured two cups of coffee. She handed him a cup after adding a smidgen of sugar, just how he liked it, then added cream and sugar to hers.

"Why do I get the distinct feeling that trying to talk Adelaide out of running a bookshop is going to be an uphill battle?" she asked.

"I imagine she'll eventually see reason if you broach a few valid points, such as it's complete and utter madness."

Camilla's nose wrinkled. "I'm sure you've already mentioned how her intentions are pure insanity, and yet here we are, and with Adelaide incredibly keen to set herself up in trade."

"She does seem enthusiastic about the idea," Gideon admitted before he smiled. "But on the bright side, operating a full-time business will most assuredly deter her from her determination to join the accounting firm."

"That's optimism at its finest because I don't get the impression

Adelaide's easily deterred, and she's determined to assist the accounting firm."

"Unfortunately, you're right about that," Gideon muttered as he took a seat beside Camilla on a settee upholstered in a pale shade of peach, a comfortable silence settling between them as they sipped their coffee until Adelaide breezed back into the room. She'd evidently been in a hurry to rejoin them because her hair was tumbling from its pins and her gown was buttoned improperly, not that she seemed concerned about any of that as she made a beeline for the large reticule she never seemed without. Opening it, she rummaged around in it, extracted a small leather-bound book, and headed across the room to join them, sitting in a chair close to Gideon.

"It didn't take you long to get dressed," Camilla said, her gaze on the buttons marching unevenly down the front of Adelaide's gown.

"I certainly wasn't going to give the two of you time to come up with a strategy to deter me from purchasing Bainswright Books."

Camilla set aside her coffee. "Purchase it? I thought they wanted to give it to you."

"They do, but I can't accept such a generous gift. Besides, giving them fair market value for their shop will ensure they won't have to be overly frugal in their retirement, but enough about the shop for now. We have more important matters to discuss." She held up the book she'd retrieved and nodded to Gideon. "This is why I wanted to stop by my house after we escorted the Bainswrights home."

He fought a sigh as he took the book from Adelaide and glanced over it before he lifted his head. "How did you come into possession of a confidential spy master-pad?"

"Is that what it's officially called?"

"It is."

"How extraordinary," she breathed. "And I found it in a

172

moldy old trunk that was abandoned in a ramshackle barn when I was exploring along the Hudson River a few years ago." She smiled. "I've studied the book cover to cover, but I haven't had an opportunity to try out any of the codes, which has been disappointing, but it appears that's about to change."

Gideon frowned. "I'm afraid your disappointment isn't going to be assuaged because I have no intention of involving you further in what is undoubtedly a complicated web involving numerous shady characters. It's far too perilous."

She lifted her chin. "I'm already in peril because unsavory characters obviously know I still have the diary. But if I were to help you crack the code, I'll be armed with knowledge that could very well see me better prepared if I'm ambushed again."

"That's some downright convoluted reasoning there."

"And that was an abysmal attempt at distracting me from the matter at hand, which suggests you're losing your touch."

Amusement had his lips quirking, but before he could formulate a response to that, Camilla rose to her feet and crossed her arms over her chest.

"Forgive me for interrupting, but we have more important matters to discuss than a cipher code that has absolutely nothing to do with what should be our top priority right now—that being our *convince-everyone-Adelaide-is-fashionable* project."

"I would think deciphering the code is far more important since it could provide us with information that could keep me alive," Adelaide countered. "There won't be much point in making me fashionable if I'm dead."

"A credible rebuttal, but even if you stay amongst the living, there won't be much point putting effort into our project if you become immersed in trade. Taking up the role of merchant will certainly see society giving you the cut direct, which is almost the same thing as being dead," Camilla countered. "Quite honestly, the only conclusion I've arrived at as to why you've decided to take over a bookstore is because you obviously relish tormenting me."

"Of course I don't relish that," Adelaide argued. "I'm taking over the bookstore because if I don't, the Bainswrights won't retire. That would place *them* in imminent danger since their shop is being used for nefarious purposes."

"But ladies of the Four Hundred don't involve themselves in commerce."

"True, but in my humble opinion, my becoming a proprietress of a shop will only cement the idea that I'm an original because you can't get more original than being a bluestocking who owns her own bookstore."

"We're trying to convince society being an original is a *good* thing," Camilla argued. "I highly doubt we'll see success with that because originality, at least in their eyes, can only go so far."

Adelaide released a breath. "I don't believe you're looking at this in the right light."

"In what light should I be looking at it, then?"

"As another challenge that will stave off your ennui for the foreseeable future as well as a test to determine exactly how strong your influence is within the Four Hundred."

"My ennui is firmly under control now, thank you very much, but tell me this—when do you think you'll have time to run a bookshop? The Season will be starting in earnest two weeks from now at the Patriarch Ball. If we're successful with your relaunch, you'll be far too busy attending luncheons, dinners, balls, and the like to devote the time needed to oversee a business."

"That's why I wouldn't reopen the shop until the Season settles down. I'm thinking late February would be the perfect time to do that, which will allow me to make some changes to the décor and have a small café added." Adelaide smiled. "I believe customers would enjoy browsing the racks while partaking of a lovely cup of coffee and perhaps nibbling on a pastry."

Camilla flung herself back onto the settee. "This is a disaster. You do not have time to become distracted by coffee and pastries, let alone everything else that must be involved with running a business, such as inventory."

"I already know all about that. I've been assisting the Bainswrights with inventory for years."

"Why am I not surprised by that?" Camilla muttered. "Nevertheless, while you may have an idea of how to go about running a bookstore, your attention needs to remain firmly on getting society to accept you in all your original glory."

"I haven't forgotten our objective," Adelaide countered. "Nor do I take for granted how kind it's been of you to take me on as your latest project. I know you're facing overwhelming odds in your quest to find success with me, and I'll forever be in your debt for attempting such a feat."

"And while that's an almost convincing speech," Camilla returned, "it hasn't escaped my notice that you seem far more excited about running a bookstore and assisting Gideon with a cipher code than relaunching yourself into society. That leads me to a question I should have pursued earlier—are you quite convinced you want to go through all the effort needed to change society's perception of you, or are you going along with this because your mother is thrilled over the thought of you becoming an innovative social success?"

"The idea of seeing my mother happy about my circumstances does hold a certain appeal."

"Enthusiasm at its finest," Camilla said before she tucked a strand of hair that had, surprisingly, escaped its pins behind her ear. "I was hoping you'd say you were thrilled by the thought of no longer being labeled an outcast."

Adelaide bit her lip. "Will it make you feel better if I admit I find the thought of not being the object of frequent ridicule rather lovely?"

A weight settled into the pit of Gideon's stomach the moment those words left Adelaide's mouth, the weight increasing when he realized she'd spoken the words in a no-nonsense fashion, quite as if her being the object of ridicule was simply a circumstance of her life.

"I didn't realize you suffered derision often," he finally said.

She shrugged. "Those of us who find ourselves the target of cruel jests normally don't care to discuss the matter. Doing so encourages the opinions of others, and since I don't enjoy people pointing out how clumsy I am, even though I would say more than half the embarrassing episodes I've suffered have been the direct result of assistance from young ladies keen on comparing their graceful natures with my penchant for ungainliness, I rarely broach the topic of the unpleasantness I've experienced over the years."

He leaned forward. "Am I to understand ladies have intentionally set up situations to make you appear less than graceful?"

"Such antics occur often, Gideon, especially considering the competition ladies face when vying for the most beneficial matches on the marriage mart," Adelaide said. "We ladies are taught from birth that our main purpose in life is to secure an advantageous alliance. It's a daunting prospect, procuring the attention of the most sought-after gentlemen, and has practically every lady on the marriage mart viewing other ladies as direct competition. That, regrettably, has pitted us against one another and caused some to resort to underhanded tactics to make themselves appear more presentable to potential suitors."

Camilla sat forward. "And that right there is exactly why you cannot even consider taking over the bookshop. Ladies will see that as a weakness and will use it to return you to a place of obscurity within the Four Hundred."

"How did I know you were going to turn the conversation back to the bookstore?" Adelaide asked.

"Because taking possession of it will create an insurmountable hurdle for us," Camilla returned. "Society may come around to the idea you're an original, and as such, should be embraced, but they'll abandon that in a heartbeat if they realize you're going to be dabbling in trade, which they'll see as a direct affront to their tender sensibilities."

"And to that I say we'll only be truly successful if society can embrace me without expecting me to conform to their strict rules of propriety," Adelaide countered. "I've been giving this a lot of thought, and while I might have originally agreed to allow you to take me on because it would make my mother happy, I'm now hoping that getting society to accept me exactly as I am may give hope to other disadvantaged ladies out there. But if I'm forced to change who I am at heart, we'll be failing what could very well be the most important aspect of our endeavor. As I've grown older, I've also been of the notion that God created me precisely as He intended." She smiled. "I'm relatively convinced one shouldn't ignore God's intentions or deviate from them simply to embrace the status quo."

Camilla released a sigh. "You know there's absolutely no argument I could possibly make to that."

"Then it's settled," Adelaide said. "I'll take up the reins of the bookstore, and you'll convince everyone that's a most innovative idea."

"You make that sound as if it'll be an easy accomplishment."

"You're the one who said you wield considerable influence within the Four Hundred."

"Not *that* much influence," Camilla muttered right as Mr. Timken, her butler, knocked on the door, stuck his head into the room, and announced that Charles Wetzel had arrived. A second later, Charles stepped into the room, his gaze immediately settling on Adelaide.

"Thank goodness. There you are," Charles said as he strode over to Adelaide. He gave her a kiss on the cheek, presented Camilla with a bow, inclined his head to Gideon, then returned his attention to his cousin. "I've been all over town looking for you."

Adelaide's brows drew together. "Because?"

"Your mother wants a word with you. She told me you left early this morning for Bainswright Books, but after I fought my way through traffic, I discovered the shop deserted. I then made my way to the Ladies' Mile, wandered around down there for an hour, then recalled you mentioned something about suffering through additional fittings this week, so . . . here I am."

"Why does Mother want a word with me?"

Charles rubbed a hand over his face. "I suppose that's on account of me. I may have—inadvertently, of course—told her, along with my mother, that you were set upon by thieves yesterday." He winced. "Given your mother's reaction, it was immediately evident you neglected to mention anything about that incident to her."

"You told my mother I was robbed?"

"In my defense, I didn't know it was a secret."

"It's not. I simply wanted to avoid worrying her, which is why I've taken pains to avoid her today." Adelaide's shoulders slumped ever so slightly. "I'm sure, though, since Mother has a tendency to overact to my misadventures, she's already making plans to hire armed guards to watch me."

"She's decided I'm going to be your guard until after she gets word to your father," Charles said. "She was composing a telegram to him as I was leaving."

"Of course she was," Adelaide murmured before she frowned. "But how did you know about my latest incident in the first place? I haven't seen you for a couple of days."

"Leopold and Vernon told me. I encountered them pulling up to your house when I returned to my carriage to fetch a shawl for Mother."

"Why were Leopold and Vernon at my house?"

178

"I believe it had something to do with them wanting to persuade your mother to speak to Camilla on their behalf."

"I knew they were taking my refusal to include them a little too easily," Camilla grumbled.

"Well, quite," Charles agreed. "But after they explained why they were there, they then wanted to know my thoughts about the theft. After I admitted I had no idea what they were talking about, they disclosed the details of what had transpired." He winced. "That's why, when Aunt Phyllis said you'd taken your carriage out early this morning, and then my mother remarked that it was odd you'd take a carriage instead of traveling on the El, I may have said something about how it wasn't odd in the least considering you'd been robbed only the day before."

"Oh no," Adelaide whispered.

"Indeed," Charles said. "Needless to say, the conversation took a turn for the concerning. On the bright side, though, Leopold and Vernon seemed very pleased, because your mother has already decided they *will* be brought on to help with your relaunch since those two gentlemen can help protect you if I'm unavailable."

"The last thing I need is two septuagenarians intervening on my behalf if I get approached by thieves again. Poor Leopold already suffered a black eye, and Vernon was limping his way out of Camilla's house last night because of an unexpected tumble over a fence."

"They might not be as physically threatening as they once were," Charles countered, "but they assured your mother they're both more than proficient with weapons. They're apparently now armed whenever they leave their respective homes, something they've not bothered to do for years, given the relative safety of traveling amongst the society set."

"One has to wonder how many years have elapsed since they've had an opportunity to practice with those weapons," Adelaide muttered.

"I was of that same thought," Charles said. "Which is why, even though I didn't get the impression they were exaggerating their skills, I invited them to join me at my rod and gun club to see exactly how accomplished they are."

Gideon tilted his head. "You're a member of a marksman's club?"

"I belong to several," Charles admitted. "I don't enjoy participating in every event offered during any given Season, so I use the excuse of prior arrangements with members of my clubs to avoid frivolities I don't particularly want to attend, such as dinners with Mother and her friends. Because of that, I've spent hours on firing ranges and have acquired, not that I care to brag, expert status with both pistols and long arms. That's why Aunt Phyllis wants me to assume the role of Adelaide's bodyguard until other arrangements can be made."

"I'm sure you'll be more than capable of protecting her," Gideon said. "And if Leopold and Vernon step in when you're unavailable, I'll have time to devote to discovering who was behind the attack on Adelaide."

Charles frowned. "Forgive me, but I'm not certain I understand why you'd do that, or why you'd have the qualifications to look into the matter at all."

"Gideon's not who he claims to be," Adelaide said.

"And doesn't that demand a few explanations," Charles said.

Knowing there was nothing to do but disclose all because Charles was going to be looking after Adelaide, Gideon took the next fifteen minutes to bring Charles up to date. After answering a few of Charles's questions, he caught Adelaide's eye. "As an added precaution for your safety, it'll be best if I take possession of the diary. I have the resources to get the word out on the streets that I now own the diary, and we can hope that word gets into the ears of whoever wants it. That should result with them turning their attention away from you."

It was not encouraging when Adelaide's nose shot straight

up into the air. "Having you take possession of the diary will only draw suspicion, since you'd have to come up with some convoluted explanation as to why you've done that."

"Some of the cases I've worked over the years are incredibly complicated. I'm sure whatever explanation I derive regarding why I'm in possession of the diary won't draw suspicion from the players in this particular debacle in the least."

"And I respectfully disagree with that nonsense because there's absolutely no reason you'd want a moldy old diary, and you know it. Besides, given that I'm apparently going to be guarded around the clock, I highly doubt anyone will chance accosting me again. And, as a last valid point, I can take care of myself."

"You were set upon by thieves only yesterday."

"True, which is why I've taken measures to ensure I'll never be robbed again."

With that, Adelaide rose from the chair, headed across the room, snatched up her reticule, opened the latch, then began to root around the contents.

Apprehension was immediate when she suddenly pulled out a pistol—a shortened black powder Colt revolver from the looks of it, a gun that wasn't very popular since a person had to stuff cotton, along with a bullet and powder, into a chamber to ready it. They then had to add percussion caps into a special spot at the back of the cylinder, something he got the feeling Adelaide had no idea was actually required to fire it.

Before he could point out anything about the gun, though, she brandished the pistol with a flourish, something that had Charles and Camilla diving to the floor.

"See?" she began as her eyes began twinkling, evidently unaware she'd just scared everyone but him half to death, Camilla even now scooting her way underneath a drop leaf table. "There's no need to worry I'll be set upon again, not when one look at this monster will surely have any miscreants fleeing for their very lives."

Fifteen

"If it makes you feel better, Adelaide, I wouldn't have known that the black panther Colt revolver needs precision cups to operate," Edna said as she sat next to Adelaide in the carriage, Camilla and Gideon sitting on the opposite seat, while Charles followed behind them in his carriage, apparently taking his job as one of her protectors seriously since he was sitting beside his driver instead of inside the coach, his pistol at the ready.

Adelaide grinned. "It's a black *powder* Colt revolver, and it apparently needs *percussion caps* to make it fire, something I had no idea about since the man down by the Battery certainly didn't explain the operational procedures of the piece when I purchased it."

The second those words left her mouth, she wanted to call them back because Gideon immediately settled an incredulous gaze on her.

"Dare I hope you were lost and ended up in the Battery by accident?" he asked.

She swallowed. "Am I in for a lecture if I admit I was down there on purpose?"

"Most assuredly."

"What if I tell you I had a perfectly legitimate reason for being in a somewhat unsavory section of the city, that being Mrs. Cassidy?"

"Unless you were rendering life-saving assistance to this Mrs. Cassidy, prepare yourself for a good old-fashioned reprimand."

"I'm afraid it wasn't a matter of life or death," Adelaide admitted. "Mrs. Cassidy was merely overwhelmed with invading rodents, which obviously required a feline intervention. Mrs. Bainswright told her I was the answer to her problem. Since I'm always trying to find homes for my little darlings, I put Winkie and Bubbles, two proven mousers, into my carriage and off I went to where Mrs. Cassidy rents rooms in a boardinghouse at the end of Bleecker Street."

"Couldn't you have dispatched a groomsman to deliver the cats?" Gideon asked.

"Not when I had to make certain Mrs. Cassidy would be compatible with Winkie and Bubbles." Adelaide smiled. "I'm pleased to report it was mutual love at first sight. But while I was making sure I was leaving my darlings in good hands, Mrs. Cassidy mentioned there was a street market not far from her house, one where many a vendor sold books."

Gideon sat forward, causing Harvey, who'd been sleeping on his lap, to send him an affronted look before he wiggled around and closed his eyes again. "Dealing with book vendors is a horse of a different color over dealing with a man who peddles weapons."

"He *was* selling books as well, along with a various assortment of kitchen items."

"And you chose to purchase a gun from a man who didn't limit his products to weapons, which should have suggested he might not know that much about the revolver he sold you?"

"It never entered my head there'd be much to learn about a revolver. I thought all I'd need to do was stuff a bullet in it and fire away." She bit her lip. "Since I didn't have the revolver handy when I was accosted, though, I wasn't nearly as prepared as I should have been."

Gideon gave Harvey's ears a scratch, earning a purr in return. "Once again I find myself astounded over the fact you're still alive because there's always more involved with operating a weapon other than stuffing and firing. I'm also finding it difficult to wrap my mind around the notion you were wandering around the Battery on your own."

"I wasn't on my own. I had my driver and two groomsmen with me. Also, I purposefully wore a traveling gown that was three sizes too large and might have been eaten by moths at some point. I didn't warrant a second glance from anyone, which was my intention all along." She tapped a finger against her chin. "Now that I consider the matter, my ability to blend into a crowd is a talent I would think you'd want to acquire for some of your covert operations."

"You should discontinue doing that type of considering because, no, I don't believe fieldwork would be appropriate for a woman with an uncanny ability of landing into trouble at the drop of a hat, or a woman who purchased a revolver from a man selling kitchen utensils."

Before Adelaide could argue with that, the carriage turned onto another road, one that was filled with bumps and had Harvey abandoning Gideon's lap and clawing his way up the front of Gideon's jacket to settle on his shoulder.

Ignoring the way her heart gave an odd pitter-patter when Gideon gave Harvey a pat instead of pulling him from where he was now perched, Adelaide lifted her chin.

"If you must know, I never had any intentions of purchasing a weapon. I'm well aware, what with my history of unfortunate events, that society would find the notion of my possessing a weapon somewhat appalling. With that said, though, I really had no choice but to buy the revolver because that poor vendor was desperate for funds, and the revolver was the most expensive item he had for sale."

"You could have simply given the man some money," Gideon pointed out.

"That might have injured his pride."

"You would have been better served buying several books that would have been equivalent to the price of the gun, or a few of those kitchen items, because after I inspected your revolver, I discovered it's in abysmal shape," Gideon argued. "I'm convinced if you'd tried to operate it, it may very well have backfired and harmed you instead of some well-deserving culprit, which is why we're now on our way to my apartment in an effort to spare you unintentional bodily harm."

"You're going to provide her with another weapon?" Camilla asked before Adelaide could respond to any of that.

"Since I get the distinct impression Adelaide now has it in that stubborn head of hers that she needs to keep a weapon in her bottomless reticule, I think it'll be best all around if I provide her with one that's more appropriate for a lady unaccustomed to handling pistols." Gideon settled a frown on Camilla. "But why did you think we were going to my residence, if not to get a more appropriate firearm for Adelaide?"

"I thought you forgot something and needed to fetch it before we repair to Adelaide's house to discuss additional security measures since she's determined to keep the diary in her possession."

"Something that's still a bone of contention for me," Gideon muttered.

"It shouldn't be, because it's the only option that won't draw suspicion from whoever was after that code," Adelaide argued.

"It's not the only option," Gideon argued back. "My idea—where we'd let it be known that you've given the book to me—would send everyone on a wild-goose chase and also afford us more time to figure out who actually wants it."

"We can't say I gave it to you since there's the possibility, what with how your secret occupation isn't nearly as secret anymore, that word is even now traveling around the street about your involvement with the accounting firm," Adelaide countered. "Whoever is after the code would certainly go to ground if they heard about your true occupation, which would then leave us with no way to ferret out the truth about the code or who was responsible for attacking me. And—" she drew in a breath—"before you blame me for so many people knowing about your clandestine activities, you need to remember that Camilla was already privy to that information, and that Leopold and Vernon figured everything out on their own."

"Vernon is a most astute gentleman," Edna said before Gideon could retort to that. "And not that I want to take sides in this matter, but I think Adelaide may be right in that having her retain the diary, at least for now, is the best course of action. Even to me it would seem odd if someone went out of their way to let it be known they'd given away a book, especially when that diary isn't valuable." She settled a smile on Gideon. "And while I understand you're simply trying to keep Adelaide safe, our dear Vernon, along with Leopold, is going to step up to help protect her as well as Charles, so I don't believe she'll be in much danger."

Camilla's nose wrinkled as she settled her attention on her aunt. "Since when have you begun thinking of Vernon as *dear* Vernon?"

Edna fluttered her lashes. "Did I call him *dear*?"

"You know you did, which suggests you've formed an attachment to the gentleman, even though I thought you swore off gentlemen forever after Uncle Morton died, and just two years after that, you got involved with Count Something or Other, who had his eye on your fortune."

"Vernon doesn't need my fortune, darling. He's independently wealthy."

Camilla opened her mouth, but before she could speak a

single word in response to that telling statement, the carriage slowed to a stop.

"We'll be continuing this discussion about Vernon later," Camilla muttered as the driver opened the door and held out his hand to Adelaide as Edna said something about there not being anything more to discuss.

Taking a second to readjust her traveling cloak, Adelaide turned back to the carriage, smiling as she watched Gideon attempt to convince Harvey he wanted to return to his basket. It quickly became evident that Harvey wanted no part with that because he dug his little claws into the fabric of Gideon's jacket and refused to budge from Gideon's shoulder.

"I believe your stubbornness is rubbing off on him," Gideon grumbled as he handed Adelaide the basket before he sent Harvey, who was still perched on his shoulder, a side-eye, then turned to assist Edna and Camilla out of the carriage as Charles strode over to join them.

"Didn't realize you lived at the Dakota, Gideon," Charles said, his gaze traveling over the impressive building in front of them, one that appeared to be at least ten stories high. "I've been considering moving out of my mother's house, but every time I broach the subject, she comes up with a million excuses why I should remain living under her roof." He grinned. "She'll deny this, but her main reason is because she fears I'll never get married if she's not present to nag me about that every day."

Adelaide returned the grin. "Aunt Petunia does enjoy a reputation for persistent nagging, but perhaps you could have Gideon speak with her and extol all the advantages of living in an apartment, such as how some of the residents here must surely be eligible ladies."

"I doubt any self-respecting lady would live in an apartment," Edna argued, scowling at the building before she settled a stern eye on Gideon. "I assumed you resided in a reputable brownstone, which is why I agreed to stop by your residence in the first place. If I'd known you lived in a seedy apartment building, I certainly wouldn't have condoned this detour."

Adelaide settled her gaze on the Dakota, which was anything but seedy and more along the lines of majestic, given the gabled roof, dormered windows, terracotta detailing, balconies, projecting turrets, and a cornice that separated the seventh story and roof from the rest of the building.

"Once you get inside, Edna," Gideon said, "you'll see that the apartments give the impression of a brownstone, yet with more spacious accommodations."

"That may be true," Edna began, craning her neck as she looked over the building. "However, I would think it's burdensome to have to traipse up endless stairways to gain access to the upper floors."

"And it would be, except that the Dakota is equipped with hydraulic elevators." Gideon smiled. "It also boasts eight apartments per floor, each of which has between four and twenty rooms, and each floor has four elevators, one designated for two specific apartments. Since I lease two apartments, I'm the only resident on the sixth floor with access to my assigned elevator, which affords me the privacy to come and go at will." He shook his head. "I would have preferred the seventh floor over the sixth because the views are better, but there were no apartments available."

"What about the floors above those?" Edna asked. "I would think those views would be even better."

"The eighth and ninth floors contain laundry rooms, along with sleeping and bathing facilities for servants, both residential and visiting, which we're supposed to limit to five or six per apartment. The tenth floor is reserved as a children's play area and laundry drying facility, and it also holds the water tanks used to operate the hydraulic elevators."

Edna's mouth went a little slack. "You can only keep five or six servants on staff?"

Gideon laughed. "I'm a bachelor gentleman. How many servants do you think I need?"

"Do you at least engage the services of a cook?"

"There's no need. The Dakota has a restaurant on the first floor, and if I'm not in the mood to dine there, I have the option of having culinary delights delivered straight to my door—for an extra fee, of course."

"I'm definitely going to have to look into acquiring an apartment here," Charles said before he cocked a brow Gideon's way. "But since you've now proven we're not about to enter a shady establishment, shall we get on our way? I'm not certain, what with Adelaide being a target, we should be lingering out in the open."

"An excellent point," Gideon said before he took a moment to instruct Adelaide's driver to pull the carriage around to the back entrance instead of waiting for them at the Dakota stables off 75th and Amsterdam since they wouldn't be long. He then offered Adelaide his arm, Charles doing the same to Camilla and Edna. Together, they strolled for the front entrance, where a doorman greeted them before they stepped into what Gideon told her was a groin-vaulted vestibule, which then led them into an impressive courtyard.

After walking across the cobblestones, Gideon directed them through an archway that led to a small foyer, where an elevator operator, whom Gideon greeted as a Mr. Jerkins, was waiting for them. Once Gideon ushered everyone inside the elevator, Mr. Jerkins closed the gilded gate and they were soon whooshing upward, Mr. Jerkins using a lever to control the speed. He pulled the level to an upright position when they reached the sixth floor, opened the grate, stepped aside, and gestured everyone out.

"Any thoughts on how I might entice Harvey into returning to his basket before we enter my apartment?" Gideon asked as they began walking down a long hallway.

Adelaide glanced to where Harvey was still perched on

Gideon's shoulder, his little head snuggled against Gideon's neck. "He seems content where he is, but is there a reason you want him in his basket?"

Gideon stopped in front of a door and fished a set of keys out of his pocket. "I told you about Moe, and I wasn't exaggerating about the fact he's an intimidating dog. As far as I know, he's never met a kitten before, so it's difficult to say how he's going to react to Harvey."

"Perhaps someone should secure Moe with a leash before we attempt an introduction," Adelaide suggested.

Before Gideon could do more than nod, the door to his apartment swung open, revealing a large man dressed in black, who had a long scar traveling down the side of his face, whom Gideon introduced as his butler, Louis.

"I wasn't expecting you back until later," Louis said, stepping aside to allow them entrance into the apartment.

"We're simply here to retrieve something from the weapons room, Louis," Gideon said. "But could you do me a favor and get a leash on Moe before we come inside? I'm not certain how he's going to react to this scrap of trouble sitting on my shoulder and—"

Whatever else Gideon had been about to say came to a rapid end when the sound of nails scrabbling over the floor reached them right before a beast of a dog, obviously Moe, appeared around a corner.

It was beyond concerning when Moe stopped in his tracks, his brown, shaggy fur standing on end, right before he started growling low in his throat as his gaze settled on Harvey.

Before Louis could do more than reach for the door to close it, Harvey suddenly launched himself through the air with no warning, landing lightly on the marble floor of the entrance-way. He then, to Adelaide's horror, began prancing Moe's way, seemingly oblivious that Moe was now snarling up a storm as drool dribbled down his massive jowls.

Sixteen

With her heart pounding in her chest, Adelaide dashed forward as Gideon did the same, both of them stopping in their tracks when Moe suddenly let out what almost sounded like a whimper before he plopped down on the floor and his bushy tail began to wag. A second later, Harvey was directly next to the beast, rubbing his little kitten head against Moe's fur, purring up a storm when Moe gave him a lick, and not one that suggested he was debating whether the kitten was good enough to eat.

"I wasn't expecting that," Louis said, brandishing a broom he'd snatched from beside the door and wielding it quite as if he'd been ready to shoo Moe away from Harvey if the dog went on the attack. "I thought for sure that kitten was a goner."

"As did I," Adelaide agreed, her heart rate returning to normal. "Fortunately for everyone involved, it appears Moe isn't in a mood for a snack but rather for a new friend." She grinned when Harvey scrambled up Moe's back and made himself at home, Moe's only reaction to that unexpected circumstance being lowering his head to the floor between two overly large paws and thumping his tail a few times.

"It seems as if Moe has gone from guard dog to kitten nanny," she said, earning a sigh from Gideon in return.

"Too right it does but know that I'm holding you directly responsible for ruining what was, up until a few seconds ago, a very intimidating guard dog."

Adelaide resisted a laugh when Moe's tongue began lolling out of his mouth. "He doesn't look very intimidating now."

"Let's hope it's not a permanent condition," Gideon said. "He won't be much use to me out in the field if he starts befriending the criminals I need him to help me apprehend."

Adelaide tilted her head. "How does he do that?"

"Normally baring his teeth is all that's needed to have suspects freezing on the spot."

"I'm sure Moe knows the difference between sweet kittens and miscreants, but . . ." She glanced at Moe again. "Isn't it simply adorable how Moe seems to have found a new companion?"

"I'm not keeping Harvey."

She gave an airy wave of her hand. "I'm not suggesting you should, although it might be nice for Moe if you'd allow Harvey to stay here temporarily. That way he'd get to develop a closer friendship with Harvey, and I'd get an opportunity to spend time with my other cats, who've been slightly neglected since I've been hauling Harvey around with me everywhere, hoping his adorability will have someone longing to give him a special home."

"You seem to be using different versions of the word *adorable* a lot, but even though I'll admit that Harvey possesses a certain charm, I'm not that someone longing to give him a special home."

Edna stepped up beside Gideon and gave his arm a pat. "You keep telling yourself that, dear, but I'm afraid you're doomed to become a kitten father." She turned to Louis. "I know it was mentioned we wouldn't be here long, but could I possibly prevail upon you for a restorative cup of tea? I fear, what with all the excitement of thinking Harvey was about to be devoured, my nerves are all aflutter."

"It'll be no trouble at all," Louis assured her. "If you'll follow me, I'll see you settled in the parlor." With that, and after assuring everyone he'd make enough tea for all, Louis escorted Edna down the hallway, Moe and Harvey scrambling after them a second later.

"Louis is notorious for sneaking Moe treats," Gideon said as Louis disappeared from sight. "I'm sure he's about to indulge Harvey as well."

"Which will leave Harvey incredibly reluctant to leave," Adelaide said.

"I'm not keeping Harvey," Gideon reiterated before he took hold of Adelaide's arm and drew her down the hallway, Camilla and Charles, who'd been lingering in the entranceway, trailing behind them.

After passing a suit of armor that Gideon told her he'd found in a crumbling old castle in Scotland, they stepped into a living room that held a fireplace with a tiled hearth, brass fixtures, and a carved mirror with a gilded frame hanging over the mantel. Displayed beside the fireplace was what appeared to be a samurai battle costume, complete with sword and helmet, an artifact that left Adelaide wondering where in the world Gideon had found such a treasure. Before she could ask, Gideon was steering her toward another door, barely giving Adelaide time to appreciate the décor of the living room, which was done up in muted shades of brown, peach, and ivory. Splashes of color on numerous embroidered pillows added a lovely touch of warmth to the room.

"Did you embroider those?" she asked, earning a nod from Gideon before they left the living room behind and moved through a dining room that had crown molding on surprisingly high ceilings and a mahogany table polished to a high sheen centered underneath a beautiful chandelier. Twelve matching chairs upholstered in red velvet surrounded the table, while fresh flowers set into Tiffany vases lent the room a dignified air.

After the dining room, they strode through what Gideon said was a second living room that seemed straight out of the pages of an architectural magazine, what with its Italian furniture, abstract oil paintings on the walls, and an Aubusson rug gracing the floor.

They soon left that room behind, walking down another hallway that led to a library. Stepping into the room, Adelaide found herself immersed in the most delicious scent of leather and paper, but before she could truly appreciate her surroundings, Gideon moved to one of the bookcases, withdrew a few books, stuck his hand into the space where the books had been, then sent her a wink when the bookcase swung open, revealing a room behind it.

She drew in a sharp breath. "You have a secret lair?"

"Given my occupation, are you really surprised?" he asked, gesturing her forward as he turned on the lights.

Her mouth had no choice but to drop open when she stepped into the room because . . . it was a room anyone who held a proclivity for matters of intrigue would adore.

A cache of weapons was mounted on the walls, from guns she'd never seen before to swords with gleaming blades as well as sabers that looked deadly. One wall held an ornate cabinet with large drawers, and her fingers itched to pull every drawer open. A pocket watch lying on a table drew her attention, and unable to help herself, she picked it up, frowning a second later.

"Is there a reason this is so heavy?" she asked.

"It's a camera disguised as a watch," Gideon explained. "It's a protype Samuel Montague, an engineer who works for us, is tinkering with."

"May I open it?" Adelaide asked.

"Of course."

Adelaide flipped open the latch and unfolded what looked like a telescope. "This is genius, but doesn't anyone get suspicious since you must have to keep it pointed at a target for an extended period of time?"

"It uses gelatin dry plates that don't need long exposures. Feel free to take it with you and try it out today if you'd like."

She blinked. "Really?"

"Since it's a camera and you can only shoot pictures with it, which poses relatively little danger to you or anyone else in your vicinity, certainly."

"And wasn't that a wonderful way to dim my excitement about the matter?" she muttered, earning a laugh from Gideon in return.

"I'm sure your enthusiasm will return after you get a peep at the rest of my collection," he said, drawing her over to the cabinet, where he began pulling out various items, barely allowing her to ooh and ahh over them before he moved on to the next.

Different cameras hidden in small bags were pulled from one drawer, then elaborate rings that could hold sleeping draughts or poisons from another, one of which got stuck on her finger when she tried it on.

"We might need some soap to get this off me," she said, giving it another tug and wincing when it wouldn't budge.

Gideon smiled. "Or you can just keep it. I have a few of those."

Pleased beyond measure to be the proud owner of a ring that might have once held a sleeping draught or even some vile manner of poison that had, hopefully, only made an intended victim sick instead of dead, Adelaide took a moment to admire her new possession, abandoning that admiration when Gideon pulled out what looked to be razor-sharp discs shaped in the form of stars.

"Oh, those would fit nicely in my reticule," she said.

"They would," Gideon agreed, "but I can't see you flinging

these at anyone because there's usually a great deal of blood involved if they meet their intended mark."

"They're probably not for me, then."

"I would have to agree with you there," he said before he pulled out a curious contraption he explained one could attach to one's wrist and strap a small weapon to. He then showed her a retractable piece of metal that allowed the user to conceal a weapon under a sleeve while still being easily accessible with a push of a button that rested by the wrist.

After demonstrating how it was to be worn, he set it aside before directing her attention to an oriental vase that stored a variety of canes. To Adelaide's delight, Gideon showed her one that concealed a sharp blade that was revealed through a twist of the ornate handle, another that shot darts out of the end of it, and a third that had a hard ball attached at the top instead of a handle, something Gideon called a skull-crusher, which sounded ominous indeed.

She picked up the cane that shot darts and tested the weight. "This might be an excellent weapon for me to use, and it would certainly lend me an air of originality if I were seen strolling around town with a cane."

"It might also land you in jail if you were to shoot a dart at someone by mistake," Camilla said, Charles nodding in agreement beside her.

Adelaide lifted her chin. "I'm sure it would be next to impossible to shoot someone with a dart cane by accident."

She was not amused when Charles rolled his eyes. "Please. You shot me with an ice chip by accident only last year when it got stuck in your paper straw."

"I didn't realize blowing on it in a somewhat earnest manner would turn the ice into an unlikely missile, but no real harm was done. I mean, it's not as if you lost an eye."

"Only because I closed it before the ice struck," Charles shot back. "And you seem to be conveniently forgetting the bruise your unintentional attack left on my face. Mother thought I'd gotten into a brawl, which resulted in an hourlong lecture about dangerous pastimes."

Camilla gave a bit of a shudder. "I now find myself wondering if providing Adelaide with any type of weapon is a good idea."

"It's an excellent idea, since even though I'll be heavily guarded, someone could very well slip past Charles, Leopold, or Vernon and try to accost me again," Adelaide argued. She glanced over some of the guns hanging on the wall before moving in front of a silver pistol with a handle inlaid with mother-of-pearl. "Since everyone seems to believe the dart cane isn't a viable option for me, what about this one? It's pretty."

"And would send you on your backside in a second because it has quite the recoil," Gideon said.

"Then what exactly do you have in mind for me?"

Gideon's gaze traveled over the wall before he nodded to an empty space. "It's supposed to be right there, but Duncan, the associate of mine you saw at Bainswright Books, used it last week on an undercover mission and must have stowed it with some of my other weapons."

"You have more weapons than what's displayed here?" Adelaide asked.

"The business I'm in demands a well-stocked arsenal," Gideon said, moving across the room and stopping beside a floor-to-ceiling shelf, filled with books that probably had something to do with espionage. He pulled the arm of a small gargoyle attached to the side of the bookshelf and then stood back as the shelf slid to the right, revealing yet another wall filled with guns that left Adelaide's mouth dropping open again.

Her attention immediately settled on a fat-barreled pistol. "Is that a blunderbuss?"

"Good eye, and yes."

She moved closer, gave the blunderbuss a once-over, and nod-ded. "I read about one of these in a story a few months back. Is that the weapon you have in mind for me?"

"Hardly," Gideon didn't hesitate to say.

"It looks manageable to me."

"Looks can be deceiving because it operates similar to a can-non. You can add nails, glass, lead shot, or any combination of those to it, which then act as projectiles when the blunderbuss is fired. It's a great weapon to use when you're faced with multiple foes because the contents spew everywhere, increasing the odds of hitting your marks."

She winced. "Spewing sounds somewhat dangerous, and I'd hate to shoot some innocuous bystander by accident." She settled her sights on a gun that had three barrels, along with three hammers, and would certainly intimidate anyone who tried to threaten her. "What about that one?"

"That's a Knights Templar, but no. The trigger is a little sensitive."

It quickly became clear that Gideon wasn't keen to let her use any of his most impressive weapons because he said no to the Assassin's Creed, although he told Charles he was welcome to take it to a shooting range. He then said no to a gun with four barrels that a person rotated after two shots to access the other two barrels, and no to a femme fatale ring that had five barrels, saying he wouldn't want her to take off a finger by ac-cident. He even said no to a pepperbox, which didn't have a barrel at all and was only meant to be used at close range but would have fit nicely into most of her reticules.

She began tapping her foot against the parquet floor. "I'm not sure why you brought us here if you're hesitant to let me borrow any of your weapons."

"I told you, I have a specific pistol in mind." He strode over to one of the cabinets and pulled open a deep drawer, rum-maged around in it, then smiled as he held up a gray hat with an unusually wide brim, paired with a large dome that had a wilted feather attached to it.

"I thought you said you had a weapon in mind for me. To point out the obvious, that's a hat," Adelaide said.

"Indeed, but it's what's stored inside the hat, if Duncan left it in here, that's important."

Before Adelaide could question him about that, Camilla was standing directly beside Adelaide, shaking a finger Gideon's way.

"If you think Adelaide is going to waltz around the city with that on her head, you're sadly mistaken," Camilla began. "It's one of the most hideous hats I've ever seen and should be relegated to a ragbag, even if it has a special button and a gun pops out of it."

"*Does* it have a special button and a hidden gun?" Adelaide breathed.

Gideon rubbed a hand over his face. "I'm afraid that gadget has yet to be invented, but this hat does have a special feature, although not one that can compare to a hat that has the capability of having a gun blast out of the brim."

"A hat that had a gun bursting out of the top would be extraordinary indeed and would certainly take an assailant aback."

"I'm sure it would, but even though you're bound to be disappointed with the special features of this hat, since there's no bursting to be had, know that Duncan found it incredibly useful when he was on an undercover case because he was able to conceal a derringer in the hidden compartment it has built into it. It was fortunate he used the hat during his assignment because the gambling den he was visiting insisted he check his reticule at the door, but they didn't blink an eye over him keeping his hat on."

Adelaide wrinkled her nose. "I would think a lot of blinking occurred if Duncan waltzed into a gambling den with a lady's hat on his head."

"Especially one that hideous," Camilla added.

"He was dressed as a lady," Gideon said. "And before you ask, he makes a somewhat passable lady—if he remembers to shave right before he goes out on assignment." He smiled. "He did complain about the fit of the garment we found for him to wear. He said it was far too constricting, and he now has a new appreciation for the discomfort ladies experience due to bustles, corsets, and stockings, which apparently fell down his legs and caused a bit of a situation when an inebriated patron insisted on helping Duncan reattach them to his garters."

"That particular problem would be alleviated if you'd simply stop being stubborn and realize the numerous benefits of adding a few ladies to your staff," Adelaide pointed out.

"Nice try, but no," Gideon said, moving to a small table and setting the hat on it. "With that out of the way, would you care to see the hidden compartment?"

"You know I would, but don't think we won't return to the advantages women could provide the firm in the near future," Adelaide said, which earned her a charming smile from Gideon before he showed her how to access the hidden compartment by pulling on an innocent-looking tab. After the false bottom opened, she peeked into the hat, blinking at the sight that met her eyes—a minuscule pistol that could fit into the palm of her hand. She scrunched up her nose. "I was hoping for something a little larger."

"I don't believe *large* is a word we're going to contemplate when it comes to appropriate weapons for you."

She glanced back into the hat. "Given its lack of size, I don't think that can actually be considered a weapon."

"It's definitely a weapon—a one-shot derringer, and it packs more of a punch than one would imagine," Gideon said. "It's also remarkably easy to handle because it only requires a user to put a bullet into the chamber, cock the hammer, then pull the trigger."

"I could probably manage that," she admitted.

"Which is why I chose this particular weapon for you." He sent her a smile. "Would you care to try it out?"

"Don't you think it's rather close quarters for me to be firing off a derringer, even if it's tiny?"

He laughed. "Not to shoot it. Just see if you can get the hat off your head and then the derringer out of the hidden compartment within a reasonable amount of time."

"Since Adelaide won't be wearing that abomination you keep referring to as a hat, I don't think there's any point in having her try it out," Camilla said.

"But it'll give her an opportunity to handle a gadget she's probably read about in one of her novels but never thought she'd have an opportunity to see, let alone experiment with. We wouldn't want to deprive her of that experience, would we?"

Before Camilla could do more than send Gideon a rather peculiar look, although what the look meant Adelaide had no idea, Gideon nodded to the hat and grinned. "You know you want to give it a try."

She was powerless to resist his grin. "I suppose I do, but after experimenting with the hat, I'd also like to try out that armband gadget you showed me earlier. You know Camilla will probably confiscate the hat at some point, but I would certainly take any assailants by surprise if a derringer suddenly slid out of my sleeve."

"I'm afraid that particular gadget is difficult to use," Gideon said. "Which means it'll be best all around, what with Camilla's aversion to the hat, to simply keep the derringer in your reticule."

"But what if someone asks me to check my reticule at the door like they did with Duncan?"

"I don't believe society makes it a habit to have ladies check their reticules while attending a ball or dinner."

"I suppose you're right," Adelaide muttered before she closed the hidden compartment and stuck the hat on her head, the mere sight of it leaving Camilla shuddering once again.

"Let's see what you'd do if you suddenly find yourself under attack," Charles suggested from where he'd taking to lounging against a wall.

Adelaide nodded, readjusted the brim of the hat, then walked around the room a few times, fighting a smile when Charles began advancing on her, evidently assuming the role of a potential assailant.

Whipping off the hat a second later, she flipped it over, fumbled a little with the tab because Charles was almost beside her, pulled up the compartment, grabbed the derringer, and—

A sharp blast was the first indication that something had gone horribly amiss, followed by bits of hat spewing into the air. The sound of something shattering then echoed about the room even as Camilla, Charles, and Gideon dove for the ground.

Seventeen

"I must apologize once again for murdering your oriental vase," Adelaide said, taking hold of Gideon's arm and pulling him to a stop in the middle of the training field he and other members of the accounting firm used to hone their skills. "I promise I'll replace it for you, although . . ." She hesitated. "The vase seemed rather old, but give me time and I'm sure I'll be able to find a suitable alternative for you to store your canes in."

Gideon drew in a deep breath, which didn't do a thing to dampen the temper that had been roiling through him ever since Adelaide had accidently fired the derringer two hours prior. He forced himself to meet her gaze. "You don't need to apologize, Adelaide. It was only a vase, and besides, it wasn't your fault."

"Since I'm the one who discharged the derringer, it was, without a doubt, my fault."

"Not when I'm the idiot who didn't check it to ascertain the hammer wasn't cocked. Derringers don't have a trigger guard on them, which means they've been known to fire when the trigger is barely touched."

Adelaide frowned. "Perhaps I flicked the hammer when I reached my hand into the hat."

"It's more likely the derringer shifted at some point, the cushioning pressing against it leaving it armed and ready to fire."

"That's hardly your fault."

He raked a hand through his hair. "It was my responsibility to make sure it was safe for you to handle. I failed in that regard, especially when I didn't even bother to make sure it wasn't loaded before encouraging you to try it out. For that, you have *my* sincerest apologies. We're fortunate you only shattered a vase. It could have been far worse."

"Is that why you're so angry? I've been worried you're furious with me for making a muddle of things yet again."

His stomach gave a curious lurch. Setting down the satchel filled with an assortment of weapons he'd brought from his apartment, Gideon took hold of Adelaide's hand. "I'm sorry if I've given you the impression I'm angry with you. I'm not. All the anger I'm experiencing right now is self-induced. I placed you, along with Camilla and Charles, in jeopardy because I wasn't diligent with taking expected safety precautions. The whole point of providing you with a weapon is to ensure your safety. Instead, I was careless. That could have cost you or the others your lives."

Adelaide bit her lip. "I think you're being a little too hard on yourself."

"Placing an armed pistol into the hands of a novice was an inexcusable error on my part."

She gave his arm a pat. "But it was an error that's completely understandable because I'm sure I was distracting you from your normal safety precautions because of all the questions I was asking you about your different gadgets."

It took a great deal of effort to not contradict her and tell her that he hadn't been distracted because of her questions—he'd been distracted simply because she'd been near him.

Adelaide's enthusiasm had been contagious, which was why, instead of locating the derringer and getting on their way, he'd taken the time to unveil piece after piece of his extensive collection, enjoying the way her eyes lit up with every new gadget.

He could have spent hours revealing all of his treasures to her but hadn't because he'd caught Camilla watching him with something interesting in her eyes, something that resembled speculation.

It wasn't much of a stretch, given that Camilla was a former matchmaker, to conclude that her speculation would most assuredly lead to a decision on her part to help him find that spark she'd mentioned not all that long ago. And while he couldn't deny, if he were honest with himself, that he felt something that might be a spark for Adelaide, he couldn't very well fan the flame, so to speak, because dragging Adelaide into his dangerous lifestyle was a certain recipe for disaster.

"Now there's a worthy distraction if there ever was one," Adelaide said, pulling him from his thoughts before he turned and couldn't help but smile at the sight that met his eyes.

Moe, with Harvey clinging to his back, was loping across the field beside Charles and Camilla, Edna having decided after the derringer debacle that she'd had quite enough excitement for the day and had asked to be delivered back to the Pierpont mansion.

"I think you may have a time of it convincing your dog to give up Harvey, Gideon," Charles said once he reached them. "Moe seems rather attached to the little fur ball."

"I've noticed," Gideon said, bending over to give Moe, and then Harvey, a pat once they came to a stop beside him. He straightened and turned to Adelaide. "I suppose it's only fair, since I'm responsible for placing you in a precarious position today, to offer Harvey a permanent home to make up for my serious lack in judgment—not that I think I have a choice in the matter now since Moe seems incredibly attached to Harvey already."

Adelaide beamed a smile at him, which left him feeling unusually off-kilter. "You're going to keep him?"

"It appears so, but . . ." He narrowed his eyes on her. "Do not think for a second that you'll get another cat into my house. One is all I'm willing to take on."

"Unless Moe decides differently," Camilla muttered as she stopped beside him, lifting up the collar of her overcoat when a gust of wind blew up. "And not that I want to point out the obvious, but we should probably get on with the how-to-handle-a-pistol lesson since it feels as if it wants to snow."

"Indeed," Gideon agreed, grabbing the satchel and heading across the field, a line of targets set up twenty-five feet away from where he was standing. He set the bag on the ground as Charles did the same with the satchel he'd brought, both of them emptying the contents, although Gideon's bag contained different guns, such as a Colt Pocket 49 revolver, and a few varieties of pistols that weren't overly heavy and could fit in Adelaide's reticule, but ones that were equipped with trigger guards, which would make them safer for her to handle.

Charles, on the other hand, had brought the Assassin's Creed, a flintlock two-shot revolver, and a very unusual gadget—a grappling hook that shot out of a pistol, something Adelaide was already eyeing with far too much interest.

"Don't even think about it," he told her, earning a sigh from Adelaide in return.

"I don't know how you expect me to ignore such a fascinating piece," she argued. "It's a *grappling hook* that *launches out of a gun*. That would come in remarkably handy when I find myself faced with rescuing cats."

"Except that it's incredibly loud when fired, which would undoubtedly complicate a rescue attempt."

"Not if I made a point of speaking very loudly to the cat before I launch the hook."

"You're reaching, and you know it. Besides, grappling hooks aren't on our agenda today. We're here to teach you the rudiments of handling a pistol."

She seemed to deflate on the spot. "Fine, no grappling hooks, but I'm still not certain why you're willing to teach me about pistols since I'm the last lady on earth who should ever brandish one again."

"You'll be less of a danger to yourself, as well as everyone else, if you learn a few basics."

"I suppose there is that," she muttered as he picked up a pocket pistol and spent the next twenty minutes explaining how to hold it, load it, unload it, and fire it.

To Adelaide's credit, her attention remained firmly on his lesson, even though Charles was practicing with the Assassin's Creed halfway across the field, the resounding boom of the rounds having Camilla put on stylish earmuffs, which apparently weren't effective because she soon repaired to the carriage.

"Are you ready to try it out?" Gideon finally asked when he felt Adelaide understood the basics.

"I suppose that's the next step, but perhaps Charles should join Camilla. There's no saying I'm going to be accurate with my shot."

"I'll simply stand behind you," Charles said, striding over to join them, the Assassin's Creed resting on his shoulder. "I should be safe there, as long as you keep your weapon pointed toward the targets."

After sending her cousin a look that suggested she'd taken umbrage over him suggesting she'd do anything else but keep her weapon pointed toward the target, Adelaide spent the next thirty minutes firing shot after shot, stumbling backward from the recoil of the pistol, but finally gaining her feet fifteen minutes in. She missed the target time and again, something that evidently frustrated her because she began narrowing her eyes, squinting at the target, biting her lip, and then firing. She grinned in delight when a bullet finally hit something besides the surrounding trees, although the target she hit hadn't actually been the one she'd been aiming for, but still.

"Did you see that?" she exclaimed, lowering the pistol to her side before she turned to him. "I hit it."

"An improvement to be sure," Gideon said. "Shall we try the pepperbox next?"

"You told me earlier that you didn't think a pepperbox would be suitable for me because it holds five shots."

"True, but I've reconsidered. You're still having some issues with hitting a target—something I know you'll resolve—but there is a very real threat against you right now. A pepperbox is meant to be fired at close range. It might not be a bad option for you since it does have more than one round, which could come in handy if your aim is off."

"Coming in handy sounds good to me," she said, her lips curving, which left her dimple popping out, something Gideon refused to allow to distract him as he began giving her a lesson on the fundamentals of the pepperbox.

Twenty minutes later, Adelaide was showing progress with her latest weapon, actually hitting her target a handful of times. But when a large gust of wind, mixed with snow, began swirling around them, they both agreed it was time to call it a day.

"Can we practice again tomorrow?" she asked as they made their way to fetch Charles, who was testing out the grappling hook on the opposite side of the field.

"Didn't Camilla's dressmaker say you have more fittings?"

"She did, but perhaps we can squeeze in at least an hour of instruction after my torture session, especially if I hold particularly still during the fitting, which should speed up the process."

Finding it next to impossible to resist the beseeching smile Adelaide was sending him, Gideon inclined his head. "I'll stop by Camilla's around two, but if you're not close to being finished with the fittings, there's little chance Camilla will be agreeable about us taking off for more target practice."

"I'll make certain to be on best behavior," she said, slowing to a stop as she watched Charles climb from a tree, the grappling hook slung over his shoulder. A trace of wistfulness flickered through her eyes. "That grappling hook really would come in handy when rescuing cats, even if it is rather loud. I mean, the worst thing that might happen would be the cat would scramble higher in the tree, but it wouldn't be an issue, what with the long rope attached to the hook."

Gideon refused a sigh, knowing what he was about to suggest was not the brightest idea he'd ever had, but once again, he found himself throwing caution to the wind—this time because he couldn't seem to ignore the wistfulness. "Would you like to try out the grappling hook before we leave?"

Her mouth dropped open. "Really?"

He smiled. "Really. But I'm warning you, the pistol the hook fires from has a strong recoil. It sent Charles stumbling backward a time or two."

"I'll plant my feet firmly in the ground and hope for the best."

"That's an encouraging thought."

Sending him a wink, Adelaide hurried to join Charles, who was jumping the last few feet out of the tree. He jerked his head up a moment later and settled a frown on Gideon.

"You told Adelaide she can try this?" he called.

"I think she'll be fine," Gideon called back as Camilla suddenly materialized by his side.

"You can't be serious" were the first words out of Camilla's mouth.

"Adelaide did far better with the pistols than I was expecting. I'm sure she'll do the same with the grappling hook."

"Or she'll lose a limb."

He fought a wince. "A valid concern. Perhaps I should rescind my offer, or . . ." He brightened. "*You* could tell her she shouldn't try the hook, saying something about how difficult it'll be to relaunch her into society if she's unable to leave her house because of an unforeseen injury."

"You want me to be the one to disappoint her instead of you?"

"I didn't say that."

"You didn't have to."

After considering him for a long moment, the hint of speculation once again residing in her eyes, Camilla finally smiled. "Fine, I'll tell her. But you're going to have to rein in this odd habit you seem to be developing for indulging Adelaide's every whim."

"I haven't agreed to bring her into the accounting firm."

"Yet," Camilla returned before she grabbed hold of his arm and began dragging him Adelaide's way, stopping in her tracks when Adelaide hefted up the pistol already reloaded with the grappling hook and took aim at the tree.

"Everyone stand back," she called over her shoulder.

Before Gideon could tell her to wait a moment, a loud bang erupted and then Adelaide was flying backward.

Unfortunately, the recoil caused the pistol to discharge the grappling hook straight up into the air, a hook that was even now plummeting to the ground.

Directly toward where Adelaide was sprawled.

Gideon was in motion a second later, skidding to a stop when Adelaide rolled to the right, the grappling hook crashing to the ground a foot from where her head had been a second before.

Instead of remaining on the ground, contemplating the fact she was still alive, Adelaide pushed herself to her feet, dusted her hands together, and sent him a grin.

"That had far more of a kick than I was expecting, but I'm sure with a bit of practice I'll eventually be able to remain on my feet."

He opened his mouth to tell her she would never handle the grappling hook again but found the argument dying on the tip of his tongue when his attention settled on the dimple that had popped out again the second Adelaide began grinning, one he had absolutely no willpower to ignore this time.

"And you claim not to believe in sparks," Camilla murmured as she gave his arm a pat, sent him a far-too-knowing smile, then turned on her heel and strode for the carriage without another word.

Eighteen

Gideon checked his pocket watch yet again, shaking his head when he realized a mere two minutes had passed since the last time he'd checked it.

"Shouldn't be too much longer," Charles said as he ambled up to join Gideon, sipping a glass of chilled champagne. "The first waltz is due to commence within the next thirty minutes, which means Adelaide should stroll through the entranceway of Delmonico's soon to make her grand entrance." He caught Gideon's eye. "Any trepidations or misgivings about Camilla's decision to present the new and improved Adelaide at the illustrious Patriarch Ball?"

"I've steeled myself to keep any expectations in check," Gideon admitted. "I, unlike Camilla, am not convinced that having me shower Adelaide with attention is going to have society concluding they should embrace her as a fashionable lady about town."

"I think you're selling yourself short," Charles argued. "My mother keeps abreast of all the gossip, and you're considered quite the catch, even more so since you've allowed it to be known

212

you have no intention of settling down soon. That right there, my friend, has turned you into a challenge for many a young lady. You mark my words, society will notice your interest in Adelaide. They'll then conclude there must be something intriguing about her they've not noticed before if the oh-so-elusive Gideon Abbott is interested in a lady they've always considered peculiar."

"I'm not certain that speaks well of society in general."

"It's not only the upper crust who are influenced by those possessed of charismatic attitudes. Regardless of social status, everyone aspires to associate with the most prominent contemporaries within their circles. It lends a certain sense of superiority over those not as comfortable in social situations."

Gideon frowned. "I've never actually considered the matter before, but perhaps you're right."

"Of course I am—just as I'm certain you've not considered it because you're obviously one of those fortunate men who've never been shunned before, been chosen last during any school activity, or had pranks played on you at the most unsuspecting of times."

"Why do I get the distinct impression you're speaking from personal experience?"

Charles took another sip of champagne. "Simply because I was born into a life of privilege does not mean I've been spared from the cruelty of others. Boarding school was a nightmare for me, but it allowed me to grow a thick skin, which has come in handy over the years." He shrugged. "Even with my Knickerbocker ancestry and large fortune, ladies have not exactly been subtle with allowing me to know of their disinterest. Frankly, the only ladies who've shown interest in me are those who have an eye on my financial portfolio, or those who didn't find success as they made their way through the first and second tiers of eligible gentlemen and eventually settled their attention on me, but only because they fear societal failure and don't want to end up spinsters."

"I doubt you want to spend the rest of your life with a lady you believe settled for you."

"Indeed, which is why I, according to my mother, am lingering in a most unfortunate bachelor state, perhaps forever."

After helping himself to a glass of champagne from a silver tray a server was offering him, Gideon took a sip and considered Charles for a moment. "I'm sure your plight on the marriage mart isn't as dire as you believe. I've seen you conversing easily with Camilla, a lady who strikes terror into the most sophisticated gentlemen and leaves them tongue-tied in her presence. That suggests you're not nearly as socially awkward as you've allowed yourself to believe."

"Camilla has no interest in marriage, which allows me to keep my nerves in check when I'm with her. I've also endeared myself to her of late because I've been instrumental with tiring Adelaide out every morning by taking her to either your training facility or my rifle club." Charles's eyes twinkled. "My cousin is apparently far less prone to complaining about being stuck with pins when she's tired. Camilla's also been delighted that I've included Leopold and Vernon with the morning weapon excursions, something that distracts them from giving Camilla pointers on how to successfully relaunch Adelaide into society."

Gideon grinned. "And while I'm sure Camilla does appreciate you distracting what she's taken to calling 'those interfering gentlemen,' Adelaide seems to be relishing their suggestions, at least as it pertains to weaponry. She told me yesterday that Leopold has given her pointers on how to use a cane to great effect, while Vernon has continued working with her on the five-shot pepperbox."

"Her skills with the pepperbox have certainly improved over the past two weeks, but her weapon of choice is still the grappling hook."

"An unusual choice, especially since it's not what I'd consider a weapon, nor is it easily concealed."

"She found a bag on the Ladies' Mile the other day that's big enough to hold it."

Gideon blinked. "She's not intending on bringing it with her tonight, is she?"

"And incur the wrath of Camilla? I think not."

"Thank goodness for that. She'll hardly enjoy success tonight if a grappling hook suddenly gets launched from her bag into the midst of the most anticipated ball of the Season."

Charles laughed. "I'm sure she considered that when she decided to leave the hook at home, although I believe what influenced her final decision was her mother." He took another sip of champagne. "Aunt Phyllis was rather vocal about Adelaide not bringing any weapons with her this evening, something I'm sure Adelaide was a touch disappointed about. But . . ." He caught Gideon's eye. "Not that Adelaide has admitted this to me, but I suspect she's also somewhat disappointed that you haven't joined our training sessions this week."

Gideon took an hors d'oeuvre from a server, pausing with it halfway to his mouth. "It wasn't my intention to disappoint her, but after I saw her eyeing that cannon that's set up on the target field, I thought it might be best if I made myself scarce."

"Afraid she'd wheedle you into letting her give it a go, were you?"

"Adelaide's very proficient with wheedling."

Charles cocked his head to the side. "And yet you don't strike me as a gentleman who can be persuaded often when it goes against your better judgment."

"I'm usually not," Gideon admitted.

"Which is quite telling and is something you might want to ponder further when you're at your leisure." Charles pulled out his pocket watch. "Now, however, is not the time for reflection because Adelaide should be making her appearance any minute now." He nodded to where Camilla was chatting with a group of guests not far from the grand entranceway. "Camilla's already here, not wanting to arrive with Adelaide because she didn't want society to conclude she's taken Adelaide on as a matchmaking client."

"I think that was Adelaide's decision," Gideon said. "She knows how successful Camilla has been with matches, and given Adelaide's decision to remain a spinster, she doesn't want to deal with the bother of fending off potential suitors if society decides to give her another chance."

"She may find herself having to do that even with her determination to remain a spinster. Gentlemen always flock to ladies who are considered in high demand."

"I doubt she'll enjoy that," Gideon muttered.

"Quite," Charles agreed. "Which means Adelaide will need us to run interference if too many gentlemen seek her out, but we'll worry about that if it happens. For now, let's concentrate on your role in tonight's scheme. According to the plan, Adelaide should arrive promptly before the first dance is scheduled because Camilla wanted the latest debutantes to have their moment in the spotlight before Adelaide makes an appearance."

Charles nodded to where a gathering of young ladies was currently surrounding Ward McAllister, all of whom were smiling, dressed to perfection, and attempting to pretend they didn't notice the many gentlemen watching their every move. "You'll notice Ward has already singled out the most beautiful of young ladies. I overheard him speaking with a reporter from *The New York Herald* earlier. He told the man there were many sparkling gems this Season—Miss Jennie Gibson, Miss Constance Kip, Miss Edith Sherman, and Miss Cynthia Barney being the lucky few who will find their names mentioned tomorrow in the society section."

Gideon tilted his head. "Doesn't your mother have her eye on Miss Jennie Gibson for you?"

"Indeed, but alas, even though Mother insisted I arrive here early in the hopes of getting my name on Miss Gibson's dance card, by the time I fought my way through the crowd surrounding her, there were no spots left."

"You don't seem overly disappointed about that."

Charles's eyes began twinkling again. "I assure you, I'm quite devasted."

"I can tell, but I find myself curious as to whether you managed to get your name on any lady's dance card this evening."

"I haven't as of yet, but I'm not all that fussed about it considering I'm not in any hurry to abandon my bachelor state, no matter that my mother nags me about that on an almost hourly basis."

"Perhaps her nagging would cease if you attempted to dance with a few ladies at any given event. You never know, you might discover one who suits you."

Charles took another sip of his champagne. "I'm not sure you're qualified to lend me lady advice since it's clear you're not keen to leave your bachelor state behind anytime soon either."

"Simply because I'm determined not to marry doesn't mean I don't have credible advice to lend about the subject. Half my friends have entered marital bliss, and they feel free to share their observations about the fairer sex with me on a frequent basis."

"Which I'm sure has lent you insight, but may I assume that has left you with an unfavorable impression of ladies in general, which is why you're opposed to marriage in the first place?"

"Not at all. I've simply made the decision to remain a bachelor for now because, given my occupation, it wouldn't be fair to become involved with any lady. I'd constantly be keeping secrets from her, and that's not the best way to sustain a happy union."

"Not every lady is incapable of handling the truth about your involvement with matters of intrigue," Charles argued. "Adelaide knows exactly what you do, and instead of being appalled by it, she's champing at the bit to convince you to bring her into the firm."

Gideon resisted a sigh because Adelaide not being put off by what he did was a notion that had been springing to mind more than he cared to admit. He'd always been of the belief that ladies were meant to be sheltered from the unpleasantness the world had to offer, but Adelaide had proven that simply wasn't true in all cases.

She seemed to thrive in the midst of chaos and had actually tried to convince him three nights before that she should accompany him to Five Points to try to ferret out information regarding what had been transpiring at Bainswright Books under the oblivious noses of poor Mr. and Mrs. Bainswright.

She'd been less than pleased when he'd flatly refused, telling him she was perfectly capable of looking after herself, then adding that it was quite presumptuous of him to make decisions about what she could or couldn't do.

Adelaide, he was beginning to discover, was rather magnificent when she was in a temper. In fact, she was quite magnificent during any given hour of any day, and . . . he couldn't seem to stop dwelling on the idea that if he were in the market for a wife, she'd be someone exactly like Adelaide, or rather, she *would* be Adelaide.

It was a thought that crept frequently to mind, rousing him in the middle of the night from the deepest of sleeps, and one that suggested Adelaide was much more to him than simply a friend.

"Given you something to ponder, haven't I?" Charles said, dragging Gideon back to the conversation at hand.

Gideon cleared his throat. "Forgive me. I fear I was lost in thought, which was quite rude since you and I were engaged in conversation."

"And that thought would be?"

He hesitated for the briefest of seconds, not knowing how much he should disclose. "I was thinking about your cousin and how she isn't intimidated by the risks I'm faced with on any given day."

"Adelaide has never been one to shy away from danger, as can be seen by how she's longing to join the accounting firm." Charles smiled. "I'm simply waiting for the day you relent to her persistent badgering."

"You'll be waiting a long time because even though Adelaide *would* be an asset to the firm, what with how she possesses unusual insight into figuring out plots, bringing her on is not a possibility, given that associates of the firm are required to interact with members of the criminal persuasion far too often."

"A valid concern, but because you do seem rather fond of my cousin, instead of bringing her on to work for you, you could always consider turning your eye to courting her instead. As we've mentioned, Adelaide is perfectly aware of what you do, doesn't shy away from the dangerous life you lead, and besides all that, I think she'd make you a more than suitable partner."

"Which is an interesting proposition, but you must realize that there's always the threat that whatever criminal I'm pursuing will turn to anyone I care about in retaliation for my disrupting any nefarious plans they have. I would never want to place Adelaide in peril, which means there's no sense continuing this conversation because I'm not in a position to offer your cousin a place in my life other than friendship, even if, perhaps, there's a part of me that wants to do exactly that."

Nineteen

❦

It really came as no surprise when Charles's mouth went a little slack a second after Gideon's admission slipped past his lips.

"That was definitely not the response I was expecting," Charles said, setting his now-empty glass on a silver tray a server held out to him. "And not that you've asked for my counsel, but I can't help but feel compelled to point out that you may very well be wrong with your decision to not explore what the possibilities could be with Adelaide. Yes, your work is dangerous, and people close to you have the potential of being affected by that. Nevertheless, I don't think you're giving Adelaide enough credit. She's incredibly resourceful and always seems to extricate herself well from the unlikely situations she finds herself in."

"The last thing I want is Adelaide placed in further jeopardy, which she would most certainly be if I began courting her. Besides, she's given me no indication her thoughts about remaining a spinster have changed."

"Perhaps you should ask her about that."

"That would be an interesting conversation because your cousin would most assuredly be curious as to why I would ask her such a thing."

"To which you could reply that you've realized you're, uh, well, perhaps somewhat, um, fond of her."

"Professing *fondness* would certainly leave her heart in a fluttering state as well as set her palms to sweating for sure."

Charles grinned. "I don't claim to be an expert on romantic prose, as can be seen by how dismal my love life has been. You, however, have most likely assumed the role of cavalier gentleman to the ladies when you're on assignment. I'm certain that experience would serve you well in coming up with something suitable to say to Adelaide."

"I don't believe my occupation has equipped me with the skills needed to glean information like *that*. I also don't think this is a conversation we need to be having right now because, if you've forgotten, there's soon to be a plan afoot, one I'm playing a key part in."

"I suppose you do need to keep your wits about you, so we'll table this conversation . . . for now." Charles glanced at his pocket watch again before turning his attention to the entranceway. "Adelaide's cutting it rather close, but perhaps her delayed entrance will work to her advantage." He nodded to Ward McAllister, who was now standing feet from the entranceway. "Ward will certainly take note of her, and if he makes a bit of a to-do over her transformation, that'll immediately get everyone talking."

Gideon narrowed his eyes in Ward's direction. "Is it just me or has Ward relaxed his strict rules regarding the Patriarch Ball and invited more than the usual number of industry titans this year? He's currently speaking with Marshall Wilson, a gentleman I know through the New York Yacht Club, but a man who's been fairly vocal about his lack of success with gaining entrance into the hallowed midst of the Four Hundred."

"It's not only you who's noticed the inclusion of numerous members of the *nouveau riche* this evening," Charles said. "My mother was appalled to witness Dudley Paulding and Anson

McKim looking pleased as punch as they made their way through the receiving line. She then almost descended into a fit of the vapors when she spotted Harold Spencer in the crowd, fawning over the debutantes." He sent a nod Marshall's way. "When Mother took note of Marshall paying close attention to Miss Jennie Gibson, she was fit to be tied and marched off to have a word with Ward and demand he get rid of the interlopers, as she called them, before the ball begins in earnest. I assume Ward didn't agree with Mother since he seems to be enjoying his chat with Marshall."

"Ward would do well to proceed with caution because his position in society isn't completely infallible," Gideon said. "High-ranking ladies might tolerate the addition of an occasional swell here or there, but an influx of them, and at the opening ball of the Season, will have repercussions for Ward, who, according to rumor, has lost a bit of favor with Mrs. Astor recently."

"That favor is surely going to diminish even more if Mrs. Astor gets wind that men who aren't worthy of the Four Hundred seem to be attracting this Season's most eligible ladies," Charles said with a nod toward Marshall, who was currently in the process of adding his name to Jennie Gibson's dance card. Ward beamed his approval at the couple, as if he'd been the one responsible for Marshall being granted a dance from a lady who was undoubtedly going to be deemed an Incomparable of the Season.

Gideon frowned as he watched Marshall return Jennie's dance card before he turned to Constance Kip, presented her with a bow as Ward performed an introduction, then added his name to her card before he moved to Edith Sherman and did the same. He then strolled with Ward to another gathering of ladies, all of whom immediately began fluttering their lashes.

Gideon turned and quirked a brow Charles's way. "I thought

you said you were unsuccessful with getting your name on Miss Gibson's card because every spot was taken."

"I've apparently been found out because, in truth, I didn't actually approach Miss Gibson and may have simply assumed she didn't have any dances left." Charles's gaze darted around the room. "Thankfully, I don't see my mother, but if she were to notice that gentlemen are still adding their names to Miss Gibson's card, I'll need to invent a suitable excuse." He brightened. "Perhaps I'll blame you."

Gideon laughed. "I had nothing to do with your inability to secure a dance with Miss Gibson."

"Mother doesn't need to know that."

Before Gideon could argue with that nonsense, Charles checked his pocket watch again and frowned. "Adelaide's definitely behind schedule. I hope she hasn't run into another unexpected and, need I add, catastrophic situation."

"We have three operatives from the firm tailing her tonight, which should alleviate any opportunity for chaos," Gideon said. "I would think Adelaide's simply stalling for as long as she can because the thought of attending her first society function since her unfortunate unmentionables debacle, paired with her swans' song performance, must be a little nerve-wracking." Gideon leaned closer to Charles. "That's why I gave her the cipher I've been unable to decode earlier today, hoping it might help distract her from thoughts of the ball, while also providing her with something to do as Camilla's stylist did her hair, an event Camilla warned was going to take several hours."

"I thought you didn't want to involve Adelaide in accounting firm business."

"I'm not really involving her because there's absolutely no possibility she'll be able to break the code, not when I've spent hours poring over it to little avail. The four men I assigned to try their hands at deciphering it haven't been successful either."

"Why would you give Adelaide an impossible task?"

"I didn't want her to spend her day worrying about what was ahead."

"You really are very solicitous of my cousin's feelings, which—"

Whatever else Charles was going to say ended abruptly when Marshall Wilson strolled over to join them, shaking hands with Charles and then Gideon before he snagged a glass of champagne from a passing server, downed a good half of the contents with one gulp, then turned a smile on Gideon.

"Good to see you at the yacht club the other day, Gideon. I was quite impressed with your little boat—*Scorpius*, was it?"

Gideon resisted the urge to snort over the notion that Marshall had just called his two-hundred-foot, three-masted steam yacht a 'little boat.' He smiled instead. "Glad you were impressed, and yes, my teeny-tiny yacht is named *Scorpius*."

Marshall took another gulp of his champagne. "Seems a little odd to name a yacht after a scorpion since those reside on land."

"Which would be a valid point if my yacht was named after a scorpion. It's actually inspired by the constellation Scorpius, which was named in the second century by Ptolemy."

"Interesting" was Marshall's response to that before he handed his now-empty glass to a passing server, snagged another flute, took a swig, and frowned. "That you know about such things suggests you're a well-read gentleman who probably attended Harvard or the like."

"Naval Academy."

"Ah, a navy man. Surprising."

Gideon opened his mouth to excuse himself from a man who was certainly trying his patience, but before he could speak, Marshall suddenly stilled with his glass halfway to his mouth as his eyes went wide.

"On my word, but who is that delightful creature who just

224

walked into the room?" Marshall demanded, gesturing with his glass toward the entranceway.

Gideon turned to where Marshall was now gaping, the room falling unusually quiet as his gaze settled on Adelaide.

Dressed in a deep shade of royal blue, the color enhanced by the sapphire-and-diamond necklace she was wearing as well as the sapphire-and-diamond tiara that was twinkling under the light cast from the chandelier, she immediately commanded the attention of everyone standing in her near vicinity—not that she appeared to notice that, since she was fiddling with her diamond bracelet, one that seemed to be attached to her mother's silk glove.

Phyllis seemed oblivious to the idea that her daughter was literally stuck to her because she was beaming and nodding to numerous guests, clearly delighted to find herself and Adelaide the subject of undivided attention, and not attention of the hostile sort.

A grin curved Gideon's lips a second later when Adelaide's arm flew up in the air from the effort she'd been using to get her bracelet free. She then teetered the slightest bit, regained her balance, took hold of her mother's arm, and stepped forward. One step was all she took, though, before she stopped and glanced around the room, apparently remembering she was supposed to wait for him to join her in the entranceway.

"You're up," Charles whispered, giving Gideon a nudge before he returned his attention to Marshall, who was now gazing at Adelaide as if she were some tasty treat, one he longed to sample.

Fighting the urge to challenge a man he'd never had an issue with before to a good old-fashioned duel, Gideon simply stared at Marshall until Charles gave him another nudge, recalling him to the fact he was supposed to be putting their plan into motion and delaying that plan was leaving Adelaide dithering in the entranceway.

After sending Charles a nod, Gideon strode into motion, resisting the inclination once again to challenge Marshall to that duel when he overheard the man saying something to Charles about needing an introduction to Adelaide as well as asking Charles if she was available.

"You're behind schedule," Camilla hissed under her breath as she glided past him, sending him a look filled with annoyance in the process.

Increasing his stride, Gideon returned his attention to Adelaide, who was still standing in the exact same spot, looking over the crowd, a smile gracing her lips when her gaze suddenly locked with his.

The renewed chatter of the guests faded away as he moved closer toward her, allowing himself the luxury of appreciating the sparkle in her eyes, the color blooming on her cheeks, and the elegant curve of a neck that was accentuated by the cut of her decolletage, a design that showed off her figure to perfection and was certain to draw the attention of gentlemen, which left Gideon with the distinct urge to shrug out of his evening jacket and drape it around her.

It was an urge he'd never felt before in his life.

"Gideon," Adelaide exclaimed as he finally reached her, holding out her hand to him, which he immediately took, pressing a kiss on it and lingering over it longer than was strictly necessary.

"Adelaide," he returned, giving her fingers a squeeze. "You are looking beyond beautiful tonight."

Her dimple immediately popped out. "Which is lovely of you to say, but . . ." She leaned closer and lowered her voice. "I feel quite as if I have a boulder attached to my head, but Mother insisted I wear the tiara, even though I thought it might be a little much."

"A tiara is never too much, dear," Phyllis said, holding out her hand for Gideon.

"You're looking lovely this evening as well, Mrs. Duveen," he said as he pressed a kiss on it.

Phyllis gave her hair a pat. "Camilla insisted I use her stylist. I must say the woman is a magician when it comes to hair, but allow us to return to Adelaide." She took a step closer. "Is it my imagination or does everyone seem to be watching us?"

"It's not your imagination, and they're looking at her with what I would certainly call genuine admiration."

"How magnificent," Phyllis breathed. "I never thought I'd see this day come to pass."

"Simply because everyone is gawking at me, Mother, doesn't mean they'll be keen to forget I've always been considered an odd duck, nor does it mean any gentleman except Gideon will want to put his name on my dance card."

"I have a feeling you're wrong about that," Gideon said, taking Adelaide's dance card and writing his name on the spots for the first and last dance, along with adding his name in the space reserved for a dinner partner.

"For Camilla's and my mother's sake, I hope you're right, but enough about dance cards, how I'm dressed this evening, or how we expect the evening to unfold. I have something much more pressing to discuss with you."

"I would think the results of this evening would be foremost in your mind," he countered.

Adelaide waved that straight aside. "Those thoughts have been firmly replaced because you will never believe what happened this afternoon."

"A traveling salesman arrived at your house and sold you a pistol you like more than the pepperbox?"

Her eyes twinkled. "Try again."

"You've added ten stray cats to your collection?"

"Not even close, although know that I'm still rather put out no one agreed with me about bringing one of my cats to the ball tonight. It would have been the perfect opportunity

227

to convince society that cats could soon be all the rage, especially when Leopold told me you had Samuel Montague, your
engineer, invent a saddlebag for Harvey that attaches to Moe
so he doesn't miss out on the runs you enjoy with your dog. I
know once everyone sees you, Moe, and Harvey running about
Central Park, cats will surely become in high demand, which
means I'll most assuredly see some of my darlings settled into
proper homes."

"I had to outfit Moe with a saddlebag because Harvey wailed
every time Moe and I headed out the door without him."

The twinkle in Adelaide's eyes intensified. "And you've become attached to Harvey and cannot abide the thought of him
being sad."

Gideon's lips twitched. "Don't even think about turning
smug when I concede that you may be right about that."

"Of course I'm right, but . . ." Adelaide's nose wrinkled.
"We seem to be getting distracted from what I've been dying to
tell you happened this afternoon as I was getting my hair pulled,
twisted, and all but yanked out of my head by Camilla's stylist."

"Would it make the torture seem better if I told you the end
results are stunning?"

The dimple popped out again. "You're doing a very nice
job of being most solicitous to me this evening, per Camilla's
request no doubt, but hairstyle aside, if I may tell you what
happened?"

"Camilla didn't suggest I compliment you," Gideon said
before she had an opportunity to disclose what she looked practically bursting to tell. "I'm being sincere when I tell you how
exquisite you look."

Phyllis raised a hand to her throat. "I must say you are in a
most charming and exceedingly delightful mood this evening,
Gideon."

"He'll be in an even better frame of mind if the two of you
would simply allow me to tell him my news."

Phyllis gave Adelaide a swat with her fan. "It would behoove you to mimic Gideon and summon up a bit of charm of your own. If you've forgotten, we've a mission to accomplish this evening, and we're currently under a great deal of scrutiny from practically every guest in attendance."

"And I'm sure I'll be able to summon up a great deal of charm *after* I tell Gideon what happened today." Adelaide settled her attention on Gideon, her eyes sparkling in a most enticing manner. "And since Mother is soon to suffer an apoplectic fit if I don't spit out what I'm dying to tell you . . . I did it."

"Did what?"

"I unlocked the code."

Twenty

❧

It was somewhat telling when Gideon's eyes went wide, but before Adelaide could expand on the cracking-the-cipher business, Mr. Muskel, one of Mrs. Astor's favorite cotillion leaders, called out that it was time for the first dance to begin. He then added that a quadrille performed by members of the Family Circle Dance Class would follow the waltz, three additional dances would commence after that, then dinner would be served at midnight.

She returned her attention to Gideon, who was now considering her quite as if she'd grown a second head, but before she could ponder that unusual turn of events, Camilla drifted past them, arched a telling brow Gideon's way, then glided away without a word.

Adelaide edged closer to him. "I fear you're soon going to find yourself suffering from the wrath of Camilla, what with how you're deviating from her well-crafted plan. To remind you, this is the point in our schedule when we're supposed to stroll across the ballroom floor and take our place in the very center of the room."

"I didn't hear the cotillion leader call for the waltz."

"Well, he did, but you're apparently experiencing shock over the idea I cracked the code, which I must admit I find disappointing, as if you never considered I might figure it out. But it may be best to not get into that right now, not when Camilla's plan revolves around you gazing at me in a smitten fashion. That's something you're definitely not doing, which suggests you should have further availed yourself of Mr. Morton Gimbel's acting instructions."

A blink of an eye later, Gideon was smiling his most charming smile, one that had her pulse hitching ever so slightly, which she ignored since her pulse was rather unruly anytime she found herself in Gideon's company. It truly served no useful purpose to dwell on it, given that he'd given her no indication that her presence caused his pulse to lurch madly about.

"Is this expression more acceptable?" Gideon asked.

She wrinkled her nose. "I wouldn't go so far as to say that's a look that screams 'I'm smitten,' but it'll have to do. With that out of the way, the orchestra has already picked up their instruments, so we need to get situated."

She took hold of an arm he'd apparently forgotten to offer her and prodded him into motion, earning a grin from him in return.

"Do you intend to lead while we dance as well?" he asked.

"If you don't snap out of whatever it is that's wrong with you, certainly."

"There's nothing wrong with me," he argued as they continued strolling through the crowd, drawing more than their fair share of speculative glances, which was an improvement over the glances she normally attracted, which ran the gamut from disapproval to pity, and in the case of her unmentionables, outright disbelief.

The thought of unmentionables had her lips twitching, which earned an arch of a brow from Gideon as they reached the center of the floor and he turned to face her.

"Care to share what's amusing you now?" he asked.

"I was thinking about unmentionables, or more specifically

the chemise Mrs. Bainswright had enough time to finish for me now that she's officially retired. She had it delivered to my house this very morning."

His eyes crinkled at the corners before he extended her a bow, which she returned with a curtsy, straightening as Gideon leaned close and lowered his voice.

"Inappropriate as this is for me to ask, may I assume you're wearing flowers tonight?"

"I certainly wasn't going to disappoint an elderly lady who is convinced these particular unmentionables are going to bring me good fortune this evening." She sent Gideon a wink. "Don't tell Camilla. She'd probably start worrying I'm going to have another wardrobe sputter and give everyone a glimpse of the lovely flowers I can now pair with the cats."

"My lips are sealed."

"Which is for the best, but since we've now adhered to Camilla's schedule and are exactly where we're supposed to be, allow me to return to the cipher and explain exactly what I discovered." She drew in a breath but before she could get a single word past her lips, the first note of the waltz rang out.

"I'm relatively certain that Camilla isn't going to be happy if she catches sight of your expression right now, which has frustration stamped all over it," Gideon said, his tone laced with amusement. "To remind you, I'm expected to gaze adoringly at you, and you're supposed to at least muster up a smile that suggests you're thrilled to take to the floor with me."

He took hold of her hand, pulled her close, then settled his other hand on her waist, which sent a tingle up her spine, one she couldn't quite ignore. In all honesty, there was something delightful about tingles, especially when they were a result of being in such close proximity to Gideon.

Summoning up a smile because Camilla truly would be annoyed if her plan failed, even though it was difficult to look cheerful when she was all but bursting at the seams to disclose more about the code, she caught Gideon's eye, and after he sent her a wink, they were off across the floor.

Waltzing past Charles, who was dancing with Miss Lucille Codman, a lady who'd been out for four Seasons and had spent many an evening wallowing against a wall beside Adelaide, she followed Gideon's lead through a turn, her pulse ratcheting up a notch when he drew her closer.

Hoping he'd think the color she knew was now settling on her face was simply a result of their exertion, she drew in a breath, which resulted with her being given a lovely whiff of a scent that reminded her of woodlands. It really came as no surprise when she immediately stumbled over Gideon's foot, suggesting she was less than capable of being barraged by his cologne and dancing at the same time.

Gideon didn't miss a beat. He simply steadied her, steered her through a complicated turn, then waltzed her effortlessly around other dancers.

"Forgive me, Adelaide," he murmured into her ear, eliciting another tingle. "I should have realized you'd be nervous this evening, and yet I'm doing absolutely nothing to distract you from your nerves."

Since she wasn't about to admit his cologne, not her nerves, was the culprit behind her clumsiness, she forced all thoughts of how delicious he smelled to the far recesses of her mind. "I must admit I'm unaccustomed to being the object of such undivided attention. I normally only incur that after one of my debacles and not because I'm fashionably dressed and being waltzed around a ballroom by a dashing gentleman. That right there could very well be why I'm less than graceful."

"I think you're doing magnificently, but I'm afraid you're going to have to get used to the attention, because if I'm not mistaken, Camilla's plan is already a rousing success and you, my dear Adelaide, have finally arrived."

She couldn't quite suppress a shudder. "That notion is doing absolutely nothing for the state of my nerves. I mean, if you really think about it, I arrived on the scene years ago, so it's not as if society is unfamiliar with me. Granted, Camilla's been doing a marvelous job convincing society I'm an absolute darling, and I am looking rather well turned out this evening. But if what you said is true and I've finally *arrived*, I'm now wondering what's going to happen next if I actually find myself in high demand."

"Haven't you taken time to consider how your life might change if you're deemed a societal success?"

She shot a glance to the edge of the ballroom floor and discovered numerous gentlemen watching her, one gentleman having the audacity to train a monocle her way. Not allowing her gaze to linger on that somewhat disturbing sight, she returned her attention to Gideon.

"Oddly enough, I didn't consider that, because I had doubts we'd be able to alter society's opinion of me, although don't tell Camilla that. Frankly, I'm not that keen to have much in my life change, but I suppose I'll have to dwell on that later. For now, we simply need to get through this dance without further stumbling on my part, which will indeed be noticed and will certainly disappoint Camilla."

"Perhaps we should find something to speak about that will divert you from your nerves."

"An excellent idea, so allow me to explain what happened with the cipher."

After Gideon gave her a twirl, he pulled her close. "You really were able to decipher the *entire* code?"

"Given the incredulousness I detect in your voice, I'm beginning to believe I was quite correct when I suggested that you didn't think I'd be capable of puzzling out the riddle in the first place."

The wariness that immediately flickered through his eyes spoke volumes and earned him a snort from her in return.

"May I assume you gave me the cipher to distract me from thoughts of this evening, which, if true, speaks well of your considerate nature but not well of your faith in my ability to solve mysteries."

He winced. "I'm afraid that *was* the case. Nevertheless, know that I'm suitably impressed by your success and disappointed in myself for doubting your abilities. You've proven time and again you have a knack for figuring out pertinent details involving matters of intrigue."

Additional warmth immediately settled on her cheeks. "Thank you for that, although I bet that was difficult for you to admit, what with your reluctance to involve me in any of your clandestine activities. I imagine you're now second-guessing your decision to give me the cipher since pestering on my part will soon commence because clearly I have some talents that would be beneficial to the firm."

"Perhaps we could come to some sort of arrangement before any pestering commences."

She stumbled over his foot again. "Does that mean you're considering bringing me into the firm?"

"No," he didn't hesitate to say. "I was thinking more along the lines of giving you the grappling hook in exchange for your agreement that you'll discontinue asking me to join the firm."

"That hook *would* come in handy with some of my more difficult rescue missions."

"I imagine it would," he said before he twirled her past a couple who were not even bothering to disguise the fact they were gawking at them.

"Could the discontinuation of the badgering have a time limit to it?" Adelaide asked, earning a laugh from Gideon.

"That's not how negotiating is supposed to work."

"But you must know it'll be difficult for me to curb the badgering. It's become a habit with you."

"Indeed, but again, if you want the hook, all you need to do is say yes to my proposal instead of launching a countermove."

"I believe I'll need to ponder the offer more before I give you a definitive answer."

His lips quirked. "I can't claim to be surprised, but are you going to do that pondering now, or would you prefer returning to the topic of how you were able to solve the cipher?"

"I'm a lady who is quite capable of thinking about more than one subject at a time, which is yet another reason—"

"You think you've earned a place in the firm," he finished for her when she faltered, his eyes twinkling in a far too compelling manner. "I'm now getting the sneaking suspicion I may be retaining ownership of a certain grappling hook."

"You may be right about that, but since I'm anxious to tell you more about the cipher, I'll curtail my nagging about the accounting firm, at least for now." Adelaide moved with Gideon across the floor, waiting until he turned them around before she continued. "I must admit that it was trickier than I thought it would be to solve."

"It took you a mere afternoon."

"Far too long if you ask me, and I had my doubts I would find any success, especially when I tried several different codes from my book, ones that spanned decades of wars and government intrigues. I was on the verge of giving up, which would have delighted Camilla's stylist, who kept complaining I was moving my head too much, when I had a thought."

"And that thought allowed you to crack a code that I and numerous associates have been working on for two weeks?"

She smiled. "Indeed, and that I found success when you and your associates were floundering suggests yet again that I should at least be considered as a future associate."

He sent her a quirk of his lips before he gave her another twirl and shook his head. "I believe the grappling hook is now firmly off the table because your tenaciousness seems to be increasing, something I'm going to broach with your mother, who will certainly have a few thoughts on that subject."

She narrowed her eyes. "Complaining to my mother is hardly fair. She completely adores you and will definitely have more than a few thoughts to share with *me* if she thinks I'm being tenacious about something while in your company."

His only response to that was to send her another charming smile, which left her treading on his shoe again.

She refused a sigh. "I beg your pardon, Gideon. I didn't mean to trample your foot yet again."

"That you did so suggests I'm being negligent with properly distracting you." He bent close to her ear. "To get us back in sync, tell me how you cracked the code."

The feel of his breath against the side of her neck sent her pulse skittering madly about. But not wanting to crush his toes again or begin stumbling all over the ballroom floor, which would probably see Camilla's plans for her dying a rapid death, no matter if Gideon was showering attention on her or not, Adelaide drew in a steadying breath.

"I figured out that someone chose a cipher from the Revolutionary War."

"And you came to that conclusion because . . . ?"

Adelaide inclined her head to Miss Martha Radcliffe, who was staring as she waltzed past with Mr. Thomas Hassel, a gentleman Adelaide had sat beside at a long-ago dinner, that circumstance never happening again after she'd thought Thomas had been choking on a piece of beef and had given him a few whacks on the back, only to discover he'd not been choking at all. Given that Thomas settled a warm smile on her, paired with what seemed to be a wink, before he steered Martha in the opposite direction, it was fair to conclude that he was finally willing to forgive her for trying to save his life when it hadn't needed saving. She returned her gaze to Gideon and frowned.

"It's very odd, isn't it, this abrupt change in how society

treats me. Thomas Hassel hasn't spoken to me in eons and yet, if I'm not mistaken, he just winked at me." She wrinkled her nose. "Do you think Camilla really had the right of it and society has collectively changed their mind about me simply because you're showing particular attention to me?"

Gideon slowed their pace. "As Charles recently remarked to me, people are drawn to those possessed of a certain level of . . . panache, if you will. Camilla understands that all too well. She knew if she could have one fashionable gentleman pay attention to you and use her own social standing to influence those around her, society would follow suit and accept you."

"Hmm . . ." was all Adelaide said to that, earning a surprising grin from Gideon. "What?"

He drew her closer. "I can see the wheels spinning, but that is causing you to scowl, which Camilla will certainly take issue with. That means we need to shelve this conversation for a later date and return to the cipher, which I'm dying to hear more details about. How did you determine the code might have been from the Revolutionary War?"

Realizing she was indeed scowling as she thought about how easy it had been to persuade society to accept her after all the years they'd spent treating her like an outsider, Adelaide summoned up a smile. "Truth be told, I should have figured it out sooner because the diary was written around the time of the Revolutionary War. I began wondering if the diary itself was a clue, perhaps one that allowed someone to know what cipher was needed to translate the code." Her smile turned genuine. "Imagine my surprise when I started working with a monoalphabetic substitution that was created during the Revolutionary War, one used by a Dr. Church, which was intercepted by Washington's army, and . . . it worked."

"What did the cipher say?"

"It's not a message, but a series of numbers. Eighteen, seven, twelve, and three. I think it's a combination to a safe, but there was nothing written about exactly what the numbers meant or a location where to find a safe."

"That's slightly problematic."

"Indeed, because we have no idea what the target is. However, I imagine if we put our heads together, we can figure it out."

Gideon led her around a couple who were trying their best to pretend they hadn't been watching them. "I hate to be the bearer of bad news, but there isn't going to be any *we* in this."

"There's that odd aversion you have with the word *we*, but no need to be hasty with rejecting my assistance. I'll give you a few days to ponder the matter, but no more than that because I'm sure this is a situation where time is of the essence."

Gideon guided her past Miss Jennie Gibson, who was dancing with a man Adelaide had never seen before. He then twirled her once and smiled another charming smile at her, done so, no doubt, because Camilla was standing on the sidelines two feet away from them, watching their every move.

"While I may have an aversion to the word *we*, you seem to have that same affliction, but with the word *no*," he said.

Before she could respond to that nonsense, although he wasn't exactly off the mark, the music drew to an end. After dipping into a curtsy as Gideon bowed over her hand, she took the arm he extended her, and together they began moving off the ballroom floor.

Her feet began to drag when she suddenly realized there were numerous gentlemen watching her with what seemed to be smiles of anticipation on their faces, which left the distinct impression they wanted a moment of her time and also suggested that Gideon had been right in that society was now quite ready to fully embrace her—a notion that left her oddly unsettled.

Twenty-One

Resisting the urge to flee in the opposite direction, Adelaide kept a smile firmly in place, relief flowing freely when, before any of the gentlemen had an opportunity to single her out, Camilla materialized by her side. After exchanging curtsies, quite as if they were merely friends greeting each other, Camilla turned to Gideon, who immediately took hold of her gloved hand and placed a kiss on her fingers.

"By your smile," Gideon began, "I have to think you're pleased with how the evening is already unfolding."

Camilla's eyes sparkled. "Pleased is putting it mildly because that was an almost flawless performance on the dance floor, except for a few stumbles and an occasional frown, something I doubt anyone took notice of because everyone is tittering about your attention to Adelaide as well as the fact you sought her out *almost* the second she entered the ballroom." She turned to Adelaide. "As I'd hoped, you're the talk of the ball, but you mustn't linger with Gideon. Gentlemen are even now waiting to add their names to your dance card, so off you go."

Adelaide shot a glance to the gentlemen in question, refusing a shudder when the gentleman still perusing her with his monocle sent her a wave. She sent him what she hoped wasn't a weak smile in return before she leaned closer to Camilla. "I'm not certain I'm up for taking on an entire onslaught of gentlemen right now."

"Of course you are, and you're going to use the onslaught right this very minute to further cement the idea you're now a most sought-after lady about town and certainly never should have faced societal ostracization in the first place."

The inclination to balk was immediate, but before she had an opportunity to do exactly that, Camilla gave her a less than subtle nudge toward the waiting gentlemen.

Sending Gideon a last glance, one he didn't notice because his eyes were narrowed on the gentlemen she was expected to approach, Adelaide forced another smile and began strolling into motion as she heard Camilla mention something about Gideon using a scowl to great effect, adding in a bit about him not needing additional acting lessons after all because he now looked somewhat menacing, which was surely going to lend everyone the impression he was completely enthralled with Adelaide.

There was a part of her that couldn't help but wish that was actually true, while another part of her, the sane part, cautioned her against longing for any such thing, because it was sheer idiocy, given that Gideon wasn't enthralled at all but was merely playing a part in Camilla's grand scheme.

Pushing aside her fairly depressing thoughts, she plowed onward, forced to a stop when Mrs. Thurman Chandler, the former Miss Suzette Tilden, stepped in front of her, blocking her path.

Adelaide refused to allow her smile to slip, even though Suzette had been the bane of her existence for years, until she'd tried to douse Adelaide with punch during the Newport Season and Gwendolyn Brinley had not only stopped her but also drawn attention to the antics young ladies got up to as they traversed the marriage mart. Fortunately for Suzette, Gwendolyn had an eye for matches and had pointed out the obvious to Suzette toward the end of the previous summer, which was why Suzette was no longer on the marriage mart, although why she was now smiling at Adelaide was definitely a reason to proceed with caution because one never knew what devious plots Suzette was up to at any given moment.

"My dear Adelaide," Suzette purred, reaching out and taking hold of Adelaide's hand. "It's been ages since we've spoken, and my oh my how you've . . . changed."

Adelaide tried to retrieve her hand, giving up when Suzette tightened her grip. "I haven't changed that much" was all she could think to respond.

"On the contrary," Suzette argued. "During all the many, many, *many* Seasons you've been out, you never attracted the notice of a man like Mr. Gideon Abbott before, nor any other worthy gentleman, but tonight, well, the gentlemen seem to be lining up in the hopes of you granting them time in your . . . interesting company."

It was immediately evident that not everyone was keen to embrace her as one of the latest darlings of the Season.

Adelaide cleared her throat. "Always lovely to see you, Mrs. Chandler."

She refused a wince when Suzette gave her hand an unusually firm squeeze before she released it and then gave her a less than gentle tap with her fan.

"Now, none of this Mrs. Chandler business. You must call me Suzette and you must agree to lunch with me at your earliest convenience so that we may catch up." Suzette smiled, although it didn't reach her eyes. "I assure you, I'm all aflutter to learn what you've been up to of late as well as learn how in the world you managed to endear yourself to Camilla Pierpont."

"I'll be certain to send a note around to arrange a time for what sounds like a delightful lunch."

"See that you do," Suzette said before she took Adelaide completely aback when she suddenly linked her arm with Adelaide's. "With that out of the way, allow me to perform an introduction to a gentleman who's incredibly anxious to become known to you."

Given the way Suzette's eyes were now gleaming in a malicious fashion, it wasn't a stretch to conclude that the gentleman Suzette wanted to introduce her to would probably not be a man she'd want to spend time with.

"How very kind of you to want to introduce me around, Suzette," Adelaide began. "However, I wouldn't want to take up more of your time."

"Nonsense," Suzette countered. "It would be my pleasure to make you known to Mr. Dudley Paulding. Granted, he's not firmly ensconced with the Four Hundred as of yet, but ladies are already whispering tonight about what a catch he is. Not only is he handsome, though in a somewhat common fashion, but he's extremely wealthy and even owns his own yacht."

"Stellar qualities to be sure."

"I think so too," Suzette said before she yanked Adelaide into motion, making a beeline for the man who'd been watching her every move through a monocle.

Thankfully, after performing a formal introduction to Mr. Dudley Paulding, Suzette sent Adelaide an innocent smile that wasn't fooling Adelaide for a second before she dipped into a curtsy and wandered away, saying something about looking forward to lunching with Adelaide soon.

"My dear Miss Duveen," Dudley said, drawing Adelaide's attention. "May I dare hope you still have dances available, given that you arrived late to the ball and I haven't seen you speaking with anyone but Mr. Abbott?"

Having no choice but to admit she did have available spots on her dance card since Dudley had been watching her far too closely, Adelaide slipped the card from her wrist and handed it to him, not wanting him to linger over her hand since he'd lingered a touch too long while Suzette performed introductions. Much to her relief, after he added his name with a flourish, additional gentlemen began clamoring for her attention, which gave her a credible reason to put some distance between herself and a man who seemed a little too enthusiastic about becoming better acquainted with her.

Additional introductions commenced with the gentlemen Adelaide was not familiar with, performed by a variety of society matrons who were smiling at her in a friendly fashion, as if they hadn't recently been considering giving her the cut direct.

To make the situation even odder, she was also approached by gentlemen she'd known for years, who took to showering compliments on her as they added their names to her dance card. Before she knew it, every spot was filled, and she then found herself in the curious position of being left to deal with disappointed gentlemen who'd not been quick enough to secure a dance with her that evening.

"Do promise you'll be at home for calls tomorrow," Thomas Hassel said as he bent over her hand, kissed her fingers, then gave them a squeeze.

Her first impulse was to say she was promised elsewhere during calling hours, but before she could get that excuse out of her mouth, she spotted her mother standing a few feet away, beaming in clear delight. Adelaide retrieved her hand from Thomas, earning a sigh from him in return. Pressing lips that wanted to curve into a grin over the ridiculousness of finding a gentleman who'd been avoiding her for years now fawning over her, she gave a brief inclination of her head. "I will indeed be home tomorrow to receive callers."

"Excellent," Thomas said as Mr. Muskel announced one of the special quadrilles was about to begin.

Taking a place beside guests now assembling on the edge of the ballroom floor to watch the eight dancers who'd been chosen by Ward McAllister to perform a Parisian quadrille, Adelaide soon found herself in the company of young ladies destined to become the diamonds of the Season. Miss Jennie Gibson, the lady Aunt Petunia had set her eye on for Charles, took the spot directly beside her.

Additional introductions, along with the expected pleasantries, were exchanged before Adelaide found herself the recipient of invitations to tea, shopping, and sleigh rides in Central Park, if the snow predicted for later in the week materialized, as well as invitations to join some of the ladies in their families' boxes at the Metropolitan Opera House.

In all honesty, it was a little overwhelming as well as disconcerting, because she'd been labeled a wallflower, and a peculiar one at that, from the moment she'd entered society. Now, however, and simply because Gideon had settled his attention on her and Camilla had been telling everyone she was delightfully original, she found herself in high demand. Although given Suzette's subtle snideness, it did seem as if not everyone was keen to embrace her newfound notoriety.

To her relief, as soon as the orchestra began playing, everyone turned to watch the quadrille, which gave her a brief reprieve from far too much attention. As the dancers swept around the floor with intricate steps that had been practiced to perfection, Adelaide's gaze drifted around the room, settling on two young ladies who were standing off by themselves against the opposite wall, positioned between two decorative ferns, as if they'd chosen the spot to afford them a small bit of protection from the guests who weren't paying them any mind. The young ladies were smiling, but Adelaide knew the smiles weren't genuine, because she'd smiled those very same sort of smiles for years.

It wasn't difficult to conclude that the ladies were awkward sorts who'd never earn the titles of Incomparables or diamonds. One lady was tall and exceedingly slender, her shoulders hunched in a way that suggested she was attempting to make herself look shorter. The lady beside her was more voluptuous than what was considered fashionable and was wearing a gown that was supposed to camouflage her figure but was instead leaving her looking as if she were far heavier than she actually was.

Unsurprisingly, even though the Delmonico ballroom was crowded with guests, no one was standing close to the ladies, who were obviously trying to pretend nothing was amiss, and in that moment, as Adelaide's stomach knotted, the plan to make her fashionable seemed small, if not downright nonsensical.

She'd always prided herself on being different, on being content with who she was, and yet she'd agreed to let Camilla take her in hand if she could remain true to herself, but . . . she didn't feel like herself in the least.

Yes, the feeling of being included, while slightly overwhelming, was nice, but the reminder that young ladies were still being slighted and excluded from the sparkling crowd left a hole in Adelaide's heart. She'd told Camilla and Gideon at one point that she was wondering if God might have a plan in store for her—one in which, if society did the unexpected and embraced her, that circumstance could be used to give hope to other disadvantaged ladies living on the edge of the upper crust. She'd forgotten all about that plan and was now left feeling as if she were disappointing God and perhaps had even failed some type of test God had given her.

It wasn't a feeling she enjoyed, and she realized in that moment that nothing of true importance had changed in society. Yes, the social set evidently no longer believed she was a pariah, but the satisfaction she thought she'd feel over gaining acceptance into the upper echelons was nowhere to be found. Instead, she felt hollow inside because it wasn't much of a stretch to realize that another unfortunate lady would simply take her place as the oddity of society, which meant—

Before she could puzzle the thought out to satisfaction,

the quadrille drew to a close, applause resounding around the room, and then Mr. Dudley Paulding, still sporting his monocle, was standing before her, his hand extended. Taking it, she soon found herself on the ballroom floor again, where Dudley proceeded to extend her outrageous compliments. He also attempted to impress her by telling her all about his yacht, then invited her to attend a play with him at the theater the following weekend before he reluctantly returned her to where Mr. James Vector was waiting to claim her next dance.

"I must say it's been far too long since we've had an opportunity to converse," James said, swirling her past Gideon, who was standing on the sidelines and watching James with a stony expression, something James apparently noticed because he changed directions and led Adelaide to the other side of the room.

"We must make plans to go riding in Central Park, or better yet," James continued, "I'm escorting Miss Cynthia Barney into dinner this evening. You must join us."

The idea that had begun to take root during the quadrille left her shaking her head. "Forgive me, Mr. Vector, but I fear Mr. Abbott and I have already promised other friends we'll join them. Perhaps you and I can share a table at another event this Season."

A touch of disappointment flickered through James's eyes before he inclined his head. "I'll look forward to that."

Thankfully, after he led her through a few complicated steps, the music came to an end, which had James escorting her from the floor, then telling her to expect him to call on her within the foreseeable future before he handed her off to Mr. Marshall Wilson.

"Ah, Miss Duveen, it appears it's our turn to take to the floor at last," Marshall said as he took her arm and towed her toward the center of the room.

He didn't bother to present her with a bow as the music

began, instead twirling her around with quite a bit of gusto, which left her feeling decidedly off-balance, not that he appeared to notice as he began marching her across the floor in a manner that suggested he wasn't comfortable dancing, which left her feeling slightly more charitable toward him. She knew only too well how it felt to not be proficient with pursuits society deemed of the utmost importance.

As they plodded around the room, Marshall wasn't at a loss for words, complimenting her on her beauty, her tiara, her necklace, and the color of her gown, suggesting he wasn't knowledgeable with ladies' fashions in general when he remarked how odd he found it that most unmarried ladies were wearing pastels when darker colors would have been more favorable, something he thought she'd obviously realized, given the deep hue of her gown. After the compliments, he then launched into asking her questions about her Knickerbocker background and if she'd seen the large home being built on Fifth Avenue that sported numerous turrets—one that, of course, belonged to him.

By the time their dance ended, she wasn't feeling nearly as charitable toward him, because the longer he talked, the clearer it became that Marshall was a man possessed of an enormous ego, and someone who didn't hold a candle to Gideon, who never bragged about his accomplishments, his wealth, his yacht, or his lofty place within society.

"Ready for dinner?" Gideon asked, materializing beside her and sending Marshall a pointed look when the man didn't immediately release his hold on Adelaide's arm.

To Adelaide's concern, the pointed look seemed to be responsible for Marshall tightening his grip on her until Camilla glided up to join them, smiling a dazzling smile at Marshall before she nodded to Gideon.

"Would you perform an introduction, Gideon?"

"I'm Mr. Marshall Wilson," Marshall said before Gideon could comply, dropping his hold on Adelaide as he took Camilla's hand

and raised it to his lips. "And you are, of course, the incomparable Miss Camilla Pierpont. I've been longing to make your acquaintance."

Camilla's smile dimmed. "It's a pleasure to meet you, Mr. Wilson. I believe everyone is making their way into the dining room. I assume you've claimed a young lady to dine with this evening?"

"Miss Jennie Gibson, to be exact." Marshall smiled and kissed Camilla's hand again. "May I dare hope you and your dinner companion will join us at our table?"

When Camilla faltered for the briefest of seconds, Adelaide cleared her throat. "Miss Pierpont is joining my table, Mr. Wilson. But now, if you'll excuse us, I believe that was the second dinner bell, so we should find our seats."

After sending her a look of what almost seemed to be annoyance, Marshall inclined his head and strode away, leaving Camilla frowning after him. "I may need to have a word with Ward McAllister because I'm not certain the parvenus he's invited this evening are gentlemen any mother would want their daughters forming an alliance with."

"I can't argue with that," Gideon returned, his gaze remaining on Marshall as the man plowed his way through the crowd. "Marshall, from what I've observed, has made it a point to only seek out introductions to ladies of fortune, and . . ." He turned and caught Adelaide's eye. "I don't know if you noticed this, but Dudley Paulding was actually leering at your sapphires through a monocle earlier."

"I suppose that's better than him leering at me," Adelaide muttered before she frowned. "But given that Marshall and Dudley seem to be singling out ladies of fortune, do you suppose either of them might not be in possession of the wealth they claim to hold?"

"Perhaps," Gideon admitted as the chime of another bell rang out. He extended his arm to Adelaide and then offered his other arm to Camilla when she admitted she'd not gotten around to agreeing to dine with anyone. "You'll, of course, dine with us."

"I would be delighted," Camilla said before they strolled out of the ballroom, down a hallway past gilded sconces dancing with gas flames, and into the dining room.

Adelaide took a second to appreciate the sight of tables draped in white linen, complete with chairs covered in white-satin slipcovers. Fine bone china graced the tables, while crystal goblets sparkled under the light of chandeliers, and hothouse flowers perfumed the air. An entire brigade of servers stood with their backs against the wall, their livery impeccable as they waited to serve a meal that would undoubtedly be at least twelve courses.

"Where and with whom will we be dining?" Camilla asked, inclining her head time and again to numerous guests who were gesturing for her to join them.

Adelaide nodded to a table situated at the far end of the room where Leopold, Vernon, and Edna were getting them-selves settled. "I thought we'd sit with them, but if the two of you will excuse me for a moment? There are a few other guests I'd like to invite to dine with us as well."

To her surprise, instead of arguing against her unlikely choice of dinner partners or against the notion she wanted to sit at a table that was meant for less-than-sparkling guests, Camilla gave Adelaide's arm a pat. "Go round up those other guests. Gideon and I will meet you at the table."

After sending her a warm smile that left her heart beating a rapid tattoo, Gideon headed with Camilla across the room as Adelaide turned, craned her neck, and set her sights on Charles, who was speaking with Lucille Codman, his first dance partner of the evening. As luck would have it, they were standing not far from the two awkward young ladies Adelaide had noticed earlier.

She was beside her cousin a blink of an eye later. "Coming?" she asked, earning a frown from Charles in return.

"Coming where?"

"To our table, of course." She turned to Lucille. "I hope Charles secured your company for dinner, and . . ." She turned to the two ladies who were pretending they weren't listening in on her conversation. She dipped into a curtsy. "Forgive me if this comes across as too forward, but I'm Miss Adelaide Duveen, and I'd like to invite the two of you to join our table as well."

Both ladies' eyes widened before one of them dipped into a curtsy. "I'm Miss Dorothy Mann, and this is Miss Marigold Welding, but wouldn't including us leave your table with an odd number of ladies compared to gentlemen?"

Adelaide smiled. "The gentlemen will certainly be outnumbered, but I imagine they'll enjoy that, don't you?"

Without bothering to wait for Dorothy or Marigold to accept her invitation, Adelaide moved next to them, linked her arms through theirs, then tugged the ladies into motion, once again earning more than her share of speculative glances from other guests, something she responded to with smiles as she strolled forward. Gideon immediately rose to his feet when she reached the table.

"I've brought new friends," she announced as Leopold and Vernon rose to their feet as well. After performing introductions, Leopold and Vernon hurried to get Marigold and Dorothy settled as Charles held out a chair for Lucille before taking a seat beside her.

After Gideon helped her into her chair, he leaned close to her ear. "That was nicely done."

"Do you think it might ruin Camilla's plan?"

Gideon leaned closer still until his lips were almost brushing her ear, eliciting a shiver from her in return, one she hoped he didn't notice.

"I don't believe showing others compassion can ever ruin anything," he said quietly. "Frankly, your actions are admirable and prove you truly are an original, and you certainly should never attempt to change who you are at heart because you, my dear Adelaide, are perfect exactly the way you are."

Twenty-Two

Over the days that had passed since the Patriarch Ball, the thought had struck Adelaide more than once that her life was turning downright peculiar, that notion reinforced by the fact she was once again having her hand kissed by a gentleman, something that had rarely happened to her over the many Seasons she'd experienced before Camilla took her in hand.

"I look forward to seeing you later this evening at the opera, Miss Duveen," Marshall Wilson said, bending over her hand and giving her fingers a second kiss, which in Adelaide's opinion was taking matters a little too far. "I'm sure I would have enjoyed the evening more though if you'd accepted my invitation instead of Gideon Abbott's, a gentleman who seems to be monopolizing your evenings of late." He leaned closer. "Everyone is wondering if an announcement is going to be made in the foreseeable future, myself included."

Adelaide retrieved her hand. "What a thing to wonder."

"And what an evasive response," Marshall returned. "I suppose it's answer enough and means I won't bother inviting you to Delmonico's to enjoy an intimate dinner with me later this week."

"Dinner with Adelaide would be less than intimate, Mr. Wilson," Phyllis snapped, bustling up to join them in the Duveen receiving room and bristling with motherly animosity. "I would, of course, be in attendance, or her cousin, Charles Wetzel, would be if I was otherwise engaged, since it would break every rule of decorum for an unmarried young lady to attend an event without being properly chaperoned."

"I didn't know older ladies were expected to be accompanied everywhere by chaperones," Marshall said, settling a frown on Adelaide.

Adelaide's lips quirked. "Just as it seems you're unaware we older ladies aren't exactly keen to have our advanced age pointed out to us."

"It wasn't an insult," Marshall hurried to assure her. "Why, I've always enjoyed the company of mature ladies. They're far more interesting than girls fresh out of the schoolroom."

"And yet I've seen you in Miss Jennie Gibson's company of late as well as a few of the other debutantes."

Annoyance flashed through Marshall's eyes before he inclined his head. "It was a *pleasure* visiting with you today, Miss Duveen, but if you'll excuse me, I've promised to take Miss Constance Kip riding in the park this afternoon."

"Yet another debutante," Adelaide couldn't resist pointing out, which had the annoyance in Marshall's eyes increasing. He turned on his heel without another word and headed across the room, stopping to speak with Jennie Gibson and Edith Sherman, who'd made a point of calling at Adelaide's house every day since the Patriarch Ball, then sauntered through the door.

"I have no idea why Ward McAllister felt inclined to include the likes of Marshall Wilson in the Season this year," Phyllis grumbled. "No matter his extreme wealth, Marshall's boorish nature wouldn't be tolerated by most people if Ward hadn't taken him under his wing. Marshall lacks basic manners and

254

didn't bother to bid me good day, a slight if there ever was one. Quite honestly, if you'd not already put him in his place, I'd have delivered him quite a dressing-down."

After giving Adelaide's arm a squeeze, Phyllis hurried to join her sister, Petunia, who was keeping an eagle eye on Charles as he conversed with Camilla. Given the smile on Aunt Petunia's face, it wasn't much of a stretch to assume that she was convinced Charles was speaking with Camilla about taking him on in a matchmaking endeavor, even though there was no possibility of that since Camilla was determined to avoid the matchmaking industry forever.

It came as no surprise when Phyllis bent her head close to Aunt Petunia's and immediately began whispering up a storm, undoubtedly about Marshall Wilson.

Smiling as she wondered how badly her mother and aunt were disparaging Marshall's character, Adelaide squared her shoulders and drew in a breath, bracing herself for more hand kissing, most likely by Dudley Paulding next, who'd been sneaking peeks at her through his monocle for the past thirty minutes.

Before she could take more than a step forward, though, her attention was captured by the sight of a monster of a black cat by the name of El Cid, named after a Castilian knight in medieval Spain she'd read about in a fascinating history book, meandering across the room. His appearance, amusingly enough, caused more than a few guests to sidle out of his way as he lumbered over the Aubusson carpet, not stopping until he reached Camilla. He immediately stood on his hind legs, gave Camilla's skirt a swat, then released a roar that resounded around the room, which drew everyone's attention. After shooting Adelaide a resigned look, done so because El Cid had made it clear from the moment he'd caught sight of Camilla that he was enamored with her, Camilla scooped the cat into her arms, where it promptly began nuzzling her neck.

"Don't think this means I'm keeping him," Camilla mouthed to Adelaide before she returned her attention to Charles, who sent Adelaide a wink.

Swallowing a laugh, Adelaide took a moment to consider the room at large, finding herself still taken aback that Camilla's plan had been a rousing success, if one discounted the handful of society ladies who'd never cared for her anyways, such as Suzette. Those ladies were not clamoring to pay calls on her, but be that as it may, society in general seemed eager to spend time in her company. The fact that there was barely standing room in the receiving parlor today lent credence to that idea, suggesting Adelaide had now been elevated to the lofty status of being considered in high demand.

It was a curious circumstance to be sure, and one that had left her with the distinct impression that being in demand was far more work than she'd ever imagined, and . . . she was beginning to get the sneaking suspicion she wasn't meant to live her life as a member of the esteemed fashionable set.

Being besieged with callers, as well as having a schedule packed with society events, left her with little time to indulge in activities she actually enjoyed, such as reading, attending to her many cats, making plans for her new bookstore, or convincing Gideon she would be an asset to the accounting firm.

Nevertheless, since her mother was elated by her emergence into the highest echelons of the upper crust, it was obvious she was going to have to make the best of the situation. If nothing else, Gideon was still insisting on accompanying her to every evening event she attended, his insistence rather odd because other gentlemen were now stepping forward with offers to escort her, ones she'd been refusing because, in all honesty, she preferred spending her time with Gideon.

There was a part of her that knew she should discourage his singular attention because Camilla's plan had already achieved astounding success, which meant there was no reason for him to continue lavishing his time on her. However, the single time she'd broached the topic with him, he'd shrugged and told her that society was fickle, and he didn't want to take the chance they'd conclude he'd lost interest in her.

She hadn't put up an argument to that because she relished the time in his company and hadn't wanted to give him a reason to limit how often he accompanied her, even though she realized she was being a complete idiot for not suggesting he get on with his regularly scheduled life instead of escorting her to the opera, theater, or the many balls society held during the winter Season.

She knew spending so much time with him was setting herself up for a hefty dose of disappointment at some point, because even though society seemed keen to embrace her status as an original, she was still simply Adelaide and he was still Gideon—a far too handsome, charismatic, and captivating gentleman for someone like her.

"Would you look at that," Jennie Gibson exclaimed, drawing everyone's attention as she nodded toward the doorway. "Mr. Abbott has arrived, and it appears he's brought some adorable friends with him today."

Adelaide's gaze darted to the doorway, her pulse ratcheting up a notch when she caught sight of Gideon. The rate of her pulse increased a second later when Moe loped into the room behind him, Harvey peeking his head out of his custom saddlebag. It wasn't much of a surprise when the sight of Moe and Harvey drew more than a few oohs and aahs from the ladies in attendance.

Her knees, curiously enough, took that moment to go a little weak, undoubtedly done so because she knew Gideon had deliberately chosen a strategic moment to introduce Harvey to society, which would hopefully persuade all the society ladies who would find the sight of him riding on Moe oh so adorable to consider taking in a cat of their own.

Her gaze returned to Gideon, and in that moment, an undeniable truth struck from out of the blue, one that left her feeling as if the ground underneath her feet had shifted.

As that truth settled, perspiration suddenly beaded her forehead because . . . she'd obviously done the unthinkable and gone and allowed herself to fall ever so slightly, or perhaps more so, in love with the man.

Before she could do more than call herself every sort of ninny for allowing such a circumstance to transpire, especially when she'd lectured herself over and over again during the past few months about Gideon being the last gentleman on earth she could hold in deep affection, he glanced around the room, caught her eye, and after telling Moe to sit and stay, began strolling her way.

"You brought Harvey," she said in an annoyingly breathless voice, one she didn't seem to have any control over, and one that left Gideon frowning as he took hold of her hand and kissed it.

"Are you coming down with a cold?" he asked.

She waved that aside. "I fear I'm merely losing my voice since I've been conversing with people almost nonstop this week."

"Perhaps you should take a break from doing that."

"I would be more than happy to do exactly that, although Camilla seems to think I need a good month of being thought of as in high demand before she'll be completely convinced we're out of the woods. Besides that, my mother is in her element." She nodded to Phyllis, who'd abandoned her sister to hurry up to Moe, giving the dog a pat before she retrieved Harvey from the saddlebag. She then snuggled Harvey close for a moment before handing him off to Jennie Gibson, who gave Harvey a kiss on the nose and refused to hand him over to Edith Sherman, who'd been holding out her hands.

"Phyllis is definitely relishing having a receiving room full of people," Gideon said.

"She's turned downright smug because even my sisters, who were immediately considered fashionable when they made their debuts, never filled up the house quite like this."

Gideon frowned. "I haven't been given the privilege of meeting your sisters yet."

"That's because they're spending the winter in Florida. Mother told them to stay put after society was set to ostracize me, but she's been considering telling them they're welcome to return home now instead of remaining in Florida for the rest of the winter."

"Because?"

Adelaide tilted her head. "I believe Mother doesn't think my sisters will believe her if she tells them I've become fashionable and wants them to see what she views as a Duveen triumph with their own eyes." She blew out a breath. "And even though I'm thrilled that Mother's enjoying this curious turn of events, to tell you the truth, I'm not sure what to make of all this attention."

Gideon's gaze sharpened on her. "Why do I get the distinct impression you're not enjoying your moment in the spotlight?"

"Is it that obvious?"

"To me it is."

She dredged up a smile. "Do I look like I'm enjoying myself now?"

He laughed. "You look more along the lines of having eaten something disagreeable."

"Perhaps I should have availed myself of the talented Mr. Gimble. Evidently I would have benefited from a few acting lessons."

Gideon tucked her hand into the crook of his arm and steered her through the room, inclining his head to numerous guests before he drew her to a stop beside the buffet table. After accepting a cup of coffee and a plate of delicacies, he held the plate out to Adelaide, waited until she took a cookie, then led her over to the fireplace, where Mr. Harold Spencer immediately abandoned the chair he'd been settled in. Mr. Spencer then presented Adelaide with a bow, sent a curt nod to Gideon, then walked away, joining a group of gentlemen callers who immediately began sending annoyed glances in Gideon's direction, ones he ignored.

Settling into the chair Harold had just vacated, she looked up and found Gideon considering her closely. "What?" she asked.

"I find myself unable to help but wonder what you'd rather be doing other than all the frivolities of the Season that have opened up for you of late."

"Any number of things spring to mind," she didn't hesitate to say. "Reading at my leisure would be toward the top of my list, something I've not had time to indulge in lately, not when Camilla insists I'm seen out and about every day." She sighed. "Do you know we spent three hours yesterday traipsing around the Ladies' Mile?"

"A trial if there ever was one."

"There was shopping involved."

"Torture at its finest."

She felt her lips twitch. "Well, quite, but besides having to suffer through the horror of shopping, Camilla only allotted me fifteen minutes to wander around a bookstore before she hauled me off to have tea at Rutherford & Company, where we were immediately inundated with requests to join numerous ladies."

"You now own a bookstore. I wouldn't imagine having your time cut short in another one was overly traumatic."

"As a bibliophile, being towed from a place where massive amounts of books are sold is always traumatic. And, to add insult to injury, what I thought would be a simple cup of tea turned into an entire afternoon fiasco because Camilla wanted to enjoy a proper tea, complete with scones, biscuits, and clotted cream. Add in the disturbing notion that our tea was accompanied by over two hours of listening to the latest *on dit* and talk of fashion from all the ladies gathered in the tearoom, well, disgruntled doesn't do justice to the mood I returned home in."

"You seemed in fine spirits at the theater last night."

"I'm apparently a more proficient actress than I've realized," Adelaide said, unwilling to admit that her mood had significantly improved the moment Gideon had arrived at her house to escort her and her mother out and about the previous evening.

Gideon smiled. "Or perhaps you simply enjoyed our conversation more since it didn't revolve around fashion."

She returned the smile. "An excellent point, because discussing different cipher codes was certainly more stimulating than the advantages of wearing jewel tones. Apparently that has been a topic of interest because of my new wardrobe. Do you know that one of the greatest advantages to wearing deeper hues, at least according to Jennie Gibson, who's evidently been pestering her mother to purchase darker colors to add to her wardrobe this Season, is the ability to disguise any unwanted stains, such as tea or, heaven forbid, droplets of rain?"

"I did *not* know that, but Jennie doesn't strike me as a lady who would experience spilled tea often."

"I'm sure she's not, but she's determined to acquire what society now believes is an avant-garde color scheme, even though there are some society mothers who are resistant to such a drastic change for their impressionable daughters."

Gideon tilted his head. "Don't you take any satisfaction from the fact that ladies are now clamoring to emulate your new style?"

"I'd rather find satisfaction from something less frivolous."

"Such as?"

"Deciphering additional codes springs to mind."

He laughed. "Why am I not surprised, but will it put you in a more affable frame of mind if I promise to seek your council if the accounting firm has another opportunity to decipher a code?"

It was difficult to resist a snort. "While I would normally be thrilled at the thought of you seeking my counsel, I find myself curious as to exactly how many ciphers the firm has ever handled."

It was rather telling when Gideon winced. "Uh, only one."

"I thought so, which means you'll likely never have a reason to make use of my assistance again."

Gideon leaned closer. "I hope you know I'm not deliberately trying to disappoint you, nor have I been refusing to bring you into the firm because I question your abilities. I'm simply determined to keep you safe."

Adelaide's brows drew together. "But I wouldn't expect you to include me in covert operations. I was thinking more along the lines of acting as an investigator of sorts, slogging through files, searching for clues in the safety of your office, which, if you've forgotten, is on Broadway, not down in the Battery. I highly doubt anyone of the criminal persuasion would burst in there and threaten me."

"A somewhat valid point."

"It's more than somewhat and you know it," Adelaide said. "You also know that your associates don't appreciate the mundaneness of research and looking through case files. I, on the other hand, would relish that opportunity. It would give me that purpose that's glaringly absent from my life right now."

"And to that I must disagree because I would think you've realized over the past few days that you have a purpose, and a noble one at that." Gideon nodded to Dorothy Mann, who was speaking with Camilla, who'd turned El Cid over to Dorothy, even though the cat was now gazing longingly back at Camilla, obviously trying to beseech her to hold him again. "You made a point of including Dorothy, along with Marigold Welding and Lucille Codman, at our table during the Patriarch Ball. Because of that, they now seem to have the confidence needed to pay calls, something I know Dorothy wasn't comfortable doing because she told me so last night at the theater." He settled a warm smile on her. "I don't know of any other lady who would have extended such a gesture, but you didn't hesitate to act, which speaks to your inherent character, and highly at that. You must know, given your recently elevated status within society, that you can have a large role with helping ladies not possessed of sparkling labels find their place in the world, and not one that keeps them invisible."

"It's not that I won't continue pulling wallflowers from their walls, but I've realized that I'm not meant to spend the entirety of my days immersed in society events. I need something more, something that will mentally challenge me."

"Won't the bookstore provide you with that?"

"To a certain extent, but I won't be opening that for a few months, not when I want to refurbish. Plus, I've struck a deal with Mother. She was adamantly opposed to me purchasing the store until I sent a telegram to my father, who's currently away on business. Father didn't hesitate to contact his bank, give his approval for me to remove money for the bookstore from my trust, and have his attorney begin proceedings to legally transfer the deed into my name."

Gideon frowned. "Your father doesn't mind his daughter launching herself into trade?"

"Not when he knows I have a passion for books. However, he insisted I agree to Mother's terms, which are that I'll hire a manager and a full staff. That means my presence won't be needed every hour of the day, so I'll have time for other endeavors, preferably useful ones."

"Such as research?"

"Exactly, which, if I haven't mentioned this already, I'm very proficient with. And not that this is a selling point, mind you, but taking on a research position at the accounting firm would allow me the opportunity to not simply read about all the fabulous adventures in my beloved spy novels, but to experience them in person for a change."

Gideon smiled. "Your enthusiasm for the accounting firm is somewhat difficult to resist."

She let her shoulders sag the tiniest bit. "But you're going to resist, aren't you?"

To her surprise, instead of immediately agreeing to that, Gideon considered her for a long moment before his brows drew together. "I'm not sure."

She blinked. "You're not?"

"No."

"Why not?"

"Because an idea just sprang to mind that may work to appease your longing for a mental challenge, although I have to state here and now that what I'm about to offer is against my better judgment. . . . What would you think about sorting through all of those case files you mentioned and perhaps setting up a more organized filing system for us?"

Her mouth dropped open. "You're offering me a job?"

"I'm considering it, but it would be on a trial basis, and you won't be working from the accounting office, even if it is on Broadway. I'll have the files sent to you here, where you can peruse and organize to your heart's content."

"That seems like it might be a bit of a bother for you."

"Bother or not, that's the only option I'm willing to consider." He settled a stern eye on her. "There will be no wheedling on your part to get you into the office instead of your house, nor any trying to convince me to let you go out into the field. This is strictly a desk job, and one you'll do in the safety of your own home, and I won't change my mind about that."

Twenty-Three

⌘

"I've clearly taken leave of my senses," Gideon muttered to Charles as he watched Adelaide flitter about the room, bidding her guests good-bye, the genuine smile on her face suggesting she was delighted by his invitation to slog through old files on behalf of the accounting firm—an offer that, frankly, had taken him just as much by surprise as it had her.

"I think your senses are fine," Charles countered. "It's more to do with you being incapable of disappointing my cousin."

"I suppose there is that."

"On the bright side," Charles began with a grin, "at least you only offered her a temporary position."

Gideon permitted himself the luxury of a snort. "As if I'm going to be able to rescind my temporary offer. That would deliver more than a disappointing blow to Adelaide."

"Which is rather telling."

"What's telling?" Camilla asked, strolling up to join them, El Cid having been returned to her arms.

"Gideon's having second thoughts about telling Adelaide she can do some filing and research work for the accounting firm, if only on a temporary basis."

Camilla's gaze sharpened on him. "You invited Adelaide into the firm?"

"It was completely unintentional, but she was feeling a little overwhelmed by all the attention she's receiving these days. I apparently felt compelled to cheer her up, and the next thing I knew, I asked her if she'd like to peruse old files and organize them for the firm."

"I suppose I'm not actually surprised you caved into Adelaide's desire to be involved with your organization, even if it sounds as if you've offered her a menial position," Camilla said, giving El Cid a pat and earning a rumble in return. "You do seem susceptible to her whims—a result, no doubt, of that spark I detected between the two of you weeks ago."

"What is it with you and this sparking business?" was all Gideon could think to respond. "You know I'm not a man prone to nonsense like that."

She sent him an overly sweet smile. "And you can keep telling yourself that, dear Gideon, but it won't make those sparks go away." She leaned closer, stilling when El Cid let out a roar, quite as if he was worried she was going to relinquish him to Gideon. She gave him another pat. "Behave, El Cid. Gideon's a friend, but where was I?"

"Sparks," Charles supplied.

"Oh, yes, quite right." She shot a glance to Adelaide, who was now in the process of handing Lucille Codman a white cat that had brilliant blue eyes, then returned her attention to Gideon. "It's not a one-sided case of sparks, if that has you worried."

His collar suddenly felt a smidgen too tight. "I never claimed to be worried, but . . . how do you know that?"

"I'm a matchmaker, or rather, a retired matchmaker. I *know* things."

"What do you know about Adelaide and sparks?"

She stepped closer, then took a rapid step backward when

El Cid gave a swipe of his paw in Gideon's direction. "Some discoveries are best left for a person to uncover on their own."

"That's less than helpful, and as one of my oldest friends, you should be more accommodating."

"It's very annoying when you pull out the friend card to get your way," Camilla muttered. "But, fine, in the spirit of our friendship, I'll say this—it's telling that Adelaide is refusing all offers she's received today to venture out with other gentlemen, using the excuse she's promised her time to you."

"She's promised her time to me because you insisted we're seen everywhere together."

Camilla gave an airy wave of her hand. "Please, if I've learned anything about Adelaide, it's that she rarely does what's expected of her. I imagine she agreed to go to Central Park with you today after calling hours because that's what she wanted to do, disappointing many a gentleman in the process."

Before Gideon could wrap his mind around that, El Cid yawned, showing massive teeth in the process and earning an indulgent smile from Camilla.

"I think the poor dear is sleepy, so I'll bid you a good afternoon and catch up with the two of you later at the Metropolitan Opera House."

Gideon's brows drew together. "What does El Cid being sleepy have to do with you?"

A hint of pink tinged Camilla's cheeks. "I may have told Adelaide I was going to take him home with me today."

"Ah, she wore you down, did she?"

"No, because it's only temporary," Camilla argued. "I couldn't very well have not taken El Cid home after Edith Sherman seemed interested in Juliet, a delightful ball of fluff if there ever was one. When Edith began questioning Adelaide about the care of cats, our darling Adelaide sent me an expectant look, which then had me proclaiming to all the ladies in my near vicinity that cats were no trouble at all, which was why I was taking El Cid with me because I couldn't bear the thought of leaving him behind."

"Adelaide's expectant looks are difficult to ignore."

"Yes, well, as I said, El Cid is only going to be a temporary guest in my house. Poor Gladys will probably be beside herself the moment Cid's paws touch the marble floor."

"Or he'll win Gladys over like Harvey did with Moe," Gideon countered. "If that happens, I'll be happy to have our engineer make another saddlebag."

Camilla gave El Cid a scratch behind the ears. "It would be better to have a bag made for El Cid because he probably outweighs poor Gladys, but allow me to get out of here before Adelaide decides El Cid needs a cat companion and I'm taking two cats home with me instead of one." With that, Camilla sent him a cheeky grin, did the same with Charles, then headed for the door, her pace increasing when she shot a glance to Adelaide, who was now holding a tabby cat and looking around the room.

After Charles excused himself, saying he needed to check on his mother, Gideon moved over to a floor-to-ceiling window and took a moment to enjoy the sight of rapidly falling snow, trying to distract himself from the sparking business. It was a difficult feat to accomplish because the idea of Adelaide perhaps feeling sparks between them was one that left him with the distinct urge to abandon decorum, stride to her side, remove the tabby cat from her arms, and . . . kiss her.

It was an unusual urge to have at this particular moment, but it was one that had undoubtedly come about due to Camilla's broaching the idea that he felt a spark toward Adelaide. In all honesty, he couldn't completely refute that because he did feel something between them, although it was more powerful than a spark, and had prompted thoughts of kissing her on more than one occasion.

"I've said my good-byes to most of the guests, but I still need to get Dudley Paulding on his way before we can head for Central Park. He seems oblivious to the fact that calling hours have come to an end," Adelaide said, materializing next to Gideon and pulling him from his thoughts, although considering his gaze immediately went to her lips, it was obvious that kissing was still foremost in his mind.

"Frankly," she continued, "I'm reluctant to approach him because he's been saying the oddest things to me."

All thoughts of kissing disappeared in a flash. "What *kinds* of things?"

"Not those kinds of things," she said with a roll of her eyes. "He's not completely inappropriate. However, today he mentioned he was disappointed I wasn't wearing that sapphire necklace I wore to the ball. He apparently has little knowledge about the rules of society, such as ladies don't wear gems during the day. I tried to tell him that as gently as I could, but instead of dropping the subject, he had the audacity to suggest he should send me a lovely ruby necklace that's been gathering dust in his safe after I told him I don't own any rubies."

A sliver of temper stole over him. "Did he now?"

"I'm afraid so." Adelaide shook her head. "I think he's determined to marry into society, and not that I know this for certain, but he may have his eye on me."

"Would you like me to discourage him?"

"I'm hoping having you escort me over to speak with him will be enough, although . . ." She tilted her head. "How would you go about discouraging him?"

"Pistols at dawn springs to mind."

Adelaide laughed, the sound lessening some of the temper that was flowing freely through him. "Pistols seem a little excessive. Perhaps you should merely take him by the arm and steer him for the door, which will then result with him standing on the sidewalk, wondering how that came to be."

"That won't be nearly as amusing as meeting him at dawn."

"Well, quite, but simply because Dudley's annoying doesn't mean he needs to suffer a bullet." With that, and with eyes now twinkling, Adelaide settled the tabby into the crook of her right arm, then took hold of his arm with her other hand, and together they walked across a nearly empty parlor to join Dudley, who was contemplating one of the many paintings gracing the parlor, peering at the brushstrokes through his ever-present monocle.

"Do you enjoy works of art, Mr. Paulding?" Adelaide asked.

Dudley immediately popped the monocle from his eye and left it dangling from a gold chain down the front of his jacket as he turned, the smile on his face dimming significantly when he caught sight of Gideon.

"Indeed I do, Miss Duveen," Dudley returned. "And if I haven't mentioned this, I'm currently in the process of working with an architect to build a residence on Fifth Avenue—close to the Vanderbilts, at that. I've decided to include a room dedicated to paintings, sculptures, and the like, so I have taken to inquiring about artists whose work is hanging in all the best houses." He inclined his head to Adelaide. "Your house is obviously considered one of those, hence my interest."

"The Duveen house does possess an impressive art collection," Gideon began, catching Dudley's eye. "But I'm afraid you won't have time to look over additional pieces today because calling hours have drawn to a close."

Dudley's lips thinned before he settled a smile on Adelaide. "Then I'll be certain to return tomorrow. May I dare hope you'll give me a personal tour of this impressive residence, where we can then discuss your art collection at length?"

The distinct desire to plant his fist in Dudley's face stole over Gideon, but before he could do more than scowl at the man, Adelaide shook her head.

"I'm afraid I won't be at home to receive callers tomorrow. I have a pressing engagement to attend to, and speaking of engagements, I must apologize because I have committed plans for the rest of the day, which means I need to bid you a good afternoon."

Dudley's smile faltered for the briefest of seconds before he hitched it back into place. "I certainly don't want to keep you, although I hope you'll spare me a few additional minutes to meet some of your cats." He leaned forward, his eyes on the tabby nestled against Adelaide's side. "I've recently spotted a few mice in my house, so a cat, which I also understand you seem to collect, may be exactly what I need to route the rodents from my house. I imagine that beast in your arms would probably suffice."

Annoyance flashed through Adelaide's eyes, and if Gideon wasn't convinced Dudley was showing interest in Adelaide's cats because of some odd manner of courting ritual, he might have felt a small sliver of sympathy for the man, given the wrath he was soon to experience.

"I don't believe Finnegan is the right, ah, *beast* for you," Adelaide returned in a voice that was downright frigid. "He's somewhat temperamental and needs affection on a regular basis."

"Nonsense," Dudley countered, brushing aside Adelaide's concerns with a flick of his hand. "Finnegan will be perfect for me because I have scads of affection to give an animal." With that, Dudley reached for the cat, earning a hiss from Finnegan in return, which Dudley ignored as he stepped closer, his proximity causing the cat to take a swipe at him with his claws exposed, which left Dudley stumbling backward, his monocle bouncing up and down against his jacket.

A yowl of displeasure resounded around the room a second later as Finnegan jumped to the ground, sent Dudley another hiss, gave a twitch of his tail, then shot out of the room.

"What a nasty cat you have there, Miss Duveen," Dudley said, lifting his arm as his eyes narrowed on the sleeve of his jacket. "It tore a hole in the fabric."

Adelaide's lips thinned. "Finnegan is usually pleasant to everyone, but I will apologize for the damage done to your jacket. I'll be happy to replace it for you."

"I suppose that's the least you can do since your cat just tried to maul me," Dudley muttered. "I'll send you the name and direction of my tailor at my earliest convenience. But now, if you'll excuse me, I believe it best for me to take my leave before your feline tries to have another go at me." After sending Adelaide a hint of a bow, Dudley didn't bother to address Gideon as he practically sprinted out of the room, checking to the left and to the right as he hurried away, obviously concerned that Finnegan might have decided to lie in wait and attack him again.

"What an unlikeable sort," Adelaide said after Dudley disappeared. "And if you ask me, there's something shifty about him because Finnegan rarely takes an immediate dislike to anyone."

"Perhaps Finnegan senses something about him that's troubling, which suggests I should make immediate plans to have the firm look into his background, especially since Dudley seems overly interested in spending time in your company."

Adelaide's cheeks, curiously enough, began blooming with color even as her lips began to curve, which caused her dimple to pop out, but before he could truly appreciate a dimple that was becoming more fascinating to him with each passing day, she ducked her head, muttered something about needing to change, and bolted out of the room.

Unable to help but wonder what had been responsible for her abrupt departure, Gideon decided to seek out Charles to discuss the matter, extracting him from Phyllis and Petunia, who were in the process of discussing how well calling hours were going for Adelaide.

After taking a moment to fetch Moe and Harvey, both of whom had been snoozing in front of the fireplace, he got Harvey settled in the saddlebag before he and Charles quit the room and moved down the hallway.

Before he had an opportunity to broach Adelaide's odd behavior, though, Charles, who'd been pressed into service once again as Adelaide's chaperone for the afternoon, nodded to a window that flanked the front door.

"Not sure this is going to be the most opportune day for strolling around Central Park," Charles said. "If you've neglected to notice, snow's coming down in earnest."

"A circumstance Adelaide's probably thrilled about because she told me she adores the snow."

Charles rolled his eyes. "And I adore staying indoors by a roaring fireplace, but since I doubt you're going to be as solicitous to my longing for creature comforts as you are to Adelaide's desire to see all of us freeze to death, know that I'll only agree to walk around Central Park for an hour—no longer, and that's nonnegotiable."

"At least the inclement weather should deter anyone from trying to accost Adelaide, which means you'll only have to assume the role of chaperone this afternoon instead of bodyguard."

"As if my cousin needs extra protection when you're accompanying her."

"Adelaide can't have enough protection, even if I'm perfectly capable of watching out for her."

Charles regarded him for a long moment, a small smile playing around the corners of his lips, but before he had an opportunity to say anything else, Adelaide hurried down the staircase, bundled up as if she were expecting a blizzard.

"I believe she may have her heart set on spending more than an hour at the park," Gideon said, earning a grunt from Charles. After giving Charles a commiserating clap on the back, Gideon shrugged into his overcoat the butler handed him before he strode to meet Adelaide at the bottom of the stairs. He then offered her his arm, which she immediately took with a smile, a circumstance that had him losing his train of thought when her dimple showed up again.

Thankfully, Adelaide didn't seem to expect anything in the way of logical conversation as she tugged him through the front door, Charles following a step behind. They made it down slightly icy steps and to the sidewalk before Gideon caught sight of a carriage parked in front of Adelaide's house. He slowed to a stop, resisting a groan when he realized the carriage belonged to none other than Sophia Campanini, which, unfortunately, meant trouble had come to call.

Twenty-Four

━━━━━❧━━━━━

Gideon blew out a breath, the cold creating little puffs of fog in front of his face, something he ignored because he had more important matters to concern himself with, such as why Sophia was lying in wait for him. Whatever the reason, though, given Sophia's demanding nature and belief her every whim needed to be appeased, he had a feeling his trip to the park was about to be delayed.

"Gideon, darling," Sophia called, leaning out of the carriage door that the groomsman had opened. "I hope you don't mind, but Roland Kelly told me where to find you."

"Is that Sophia Campanini?" Adelaide asked, squinting against the snow that was swirling around them.

"I'm afraid so."

"She's wearing her platinum wig."

"That does appear to be the case."

"Mother believes I would look very fetching as a blond."

Gideon swallowed a laugh. "Is that your way of suggesting I get Sophia on her way before your mother has an opportunity to catch sight of Sophia in all her blond glory?"

"If it wouldn't be too much of a bother."

275

"No bother at all," Gideon said, handing Moe's leash to Charles. "I'll be right back, and before you ask, it's not that I don't care to introduce the two of you to Sophia, but she's notorious for turning into the biggest flirt when gentlemen are in her vicinity, especially gentlemen involved with the Four Hundred."

Before Charles could do more than blink, Adelaide crossed her arms over her chest. "Does that mean we should be prepared to watch her flirt with you?"

A distinct trace of something that almost felt like satisfaction flowed through him, no doubt a direct result of Adelaide's tone, which could certainly be described as annoyed, which suggested . . .

"Gideon! I'm waiting," Sophia yelled, interrupting his train of thought.

"I'll be right back," he said, striding into motion and reaching Sophia's carriage a few seconds later.

Sophia immediately held out her hand, a coquettish smile already gracing her face. After placing the expected kiss on her gloved fingers, he released her hand and caught her eye. "You needed a word?"

Sophia batted her lashes. "Indeed, but it's more along the lines of a lengthy chat, so do join me for a drive so we'll be able to speak at our leisure."

"I'm afraid that won't be possible since my friends are waiting for me to walk with them to Central Park."

"In this weather?"

"Miss Duveen, a dear friend of mine, enjoys the snow."

Sophia's gaze immediately shot to where Adelaide and Charles were standing, her smile fading as she considered Adelaide for a long moment.

"How dear a friend is she?" she finally asked.

"Dear enough."

Sophia pursed her lips before she gave a languid wave of her hand toward Adelaide. "I now find myself intrigued by this *dear* Miss Duveen. I must insist she join us for a ride about the city."

"Joining you for a ride would defeat the purpose of taking a walk."

Sophia began to pout. "Don't be like that, Gideon. It took me a good hour to track you down, and I have limited time at my disposal today because I have a performance later. I know you wouldn't want to disappoint me by not accommodating my itsy-bitsy little request of your attention right now." She let out a breathy sigh. "It's been forever since we've spoken, and I've been dying for an update on that deceitful chit I hired out of the goodness of my heart when she came to me with no dressing experience, spouting a sorry tale of woe about her desperate financial circumstances."

"You know you hired Lottie McBriar because you frequently have members of your staff abandon you with no notice, Lottie being no exception to that. As for it being forever since we've spoken, I've attempted to schedule a meeting with you for weeks, but you've been avoiding me."

Sophia raised a hand to her chest. "Avoid you? I've been doing no such thing. I'm a very busy lady. With that said, I have time now to devote undivided attention to you, just as soon as you either ask your friends to join us or get rid of them."

Gideon refused a sigh. "I see you're in an unreasonable frame of mind today, but since Miss Duveen, along with her cousin, Charles Wetzel, are aware of my association with the firm, I'll ask them if they'd like to join us. However, if their answer is no, I won't be reneging on my commitment to walk with Miss Duveen, which means we'll have to find another time to speak."

"It would be an unusual event indeed if they'd pass up the opportunity to spend intimate time in my company," Sophia said, right before her eyes began to sparkle. "You mentioned Miss Duveen's cousin is a Mr. Charles Wetzel. Would that be the same Charles Wetzel who is not only an esteemed member of the Four Hundred but worth millions as well?"

"You will not set your sights on him," Gideon said firmly.

"Did I say I was going to?"

"Not out loud, but I'm definitely reconsidering asking them to join us."

The smile that immediately curved Sophia's lips was not an encouraging sign. "Then I'll simply invite them myself, which I'm sure they'll see as a great honor."

"You're trying my patience."

"It's one of the many talents I've cultivated over the years."

"I'm not certain that's something you should be proud of."

Sophia released a tinkle of laughter and held out her hand, clearly with the expectation he was going to assist her out of the carriage.

Instead of obliging her, he released a bit of a harrumph instead. "Will you at least attempt to behave if I ask Adelaide and Charles to accompany us for a short ride?"

"Behaving is seriously overrated."

"I'm going to pretend that was a yes, and now, if you'll excuse me, I need to speak with my friends."

Sophia's smile turned smug. "How very accommodating you always are of me."

"I'm not sure it's accommodation. More along the lines of resignation," he muttered before he turned and made his way down the sidewalk.

"You weren't jesting about her ability to flirt," Adelaide said once he stopped in front of her. "I was afraid I was going to have to intervene on your behalf, given that it appeared at one point she was considering throwing herself out of her carriage and straight into your arms."

His lips quirked. "How chivalrous of you, but I'm perfectly capable of sidestepping Sophia's advances, a talent that annoys her whenever I'm in her company."

"I'm sure it does. I wouldn't think Sophia Campanini is accustomed to being rejected." Adelaide's gaze returned to Sophia, who was still leaning halfway out of her carriage. "Perhaps that explains why she's lingering, or does she want you to join her and you're about to tell me our trip to the park is going to be delayed?"

"It truly is uncanny how accurate your deductions are at times. But while Sophia did suggest I delay my walk and abandon you, she's now changed her mind about that because she wants you and Charles to join us for a ride about the city."

Adelaide arched a brow. "Because?"

"I may have called you my dear friend, which apparently piqued her interest."

"Or infuriated her, since she's now undoubtedly concluded that we share some manner of romantic, er, involvement—not that you view me in a romantic light, of course, but she doesn't know that."

He felt an unusually strong inclination to contradict her about that.

"Gideon! It's not getting any warmer out here," Sophia yelled before he could get a single word of contradiction out of his mouth.

"She's a very demanding sort, isn't she?" Adelaide said before she lifted her chin. "However, having her shriek like a fishmonger is certain to attract my mother's attention since Sophia does have a voice that carries. I believe it'll be best all-around if we join her for that ride. Truth be told, I'm beyond curious to discover what she wants to have a word with you about. I'm hoping it has something to do with Frank Fitzsimmons. Perhaps he's reached out and proposed having another tête-à-tête with her."

Gideon took hold of Adelaide's arm, and with Charles walking on her other side, and Moe keeping pace with Charles, they began moving down the sidewalk. "From what I've learned about Frank over the past month, besides being adept at remaining out of sight, hence the reason I've yet to run him to ground, he's an incredibly savvy man who's got a reputation for knowing exactly how to keep his involvement in criminal endeavors sequestered. He won't attempt to personally meet with Sophia again because that would be too great of a risk. That is exactly why I assume he sent Lottie McBriar to take up a position with Sophia, probably to either steal whatever it is Frank was hired by someone to steal from her, or to at least extract information that he needed."

Adelaide came to an abrupt stop, wiping snow from her face. "Sophia's the client who asked you to locate Lottie?"

"She is."

Adelaide's eyes began to gleam. "I'm suddenly feeling far more enthusiastic about meeting this woman." With that, she surged into motion, tugging him along at what could almost be considered a trot.

She released her hold on his arm the second they reached Sophia and dipped into a curtsy. "Madame Campanini," she all but gushed. "How lovely to make your acquaintance. I'm Miss Adelaide Duveen, and may I simply say that I am one of your greatest admirers?"

As Sophia began to preen before pressing Adelaide on why she was such an admirer, Charles moved close to Gideon and lowered his voice. "I thought you were determined to keep Adelaide far removed from any fieldwork."

"I am."

"You're failing miserably with that then, because Adelaide isn't the type to fawn over anyone. That she's doing so now suggests she's about to launch into an attempt to extract any information she can about Lottie."

"I'm afraid you may be right."

"Indeed. So why did you ask us to join you if you knew Sophia wanted to discuss Lottie in the first place?"

Gideon rubbed a hand over his face. "Adelaide asked me to get Sophia on her way as quickly as possible, what with the wig business and all, and—"

"You couldn't refuse her request," Charles finished for him as Sophia swung her attention to them, or rather Charles, beaming a smile at the man as she fluttered her lashes.

"You must be Mr. Charles Wetzel, darling Adelaide's cousin." Sophia thrust her hand Charles's way, waiting until after he'd kissed it before she blew out a breathy sigh. "How charming you are, Mr. Wetzel, or should I call you Charles?"

When Charles merely stared at the woman as if he had no idea how to respond to that, Adelaide edged closer to Sophia and smiled, although the smile didn't reach her eyes—not that Sophia noticed. "I fear my dear cousin has found himself tongue-tied in your presence, Madame Campanini, and who can blame him? You are, after all, the most renowned opera singer in the country, if not the world. But perhaps we should continue discussing that from the comfort of your carriage? It's beginning to snow harder, and I would hate your lovely voice to suffer any damage from the cold."

Sophia shot a look to Gideon. "I now understand exactly why she's your *dear* friend." With that, she retreated into the carriage, but not before telling her driver she wanted him to drive them around the city. A second later, she called for Adelaide to join her, and after sending him a grin, Adelaide climbed into the carriage, Charles following behind her.

Whistling for Moe to jump in after Charles, Gideon took a second to get Moe settled on the floor before he sat down beside Charles, looking up to find Sophia scowling at him.

"I didn't realize your mutt would be joining us," she said.

"I couldn't very well leave him or Harvey behind."

"Harvey?"

Gideon nodded to where Harvey was peeking out of his saddlebag. "My cat."

"I never took you for a cat person."

"I wasn't one until Adelaide convinced me, as well as a good portion of society, that cats make extraordinary companions."

"Society is now clamoring to add felines to their households," Adelaide added before she leaned forward, scooped Harvey out of his holder, then turned to Sophia. "Would you care to hold him?"

Before Sophia had an opportunity to refuse, something her expression suggested she was about to do, Adelaide dropped Harvey straight into Sophia's lap. To Gideon's amusement, Harvey immediately began kneading the folds of Sophia's traveling cloak, curling himself into a ball a moment later and closing his eyes, apparently in the mood to nap on a lady who certainly didn't seem receptive to that idea.

"How wonderful," Adelaide exclaimed, drawing Sophia's attention. "He already adores you, and given that cats are incredibly finicky, I think I can safely say that you, quite like Gideon, are a lover of cats at heart. But kitties aside, now that your carriage has gotten underway, I believe there was something you wanted to discuss with Gideon, perhaps about Lottie McBriar?"

Sophia frowned. "You know about Lottie?"

"Not any particulars, just that she may have been in your employ under dubious circumstances."

"You really are dear to Gideon, aren't you?" Sophia murmured before she turned her full attention on him. "Adelaide is quite right, though, about me wanting to discuss Lottie."

"I have nothing new to report," Gideon said. "We've had her under constant surveillance, but Lottie's been a model citizen of late, barely leaving her apartment except to wander around Bleecker Street."

Sophia released a huff. "Why haven't you simply snatched her off Bleecker Street to demand she explain why she sought out employment with me?"

"Snatching someone from the street would be kidnapping, which is, as I'm sure you know, illegal."

Sophia waved that aside. "I doubt Lottie would file a complaint."

"Perhaps not, but I won't have her apprehended until I have solid proof she's been up to something. Yes, I think she's working for Frank Fitzsimmons, and appears to collect extortion money from a variety of businesses on his behalf. However, that's not enough to have her arrested."

"What if there's a possibility she broke into my dressing room? Breaking and entering, if I'm not mistaken, is a crime."

"Why do you believe she broke into your dressing room?"

"Jane, or rather Lottie as I guess her real name is, wears a distinctive scent. I smelled it straightaway when I entered my dressing room yesterday after my performance." Sophia released a dramatic sigh. "You cannot imagine my distress when I found my vanity table in shambles, although oddly enough, I've yet to find anything missing."

"Do you have any suspicions regarding what Lottie may have been searching for?" Adelaide asked.

"I have not the slightest idea," Sophia returned. "It's not as if I keep anything of value in my vanity at the Metropolitan. Anything I consider reasonably valuable remains safely ensconced in my safe in the suite of rooms I keep at the Fifth Avenue Hotel."

Adelaide tilted her head. "And this safe of yours—is it a combination one, or a lockbox that has a key?"

"I would never keep anything of worth in a lockbox. And according to the locksmith I purchased it from, my safe is considered practically impenetrable if one doesn't have access to the combination."

Adelaide reached for her reticule and began digging through the contents as Charles leaned closer to Gideon and dropped his voice.

"And just like that, Adelaide has gotten herself involved in fieldwork." Charles's eyes began to twinkle. "I have a feeling we're soon to be in for a treat as my cousin gets down to business."

Given that Adelaide was already thumbing through the small notepad she'd retrieved from her reticule and seemed to be almost humming with excitement, Gideon had a feeling Charles was quite right with his assessment and that Adelaide had almost effortlessly gotten herself involved in the thick of an investigation yet again.

The question that remained now was how he was going to get her removed from Sophia's case without disappointing her too much in the process.

Twenty-Five

As Adelaide continued flipping through her notepad, Gideon drew in a breath, set his sights on Sophia, who was looking bewildered, and said the first thing to spring to mind in a desperate attempt to redirect the conversation.

"I don't believe I've complimented you on your hair color today, Sophia," he began, earning a smile from Sophia, an arch of a brow from Charles, and an honest-to-goodness snort from Adelaide as she lifted her head and narrowed her eyes on him.

"This is hardly the moment to discuss wigs," Adelaide said, which left Sophia's nose wrinkling, as if she couldn't fathom a time when wig discussion wasn't of paramount importance. "I think I'm on to something important, but before I disclose what that is, know that your distraction tactics seem to be somewhat flimsy of late because that was an abysmal attempt at best."

"She has a point," Charles muttered.

Unfortunately, that was nothing less than the truth because while he'd once been a master at redirection and distraction, ever since he'd become involved with Adelaide, his talent with those specific tactics seemed to be somewhat lackluster. Before he could dwell on that further, though, Adelaide stopped on one of the pages, ran her finger over it, then smiled.

"Ah, here it is." She turned to Sophia. "I've actually committed this information to memory, but I wanted to be certain I had everything just right, so tell me—is it possible the first number of the combination to your safe is eighteen?"

Sophia's brow furrowed. "How would you know that?"

"Long story, but since eighteen *is* the first number, may I assume the last number is three?"

"I haven't committed the entire combination to my safe to memory, but it might be."

Adelaide turned to Gideon, her excitement almost palpable. "It appears we've just discovered what those numbers were for that were hidden in the cipher." She redirected her attention to Sophia. "May I presume that when Lottie worked as your dresser, she asked questions about your impressive jewelry collection, one you would undoubtedly store in this almost-impossible-to-open safe?"

"As I said, I only keep items of reasonable worth in my safe. My jewelry is outrageously expensive, which is why I keep the majority of my collection in a safe-deposit box at my bank, using one of my personal guards to switch out pieces according to my whims. But to answer your question, Lottie might have remarked on a few of the pieces I wore on any given night, but that's not unusual, given the extravagant nature of the jewels my many admirers have lavished on me over the years."

"Did she ever make a point of asking you where your safe is hidden?"

"I don't recall speaking about my safe, but I don't believe it would take a genius to realize it's located in the suite of rooms I keep at the Fifth Avenue Hotel."

"If you didn't spend your time speaking about your jewels, and don't recall Lottie broaching the matter of your safe, what did you usually talk about?"

Sophia shrugged. "The usual—fashion, the weather, but most of all, books." She began fiddling with a button on her glove. "I thought we'd formed a bond over our shared literary preferences, but I was certainly wrong about that."

"Did you tell Lottie about any rare books you own?"

"I don't own any rare books because my tastes run more to Jane Austen or Charlotte Brontë." Sophia tucked a strand of blond hair behind her ear. "Foolish as this seems to me now, even though there was a part of me that knew Lottie hadn't left my employ because of an ill mother, I was hoping I was wrong and that she would return to me because she promised to help me with a project she suggested I take on."

"Project?" Adelaide pressed.

"Lottie thought I could make a fortune—not that I'm ever short of funds—if I were to write my life story and get it into print."

Adelaide settled back against the seat. "Did she question you a lot about your life experiences?"

"Not really. She suggested I begin jotting down the adventures I'd experienced ever since becoming an opera singer." Sophia smoothed a hand against the sable lapel of her overcoat. "I told her there was no need for me to do that because I've been keeping journals for years and make a habit of writing in them daily."

"Did you share any of your journals with Lottie?"

"Absolutely not. The contents of my journals are far too personal to share with anyone because I've written down my dreams, my thoughts, and my time spent with my many admirers. And before you ask, because of the sensitive material I've written down in them, I keep them locked in my safe, except for whatever journal I'm currently writing in, but that also goes into the safe every night."

Adelaide glanced out the window, traced a finger through the frost that was marring the glass, then turned her head, her gaze sharpening on Sophia. "I find myself reluctant to ask this, but it may bear significant importance to your case. Is there a possibility you've included information about those admirers in your journals that could, hypothetically, of course, be used to persuade them to lavish all those jewels on you?"

Sophia's eyes flashed with temper. "That almost sounds as if you're accusing me of blackmail."

"I believe I used the word *persuade*, but your indignation suggests I'm not off the mark."

"You're not nearly as darling as I thought you were," Sophia grumbled before she crossed her arms over her chest. "But since I get the distinct impression you're annoyingly persistent when you set your mind to it, know that I *may* have persuaded a few gentlemen to purchase me trinkets after reminding them of certain delicate matters they mentioned to me over candlelit dinners."

"Which would be considered blackmail."

"That's your opinion, but increasing the size of my jewelry collection isn't the only reason I've scribbled information about gentlemen into my journals. A woman in my position must have means of protection, especially when some gentlemen want to further their acquaintance with me and I'm not receptive to their overtures."

"Perfectly understandable, but how often do you write about gentlemen?"

"I uncover secrets and scandals on a nightly basis and go through at least a half-dozen journals a year."

Adelaide shot a look to Gideon. "I believe we're finally getting to the bottom of why Lottie took up a post as Sophia's dresser." She leaned closer to Sophia. "Do you imagine that your journals may have been why Frank Fitzsimmons wanted to speak privately with you at the Nelson event a few months back?"

Sophia shifted on the seat. "That notion did cross my mind

after learning Frank tried to murder Gideon—to no avail, of course, because . . ." She fluttered her lashes Gideon's way. "You are certainly a gentleman who knows how to take care of a murderous villain, something I, for one, find incredibly compelling."

"Of course gentlemen like Gideon are compelling, but getting back to the real issue here," Adelaide said through what seemed to be clenched teeth, something that left Gideon's lips quirking, "are you certain that you never mentioned to Lottie that you keep these journals in your safe?"

"I suppose I might have mentioned that in passing, but I can't be certain."

"Could you have also disclosed that you make a habit of writing about your gentlemen admirers?"

"I would never be so careless as to do that, although . . ." Sophia frowned. "I have a tendency to speak out loud as I write in my journals. Lottie might have been in my dressing room when I was writing a particularly delicious tidbit I'd learned about one of the recent additions to the opera scene—a Mr. Marshall Wilson. He graciously took me to Delmonico's after a performance and was quite the talker."

Gideon sat forward. "What did you learn about Marshall?"

"Just that he grew up poor, made a fortune in oil or something of that sort, and has an eye for the ladies, even though he's determined to marry into the society set, no matter if he has to settle for a less-than-fashionable lady in the process."

"That right there may be reason enough to flag him as a potential suspect," Adelaide said, tapping her finger against her chin. "I'm sure Marshall knows that if he sets his sights on a wallflower and the mother of that wallflower learns he's got a roving eye *and* that he might only be marrying this wallflower to improve his social standing, his plans could be disrupted. He might even find himself banned from future society events, something I'm sure he would go to great lengths to ensure never happens."

Sophia's mouth pursed. "While I can certainly understand why Marshall Wilson wouldn't want that information to get out, Lottie was already working for me when I allowed him to take me to dinner. Besides that, the tasty tidbits Marshall let slip were actually incredibly tame compared to the downright scandalous revelations I've learned about from other men."

"Which suggests there could be numerous suspects who might have the proper incentive to hire a man like Frank Fitzsimmons to steal any evidence regarding their wrongdoings, which means . . ." Adelaide worried her lip for a moment, then nodded. "I bet Lottie was sent to take up a position as your dresser so she could uncover whether you truly do keep journals, how often you write in them, and where you store your journals when you're not scribbling tidbits into them."

Gideon fought a smile because clearly Adelaide was on to something, and even though he couldn't in good conscience bring her fully into the accounting firm, it was fascinating to watch her puzzle out particulars regarding Sophia's case.

"You're not missing one of your journals, are you?" Adelaide asked next. "Perhaps the one you're currently writing in?"

Sophia shook her head. "After Gideon sent word that Lottie was not the down-on-her-luck girl she presented herself to me as, I began to worry that something was amiss, especially after Frank Fitzsimmons wanted to meet with me. Since then, I always keep my current journal on my person during the day, and the others never come out of the safe, so no, I'm not missing any of them."

"One would have thought you'd bring your concerns about Frank to Gideon," Adelaide said.

It really wasn't a surprise when Sophia began fluttering her lashes at Gideon again. "I wanted to tell you, Gideon, truly I did, but then I would have had to admit what I'd written in those journals and . . . I thought you might think poorly of me."

Given all he'd seen during his time as an intelligence agent, learning Sophia dabbled in her own peculiar form of blackmail wasn't exactly a surprise.

He caught her eye. "I knew you were deliberately avoiding me, and at least now I understand why."

She gave another flutter of lashes. "Does that mean you'll overlook my somewhat questionable behavior when it comes to the contents of my journals?"

"Blackmail, just like breaking and entering, is actually against the law," Gideon said, causing Sophia's eyes to widen.

"Surely you're not intending on having me arrested, are you?" she breathed.

"Not if you discontinue using privileged information to increase the size of your jewelry collection."

"I'll be on my best behavior from this point forward."

"See that you are," he said, suppressing a grin when Adelaide rolled her eyes before she gave a pointed clearing of her throat.

"Bad behavior aside," Adelaide began, waiting until Sophia stopped batting her lashes at Gideon and returned her attention to Adelaide before she continued. "I don't believe it's much of a stretch to conclude that Lottie was unable to get her hands on your journals, so she then set her sights on discovering what the combination to your safe was. You mentioned you haven't committed the combination to memory, which leaves me concluding that you've written it down somewhere."

Sophia winced. "I might have kept it written on a scrap of paper I tucked into the back of my vanity, although I took it out after I learned that Lottie had taken up a position with me for some nefarious purpose."

"Which would explain why someone rifled through your vanity last evening," Adelaide said.

"But I would think Lottie left her position with me because she found the combination. Why come back again?"

"There's a distinct possibility that the combination Lottie undoubtedly stole the first time around was lost," Adelaide said before she caught Gideon's eye. "I'm sure you'll agree that it's highly probable that someone who is written about in the journals has decided they need to get rid of whatever nastiness Sophia's jotted down about them. The question that remains, of course, is who that someone is."

"I agree." Gideon nodded to Sophia. "Unfortunately, the only way we're going to have a chance of solving your case is if you give me access to your journals. I'll need to read them in order to discern which gentleman you've written about stands out as the most viable culprit."

Sophia raised a hand to her throat. "I can't allow you to read my journals. My life in glaring detail is written on the pages, some of those details shockingly personal."

"I'm sure Gideon understands your reluctance to share your journals," Adelaide said, leaning forward. "But perhaps you could jot down the names of some of the gentlemen you dined with right before the time Lottie came to work for you—specifically men who may have imparted sensitive information."

"I'm afraid I don't have the luxury of the time that would be needed to accomplish that," Sophia admitted. "I dine with numerous gentlemen a week, and even the journal I'm writing in now probably has tidbits on at least thirty, if not fifty, men in it."

Adelaide's eyes widened. "It's no wonder you have a vast collection of jewels, but investigating fifty men would indeed be time consuming, which is problematic, given that someone is obviously determined to destroy whatever you've written about them as soon as possible."

"So I truly am in danger?" Sophia breathed.

"It would be foolish to believe otherwise, and you should make certain you have a guard on duty to protect you at all times, as well as someone to watch over your safe."

"One of my many bodyguards is sitting beside the driver on top of this very carriage as we speak, and my suite of rooms

is under twenty-four-hour surveillance because I seem to frequently attract attention of the dubious sort. I assure you, my
safe is in no danger of being opened, except by me or by one
of my trusted guards."

"Which is reassuring, but you still might want to consider
changing the combination and then committing that to memory
instead of writing it down," Adelaide said before she turned
her attention to the window, tracing her finger against the glass
again before she suddenly stilled.

A second later, she settled a gaze filled with what seemed
to be anticipation on Sophia, something Gideon couldn't help
but take as clear cause for concern.

"I've just noticed we're riding adjacent to Central Park, so
if there's nothing else you needed to discuss with Gideon,"
Adelaide began as she removed Harvey from Sophia's lap, "I
believe now is when we should bid you good afternoon and get
on with that walk I've been longing to take."

"Just like that—you want to abandon me?" Sophia asked.

"I'm sure you need to get ready for a performance tonight,
just as I need to enjoy some brisk air before I attend a dinner
at Mr. Stanford Mellon's house later."

Sophia turned to Charles and immediately began batting her
lashes at him. "While I do have a performance later, I always
enjoy a cup of tea at Rutherford & Company before I begin to
get ready. I find the lemon soothes my throat before I perform.
I'd be delighted if you'd accompany me there."

"Ah" was Charles's only response to that before he sent a telling glance to Adelaide, one that had her squaring her shoulders
before she inclined her head Sophia's way.

"I'm sure darling Charles would adore nothing more than tea
with you, Madame Campanini, but he's my chaperone for the
day, so tea with you is out for now." With that, Adelaide gave
a sharp rap on the ceiling, the carriage immediately skidded
to a stop, and before Gideon knew it, he was standing on the

sidewalk, watching Sophia's carriage trundle away, removing a very disgruntled opera singer from them in the process.

"I don't think she's going to be calling you her *darling* Adelaide anymore," Charles said, earning a grin from Adelaide in return.

"And thank goodness for that, but enough about Sophia. I've had a brilliant idea I'm all but bursting to share with both of you regarding how we can solve the mystery surrounding Sophia's case."

"You just said you've had enough talk about Sophia," Gideon pointed out.

"The lady, yes. Her case, no." With that, Adelaide took hold of Gideon's arm, and with Charles taking her other one, they moved down a snow-covered sidewalk, Moe leading the way with Harvey once again riding in his saddlebag.

After checking to the left, and then to the right, as if she wanted to ascertain no one was within listening distance, which they weren't because the snow was coming down harder than ever and most people had the good sense to seek out warmer places to congregate, Adelaide caught Gideon's eye.

"Since Sophia obviously isn't keen to share the sordid recollections of her life with us, I think our only option to discover who wants to get their hands on her journals is to get that information directly from Lottie."

"We're not snatching Lottie off the street."

Adelaide released a snort. "I'm not suggesting we kidnap her. If you'll recall, I broached the matter of hosting a book salon with Lottie before the holidays. She voiced an interest in attending such an event, and if I invite all the book agents and leave a note on the bookstore door, I don't think her suspicions will be aroused. If she shows up, we can then get down to asking her some pertinent questions, and that certainly wouldn't be considered kidnapping since she'll be at the book salon of her own free will."

Gideon frowned. "I've never had a suspect disclose information without due cause, and I can't see Lottie blithely admitting she got herself hired as Sophia's dresser for nefarious purposes just because we start asking her questions."

"A valid point, so . . ." Adelaide tilted her head. "What if we offer some bait in the form of the Juliette Watson diary? Given that Sophia's vanity table was ransacked, it stands to reason that Frank Fitzsimmons needs to get his hands on that combination again."

"But wouldn't Lottie have written that down somewhere?" Charles asked. "Or, better yet, if she uncovered the combination, why didn't she simply break into the safe on her own?"

"Perhaps her talents don't lie with breaking into safes or rooms at the Fifth Avenue Hotel," Adelaide said.

"It's more likely that Frank doles out assignments to different criminals so that no one can double-cross him or to make it difficult to trace criminal activity back to him," Gideon countered.

"Which makes sense, and perhaps Lottie didn't bother to write the combination down because after she put it into a cipher or took the combination to whoever does ciphers for Frank, she didn't think she'd have need of it again." Adelaide wrinkled her nose. "I also imagine she wouldn't want the combination in her possession in case something went amiss with the actual heist of the journals."

"Which is sound reasoning," Gideon conceded. "However, to return to the book salon, I don't understand how that would work because the store isn't open yet, and Lottie seems a wary sort. Won't she view an impromptu book salon as suspicious, especially one where a diary she might need is suddenly coming out into the open?"

"Not if we let it be known that I've decided to host a pre-reopening event geared to the most avid of readers and book agents. We can also add that as a special treat, I'll be offering up some of my personal book collection for sale—books that no longer hold my attention, such as diaries, herbals, and poetry."

"Since when have you decided you don't enjoy poetry?" Charles asked.

She dashed some snow from her face. "I adore poetry, but it's a genre the book agents are always keen to acquire, which will ensure most of them will attend the event." She smiled. "I can guarantee you that Lottie will come if she hears I'll be offering up a few diaries for sale, especially if Frank is currently being pressured by whoever hired him to find Sophia's journal in the first place."

"While I will admit it's a credible plan," Gideon began, "having the diary out in the open will place you in far too much danger."

"Except that I doubt Lottie, or anyone else for that matter, would make a play for the diary in the midst of the salon," Adelaide countered. "You mark my words, any danger that may occur will happen after the book salon disbands, when I'll be safely at home."

Gideon pulled her to a stop. "Having you anywhere near the book salon is not an option because that, as you very well know, would be considered field work, something you promised me you'd avoid."

"I know I promised that, but in this particular circumstance, I'm essential to finding success with this scheme," Adelaide argued. "It would look beyond suspicious if I'm not involved." She drew in breath before she smiled. "However, I'll swear here and now that I'll head for home the second the salon is over and will even use one of my carriages to get there that evening instead of taking the El."

Gideon rubbed a hand over his face because even though her plan was probably the most viable solution to getting information out of Lottie, or to flush out anyone else who was interested in acquiring the diary, he knew Adelaide—and knew if something could go wrong, it would.

Nevertheless, when he caught her gaze and discovered that her eyes were sparkling with anticipation, instead of telling her there was absolutely no way she was going to become actively involved with planning and hosting a book salon, he inclined his head ever so slightly.

"Excellent," Adelaide exclaimed before she suddenly threw her arms around him and gave him a tight hug, and just like that, any thought of taking back his agreement to let her host a book salon disappeared into the chilly air.

Twenty-Six

"I'm certain I don't need to remind you of this, Gideon, what with how many years you have vested in the intelligence world, but possessing such a miserable demeanor right before everyone arrives for an exciting new venture for the bookshop is certain to draw more than a few questions," Adelaide said, earning a wince from Gideon before he was smiling one of his most charming smiles.

"Better?"

"If you can maintain that look once our guests arrive, certainly, although I have no idea why you're looking so worried in the first place. You should be impressed as well as satisfied that we were able to fine-tune our plan and see it executed a mere three days after our meeting with Sophia."

"It's not as if we had any choice about that," Gideon pointed out. "Camilla allotted us only three days to get everything in order, threatening to convince your mother you needed additional ball gowns made if you weren't back to attending all the social events she scheduled for you."

"She can be ruthless when she sets her mind to it," Adelaide muttered before she brightened. "But since we met her deadline, I have no need to fear the horror of more fittings. And as an added bonus, because I was given a small reprieve from the frivolities of the Season, I'm sure I'll be far more affable in general once I return to attending numerous society events per day."

"I'm not sure you should mention that last bit to Camilla. She might take that as affirmation she was right about you not being fully committed to the plan of having society embrace you as an original."

Adelaide waved that aside. "It's not as if I don't enjoy being invited to numerous events because people actually want me there instead of receiving invitations because it's expected, given my Knickerbocker lineage."

"I'm sure that is a novel experience for you, but I know you enjoy your bookstore more, along with being involved in a case for the accounting firm."

"I wouldn't think that would even be in question," Adelaide said, smiling as her gaze traveled over the bookstore, pleasure running through her as she took in the tidiness of the shop, the gleaming surfaces of all the tables, and the scent of lemons that permeated the air. "There's something remarkably gratifying about getting this shop in hand, although it's not nearly to where I want it to be. I must admit I'm looking forward to starting a true renovation just as soon as the Season winds down."

"I'm sure the Bainswrights are pleased to have left their shop in such capable hands."

"Indeed, although selling it to me was a bittersweet moment for them." Adelaide bent to retrieve a few books from a crate she'd packed up from her private collection and set them on the counter. "Mrs. Bainswright got rather teary when she handed over the keys to the shop after Father's attorney went with me to settle the purchase." Adelaide grinned. "That state didn't last long after Mr. Bainswright announced he was taking her off to warmer shores for the entirety of the winter, followed by spring in Europe, something they'd only dreamed about but are now able to afford after selling their shop to me."

Gideon returned the grin right as the front door opened and Vernon and Edna strolled in, followed by Leopold, with Jeromy Hopkins, William Osborne, and Clement Robards trailing after them.

"Looks like you were successful in getting the word spread," Adelaide said.

"Only if Lottie shows up," Gideon countered before he strode forward to greet the arrivals, barely having time to release Edna's hand before Vernon thrust a covered dish his way.

"I know Adelaide said she was going to provide the refreshments," Vernon said, "but my cook makes an excellent shrimp hors d'oeuvre I thought everyone would enjoy."

"I'll put it with the rest of the food Adelaide's staff has set up near the biography section," Gideon said, moving across the room to hand the dish to one of the Duveen maids who was manning a table that sported pastries, cheese, fruit, and a variety of other treats, along with beverages.

"Are refreshments going to be a regular circumstance once the store reopens for good, and we can hopefully hold regularly scheduled salons?" Clement asked, moving up next to Adelaide.

Adelaide smiled. "I believe that'll be a given since you and I both know that once we begin discussing books, we could be here for hours."

"Indeed we could, and speaking of books, I heard through the grapevine that you were going to be putting up some of your personal collection for sale this evening."

"Rumor would be right about that because, yes, I am."

"Why?"

She gave an airy wave of her hand. "I've decided I have too many books, and many of them are very similar in nature. Besides, books should be appreciated to their fullest, not stored on shelves where they're not getting the attention they deserve."

She smiled. "I thought, what with the annoyance I evoked when Mr. Bainswright gave me permission to snoop in that crate and pick out a few treasures before anyone else, that I should offer all of you first access to my collection before I begin putting those books on the shelves for other customers to purchase."

"Since you just said *you'll* be putting books on the shelves, should I take that to mean the other rumor I heard about this shop is true and that you've taken over ownership from the Bainswrights?" Clement asked.

"They wanted to retire."

"Can't say I'm surprised about that," William Osborne said as he moseyed up to join them. "The Bainswrights were positively ancient, and over the past few years, Mr. Bainswright was less than receptive to little suggestions we tried to impart to enhance this fine store. I know I'm not alone when I say I'm looking forward to any improvements you may care to make, Miss Duveen. If you need any assistance with tracking down suppliers to purchase books from, national or international, I'd be more than delighted to help."

"As would I," Clement hurried to say. "I'd also be willing to help you shelve any books you may acquire. You'll just need to send a note around to my office, and I'll be here at my earliest convenience."

"Of course you will," William drawled before Adelaide could respond. "Shelving new additions would allow you the opportunity of the right of first perusal."

Adelaide held up her hand, stopping the argument she knew was about to commence. "While I appreciate your offers, gentlemen, I'm intending on hiring a full staff, complete with a manager who will be given the responsibility of procuring new books for the shop. However, since I only recently took over ownership, I'm still in the infant stages, although I will welcome any suggestions you may wish to make. For now, though, I still have a few details left to attend to before we can begin our first meeting."

"Do you need any help with those?" William asked.

She laughed. "Thank you, but no. You're here to enjoy yourselves this evening, so I suggest you begin doing exactly that by looking around the store at your leisure." She grinned. "I'll be more than happy to relieve you of your money if you happen to find any books you simply can't live without."

"Can we look through your collection?" Clement asked.

"And start a war once other agents arrive and learn you've gotten the jump on them? I think not. You'll need to wait until everyone is here."

"It's hardly our fault we arrived on time," William grumbled before he clapped Clement on the shoulder. "Nevertheless, since Miss Duveen is probably right about the war, and a book salon shouldn't turn into a contentious affair before it even starts, I saw Leopold Pendleton head up to the second floor. What say we go and see if we can assist him with finding some excellent books to add to his collection?"

"Should I expect you to remind him you're a book agent?" Clement asked.

"Undoubtedly," William said, earning a chuckle from Clement before the two men strolled off across the room, disappearing up the stairs a moment later.

Shaking her head, Adelaide returned to emptying the crate she'd brought with her, glancing Gideon's way a second later to find him in conversation with Jeromy Hopkins.

"My dear, you look positively radiant this evening," Edna said, drawing Adelaide's attention as she glided up to join her. "Camilla certainly knew what she was about dressing you in jewel tones because that emerald green suits you to perfection, although . . ." She lowered her voice. "I have a feeling you're looking luminous because a certain gentleman is present."

Adelaide shot another glance to Gideon, who was, unfortunately, watching her as he continued speaking with Jeromy, the smile he immediately sent her causing heat to crawl up her neck and settle on her cheeks. She sent him a small smile in return before turning back to Edna. "I'm sure if I'm glowing, it's merely because this is my first official event as the proprietress of this shop and my nerves are somewhat jittery."

"You keep telling yourself that, dear, but I don't believe it for a moment." Edna's eyes took to sparkling. "As a woman who's recently become enamored of my own gentleman, I recognize the expression residing on your face, one you sport often of late. You, my darling, hold Gideon in great affection, and if I'm not mistaken, which I assure you I'm not, that sentiment is returned."

Adelaide's pulse, unsurprisingly, began racing madly about, but before she could press Edna for more details, the door to the shop opened again and Lottie breezed through it in the company of a handful of other book agents, none of whom Adelaide was overly familiar with. They were followed by two dapperly dressed men Adelaide had never seen before, both of them hesitating just inside the doorway, as if they weren't certain where they should go from there.

Gideon was moving across the store a second later, the two men in his sights.

Telling Edna she'd be right back because she wanted to greet the new arrivals, to which Edna told her not to hurry because she was off to speak with Vernon, Adelaide made it halfway through the store before Lottie intercepted her.

"Miss Duveen," Lottie exclaimed. "How delightful to see you again."

Adelaide summoned up a smile. "Miss . . . Smith. It's wonderful to see you as well. I'm so pleased you were able to attend our very first book salon."

"I rearranged my schedule as soon as I saw the notice posted on the door, but tell me this." Lottie moved closer. "Are the rumors true? Are you really the new owner of this shop, and if so, I must admit I'm dying of curiosity to learn how society reacted to that scandalous development."

"I'm afraid they've yet to become apprised of what I'm sure they'll consider an outrage, so I must beg your discretion in this matter. However . . ." She caught Lottie's eye. "I don't recall telling you that I was involved with society the last time we spoke."

"William Osborne mentioned it while we were rummaging around that crate, searching for treasures."

"And did you find any treasures that day?"

"Alas, I went home empty-handed," Lottie said before she glanced around the room, her gaze lingering on Gideon and the men he was speaking with. Her eyes narrowed ever so slightly, but then she blinked and returned her attention to Adelaide. "I hope I don't come across as too forward, but wasn't that gentleman standing over there the same one you were with when I first made your acquaintance?"

Unable to help but wonder why Lottie would be interested in Gideon, or if she might have somehow learned he was not simply a gentleman of leisure, Adelaide forced herself to keep her smile firmly in place. "He is indeed. He's an avid collector and simply couldn't resist attending tonight."

"I thought I overheard him telling the book agents he collected art and ancient weaponry."

"What a wonderful memory you have, Miss Smith, as well as a talent, if I'm not mistaken, for overhearing conversations."

"And what a wonderful talent you seem to possess for distraction, Miss Duveen," Lottie said before she dipped into a curtsy, shot another glance to Gideon, although it seemed her gaze darted ever so briefly to the two men Gideon was still speaking with, then said something about perusing some books and ambled away.

Blowing out a breath while hoping she hadn't drawn Lottie's suspicions or put her on high alert regarding the evening ahead, Adelaide checked her watch just as Gideon strode up to join her.

"Everything alright?" he asked.

"I might have sent Lottie's suspicion meter ratcheting up a notch," she admitted.

"She just got here."

"True, but she's evidently very canny, and she caught me in a lie when I told her you were here to add to your collection. Unfortunately, she overheard you tell the book agents you don't collect books."

He reached out and gave her arm a small squeeze. "I wouldn't worry overly much about that. If she's here to scope out the diary, she won't be leaving anytime soon."

"But I was hoping to make her comfortable around me and perhaps slip about something important."

He grinned and leaned closer. "Girls like Lottie don't slip, but again, don't worry about it. She won't be going anywhere for a while."

Adelaide checked her watch again. "I hope you're right, but to err on the side of caution, I think we should gather everyone and start the salon. The sooner we get down to business, the sooner we can get this ended, and then hopefully someone will make a move after everyone leaves."

"And you will be leaving as well."

"I know," she muttered.

"There's no need to be forlorn about that, Adelaide," Gideon said quietly. "I promised you I'd tell you every detail if something happens. For now, though, let me fetch everyone who went upstairs. Then I'll stop by the back room and check in with Charles. He'll only need to guard the back door until Roland and some other associates take over for him. I told them to wait to take their places until quarter past the hour, thinking that anyone who's coming to the salon should be here by then." He sent a glance to the dapperly dressed men he'd recently been speaking with. "I think I'll ask Charles to strike up a conversation with those gentlemen. They told me they're book agents visiting the city from Boston, on the lookout for old diaries, which suggests Frank has let it be known far and wide that he's on the lookout for a specific diary. I didn't want to press them on the matter, but perhaps we can have Charles say something about being here because he's looking for a diary and see how those men react."

After Adelaide nodded, Gideon strode for the stairs, leaving Adelaide to return to the pile of books she'd been unpacking. It took her three trips to get all the books settled on an empty table, making certain to place the diary she'd rewrapped in brown paper to make it appear as if she'd never opened it on the top of one of the stacks she'd made. Retrieving her reticule from where she'd stashed it on a chair, she jumped ever so slightly when Lottie, in the company of Jeromy Hopkins, was suddenly standing beside her, both of their gazes settled on the wrapped package.

"My dear Miss Duveen," Jeromy began, nodding to the diary. "May I dare hope you've decided to offer a door prize this evening, a mystery book that will only be revealed once you choose a winner?"

"What a wonderful idea, but alas, I didn't even consider that," Adelaide said as she picked up the diary. "Sadly, there's nothing mysterious about the book underneath the paper. It's a dilapidated old diary written by a young girl—Juliette Watson, if memory serves me correctly. I found it a few weeks back in that crate everyone was wrangling over and never got around to unwrapping it. I decided, as I was sorting through some of my books to find ones to offer up for sale this evening, that I might offer this one as well. I have at least twenty old diaries left in my collection and don't actually have room to add more, especially not one that has a broken binding and is probably missing a great many pages." She shook her head. "There's nothing quite as frustrating as trying to read a diary and missing out on key elements regarding the author's life."

"How much do you want for it?" Jeromy asked.

Adelaide wrinkled her nose. "You haven't even seen it yet."

"Who could pass up a book that's old, dilapidated, and probably missing pages?" Jeromy countered.

Adelaide tilted her head, wondering what Jeromy would do if she quoted an outlandish price, but before she could do exactly that, William Osborne came barreling across the store, his color high and temper in his eyes.

"Do not say you're already trying to beat out the rest of us of a book we may want to acquire for one of our clients, are you?" William demanded as he reached the table, Clement Robards by his side.

Jeromy smiled even as he shrugged. "All's fair in love and book acquiring, gentlemen, as you very well know." He turned an expectant eye on Adelaide. "Do you have a set price in mind?"

"I was thinking fifty," she said, mostly because she was curious to see what would happen after asking such an exorbitant price for a diary she'd paid less than a dollar for.

"Done," Jeromy didn't hesitate to say.

"I'll give you sixty," William said.

"Seventy-five," Clement countered.

"Eighty-five," Jeromy offered next.

"One hundred," William said before he sent Adelaide an unexpected wink. "I'll also offer to keep an eye out for treasures for you the next time I'm in Europe without charging you my usual agenting fee."

"That's a low blow," Jeromy grumbled. "You know Clement and I don't have plans to travel internationally until late spring."

William smiled. "As you said, all's fair in—"

Before he could finish the sentence, a loud ruckus sounded from the back room, and a few seconds later, five men dressed in black, and with their faces covered, rushed into the room, pistols at the ready.

"Hands in the air!" a burly man shouted.

Adelaide's hands, along with the book agents', shot into

the air, whereas Lottie dropped to the floor and disappeared from sight.

"You," the man yelled, brandishing his pistol Adelaide's way. "Get the money from the till."

Adelaide shot a look to Gideon, who was edging ever so slowly toward her, his hands in the air, freezing a second later when one of the men trained his pistol on him.

"Stay where you. No sudden moves."

"Get going," the burly man ordered, gesturing to the cash register even as he kept his weapon aimed at Adelaide.

"I can open the cash register, but there's no money in it because the store isn't open for business," she began, taking a step forward and then freezing on the spot when the largest man in the group joined the one with the gun trained on her.

"Then I guess you'll just need to give us what we're really here for—a diary," he growled. "It's old and it's got an X on the spine. Might have been written by some girl."

"I knew that diary was going to be worth at least a hundred," William muttered, his complexion turning chalk white when the man leveled his pistol on him.

"You know the diary I'm talking about?" the man demanded.

"Not for sure, but it might be . . ." William nodded to the wrapped package lying on the table, keeping his hands in the air.

"Unwrap it," the man demanded, jerking his head toward Adelaide.

With hands that were trembling ever so slightly, Adelaide reached for the diary, tore off the wrapping, and held it up.

"Is there an X on the spine?" the man asked.

She held it up so that the X was visible.

"That's the one. Hand it over—real slow like."

Taking a step forward, Adelaide faltered when, from out of the corner of her eye, she saw the two dapperly dressed gentlemen draw pistols from beneath their jackets.

A second later, shots erupted around the room.

"Get down!" Gideon yelled.

Chaos was immediate as William, Clement, Jeromy, and the rest of the book agents dove for the floor as the Duveen maids dropped behind the refreshment table. Vernon pushed Edna under a table even as he pulled out a pistol, while Leopold's weapon was already in his hand as he crouched behind a chair and began taking aim at the two groups of men who were now engaged in what seemed to be a showdown.

"Get down!" Gideon yelled again to Adelaide, two pistols in his hands as he leaned around from behind a bookshelf and took aim.

Needing no other encouragement to get out of the line of fire, Adelaide dropped to the floor before she reached up, snagged hold of her reticule that was still on the table, flipped the clasp open with fingers that seemed to be all thumbs, and extracted the pepperbox she'd been carrying everywhere with her of late.

Drawing in a deep breath, she peeked over the edge of the table, horror flowing through her when she saw Charles stumbling into the room, blood running down his face, a pistol in his hand, his appearance drawing the attention of one of the men in black. As that man aimed his gun at her cousin, Adelaide cocked the hammer and began to fire.

It soon became clear why Gideon had cautioned her about only using the pepperbox at close range, because without a long barrel, her shots went wide. One shattered a front window, another hit the man advancing on Charles, while another dropped one of the dapperly dressed gentlemen to the ground. Unsurprisingly, the irregularity of her shots sent everyone else who'd come into the store with mal intent on their minds fleeing out the front door as fast as their legs could carry them without a backward glance.

Twenty-Seven

Rage coursed through Gideon as the scent of cordite from the many firing weapons seared his nostrils, all the men except two having fled, trailing blood behind them. He set his sights on one of the remaining men, a man dressed in black who was writhing on the floor, a direct result of Adelaide having shot him.

His gaze immediately sought out and found Adelaide, who was rushing across the room toward Charles, who was bleeding profusely from his temple, tearing the cuff off her sleeve as she ran and pressing it against his head once she reached him.

Realizing she was safe, he strode to the man on the ground, bent down, and yanked the covering from his face, revealing none other than Frank Fitzsimmons.

"We meet again," he said, earning a grimace from Frank in return.

"I need a doctor" were the first words out of Frank's mouth. "I've been shot."

"And I'll be happy to summon one for you after you answer a few questions."

"I could bleed to death by then."

"Then I suggest you answer quickly," Gideon said, his gaze

settling on a rapidly widening bloodstain on Frank's leg. He pulled off his cravat as Leopold knelt to join him.

"We should cut his trousers away," Leopold said. "He won't be any use to us if he dies."

"You think I'm really going to die?" Frank all but sputtered.

Leopold pulled a knife from his boot, made short shrift of cutting away part of Frank's trousers, then took a moment to probe around the small hole in Frank's leg, earning a howl from Frank in the process.

"The bullet went straight through," Leopold said, taking the cravat from Gideon and then wrapping it around the leg, tying it off a second later, which earned another howl from Frank. "Still, we'll need to have it taken care of soon." He sent Gideon the barest hint of a wink. "As I said, he won't be any good to us if he's dead."

Knowing full well Frank's injury was not life-threatening, not that Frank seemed to realize that, Gideon crouched down next to the man. "Who are you working for?"

"You clearly haven't taken time to learn who I am if you have to ask that because I don't work for anyone."

"You're Frank Fitzsimmons, one of the touted up-and-coming bosses of the Lower East Side," Gideon said. "With that out of the way, you may not actually work for anyone, being the big boss and all, but I know someone sought you out to procure the particular type of services you offer—someone who needs to get their hands on one of Sophia Campanini's journals."

Frank's eyes glittered. "I'm not saying anything until my attorney is present, a man who'll have me released and back in my bed before morning."

"Not to disappoint you, Frank," Gideon began, "but I don't think your attorney is going to be able to pull any magic get-out-of-jail-free rabbits from a hat anytime soon. If you're unaware, you and your associates could have killed ladies of the

Four Hundred. Frankly, I wouldn't be surprised if your attorney neglects to take on your case because of the daunting odds he'll face trying to represent you."

"I wasn't the one who started shooting first," Frank said, jerking his head toward the other man who'd been shot, who already had his hands tied in front of him, compliments of Vernon, a circle of blood staining the shoulder of his well-cut jacket. "Bernie and Johnny were the first to shoot, so maybe you should be directing some questions their way."

"Shut your mouth," Bernie growled.

Gideon frowned. "You know this man?" he asked Frank.

"He's Bernie—works for Victor Malvado."

Gideon nodded to Leopold, who pulled his pistol out again and trained it on Frank before Gideon straightened and made his way over to Bernie, ignoring the glare that man sent him.

"You work for Victor Malvado?"

"Frank doesn't know what he's talking about," Bernie growled.

"It's always been my observation that when a man is cornered, he's likely to give up a few truths in order to save his skin," Gideon said. "And if rumor has it right about Victor, he runs an established crime syndicate, which I imagine puts him in direct competition with Frank. The question of the hour is why Victor became involved in this situation and who approached him to do so."

Bernie turned his head, giving the distinct impression he wasn't going to be forthcoming with any details.

Gideon stalked back to Frank, his temper rising with every step. "Since Bernie doesn't appear to be in a cooperative frame of mind, I guess it's up to you to explain who wants Sophia's journal."

"It wouldn't be in my best interest to say anything else."

Gideon smiled. "Probably not, but you see, Victor's reputation precedes him, and I doubt he appreciates your encroachment on the Lower East Side and has probably been making plans to deal with you. That you just gave me the name of two of his employees and disclosed that Victor himself is somehow involved in this, well, I don't believe he'll take that lightly."

"I don't know anything about Victor's involvement, save for the fact two of his most trusted men showed up here tonight and began firing at me and my boys." Frank narrowed his eyes on Bernie. "For all I know, Bernie and Johnny showed up here tonight because of what you said—Victor's furious about me taking over some business on the Lower East Side."

"Or he was approached by *the man* because you're incapable of retrieving an opera singer's scribbles," Bernie muttered, pressing his lips together a second later, as if he'd just realized he shouldn't be saying anything.

"Who's *the man*?" Gideon demanded, leaning closer to Frank.

It was infuriating when Frank, obviously taking a page out of Bernie's book, pressed his lips together and turned his head.

Adelaide suddenly cleared her throat, drawing Gideon's attention. His brow furrowed when she sent him a hint of a smile before she began wiping Charles's blood from her hands with a handkerchief Edna handed her and walked across the room, stopping directly next to him.

"I don't believe Frank is grasping the direness of his current predicament," Adelaide began in a voice that held not the slightest tremble in it, which was impressive given what she'd just experienced. "He evidently doesn't seem to understand the extent of what we already know about his little criminal organization."

Frank released a snort. "You're bluffing."

Adelaide arched a brow. "If I were bluffing, I wouldn't know that you've been using this very bookstore as a hub to exchange messages and instructions regarding illegal activities. And if I'm not mistaken, you also supplied a Mr. Elmendorf with crates of books to sell to Mr. Bainswright, probably giving that poor man a few dollars to traffic your messages for you for his trouble. Do know that we'll be tracking that man down in the near future, although I highly doubt that he, quite like Mr. Bainswright, had any idea he's been assisting your criminal endeavors."

"I don't know any Mr. Elmendorf."

"Just like I'm sure you're going to claim you don't know Lottie McBriar, even though we're aware she works for you and was sent to take up a position with Sophia Campanini with orders to steal a journal. She was clearly unsuccessful with that, but she did succeed with uncovering the combination to Sophia's safe, didn't she?"

"I don't know Lottie McBriar."

Adelaide smiled. "Now, Frank, lying is not going to aid your case, and know that it's an easy matter to verify you're lying since Lottie's here, right at this very moment, and can certainly clear up whether or not she works for you."

She glanced around, her smile fading a second later. "Where *is* Lottie?"

"I saw her hightail it through the front door a second after the bullets began flying, but not before she grabbed something from the table," Vernon said from where he was keeping his cane, one that had a sharp blade attached to the end of it, trained on Bernie.

"The diary," Adelaide muttered, glancing to the table before she blew out a breath. "And doesn't that complicate matters, but we'll have to deal with that later." She turned to Gideon. "Would it be alright with you if I take another few minutes to delve into a more in-depth interrogation with Frank? He really hasn't been as forthcoming as he could be, and I'm finding that rather annoying."

"Annoyance can be a constant companion in the intrigue business," he said.

"I see that now, but you know how irritable I become when I'm in an annoyed state." Her lips began to curve again. "I'm certain uncovering at least a few answers will have my annoyance decreasing, but besides that, this may be the only opportunity I'll ever have to fully interrogate a known criminal, and you wouldn't want to deprive me of that, would you?"

He fought the most unusual urge to laugh. "I don't suppose asking Frank a few more questions could hurt, but you might want to make it quick. You did, after all, shoot Frank, and we probably should get him to a hospital soon."

"Too right we should," Frank agreed, earning a roll of the eyes from Adelaide before she grabbed hold of a chair, dragged it over to Frank, pulled the pepperbox from her pocket, then took a seat.

"If you haven't realized this, Mr. Fitzsimmons, or . . . shall I call you Frank?" she asked.

"Frank's fine, but you have me at a disadvantage because I have no idea who you are."

"I'm simply the lady who's determined to get to the bottom of what led to the events of this evening."

When Frank settled a scowl on her, Adelaide's lips twitched before she cocked her head to the right. "Where was I going with all this?" she began. "Oh, yes, your injury, which I'm going to assume isn't as dire as you believe, otherwise you'd already be on your way to a doctor because we, unlike you, aren't monsters."

"The pain I'm in suggests otherwise," Frank muttered.

"Pain that will be addressed just as soon as you answer my questions." She gave the pepperbox a tap. "I should disclose, before I begin, that I'm a novice with weapons. I've been known to fire off weapons unintentionally, which should provide you with the proper incentive to tell me the truth."

"Are you sure that's even armed?" Frank asked. "It's a five shot. I would think you fired all those rounds earlier."

She shrugged. "Perhaps I did, or perhaps I only shot four rounds, which would leave me one. And while hitting you earlier was not exactly intentional on my part, I doubt I'd be able to miss now, given my close vicinity to you." She inclined her head. "With that out of the way, on to my questions. I'm curious as to why there's still such interest in that diary. One would assume that whoever left that cipher code in it—and yes, we do know there was a cipher—would have re-sent it."

"How'd you know about the cipher? That diary was still in its wrappings."

"I'm clever" was all Adelaide said to that before she arched a brow at Frank and simply waited.

After a full minute passed, Frank blew out a breath. "The idiot who created the cipher got himself arrested not long after he placed it in the diary. He then started a fight while in jail and was thrown into solitary confinement. He hasn't been able to smuggle another cipher out of jail to replace the one that was lost or to even send the numbers I had Lottie leave in this store for him to retrieve."

"Ah, so Lottie does work for you. But why didn't she keep a copy of the combination to prevent this unlikely situation happening in the first place?"

Frank released a grunt, probably because he'd not been intending on admitting Lottie worked for him. "Maybe she knows that keeping information like that could be incriminating evidence if she ever got caught."

"Or you told her to destroy the combination after she left it for someone to fetch in this store, an order that I would assume was given to alleviate the possibility that Lottie would sell the combination to a rival crime boss."

"She wouldn't dare."

Adelaide tilted her head. "Ah, so she's afraid of you, which explains why she obeyed your order and didn't hide a copy of the combination somewhere just in case."

"I do hold the reputation of being the most frightening man on the streets these days," Frank admitted, a distinct trace of smugness in his tone.

A snort from Bernie drew Gideon's attention.

"Was there something you wanted to add to the conversation?" Gideon asked him.

"Frank's not the most terrifying man in the Lower East Side, no matter that he apparently believes he is," Bernie scoffed. "There are other far more powerful and frightening men out there, ones who'll be retaking Frank's territory after he gets carted off to jail."

"As I said before," Frank snarled, "I'll be out before morning, just as soon as I contact my attorney."

"You'd be smarter to stay in jail," Bernie countered. "Not only did you mention Victor tonight, but you've also botched a job for a man who makes even Victor nervous. If you get back on the streets soon, I have a feeling you won't be breathing for long."

It was incredibly telling when Frank's face drained of color, but before Gideon could ask a single question, Adelaide tapped a finger against the pepperbox, an action that immediately drew Frank's attention. "You seem like an intelligent man, Frank, since you've carved out a place for yourself, and done so against great odds, given that you must have provoked men like this Victor Malvado and yet managed to stay alive over the past few years. It then stands to reason, what with how you completely bungled this particular job, that, as Bernie mentioned, your life is certainly in jeopardy now. However, if you cooperate with us, you may have a slight chance of surviving this ordeal. Granted, you'll definitely find yourself behind bars soon, but I assume you'll find that better than being dead."

It was impossible for Gideon to not be impressed by Adelaide's calm demeanor or the straightforward way she was dealing with Frank, especially after she'd been thrust into a situation that would have rattled some of the most seasoned of operatives.

Frank's eyes narrowed on the pepperbox, giving a bit of a shudder when Adelaide lifted it up and casually aimed it his way before he darted a look to Gideon. "I'll need some reassurances before I say anything else."

"Reassurances about what?"

"That you'll arrange for me to have a lenient sentence if I cooperate and that you'll arrange for me to be housed in a jail that's not in New York. I'll be dead come morning if certain people learn I've talked."

Gideon inclined his head. "I can manage that."

Frank considered Gideon for a long moment before he nodded. "What else do you want to know?"

"I believe the most important thing right now is the name of the man who wants Sophia Campanini's journals."

"He's a nasty piece of work," Frank began. "He has access to enormous wealth, and I know he's ruthless. He once bragged to me about how he secured that wealth, and when I say he used any means possible to increase his bank account, I'm not exaggerating. Sanctioned killings of men he viewed as competition was apparently common."

"His name?" Gideon pressed.

Frank shot a glance to Bernie, who gave a quick shake of his head, which Frank apparently decided to ignore as he returned his attention to Gideon. "You promise you'll honor my requests if I divulge that?"

"I have connections in very high places. Your requests won't be a problem."

Frank drew in a deep breath and slowly released it. "It's worth my life to tell you this, but the man who wants Sophia Campanini's journal is . . . Marshall Wilson."

"Marshall Wilson?" Gideon repeated.

"He's your man" was all Frank said before the front door

burst open, Gideon training his pistol on it a second later, only to lower it when Roland, along with a brigade of associates, rushed in.

Roland glanced around before his attention returned to Gideon. "Seems we're late to the party. We got held up because we ran across men fleeing down Bleecker Street. I had a feeling, so we gave chase. Rounded all of them up, not that it was too difficult since most of them had been shot." His gaze darted around the room, narrowing on Frank. "Is that Fitzsimmons?"

"It is. Adelaide shot him in the leg, making it impossible for him to escape with the men he came with."

"Good job, Miss Duveen," Roland said, his lips curving. "Seems as if those mornings spent at the shooting range have really paid off."

Adelaide winced. "I wasn't actually aiming to hit him, or the other man I shot, but in my defense, bullets were ricocheting around the room. I may have simply started firing willy-nilly."

"Perfectly understandable," Roland said before he began barking out orders to his men, directing Duncan and another associate to see Frank and Bernie off to a doctor, and then to jail. As Duncan strode over to Frank, Roland turned to the book agents. "We'll need all of you to remain for a while because we'll need to question everyone."

Jeromy blinked. "None of us had anything to do with this."

"You do if any of you claim Marshall Wilson as a client," Adelaide said, rising to her feet and advancing on the book agents, who'd all gotten up from the floor and were now sitting around a table, looking rather stunned.

"I've never heard of Marshall Wilson before," Jeromy said.

"Me either," Clement proclaimed.

"Nor I," William said, as the other five book agents, who'd been keeping themselves well-removed from the interrogation, nodded in unison.

Adelaide arched a brow. "You expect me to believe that none

319

of you were told to keep an eye out for a specific diary for one of your clients?"

William shifted in his chair. "I wasn't approached by a client, per se, but I did hear rumors there was interest in an old diary penned by a young girl. We agents hear things, and then, well . . ."

"We see if we can get our hands on the coveted piece before anyone else," Clement said.

"And none of you have ever heard of Marshall Wilson before?" Adelaide asked again.

William rubbed a hand over his face. "Now that I think about it, I read a Marshall Wilson got himself invited to the Patriarch Ball in the society section of the *Times*."

Adelaide deposited the pepperbox into her pocket and crossed her arms over her chest. "Should I assume some of you are here because you thought I purchased that diary?"

"You *told* us you'd bought a diary," Jeromy said. "You didn't remember the title of it, and we didn't actually see it, but if I'm being honest, I was going to make a point to ask you about it tonight, see if you'd be interested in selling it."

"Which is why you didn't hesitate when I asked fifty dollars for it," Adelaide said.

"'Course I didn't. That would have been a bargain."

"It would have been a bargain at one hundred," William said.

"I would have gone two hundred," Clements added.

As the book agents began debating how high they would have gone, Roland stepped in, the conversation coming to a rapid end the moment he suggested it might be more productive if they accompanied him to the police station to get official statements.

"I think Roland has that well in hand," Gideon said, taking hold of Adelaide's arm. "Now all that's left to do is get Charles off to see a doctor. After that, I'll send someone to find Lottie, and then I'll see you home before I run Marshall Wilson down."

A storm began brewing in Adelaide's eyes. "If you think I'm going home while you continue with matters, you're sadly mistaken. I'm going with you to find Marshall."

"Absolutely not. You heard Frank. He said Marshall's ruthless, and ruthlessness only intensifies when a man finds himself cornered."

"Then I'll go with whomever you're sending after Lottie. She'll be far more comfortable divulging her secrets to me than any of the other agents."

"I'm not concerned with how comfortable Lottie might be."

"Perhaps not, but you can't simply pat me on the head, tell me what a good girl I was for shooting Frank and Bernie—which allowed us to secure some important information, I might add—and then send me home. That's not fair, and you know it."

Gideon raked a hand through his hair, trying to quell the fury that had been threatening to overwhelm him ever since Frank and his cohorts had rushed into the bookstore.

He'd placed Adelaide, along with Edna and everyone else for that matter, in grave danger this evening, convincing himself no one would be so bold as to ambush them during the book salon.

It was unlike him to be so careless, and he knew he'd done so because he'd been incapable of refusing Adelaide's enthusiasm to participate in what had amounted to nothing less than a sting operation.

His decision to accommodate her longing to be involved with a genuine investigation had been sheer stupidity on his part, a direct result of his inability to resist granting her every whim, no matter how dangerous the results of those whims might be.

Why he couldn't seem to deny her anything wasn't exactly a mystery, because she was the most enchanting lady he'd ever known, possessed of an intellect he admired as well as courage he'd never expected to see in a lady.

She thrived under the most unusual situations, but she could have been killed this evening, and that was something he would never forgive himself for. He would also never, no matter how irresistible he found her, allow her to be placed in harm's way again.

"I believe we should discuss this in private," he said before he tugged Adelaide through the bookstore and steered her into the back storeroom.

"Why do I get the distinct feeling I'm not going to enjoy what you have to say to me?" she asked as he released her arm and moved to shut a door that was hanging on its hinges and allowing snow to blow into the room.

He turned and took a moment to simply consider her, emotions he'd never felt before threatening to overwhelm him— sadness being the worst of them, mixed with a great deal of regret.

Stepping closer to her, he took hold of her hand. "You must surely realize how very dear you've become to me," he began, earning a frown from her in return.

"And?"

He drew in a breath and slowly released it. "I made a vow when I joined the service years ago to protect those more vulnerable than myself. I failed miserably with that tonight, placing you and the others in a situation where you could have very well lost your lives."

"Being unprepared for an ambush was my fault," Adelaide argued. "I'm the one who insisted there'd be no danger to anyone while the book salon was in session."

He shook his head. "I've been involved with men who are the lowest forms of humanity imaginable ever since I joined the navy. I've seen the lengths they'll go to get what they desire, and I should have, at the very least, prepared accordingly. I'm the one who made the decision to have Roland and our other operatives wait to position themselves around the store until after everyone arrived for the salon. That was an inexcusable error on my part." He raked a hand through his hair. "I placed you in grave danger."

"You saved me from harm tonight," she countered.

"You saved yourself, along with everyone else, when you let loose with your pepperbox."

"You were holding off the assailants as well."

"But assailants shouldn't have been a factor at all this evening. I shouldn't have agreed to the book salon plan to begin with, but I did because . . ." His voice trailed away, earning a narrowing of her eyes in the process.

"Because why?"

"That's not important. What is important is that I should not have let you become involved with fieldwork in the first place. It was irresponsible on my part, but my irresponsibility toward you ends as of this moment."

"What does that mean?"

"It means you can no longer be involved with the accounting firm, not even looking over old files for us."

"That's not fair."

"It may not be fair, but it'll keep you alive. It was only sheer luck you weren't killed tonight."

Her eyes flashed. "And to that I say rubbish. Besides, if you've forgotten, because of my actions, even if they were unexpected, we were able to uncover answers that have evaded us for weeks."

"You're not going to change my mind."

"You're being unreasonable."

"I'm being realistic. I decided years ago that I wouldn't become involved with a lady until I was much older, but then . . . you stumbled into my life when you caught on fire, and from that moment forward, I have felt driven to protect you. I've done an abysmal job of that, ignored my better instincts, and have pulled you into my world, where I've now realized, without a shadow of a doubt, that you don't belong."

"What if I promise to never venture into fieldwork again, and content myself with those old files?"

He closed his eyes for the briefest of seconds. "You know, because it's you, that you'll end up stumbling upon something you shouldn't know or figure out a clue that'll land you in direct danger again. I can't be responsible for frequently placing your life in jeopardy. With that said, and as much as I hate to say this, it'll be for the best if we make a clean break of everything and say good-bye."

Her mouth quivered the slightest bit. "Good-bye? As in you not only don't want me involved with the accounting firm but you also no longer care to be my friend?"

He drew in a deep breath, determined to keep his resolve, no matter that the distress visible on her face was driving a knife through his heart. "I will always consider you one of my dearest friends, but I can't continue seeing you, Adelaide. I have enemies who, if they realize you're important to me, will use you to get to me. I can't allow that to happen."

"And I have no say in this? If you've forgotten, it's my life. You can't tell me how I should live it or expect me to return to the monotony of society after experiencing the world you inhabit. I won't agree to that. I need more."

"You'll have your bookstore and more cats to save since society seems to be taking an interest in them. You'll also have young ladies to rescue, ones who would be lingering against walls without your assistance."

"Which is all well and good, but again, it's not enough."

"It going to have to be, because I cannot subject you to the hazards of my world ever again." He leaned forward, drew in a breath, committed her scent to memory, then placed a kiss on her forehead before he drew back. "I'll tell Camilla to begin spreading whispers that you've decided we won't suit." He forced a smile. "I'm sure there will be many relieved gentlemen who'll be more than anxious to step up and escort you around town."

He wiped away a single tear that was trailing down Adelaide's cheek. "I hope someday you'll be able to remember me with some fondness, but I understand you probably won't feel anything but anger toward me for a very long time. Know that I will cherish the time we've spent together and know that I wish things could be different." He caught her eye. "If you could promise me one thing before I go?"

"That would depend on what you want me to promise."

His lips curved on their own accord. "There's that practicality I'm going to miss. But if you could promise to try and keep yourself out of trouble, I'd sleep better at night since I won't be around to watch over you."

"I don't need anyone to watch over me. Besides, I always seem to land on my feet after my debacles, which certainly aren't going to end simply because you're not around. However, if it makes you feel better, I'll try to stay out of trouble, but I don't go looking for trouble. It simply finds me." She jerked her head toward the door. "I don't believe we have anything left to discuss, so you should go find Marshall. I'll have Leopold and Vernon see me safely home."

Knowing he'd been dismissed, and rightly so, Gideon pressed a kiss against her fingers, released his hold on her hand, then strode for the door, his vision blurry as he let himself out into the snow-covered alley behind the bookstore.

As he strode down it, he realized that saying good-bye to Adelaide might be the hardest thing he'd ever have to do in his life. And even though he wished he could rush back to her and beg her forgiveness, tell her that he was in love with her, since he'd realized as he was saying good-bye to her that he certainly was, he knew he'd made the only decision that would keep her safe—even if that decision meant he would not get to spend the rest of his life with the one lady who suited him in every way.

Twenty-Eight

"I made excuses for you at Mrs. Aldrich's tea," Phyllis said, strolling into the music room, her eyes widening when she caught sight of Adelaide sitting on the bench in front of the piano. "You're playing the piano?"

"Isn't that what we ladies are supposed to do? Play the piano, sing, complete needlepoint samplers, and chat about the weather?" Adelaide nodded to the window. "Per the weather report in the newspapers today, it has, indeed, stopped snowing."

"You never read the weather forecasts."

"I've turned over a new leaf."

Phyllis moved to join Adelaide on the bench, releasing a sigh after she got herself settled. "I'm not certain this is the way to do that turning, dear, although I understand your somewhat odd state of mind. You're disappointed with Gideon's decision."

"I'm more disappointed for allowing myself to fall for his charming nature."

"You certainly shouldn't be upset that you grew fond of Gideon. He's a very likeable sort, and I would have been surprised if you hadn't developed feelings of the affectionate type

JEN TURANO

for him. The two of you were incredibly well suited, and I'm not the only one who realized that. Everyone remarked on it, including Camilla, who, if I'm not mistaken, had her eye on making a match between you and Gideon from the moment she saw how you interacted with each other."

"I think you *are* mistaken about that because Camilla's first opportunity to observe us interacting was when I was sitting in a tree in my unmentionables."

"And I believe that circumstance is when she realized you'd be perfect for Gideon because you're unconventional. That's what he needs in his life."

"According to Gideon, he doesn't need a lady in his life at all since the nature of his business is far too dangerous for members of the weaker sex to be exposed to."

Phyllis smoothed a hand over Adelaide's hair. "I understand why you're angry, but don't give up hope, my dear. It's only been two days since you and Gideon parted ways. I assure you, he's having second, if not third and fourth, regrets by now."

"He won't act on those regrets even if he has them because he's apparently made some sort of personal vow to hold danger at bay for as many people as he can, myself included."

"Gentlemen can get the most ridiculous ideas at times," Phyllis said, her lips curving ever so slightly.

Adelaide's lips curved as well. "I'm not saying his chivalrous attitude is ridiculous, but his decision to set me aside because of that attitude is complete nonsense. I'm not some delicate china doll that needs to be placed on a shelf, because contrary to Gideon's belief, I'm not that fragile." She trailed her fingers over the keys, eliciting some horrid notes in the process and earning a wince from Phyllis in return. "What bothers me the most, though, is that the annoying man alluded to the notion he's rather fond of me but won't allow that fondness to sway his decision because it wouldn't be in my best interest."

327

"Gentlemen do embrace nonsensical reasoning at times."

"Which is why I'm now going to embrace my spinster status and spend the rest of my years surrounded by my cats."

"A troubling image, to be sure."

Adelaide grinned. "Perhaps I'll even take to wearing a platinum wig around town."

"Another disturbing image."

"You're the one who thought I'd look marvelous with blond tresses."

"True, but when I pictured you with that color, I wasn't counting on you being flanked by cats."

"They'll be far better company than any of the gentlemen who've decided I'm all the rage this Season, Gideon included."

Phyllis checked the watch encircling her wrist and caught Adelaide's eye. "What you need, my dear, is a change of scenery. It just so happens that I'm due at Petunia's house in less than thirty minutes. I'm sure she'd love to see you, as would Charles, since he's still recuperating from all those stitches he now has in his head."

"I'm not very pleasant company at the moment, but tell Charles I'll come around later."

"What are you going to do instead?"

"Play the piano for another hour or so, then maybe do some reading."

Phyllis glanced at the piano, winced again, then gave Adelaide a kiss on the cheek before she rose from the bench and moved across the room.

As her mother shut the door firmly behind her, likely to spare the staff the horror of listening to Adelaide play, Adelaide resettled her fingers over the keys, launching into one of the few songs she somewhat remembered from when she'd taken lessons eons ago, lessons her mother eventually discontinued after deciding proficiency with musical instruments might not be a talent Adelaide would ever acquire. As she massacred one note after another, her thoughts, to her annoyance, returned to Gideon, something they did with maddening frequency of late.

He'd decided, and from out of the blue, that he wanted nothing to do with her—as in ever.

No more dancing around a ballroom, no more enjoying time at the shooting range, no more watching him with Harvey, no more . . . anything.

And while she understood, to a certain extent, his reasoning for shutting her out of his life, she didn't agree with it, nor could she believe he'd admitted he might hold her in some manner of affection, and yet that hadn't been enough for him to consider maintaining any type of relationship with her.

He was the most annoying, irritating, misguided, and idiotic gentleman she'd ever met, but even knowing that . . . she still loved him—had loved him for months, if truth be told, which was why she'd been crying herself to sleep every night, which was a curious circumstance because she wasn't a lady who cried often.

A knock on the door had her fingers lifting from the keys and turning her head, finding Susie, one of the downstairs maids, poking her head into the room.

"Begging your pardon, Miss Duveen, but a message just arrived for you," Susie said, advancing across the room to hand Adelaide the message.

After thanking her, Adelaide flipped the piece of vellum over, finding it sealed with a flower stamped in wax. After she found a letter opener lying on a side table and slid it through the wax, she unfolded the paper. She was frowning a second later when she realized the message was from Sophia Campanini and . . . she had an urgent matter to discuss with Adelaide and would send a carriage around to pick her up at four o'clock sharp.

"She didn't leave me much time, since it's a quarter to four now," Adelaide muttered before she strode out of the music room, fetched a warm overcoat, along with her reticule, then headed for the front foyer. She was met at the door by the family butler, Mr. Hodgkin, who immediately helped her into her coat.

"Shall I ring for a carriage, Miss Duveen?" he asked.

"No need, Mr. Hodgkin. Madame Campanini is sending a carriage for me. If my mother returns before I do, tell her I shouldn't be long because I'm sure Sophia has a performance tonight."

"Very good, Miss Duveen, although . . ." Mr. Hodgkin frowned. "Given the unusual circumstances that have befallen you of late, do you believe it wise to travel without a chaperone?"

"Since Mother isn't here and Charles has been instructed to take it easy for the next week, per his doctor's order, I'm afraid there's no one readily available. But no need to fear about my safety. No one has any reason to harm me now."

He inclined his head. "I suppose you would know best about that."

"Indeed, but to alleviate any lingering concerns you may have, know that I'm armed."

Mr. Hodgkin smiled. "From what I hear, you've gotten better with your aim of late, or at least I imagine you have, since rumor in the servants' hall is that you recently shot a man."

"It was two men, but I wasn't actually aiming for either of them."

"Perhaps I *should* accompany you."

"I'll be fine," she reassured him as the sound of a carriage rumbling to a stop in front of her house met her ears. Accepting the umbrella Mr. Hodgkin handed her in case it began snowing again, she walked through the door and down the steps, met by a groomsman who hustled her directly over to the carriage.

To her complete surprise, he then opened the door and all but tossed her inside, slamming the door shut the second she landed on the seat.

A sense of unease washed over her when her gaze settled on Sophia, who was pressed up against the far side of the carriage, clear terror in her eyes, the terror a direct result of being held at pistol point by . . . Mr. Dudley Paulding.

"How nice of you to join us," Dudley drawled as the carriage jolted into motion, sending her sprawling across the seat beside Sophia, who didn't move a muscle and continued staring at the weapon in Dudley's hand.

After pushing herself up, Adelaide kept a firm grip on the umbrella as she lifted her chin. "I believe you have the advantage on me, Mr. Paulding. I cannot imagine why you'd care for me to join you in the first place or why you're holding a gun on poor Madame Campanini."

"Don't be coy, Miss Duveen. It doesn't become you. I'm sure you've already concluded I'm in the company of the oh-so-devious Madame Campanini because I'm in need of her journal."

Adelaide stilled. "Frank Fitzsimmons said Marshall Wilson was the one who was desperate to get his hands on Sophia's journal."

"Nice to hear Frank's not a complete idiot," Dudley returned. "He obviously realized his life would be in jeopardy if he told you my name. But how clever of him to point a finger at Marshall Wilson—done so, no doubt, because I once remarked to Frank that Marshall Wilson was a complete dolt who many in society find to be a boor. I imagine Frank decided Marshall would be a handy scapegoat after he got shot, and by you, from what I've heard. Speaking of that incident, though, I'll take your reticule, if you please. No sense taking the chance you'll whip out a pistol at some point, and you might as well hand me the umbrella as well."

When Dudley turned the pistol on her, Adelaide knew there was nothing left to do but comply, so she handed over her umbrella, then her reticule, earning a nod from Dudley in return.

"That's a good girl." He opened the reticule, rustled around inside it, then lifted his head. "It's not here."

"What's not there?"

"Sophia's journal."

"Why would I have Sophia's journal?"

"Sophia told me you took possession of it, instead of Gideon, as a way to confuse whoever was after it."

Adelaide swung her attention to Sophia. "You told him that?"

Sophia's lower lip began to tremble. "He showed up in my dressing room after rehearsal for tonight's performance, and that was after some of his men knocked out my security guards at the Fifth Avenue Hotel and broke into my safe. The journal he's after wasn't there and because he took me by surprise, I just blurted out the name of the person who's holding it for me."

"You couldn't have blurted out that Gideon has your journal?"

"You know Gideon doesn't have my journal, and besides, he's not in town. He went after Marshall Wilson, who left two days ago because of a problem with one of his factories in Pittsburgh."

Adelaide blew out a breath, having no idea how to extricate herself from this latest debacle, or how to convince Dudley she didn't know where Sophia's journal was. She forced herself to meet his gaze. "I'm afraid Sophia's wrong about me having the journal. She obviously panicked when she found herself on the wrong end of your pistol and told you what she thought you wanted to hear."

"I've always found that when a person's life is threatened, they tend to tell the truth," Dudley said. "I'm sure Sophia was being truthful when she said you have her journal. All that's left now is for you to divulge where you've stashed it."

"I didn't stash it anywhere."

He regarded her for a long moment before he smiled. "I imagine it's hidden in your little bookshop because that would be the easiest place to hide a book, what with how many books are there."

"True, but again, I didn't hide it. I've never even seen it, although . . ." She drew in another breath, willing her thoughts to settle so she could get down to devising a plan to extricate herself from what was clearly a perilous situation. "May I assume you're personally seeing to this matter because Frank made such a muddle of everything?"

"I should have never sought out Frank's services to begin with," Dudley grumbled. "I should have used Victor Malvado all along, but Victor was out of town when I first became aware of Sophia's duplicity. Talk on the street suggested Frank was the next best choice." Dudley's lips thinned. "His work was less than satisfactory, which is why I reached out to Victor Malvado the second I learned he was back in town. Victor's men were able to secure the diary and code the night of your book salon. Unfortunately, the journal I desire was not in the safe. Since I've lost all patience with this situation, I decided it was time for me to take matters into my own hands."

He glanced at Sophia. "It really is regrettable that you had the audacity to ply me with far too much wine during our dinner, then scribble down the information I let slip while in a highly inebriated state."

"I told you," Sophia whispered. "I didn't write down anything you said that night."

"Don't be ridiculous, my dear," Dudley scoffed. "Word on the street has it that you jot everything down, then use that information to secure yourself a fortune in gems, something that was confirmed after I glanced through the journals Victor Malvado's men took from your safe earlier. I must say, I was pleased to see you'd put the dates on the front of all your journals, which made it remarkably easy to discern that the journal I want was not in your safe."

"But once you get the journal you want, can I expect you to

return my other journals to me?" Sophia asked, a rather bold question in Adelaide's opinion, because it wasn't as if the lady was in a position to expect much of anything at this point.

A chortle was Dudley's first response to that before he leaned forward. "How delusional you are, Madame Campanini. I have no intention of returning your journals because with the information stored in them, I'll be able to secure one business deal after another, and without any bloodshed, by using the tawdry information you've amassed against an entire brigade of wealthy gentlemen." His eyes hardened. "If you haven't realized this yet, you silly chit, you've met your match in me. I'm not a man to trifle with, and I did not build a fortune by being soft, nor would I ever countenance a mere woman attempting to blackmail me by using information I never intended to divulge in the first place."

"What did you divulge?" Adelaide couldn't resist asking.

Dudley gave a dismissive wave of a hand. "I might have mentioned something about acquiring a steel mill through somewhat questionable means."

"You had the owner of that mill assaulted, then had the men who assaulted him threaten his life if he wouldn't sell the mill to you at a fraction of the worth," Sophia said.

Dudley narrowed his eyes to slits. "And you would have me believe that you didn't jot that information down to be used against me at a later date?"

"I swear on my mother's grave that I didn't," Sophia exclaimed.

"Your mother is alive and well, living in a cushy apartment you bought for her in Boston."

Any color that was left in Sophia's face drained away as she began shaking like a leaf, evidently having no credible response to make to that.

"You've clearly done your due diligence when it comes to Sophia," Adelaide said, drawing Dudley's attention. "And because of that, surely you learned that Sophia never publicly spreads tales about any of the gentlemen who've been somewhat loose with what they've told her."

Dudley inclined his head. "True, but that's only because they always capitulate and shower her with jewels. And even though she's now claiming she would never attempt to blackmail me, greed is a powerful motivator, Miss Duveen. It would only be a matter of time until she'd try to weasel a diamond necklace out of me, then demand another piece a few weeks, months, or even years later. I don't deal well with people who threaten me, nor can I afford to allow someone else to gain access to her journal—especially not Gideon Abbott, who I was so surprised to learn is no mere gentleman about town. He could destroy my reputation if he reads what Sophia wrote about me. I won't stand for that because banks will then refuse to extend me credit and then my investment partners will insist I repay the money they've poured into my ventures. That'll ruin me since I'm cash poor at the moment."

"Is that why you convinced Ward McCallister to get you invited to the Patriarch Ball?" Adelaide asked.

Dudley shrugged. "A wealthy wife with high standing in society would solve most of my problems. Everyone knows Ward is a man easily impressed. It didn't take much to get my invitation. I simply showed him the plans for the house I'm intending to build on Fifth Avenue, and he had an invitation to the ball delivered to me the next day."

"I doubt you'll be able to secure a society wife after they learn you abducted a premier opera singer, along with one of their own," Adelaide said.

Dudley's lips curved into a smile that left Adelaide's blood cold. "How naïve that you seem to believe society will ever learn the details of what happened to you or Sophia. You surely must realize I can't let either of you live."

Adelaide narrowed her eyes. "You probably should have

waited to tell us that until after you got your hands on the journal. What possible incentive do I now have to fetch it for you?"

"An excellent point, Miss Duveen," Dudley said with an inclination of his head. "But as an incentive to encourage you to cooperate, know that I give you my word I won't harm your family if I get the journal." He settled back against the seat, his eyes glinting. "Make no mistake, though, if I don't have the journal in my hands precisely five minutes after we reach the bookstore, I'll contact Victor Malvado again. Believe me, he'll be only too happy to make certain that anyone with the name Duveen suffers a most horrible demise."

Twenty-Nine

Gideon strode into the Union Club and inclined his head to a few of the members lingering in the foyer before heading down the hallway, intent on grabbing a quick meal before he headed out again to search for the oh-so-elusive Marshall Wilson.

To say he was in a dark mood was an understatement.

After parting ways with Adelaide, one of the worst nights in his existence, he'd gone directly to the brownstone Marshall owned near Washington Square Park, only to be told by Marshall's butler that his employer wasn't in New York, having left for Pittsburgh to attend to matters of business.

Since there were no trains departing to Pittsburgh until morning, Gideon had returned to his office on Broadway, slouched into a chair, and taken to brooding until Roland showed up.

Roland, instead of wanting to discuss the recent events that had transpired, had immediately launched into a diatribe about how Gideon was a complete and utter fool because Adelaide was perfect for him in every way and yet Gideon had walked away from her.

Even after explaining exactly why he'd parted ways with the lady he knew was the love of his life, Roland still called him an idiot and told him to go home and sleep on matters, which would hopefully have him coming to his senses by morning, at which point Roland expected he'd make matters right with Adelaide.

It had taken everything Gideon had in him to not seek Adelaide out before he left for Pittsburgh, knowing if he did so he'd end up begging her forgiveness and asking her to give him a second chance.

That ridiculousness would only see her placed in danger again, and no matter how much he longed to be with her, he wouldn't be able to live with himself if any harm befell her on his account.

By the time he'd reached Pittsburgh, he'd been prepared for a fight with Marshall, only to be told at Marshall's factory that the man had been there that morning but had been called away to deal with another problem in another city.

No one knew exactly which factory Marshall had traveled to, which was why Gideon boarded another train back to New York.

He'd spent a restless night, tossing and turning as he replayed the look on Adelaide's face when he told her he couldn't see her again over and over in his mind.

Her eyes had sparkled with tears, something he doubted she experienced often, and her tears suggested she *had* held him in affection as well, and perhaps had even felt that spark Camilla frequently mentioned, one Gideon knew he felt for Adelaide but would now never be able to act upon.

Shaking aside his thoughts when he realized he was attracting more than a few curious glances from members of the club, probably because he was undoubtedly scowling, Gideon strode into the dining room, hesitating as he glanced around the room until someone called his name.

Turning, he discovered Leopold and Vernon sitting at a table beside a window, Vernon gesturing for Gideon to join them.

"Gideon," Vernon exclaimed, shaking Gideon's hand once he reached the table. "May we dare hope you ran that scoundrel Marshall to ground and he's even now safely behind bars?"

After shaking Leopold's hand, Gideon took a seat and shook his head. "Marshall had already left Pittsburgh by the time I got there. No one seems to know where he went after that."

"He'll turn up eventually," Leopold said. "But Marshall aside, we're delighted you stopped at the club today because Vernon and I have a few things we'd like to discuss with you— more specifically, the concern we have that you've lost your mind. What were you thinking, parting ways with Adelaide?"

"I see the two of you don't care to exchange the expected pleasantries today," Gideon said, fighting the urge to fidget, a somewhat novel experience for him. "But to address your concerns, I haven't taken leave of my senses, as both of you are very aware since you must understand why I made the decision I did. Adelaide could have been killed the other night."

"But she wasn't," Leopold argued.

"True, but she wouldn't have been in that situation if not for me."

Vernon rolled his eyes. "It's Adelaide. She possesses a proclivity for courting trouble."

"Which is why I'm the last gentleman on earth she should associate with, given my occupation."

"You're the only gentleman she should be with because you can protect her."

"I didn't protect her very well at the bookstore. In fact, she was the one who brought the situation to an end when she began firing that pepperbox."

"Which suggests you're underestimating her," Vernon said.

Gideon frowned. "I'm surprised you'd encourage me to return to Adelaide, Vernon. Edna was placed in peril as well, and that was my fault."

"Edna came at my request," Vernon argued. "However, she

certainly doesn't blame me for placing her in a dangerous situation. It was a book salon. No one could have anticipated that Frank Fitzsimmons would decide to burst in with guns drawn. Any normal criminal would have waited until everyone left to make their move."

"And," Leopold added, "Frank told Roland they *had* been intending on breaking into the bookstore once it was unoccupied but changed their plans when one of his men thought he recognized those two men Victor Malvodo sent." He caught Gideon's eye. "Word on the street has it, if you were considering having the accounting firm investigate that slippery criminal, that Victor left town."

"An unfortunate circumstance, since we could have used Victor to establish firm evidence against Marshall Wilson," Gideon said.

"Victor Malvado will eventually resurface," Vernon said. "Men like him always do, but if we could return to the subject of Adelaide?"

Gideon slouched into the chair. "There's nothing else to say about her."

"There's plenty to say because you, my boy, are making the worst decision of your life," Vernon argued. "Adelaide is perfect for you. You can't let her go simply because you're afraid you'll lose her in the end."

"I'm afraid I'll lose her because of her association with me."

Leopold sat forward. "Life comes with risks, Gideon. Yes, you take more risks than most, but Vernon and I were the same in our younger days. We traveled the country, seeking out new adventures, did some work for the government at times, and then returned every so often to the city because our mothers demanded we show up for holiday dinners." He smiled. "We were fortunate to meet our wives during one of those visits, and Adelaide reminds both of us of our late wives."

"How so?"

Vernon took a sip of his drink before he smiled. "My Veronica and Leopold's Darcy were women not fond of the expected feminine graces. They both enjoyed escapades, which is why they were drawn to us in the first place. Veronica and I got married a month after being introduced, and Leopold married Darcy a month after that. Both of our wives insisted on traveling with us, and what adventures all of us enjoyed together."

"Darcy and I got chased by bears once," Leopold added, his eyes twinkling. "We reached the edge of a cliff, and Darcy didn't hesitate to jump, landing in a pool of water at least twenty feet below us. I, of course, followed her, and we could have lost each other then, but we didn't." The twinkle faded from his eyes. "I lost her to an illness ten years ago, but you see, Gideon, one of the last things she said to me was to thank me for allowing her to lead such an extraordinary life and to not curtail her adventurous spirit simply because she was born a woman."

"Veronica was the same," Vernon said. "She died of a weak heart some five years ago, but like Darcy, she told me before she died that she wouldn't have changed a thing about our lives. That she loved sharing everything with me instead of being left behind to tend home and hearth."

"Adelaide deserves an extraordinary life," Leopold said. "And you're the only one who can give that to her."

"But what if she's harmed?"

"I've always believed God looks after us, and I think you can see that's certainly been the case with Adelaide, given the life-threatening circumstances she finds herself in." Leopold leaned closer to Gideon. "Don't deprive yourself and Adelaide of an exceptional life simply because you think you're being chivalrous by turning away from her to keep her safe. Adelaide is a woman who was born to live life to the fullest, and I'm convinced she wants to live that life with you."

"I'm not sure I agree with that," Gideon argued. "She never gave me any indication she was anything other than fond of me, even if she *was* somewhat distraught when I told her I wanted to discontinue our friendship."

"She's definitely not fond of you now if you actually told her that," Vernon said dryly. "But luckily for you, Adelaide possesses a generous soul and a kind nature. I imagine she'll forgive you, although some groveling might be in order."

Gideon glanced out the window as he tried to gather his scattered thoughts, stilling when he caught sight of Lottie Mc-Briar, who was, oddly enough, waving at him from the other side of the glass.

"Isn't that . . . Lottie?" Leopold asked, peering through the window.

"I'll be right back," Gideon said.

"We're coming with you," Vernon said, rising to his feet as Leopold did the same, the gentlemen falling into step behind Gideon as he made his way through the dining room and then out a door that led to a snow-covered terrace, Lottie hurrying to join him.

"This is an unexpected surprise," Gideon said once Lottie stopped in front of him.

"I'm sure it is," Lottie said, "but I had to come because . . ." She stepped closer to him, laying a hand on his arm. "It's Adelaide. He's got her, along with Sophia Campanini."

Gideon's heart missed a beat. "Marshall Wilson has Adelaide and Sophia?"

Lottie frowned. "Why would Marshall Wilson have them?"

"Because Marshall's the man who hired Frank to retrieve Sophia's journal."

"Dudley Paulding paid Frank to steal the journal, and he's the one who has Adelaide and Sophia." Her brows drew together. "Why did you think Marshall is behind everything?"

"That's what Frank told me."

Lottie wrinkled her nose. "I suppose that's not surprising, given that Frank, who isn't afraid of much, is deathly afraid of

Dudley, but we're wasting time. As I said, Dudley has Adelaide, along with Sophia."

"Has them where?" Gideon demanded.

"Last I saw them, they were heading toward Bleecker Street. I think he's taking them to the bookstore. I was following them, but then I saw you riding in the opposite direction and came after you because I wouldn't have a chance of saving them on my own, not when they're with Dudley."

He shot a look to Leopold. "Did you bring your carriage today?"

"It's around front."

Five minutes later, they were racing down Park Avenue, Lottie explaining everything she knew.

". . . and then Frank demanded I get a job with Sophia after he was unsuccessful meeting with her, the fact that he decided to get personally involved in this affair speaking volumes about just how intimidated he is by Dudley. I was tasked with the job of discovering where she kept her journals, and then I was supposed to steal her current journal and whatever journals she'd written over the past four months." Lottie dashed a strand of hair out of her face. "Unfortunately, Sophia doesn't keep her journals lying about, putting them in her safe. After telling Frank that, he insisted I stay on as Sophia's dresser until I uncovered where her safe was and located a key or a combination to said safe—a difficult assignment if there ever was one because Sophia's a suspicious sort."

"Sophia told us she couldn't recall speaking to you about her safe," Gideon said.

"She didn't say much about it," Lottie admitted. "However, I overheard her directing her most trusted guard to fetch some jewels for her from a safe-deposit box, which concerned me because it's never easy to break into a bank. I thought for certain it would be impossible to get my hands on her journals, but then she sent this same guard to fetch something from her suite at the Fifth Avenue Hotel. That's when I saw her riffle through her vanity table, pull out a small piece of paper, scribble something onto another piece of paper, and hand that to her guard. She then reminded him to dispose of what she'd given him after he was done. It wasn't a stretch for me to assume he was off to retrieve something from a personal safe. I waited until Sophia was onstage, snooped around her vanity table, found four numbers written down on a slip of paper, and sent those numbers off to a man Frank uses who converts messages and the like into codes."

"But why go through the bother of having the combination put into a cipher?" Vernon asked, sitting forward. "Why didn't you simply find a way, since you were Sophia's dresser, to gain access to her rooms in the Fifth Avenue Hotel?"

Lottie rolled her eyes. "That's what most people *would* have done, but Frank fancies himself a master criminal, using a web of convoluted schemes to control his network of hoodlums. He likes to dole out assignments in a piecemeal fashion, keeping the players apart so that no one can double-cross him. The problem with that, though, is there are numerous opportunities for problems to occur, and in this case, the man who creates all of Frank's ciphers got himself arrested and thrown into jail not long after he put the cipher he created to hide the combination to the safe into a diary that was slated to be delivered to Bainswright Books. His arrest turned problematic after Adelaide got her hands on the diary. That caused all sorts of complications because I didn't keep a copy of the combination because Frank expects me to destroy such things, and I know better than to cross him. Frank's man who was given the job of breaking into Sophia's safe couldn't complete his part of the plan, so Frank sent me back to the opera house to get the combination again, but Sophia had removed the slip of paper from her vanity table."

Lottie's shoulders slumped the tiniest bit. "I was hesitant about the book salon when I saw that notice posted on the door. I told Frank I thought it was a little too convenient that we were desperate to retrieve that diary and Adelaide Duveen just happened to decide to liquidate some of her collection, diaries included, giving her book agent friends the benefits of perusing her collection during the first salon event. Frank wouldn't listen to me—he never does, believing a girl doesn't warrant consideration of what turned out to be a prudent concern." She blew out a breath. "I wasn't expecting Frank to burst into the meeting, and I definitely wasn't expecting to see a few of Victor Malvado's known associates there. However, when everything went south and I saw an opportunity to flee with the diary in my possession, I thought I would finally have a way to get out of Frank's clutches once and for all by presenting him with the coveted diary and telling him I was done. Unfortunately, I was nabbed by additional men Victor Malvado had sent to watch the street. They relieved me of the diary, thus depriving me of a way to get out of Frank's syndicate, although that might not still be the case since Frank's been arrested."

Leopold exchanged a glance with Gideon before he returned his attention to Lottie. "You're not willingly in Frank's employ?"

A hint of a smile curved Lottie's lips. "Being involved with the criminal set was never my intention. My father, God rest his soul, was a tutor for a wealthy family for years. And while we never had much money, he gave me something far more valuable—an education. I was intending on continuing with my education, perhaps becoming a teacher, but then Father died. Mother and I were left in dire straits once the family my father worked for insisted we abandon the small apartment we lived in over their carriage house. They then didn't bother to give my mother so much as a dime to help her secure other accommodations."

"You'll need to give me the name of that family," Gideon said, earning a touch of a grin from Lottie in return.

"There's no need for you to speak with them about their abysmal behavior toward my mother and me," she said. "It's not as if what they did to us is an uncommon occurrence, and we did have a small amount of money to get an apartment, albeit in Five Points." Her grin faded. "Frank's always on the lookout for talented people to join him, and he took note of me a few weeks after my mother and I got settled. Mother had managed to find a job in a shirtwaist factory, and I found one at a telegram office. Frank came in one day, realized I could read, and set out to bring me into his operation." Her eyes turned hard. "I wasn't interested, but he doesn't take no for an answer. He arranged for my mother to get fired and then offered me three times what I was making at the telegram office if I'd agree to do little jobs for him. I really had no other choice, but I was hoping I'd be able to save up my money and escape with my mother to another state before too long."

"It's next to impossible to get out of a criminal organization once you've been pulled into it," Gideon said.

"Something I wasn't aware of until I discovered Frank had his people watching me to make sure I wouldn't try to sneak off. He also threatened to harm my mother if I left him, promising he'd hunt her down and make me regret what he would see as an unforgiveable betrayal."

The carriage made a sharp turn, and after glancing out the window, Gideon realized they were only about five minutes away from the bookstore. He returned his attention to Lottie. "You've yet to tell me how you became aware that Dudley has Adelaide and Sophia."

Lottie shifted on the seat. "After Victor's men took the diary away from me, I knew it wouldn't take long for the cipher to get into Dudley's hands. I also knew Dudley would want to personally handle Sophia, given the trouble she's caused him, and I didn't want to see her dead. That's why I set off to tail Dudley early this morning. He went with some men to the Fifth

Avenue Hotel but apparently didn't find the journal he's after, which I'm not actually surprised about because Sophia keeps her current journal close at hand while she's rehearsing."

"Why didn't you simply steal that journal when she took to the stage?" Gideon asked.

"I could never find it, leaving me with the impression she might stash it on her person—not that I ever told Frank that because that information could have gotten Sophia killed." She blew out a breath. "I knew Sophia was in danger when Dudley stormed out of the Fifth Avenue Hotel and his carriage raced off a second after he got into it. I followed him to the Metropolitan Opera House, where he pulled Sophia from it five minutes later. They then went to a mansion on Fifth Avenue. Adelaide Duveen walked out of that mansion and got into the carriage, although Dudley's groomsman didn't seem to be giving her a choice in that matter, and off they went. I was following them in a hired hack, but as I said, I spotted you and decided to ask for help."

"Why do you think Dudley took Adelaide?" Leopold asked.

Lottie bit her lip. "The only reason I can think of is that Sophia was trying to buy some time. She's far more cunning than people know, and she would have realized that Dudley would kill her the second she turned her journal over to him."

Gideon frowned. "You believe Dudley's capable of murder?"

"Since Frank, one of the most dangerous men I know, is frightened of him, yes, Dudley's capable of murder."

Gideon drew in a breath, then another, trying to control the rage that was coursing through him.

"We're almost there," Vernon said, looking out the window. "About a block away if I'm judging correctly."

"Have the driver pull over here," Gideon said.

A second later, he was out of the carriage, telling Lottie to wait in it until he returned. Breaking into a run, leaving Vernon and Leopold behind, he darted down the alley leading to the back of Bainswright Books, stopping when he noticed the back door was open. Edging through it, he pulled out his pistol and inched toward the main room but stilled when he heard Adelaide's voice, one that didn't sound frightened in the least, her tone more along the lines of lecturing.

"Stop whining. It's barely a scratch," she said.

"You shot me with a grappling hook."

"It was the only weapon I had at hand."

"Who uses a grappling hook as a weapon?"

"Someone who no longer had access to their pistol. I must say it was fortuitous indeed that I've learned to handle the grappling hook properly and that I forgot to return it to Gideon, leaving it here in my store instead."

"Aiming a grappling hook at a person is not using it properly."

"True, just as I'm sure you don't find my using the rope that attaches to the grappling hook to bind you up as proper either. From where I stand, though, it worked out very well indeed."

Relief surged through Gideon as he strode forward, holding up his hands when he caught sight of Adelaide, who'd apparently heard his footsteps and was now aiming her pepperbox his way.

"Don't shoot, even though I know you're more than annoyed with me right now," he said.

"Gideon," she exclaimed, lowering the pepperbox. "What are you doing here?"

"I thought I was coming to rescue you, but you seem to have rescued yourself." He glanced at the grappling hook anchoring Dudley to one of the bookcases. "Nice."

Her lips curved. "I know. I bet no one has ever taken out a criminal with one of those before."

"I can't argue with that," he said, stepping closer. "Nor can I argue that this isn't exactly the proper moment for what I'm about to do, but I thought you were going to be dead, and—"

"I'm not dead, and before you launch into a diatribe about

how my current situation is obviously somehow your fault, it's not. It's hers." Adelaide nodded to Sophia, who was sitting in a chair, tears running down her cheeks, looking dejected.

"I wasn't even considering any sort of tirade because what's foremost on my mind right now is apologizing to you."

"Apologizing?" she repeated slowly.

"Indeed." He raked a hand through his hair. "I've been a complete and utter fool and have been absolutely miserable since I told you good-bye."

"Serves you right," she muttered.

"Well, quite, but I'm hoping my state of misery will lift if, after I tell you I want to give you an extraordinary life, you'll let me."

She wrinkled her nose. "I'm not certain I'm following you."

He reached out and took the pepperbox from her hand, stowing it in his jacket pocket to be on the safe side in case she was inordinately annoyed with him, then smiled. "I'm saying, in a rather roundabout way, that I'm in love with you—and *madly* in love, at that. I don't want to live without you, and if you can find it in your heart to forgive me, I'm desperate to marry you."

Her eyes grew wide. "You want to marry me?"

"More than anything."

Her brows drew together. "And you love me?"

"Indeed. I'm also incredibly sorry for reneging on your temporary position of sorting through old files for the accounting firm."

"That was not well done of you."

His lips twitched. "I know, but would it make it up to you the slightest bit if I promised to teach you how to operate the Assassin's Creed, a weapon I know you've had your eye on?"

"I may have had my eye on it, since it's quite an impressive-looking weapon, but in all honesty, the Assassin's Creed frightens me half to death." She smiled. "I wouldn't be opposed, though, to learning how to shoot darts properly out of that one cane, especially when I think canes could very well turn fashionable for ladies and would allow me to have a weapon easily accessible whenever I'm in Central Park."

"I shall personally take you to the range tomorrow with that cane in hand, but now, if we could return to a more pressing issue?"

"What we're going to do with Dudley?"

"He's not pressing in the least, since you've done an excellent job of securing him. A more important matter is this— whether you're going to put me out of my misery and tell me your thoughts about my requesting your hand in marriage."

"Is this really the time for any of this?" Dudley suddenly demanded, drawing Gideon's attention as well as his annoyance, because now wasn't exactly the moment for an interruption. Not when Adelaide was keeping him in high suspense regarding the marriage business.

He narrowed his eyes on Dudley. "It might not exactly be the proper moment since it's not as if I've chosen the most romantic of settings. However, since you decided to abduct the love of my life, I'm not willing to waste another second wondering if she'll agree to spend the rest of her days with me. That means you're going to sit there, be quiet, and let me get on with things."

Before Dudley could do more than release a disgruntled-sounding snort, Leopold and Vernon rushed into the room, both men wheezing. They skidded to a stop, Leopold bending over in an obvious attempt to catch his breath.

"Seems like we missed all the action," Vernon said, rubbing his side as if he'd developed a stitch. "We might need to take up running on a more frequent basis because we're obviously a lot slower than we used to be."

"There wasn't any action to miss because Adelaide had the situation well in hand when I came charging in here," Gideon admitted. "Nevertheless, if I could prevail upon the two of you to guard Dudley for a moment, I need to return to a most *extraordinary* discussion I'm having with Adelaide, one I'm desperate to continue."

Vernon was suddenly all smiles. "By all means, get on with it," he said with a wave toward the door, paired with a wink, before he whipped a pistol out of his jacket and trained it on Dudley. "Leopold and I will take over for you here."

After sending Vernon a nod, Gideon took hold of Adelaide's hand and pulled her into the back room, turning to face her. "Where was I?"

She smiled, her dimple immediately popping out. "I believe you told me you loved me—and madly, at that—and mentioned you'd like to marry me, offered me my job back at the firm, although I'm not completely certain about that one, and left me under the impression you need to be put out of your misery."

"A state I'm currently languishing in because you never said whether you want to marry me, or even if you might hold me in some esteem."

A roll of her eyes was not what he'd been expecting, nor was he expecting her to step directly up to him and loop her arms around his neck.

"I hold you in more than some esteem, Gideon," she began, her eyes twinkling in a most delightful fashion. "In fact, I believe I fell in love with you when I went up in flames, which Camilla would probably say was a precursor to the sparks she keeps mentioning are between us."

"I think she may be right about the sparks."

Adelaide smiled. "I also think she was always hoping to spark a match between us when she agreed to take me on, even though she swore she was done with matchmaking forever."

"You might be right about that, but you haven't answered my question. *Will* you marry me?"

"It depends."

He blinked. "On what?"

"Will you promise to let me experience life with you instead of trying to put me on a shelf in an effort to keep me safe?"

He leaned closer to her. "If you'll promise me you'll at least try not to intentionally place yourself in danger."

"I never *intentionally* suffer any of my mishaps."

"I suppose that's a valid point, and I'll take that as an affirmative."

"You won't leave me behind when you go off on an adventure?" she pressed.

"It wouldn't be much of an adventure if you weren't with me."

Her eyes turned suspiciously bright. "Then yes, I'll marry you, but . . ." Her dimple popped out again. "Do you think now's the time we should investigate whether there's any truth to that sparks-between-us business?"

"Now is definitely the time," he didn't hesitate to say.

With that, he drew her close, lowered his head, and claimed her lips with his own.

The second his lips met hers, he realized Camilla had been right all along, and that the spark between them was much more than a spark, and with a simple kiss, it had turned into an inferno he knew was going to keep them ablaze for many, many years to come.

Thirty

THREE WEEKS LATER

"I hate to point out the obvious," Camilla began, picking her way through the stacks of books Adelaide was sorting, "but I can't help but notice that you seem far more enthusiastic about wading through moldy old books than you ever were about improving your social status. I'm not sure if I should be insulted or delighted about that unusual state of affairs."

Adelaide looked up from the book she'd been thumbing through and grinned. "I would opt for delighted, because you and I both know being a fashionable lady about town was never really for me."

"But you *are* a fashionable lady about town, even with the upper crust discovering you're now the owner of this fine establishment, which has yet to reopen or be renamed for that matter."

"I haven't been able to come up with something clever, but I'm sure that'll change once the renovations begin in earnest." Adelaide picked up another book. "Richard Morris Hunt has agreed to take on the project, and I'm certain a name will spring

353

to mind once he completes his designs." She shook her head. "Poor man. He was appalled when he took note of all the bullet holes on the first floor."

"I'm sure he was, but those will soon be fixed, and then you'll be ready to open your doors."

"It'll still be a few months before that happens." She set aside the book. "Did I tell you that Charles has offered to oversee the renovations while Gideon and I go off on holiday after the wedding next week?"

"Charles did mention that, right before he warned me his mother is planning to pay me a visit to convince me to find a match for him like I did for you."

"So you *did* have a match in mind all along, didn't you?"

A snort was Camilla's first response to that. "Of course I did, which is why I'm taking credit for your happy union." She sent Adelaide a wink. "I knew the moment I saw the two of you interacting when you were up in that tree that you were meant to be together, which means I may have been a little hasty with abandoning my matchmaking endeavors." She caught Adelaide's eye. "I've been thinking I should take Charles on."

"Aunt Petunia would adore that."

"She would indeed. And not that Charles is aware of this, but Petunia already sought me out the other day while I was enjoying tea at Rutherford and Company. She mentioned that the ennui everyone apparently realizes I suffer from was certain to return since life will undoubtedly be rather dull now that you and Gideon are settled. She then told me Charles, being somewhat difficult when it comes to setting his sights on a particular lady, would be a challenge for me, staving off my boredom." She blew out a breath. "She then broached the matter of my aunt Edna, telling me how I could banish the disappointment I was sure to be feeling over not matching up my own flesh and blood with a man Aunt Edna was destined to marry—that being Vernon of course."

"Were you disappointed to not have had a hand in that romance?"

Camilla waved that aside. "Aunt Edna had no need of a matchmaker, not when she and Vernon fell for each other after spending an afternoon together."

"Edna does seem incredibly pleased with herself."

"She also seems twenty years younger since Vernon proposed to her and is happier than I've ever seen her." Camilla's lips curved. "She told me she's highly anticipating the adventure she's certain to experience when Vernon takes her on a European tour. She mentioned something about hiking in the Alps and then going off to Egypt to view the pyramids."

"Leopold will certainly miss their company while they're gone."

Camilla tilted her head. "Perhaps I should take him on to find him a match as well."

"You definitely wouldn't suffer from boredom then because Leopold, as I've learned, can be a handful. But returning to Edna, since she's no longer your chaperone, are you considering hiring someone to fill that role?"

"I already have." Camilla smiled. "Although technically Lottie McBriar is now my paid companion, not chaperone."

"You've hired Lottie?"

"I certainly wasn't going to allow the poor girl to find herself working for Victor Malvado next, something I got the distinct impression Lottie was worried about because it seems every criminal boss in Five Points longs to have well-spoken girls who can read working for them." Camilla dashed a strand of golden hair out of her face. "I've already taken the liberty of resettling Lottie and her mother in the apartment above my carriage house here in the city, but know that I'm having improvements made to a delightful cottage that resides on the grounds of my Hudson estate. Mrs. McBriar will move there when it's ready, and I've assured Lottie she'll be able to visit her mother whenever she pleases."

"Aren't you concerned that this mysterious Victor Malvado may take issue with that if or when he returns to the city and discovers he won't be adding Lottie to his stable of thieves and hoodlums?"

"I don't believe anyone of the criminal persuasion would think I, a well-established member of the Four Hundred, would even consider hiring someone with Lottie's history." Camilla sent Adelaide a hint of a wink. "However, if that's not the case, I do have connections with the accounting firm."

"Gideon's already determined to learn more about Victor Malvado."

"I'm sure he is, but enough about that troublesome criminal." Camilla moved to take hold of Adelaide's arm. "Tell me, has Gideon told you yet where he's taking you after the wedding?"

"I'm afraid not, but I've devised a plan to coerce that information out of him."

"A plan, you say? How intriguing."

A tingle ran up Adelaide's spine as she turned and found Gideon walking her way, a large box in his hand and a twinkle in his eyes. As he set the box atop of a stack of books, she moved to join him, the tingles increasing when he leaned forward, kissed her ever so softly on the lips, then drew back and arched a brow.

"So?" was all he said.

"So . . . what?" she had to ask because his kiss had left her thoughts a bit muddled.

"Your plan?" Gideon prompted.

She wrinkled her nose. "I'm not telling you that. It won't work if I do."

"She makes a most excellent point," Camilla said, earning a scowl from Gideon in return.

"Don't you have somewhere you need to be?"

Camilla sent him a cheeky grin. "Since Adelaide has no one

else to chaperone her at the moment, I'm afraid I don't have anywhere else to be except here."

"I hear the back room calling you," Gideon countered.

Camilla tapped a finger against her chin. "I suppose it could be calling, but I'll only answer that call if you agree to teach me how to use the Assassin's Creed."

"You're not nearly as proper as everyone believes because that sounds exactly like blackmail," Gideon grumbled. "Besides, the Assassin's Creed is far too much gun for you since you just learned how to operate a basic revolver."

"I'm not blackmailing you," Camilla countered. "I'm merely suggesting a bit of a favor, something you now owe me because I granted you a favor and look how well that turned out."

"That is a compelling argument," Adelaide said.

Gideon smiled. "Perhaps, but I'm still not letting her use the Assassin's Creed because she's liable to lose a limb. What kind of a friend would I be if I was responsible for something like that?"

"I'm not going to lose a limb," Camilla argued. "And it's the Assassin's Creed or no five minutes alone with Adelaide."

Gideon's brows drew together. "I don't believe there needs to be a time limit to this because if you've forgotten, Adelaide and I are getting married next week. Frankly, there's really not much point in even having you around to chaperone us."

"Au contraire," Camilla returned. "There's every need to have me chaperone the two of you because this is *not* next week."

Adelaide grinned. "She's a tough negotiator, Gideon. I say you're going to have to capitulate to her demands if you want to spend even five minutes alone with me."

Gideon sent Adelaide a warm smile before he turned to Camilla. "Fine. I'll teach you how to shoot the Assassin's Creed but not until Adelaide and I get back from our holiday."

"I better not find out you've decided to spend months away" was all Camilla said to that before she turned on her heel and headed for the back room, looking over her shoulder before she reached the door. "And no stealing additional kisses."

"It's not stealing if I do it out in the open."

"No kissing," Camilla reiterated before she headed through the doorway.

"She's very annoying," Gideon muttered.

"But you adore her."

"I do, but I'd adore her more if she'd given us more than five minutes."

"We'll have all the time in the world to be alone after next week."

He smiled and drew her near, placing his arms around her waist. "It seems far too long to have to wait," he murmured before he bent his head and placed his lips on hers. The world disappeared as she leaned into him, savoring the feel of his lips against hers.

Far too soon, he pulled away, but not before placing a feather-light kiss on her forehead. "Next week cannot arrive fast enough."

She grinned. "I agree, but tell me, what are you doing here? I thought you were taking today to make additional arrangements for wherever it is we're going on holiday after the wedding, which, I have to say, is very romantic on your part, keeping it a secret, but rather difficult for me to know how to pack for the trip."

"Your mother was going to pack for you because she knew where we were intending to go, which was Egypt, but . . . there's been a change of plans."

"We were going to Egypt?"

"I thought you'd enjoy traveling there because of that mummy book you were reading when you caught me in the library at the Nelsons' dinner party. However, don't fret that we won't make it to Egypt. We simply have somewhere else we need to go first."

He walked over to the wrapped box he'd brought in with him, returned to her side, handed it to her, and grinned. "Open it."

"Is it going to explain the change in our plans?"

"You'll see."

With her lips curving into a grin, Adelaide untied the bow, pried the lid off, then pushed aside some paper, her eyes widening when she caught sight of a hat resting inside the box. Pulling it out, she discovered it was similar to a gentleman's top hat, but it was done up in a deep emerald green, with a simple piece of black satin wrapped around the base, a black feather attached to the satin.

"It's a protype I had made for you."

Adelaide raised a hand to her throat. "Do not say there's a gun stored inside that pops out of the top."

"There is, but that's not the only gift for you in the box. Look underneath the paper at the very bottom."

Adelaide set aside the hat, which she knew even Camilla wouldn't have an issue with because it was incredibly fashionable, and withdrew another wrapped package.

Sending him another grin, she attacked the wrapping, then blinked and blinked again when she pulled out a wig—or more specifically, a platinum wig that looked remarkably like the one Sophia had been wearing around town.

She arched a brow Gideon's way. "And . . . why have you given me this?"

He moved closer to her, took the wig out of her hands, plopped it on her head, and nodded. "Perfect, but just so you know, that's actually a gift from Sophia. She's apparently still feeling contrite over almost getting you killed, which was why she didn't hesitate to give me her very favorite platinum wig when I went to inquire where she purchases them."

"And you thought I needed a wig because . . . ?"

"It seems as if there's an aristocrat in England who may be dabbling in trading American secrets. This man is married to an American whose father is often courted by English gentlemen because he possesses a very large fortune. From what little we know, this aristocrat stole sensitive information from his

father-in-law and is even now searching for a buyer. He's hosting a costume ball three weeks from now and . . . you'll need
a costume."

Adelaide forgot to breathe for the briefest of moments.
"You're going to take me out in the field with you?"

"And make you an official associate of the accounting firm."
He smiled. "I thought it might be a wedding present you'd enjoy."

A laugh escaped her before she threw her arms around his
neck and pulled him close. "It's the best wedding present you
could have ever given me."

"Better than the diamond necklace I sent over last night?"

"Indeed."

"What about the building I purchased for you a few doors
down from this very shop that you can now turn into a sanctu-
ary for cats?"

"That was an amazingly sweet gesture, but yes, even better
than that."

"What about—"

She placed her finger over his lips. "You've overindulged me
tremendously since I told you I'd marry you, which means we
could be here all day discussing how much better your officially
making me an associate of the accounting firm is compared to
everything else you've lavished on me."

"Why do I get the distinct feeling you'd rather spend the
scant few minutes we have left before Camilla returns doing
something other than talking?"

She smiled. "You do know me well, my darling Gideon, because yes, I have something else in mind."

His lips curved. "And that would be?"

"An experiment, so to speak, one to make certain that the
sparks between us are increasing with time, not diminishing."

"I don't believe it's possible for them to diminish."

She leaned closer. "I'm sure you're right, but no sense losing
an opportunity to put that theory to a test."

As Gideon settled his hands around her waist, Adelaide drew his head closer and pressed her lips to his, realizing in that moment that she'd been completely wrong in her belief she was meant to remain a spinster because Gideon was certainly the spark she'd needed in her life, one she knew would never be extinguished.

Named one of the funniest voices in inspirational romance by *Booklist*, **Jen Turano** is a *USA Today* bestselling author, known for penning quirky historical romances set in the Gilded Age. Her books have earned *Publishers Weekly* and *Booklist* starred reviews, top picks from *Romantic Times*, and praise from *Library Journal*. She and her family live outside of Denver, Colorado. Readers can find her on Facebook, Instagram, and at jenturano.com.

Sign Up for Jen's Newsletter

Keep up to date with Jen's latest news on book releases and events by signing up for her email list at the link below.

FOLLOW JEN ON SOCIAL MEDIA

Jen Turano   @jenturanoauthor   @JenTurano

JenTurano.com